Jade's Blood

Edited by Charles W. Ott

Cover Photo by D-Keine
Cover Photo by neoblues
Back Cover Photo by Stacey Gabrielle Koenitz Rozells
Cover Design by Kat Huddleston

Printed in the United States of America

A Max Maguire Vampire Novel

Jade's Blood

by Kathie Huddleston

To my wonderful husband and editor,
Charles W. Ott
and
To all the writers' groups
and writers who have helped
me tell a better story.

PROLOGUE

Jade pushed Max down on the bed. Her eyes captured him and his plans to escape vanished. His body betrayed him and Max's growing desire pushed away the nagging thoughts about what he knew she was.

She pulled off her dress. She wasn't wearing anything underneath. He studied her body for a moment and she was so perfect… captivating deep blue eyes, curls of cascading blonde hair cupped her beautiful breasts, legs long enough to wrap around him and never let go. She reached down to unbutton his shirt, but he stopped her and unbuttoned it himself.

As Jade unzipped Max's pants, he knew it was wrong. He knew she was evil and that she would take away everything that was precious to him. But then she started to touch him.

She straddled him and bent down kissing him with a hunger he'd never known before. Her desire welled up in him until it was his own. She kissed his neck, and Max gasped fearing what would happen next. He could feel her fangs brush against his skin…

They weren't going to like it. The students were probably going to complain, at least at first. Max Maguire looked out over his classroom as the students piled in, their mismatch of clothing styles and color schemes creating a kind of modern art. There was something about high school students, how they could appear endlessly energetic and bored at the same time. Well, he was going to shake them up today.

Sun streamed through the windows, the leaves from the trees outside creating a mosaic across the students' faces. A couple of broken desks sat in the corner, one on top of the other. The school was worn down, like many in the Chicago school system, without hope of ever being anything more.

At 33 and filled with energy, Max knew he wasn't the normal Chicago public school teacher. He had dark brown hair that was a little too long to make him a respectable teacher, hazel eyes that changed color depending on the light, and a slight exotic look thanks to a mixed gene pool. But the main thing that set Max apart was that he loved teaching.

He went to the whiteboard and wrote "The French and Indian War" as the bell rang. Some of them began to quiet down, which only made the few who continued to talk seem louder.

Max wrote on the board, "You get an A on the quiz if you stop talking now." Silence began to spread through the room, even though he could hear whispering as some conversations continued at a lower volume. They settled into their seats.

Jamal, the class comedian, was as animated as ever and when he realized that Max was staring at him he grinned. "So what we talking about today, Mr. M?"

"I don't think you're getting that 'A', Jamal," said Max. Jamal closed his mouth and shrugged. "What would you like to talk about today, Jamal?"

"Not the French and Indian War. I just think there are other, you know, bigger and more important wars." Hushed laughter broke out around the room.

"Really, why don't you tell me which war you'd like to cover. That way we won't bother with, you know, the insignificant ones. Why, we don't even have to do them in order, do we?" The laughter got louder.

"That's exactly what I was thinking. I mean we can always go back to get the little ones later on if there's time at the end of the semester."

"Thanks for your input, Jamal. If you or anyone else in class would like to add any additional thoughts on the subject, I'll expect a five page report which can be presented to the class on the underlying currents of…"

Max pointed to Jamal. "The French and Indian War," Jamal said.

"Yes. That's right. The French and Indian War," Max repeated.

"You are the teacher, Mr. M. If you think we need to learn about the F and I War, then we're with you." He looked around at the other students but they weren't joining in.

Max laughed. "You're sure then? I wouldn't want to bore you."

"Really, it's no trouble at all, Mr. M," Jamal said.

"Well, good. Everyone else gets an A on the quiz, except you, Jamal. You get to take the quiz." Jamal stopped talking and there were some quiet laughs around the room. "Guess what class, we're not going to talk about the French and Indian War today." The class was silent. Now, he had everyone's attention. Max glanced at the doors and leaned toward them. "That's just a cover."

Sara, a normally shy girl with thick black glasses, spoke up. "A cover for what?"

"I'll have to swear you all to secrecy."

"What's going on, Mr. Maguire?" It was Kevin, who was bound to be a future Republican. Max was in his glory. He had them now.

"The problem is, I have to believe you're trustworthy. If even one student blows the whistle, I'm just afraid…"

"Afraid of what?" Sara asked.

"Afraid we might be talking about the French and Indian War for… oh… a long, really long time."

"Lord knows, we don't want that, Mr. M," Jamal said. "Believe me, we are going to be so quiet about your secret, we won't even talk to each other about it."

"Absolutely," said one of the students from the back of the room.

"So, we're all in agreement then?" Max asked. Nods met him around the room. "If anyone doesn't agree, just speak up." There was silence. "Okay."

Max returned to his desk at the front of his class. He let the silence hang in the air like a basketball balancing on the rim of a hoop. Max just loved this part. The students waited expectantly. He opened the large bottom drawer of his desk, and then glanced suspiciously at the doors. He looked back at his class.

"You're sure now?" Max asked. A sudden and vocal uproar met his question. They were squirming in their chairs, laughing and complaining. Max loved the smell of victory in the afternoon.

"All right," Max said sharply to silence them again. He leaned toward them and lowered his voice. "Here's the deal, we're going to do something a little different."

Max pulled the bottom draw open a bit more and pulled out a cowboy hat that was upside down. He rested it on the desk in front of him. Inside the hat were strips of paper that had been folded a couple times.

"Mr. M, that is a cowboy hat," Jamal said.

"Thank you, Jamal."

Max stood up and grabbed the hat. "Inside the hat are slips of paper. Every student will take one slip. On that slip of paper is your assignment, which will be explained shortly.

No talking until everyone has their slip… I mean that."

Max went to the first row and one by one the students took a slip of paper out of the hat. After the first few students had chosen, the whispering started.

"Shush!" Max said sharply.

In a few minutes everyone had a piece of paper and the confused students looked from their slips to Max, and then around the room to each other. Max faced them and leaned back against his desk.

"For the next four weeks you will, while you're in this class, take on the career that's written on your slip of paper… Jamal, what is your career for the next four weeks?"

Jamal laughed. "It says, Stockbroker."

"There we have it. Jamal is a stockbroker." Max started down the aisle and glancing at the papers as he went. "Rita is a novelist. Jason is a surgeon. Latoya is a firefighter. Ricardo is an astronaut. Mike is a chef… Everyone here has been given a fine career." Max ended up at the back of the room, but he kept talking and heads followed him as he walked back to his desk. "All right, who has it? Come on. Spill. You know who you are."

Sara raised her hand slowly. "I'm guessing maybe it's me."

"Let's see," Max said.

Sara stared down at her desk as she lifted the paper so Max could read it.

"We have a winner. There she is folks, the President of the United States, Sara Kelly." Max began applauding.

"Oh, come on, Mr. Maguire. That's silly," Kevin said.

"Why? I think Sara would make a great President. You're not saying that because she's a woman, are you?"

"Uh, uh, no…" he stammered.

The girl sitting in front of him turned around to glare at him.

"Yeah, Kev. Why is it silly?" she asked.

"Maybe she's not the next Barack Obama or Kamala Harris. That's all I'm saying."

Max laughed. "Then again, maybe she is… Now that you know what career you'll have in this class for the next four weeks, your job, whether you choose to accept it or not, is to do some research on that profession." Mumbled complaints came from various points of the room. "Yes, there will be some work. We'll spend the last few minutes of every class talking about those careers, and you are responsible for answering the questions your fellow students come up with. So, for example, Jamal needs to find out what it takes to become a stockbroker. Sara needs to find out how old you have to be to become the President. And Jason needs to find out how many years you have to go to school to become a surgeon."

"But Mr. M, I don't know what a stockbroker does," Jamal said.

"Yeah, Jamal's thinking a good career would be flipping burgers at Mickey D's," said one of the students from the back of the room. Laughter broke out again.

"It's your job to find out," Max said. "Everyone in this room has a shot at any of these careers, even President of the United States. Who's the Vice President?"

Kevin smirked and reluctantly raised his hand.

"There you go," Max said. "Now we can all rest safely knowing that if President Sara can't fulfill her duties, Vice President Kevin will step in."

"Somehow that doesn't make me feel safe," Jamal said.

"Can we trade?" asked one of the girls.

"No," Max said. "However, who would like to trade if he or she could?" Several hands went up. "I do have one more that can go to anyone who wants it."

Max grabbed the paper from his desk. "Let's see what this one is…" Max opened up the paper for all to see. "Anyone want to be a 'high school history teacher?'" All the hands vanished.

The students were laughing and shaking their heads. Max feigned offense. "You guys are breaking my heart." Then he offered a big smile.

"Now, just so this does fit into the realm of a history class, don't forget that part of what you have to find out is about the history of your career."

Max continued the class with a discussion on careers and college. They argued, they complained, they considered lives they'd never imagined before. Max looked out at the faces that held the key to the future.

As the bell rang the students were still talking about their assignment on the way out. Jamal hung back for a moment until everyone left.

"Mr. M, do you know why Crystal hasn't been to class?"

"No, I haven't heard anything."

Jamal nodded, concern flickering across his face. He turned to walk away, but then looked back. "Mr. M, what career did you want to have when you were in high school?"

Max sat back in his chair and picked up the hat. He turned it over so the few remaining strips of paper fell onto his desk. In a practiced motion, he flipped the hat by the rim and it landed perfectly on his head. With his forefinger he pushed the hat up slightly. Then he put his feet up on the desk. Jamal saw that he was wearing cowboy boots.

"Me... I always wanted to be a cowboy," he said with a perfect southern drawl.

"You are the strangest teacher I have ever had."

"Why thanks. Maybe we could listen to some country music in class on Monday. What do you think? Maybe you could take that quiz?"

Jamal shook his head and retreated, laughing. Max loved his job.

# # #

Max dashed into the administration office to face Mrs. Vigars, the principal's secretary.

"No running in the halls, Mr. Maguire."

"Yes, Ms. Vigars," Max said.

"You did it again, didn't you?" she asked.

"What?"

"You're doing that career thing again. You know what happens when you rile up the wildlife."

Max shrugged his shoulders. "I couldn't help myself."

"At least you didn't dress up like Abraham Lincoln this time."

"You have to admit, I made a stunning Lincoln."

"No. You made a short Lincoln. He was 6'4". And I sincerely doubt he ever danced to hip-hop."

"So I was a couple inches short," Max said. Mrs. Vigars cleared her throat. "All right, four inches short." Max made a fist and tapped the counter top a couple times. "If only they'd let me get some really interesting books to teach from. Thank God I have the internet."

"Max, you are incorrigible. Next thing we know those kids will actually start believing they can do anything. Then where will we be?"

"It's too scary to imagine."

"What can I do for you today, Max?"

"Crystal Stevens has missed my class the last three days. Have you talked to her grandmother?"

Mrs. Vigars flipped through the folders on her desk. "Crystal Stevens… No one's called from the family. I left a message on their answering machine yesterday and today, but haven't gotten any calls back."

Max was worried. Crystal was a good kid. Very bright, although she pretended she wasn't. She'd missed some time after her grandmother ended up in the hospital, but she'd been working hard to make that up. "Okay. I'll check back on Monday if she's not in class."

"It's probably nothing, Max. You know how it goes," Mrs. Vigars said.

"Can I get an expense voucher?"

She tapped Crystal's folder and nodded. "Sure. I'll just go to the other room and get one for you."

She wasn't supposed to give out the kid's information, not

even to a teacher. There'd been an incident a couple years back and some rules had been put into place to keep the student's addresses private. As Mrs. Vigars left the room, Max picked up Crystal's folder and opened it. He didn't have a piece of paper, so he grabbed a pen and wrote her address on the palm of his hand. He returned the folder to its place. Mrs. Vigars gave him another moment and then returned with the form.

"Here you go," she said.

"Thank you, Mrs. Vigars," he said.

"You're welcome," she said with a knowing glance before returning to her work.

As Max left the office, he looked at the address. It wasn't far away. It wouldn't hurt to run by Crystal's apartment after school, just to check things out.

# # #

Max had some work to do after his classes, so it was dark by the time he left. He turned on the overhead light in his car and looked at his palm, checking the address. It was only a 15-minute drive according to the Maps on his phone. He called before leaving school, but he got voice mail. More than likely he'd get to her building and find nobody home.

The neighborhood was mostly made up of ornately crafted apartment buildings and stores from another era, with the occasional modern building mixed in. Max had to drive around the block to find a parking space.

When he got to the old but well maintained building, Max found the buzzer for Stevens. He tried it several times, but there wasn't any answer. He stepped back and looked up at the tall building. Max took a breath and considered his options. The best bet was to see if someone else would let him in, maybe one of Crystal's neighbors. He tried a couple of buzzers, before he heard the loud buzz that released the door. He let himself in. He'd been expecting to be interrogated, but had gotten lucky.

Crystal's apartment was on four and Max was slightly out

of breath when he reached her floor. Looked like it was time to get back to the gym. He found her door and saw that it wasn't pulled all the way shut. He knocked gently so as not to jar it. But standing there, he smelled something that made him pull back. Max had been in the Army and had the misfortune to know what a dead body smelled like. The body must have been there for a while, like maybe three days.

Max really didn't want to open the door. No matter what he saw in the room, it wasn't going to be good. Logically, he knew there was no way, if Crystal was in the room, he would to be able to help her. He should just call the police. But he couldn't leave.

Max gently pushed the door open and the smell came at him full force. His head snapped back. It took him a minute, but he forced himself to peer into the small one room apartment. An elderly woman lay in the bed dead, her eyes wide open staring at him. Max thought he might lose it for a moment. He breathed through his mouth, but the odor rolled over his tongue and he gagged. Not breathing was a better choice if he could manage it.

He stepped in and looked around and tried to avoid looking at Crystal's grandmother. The bed took up most of the apartment, with a kitchen table and an easy chair being the only other major pieces of furniture. Boxes were piled up along the walls. It was a neat and organized, but very full apartment.

He walked around the bed and glanced in the bathroom. There was no place to hide, but he did check out the open closet and looked under the bed, just in case. Max didn't touch or disturb anything.

Max needed to call someone, but he'd forgotten his phone in the car and the apartment phone was laying in pieces on the floor. It was the only sign that violence might have happened.

On the kitchen table sat a weighty library book about the French and Indian War. Max left quickly. He couldn't wait to get out of the apartment. Since his cell phone was in the car, he'd have to use one of the neighbor's phones. Max used the sleeve of his coat to pull the door shut so he wouldn't disturb any fingerprints or evidence the police might find.

He walked several steps away from the apartment as he tried to get away from the smell. He really shouldn't have gone in. Running his hand through his hair, Max took a few moments to try to gather himself. Where was Crystal? Had she run away when her grandmother died? Was she hurt? What could have happened? Max went to the first apartment and knocked. No answer. He tried another door, but even though he could hear a TV inside no one answered. After the third try, he knew he had to get out of there. The smell made him sick even from the hall. He had to get his cell phone to call the police. Let them sort it out. He needed fresh air.

Max ran down the stairs. Crystal was in trouble. That much he knew. He pushed through the outside door and rested heavily against the building. "Oh, God. Pull together. Pull together," he told himself. A few deep breaths of fresh air calmed his stomach down.

Right now he had to call the police. Time could mean everything if Crystal was in danger. Max rushed toward his car. Half a block down, he saw Crystal standing in the alley between two apartment buildings. He could just make her out in the darkness, with her tiny frame and her hair pulled back the way she often wore it. He tripped over a crack in the sidewalk and almost fell on his face. By the time he got his balance she was walking away from him.

"Crystal," he called. "Crystal, stop… it's me, Max Maguire." When he reached the alley, she turned the corner toward the back of the building. "Crystal," he yelled.

Max ran after her. Something was very wrong. She hadn't even acknowledged him. As he rounded the building, Max saw her standing with a well dressed man and women. The dim light on the building barely cast enough illumination to make them out. Crystal was black and they were white. He stopped, trying to comprehend the situation. Were they taking her into foster care? But it felt wrong somehow. Max didn't understand what was going on.

Every instinct inside him told him to keep his distance. "Crystal, are you all right?"

"I'm fine, Mr. Maguire. You really shouldn't have come."

"I was worried about you. Your grandmother…" Max glanced away and couldn't help but take a step back when he looked at the couple with her. Something was peculiar about them.

"I know," Crystal said. Her young, fresh face looked so calm.

Two men came up behind him and he was surrounded. Max backed up against the wall of the building. "What's going on here, Crystal?"

"These are my friends. They're my family now."

"I see." Max looked from face to face, all with a strangeness about them. One of the two that had come up behind him was a man with African American features, but almost white skin. The woman's eyes had a red tint to them. If they were a gang, it was the weirdest gang he'd ever seen because the people didn't seem to fit together. Even Crystal seemed different. Whatever was going on, she was a part of it. "Look, um, maybe you could come with me. Help me, you know, take care of your grandmother."

"She doesn't need anything anymore."

"That's not true. She needs a funeral, and, uh…" Max saw that they were starting to close in on him.

Crystal walked up to him and held out her hand. Max reached out to take it. He had to get her out of there. Crystal smiled and then grabbed him with an impossibly hard grip.

"Crystal!" he yelled. Then Max saw the fangs that slipped between her lips. He couldn't quite bend his mind around what he was seeing. With a flick of her wrist, Crystal threw him against the building and he banged his head hard. He fell to the ground. Max vision blurred for a moment, but when he looked up he could see they all had fangs.

## CHAPTER 2

The first thing Max noticed after the pounding in his head died down somewhat was the smell. He couldn't open his eyes, but the stench of decay was mixed with other unpleasant odors, some of which Max could recognize, some which he couldn't. The acid taste in his mouth told him he must have vomited at some point.

His arms hurt. In fact, just about every part of his body hurt. Max forced his eyes open slightly and realized that he was in a standing position, tied to something, with his arms out to his sides. Ropes cut into him, holding him up.

He turned his head to see if he could make out where he was. Pain shot through him and he almost lost consciousness again. Moving his head was a bad idea. He was in some sort of large room. A spotlight lit up the center of the area he was in, but the rest of the room vanished into darkness. He could hear movement and whispers in the background, but couldn't make out how many people might be there.

A large cross stood a dozen feet in front of him, and Max realized he must be tied to a similar one himself. A huge ornate chair Max could only compare to a throne, sat off to his left side on a platform with several steps leading up to it.

Crystal had gotten herself into something, and now he was involved too. Begging for his life wasn't going to change anything. He'd discovered that a long time ago as a child. When some evil son of a bitch wants to cause pain, pleading and begging only made it worse. Whatever happened, he'd better think fast. That might not prove to be easy, but at least the pounding in his skull had slowed a bit. He closed his eyes.

Several minutes passed and Max settled in to wait. Dozens of thoughts ran through his mind. None of them were good. Maybe the people who had him killed Crystal's grandmother. He wasn't tied up for his health. Most likely, they were planning on killing him.

"Teacher, you've come back to life," a woman's voice spoke, deep and rich. He heard a slight echo, and Max realized the room was quite big. As she came out of the darkness to face him, he was surprised. She had long blonde hair, beautiful exotic features, stunning deep blue eyes and skin as white as ivory. She wore a skintight burgundy dress that went to the floor with a long slit up the side. It left little to the imagination. He expected some gangbangers or religious fanatics, but this was something else.

"Where am I?" Max asked, his voice thick and rough.

She cocked her head and came to within a few inches of him. A slow smile overtook her and she turned and went to her throne. "One of your former students has requested that we make you part of my little family. That would be instead of killing you. How would you feel about that?"

Max carefully turned his head toward her. "Survival is usually preferable," he said.

She considered him again. "Crystal," she said. Crystal walked out of the darkness and went to her side. "I think you're right. Let's do keep him." Crystal nodded once, and then stood silently by the woman's side. When he saw Crystal his heart broke. He wasn't going to be able to get her out of this.

"Tell me, Teacher, what do you think this is all about?" the woman asked.

"Why don't you tell me," he said. "It appears I'm not going anywhere." Max felt dizzy and sick.

She laughed. "So it does. In fact, you have all the time in the world."

"You know, I'll be missed. People will be looking for me and for Crystal too."

"No one's looking for Crystal. Since her grandmother passed away, she's gone to live with a relative. She's part of my family, so that part's not even a lie. She's called some of her friends to say goodbye… As for you, we're going to take care of all that too. It's really nothing you need to worry about."

"So you've got it all figured out."

"All people really need is a good explanation and they'll accept anything."

"What do you want from me?" Max asked. The room was swaying and he closed his eyes to stop it.

"I have everything I want."

"I'll bet. You've got a nifty throne and if I'm not hearing things it sounds like you've got some minions hiding in the dark just waiting to do your bidding. What more could a girl ask for?"

"You understand me, then."

"I don't suppose you'd want to let Crystal go?"

"I don't think she wants to leave. Do you, little one?" she directed her question to Crystal.

"I'm home. Why would I want to leave?"

Max took a breath. What had they done to her? "Well, then since you're all one big happy family, how about letting me down?"

She laughed.

"I didn't think so. It's okay. I'm going to pass out in a minute anyway."

"Don't pass out too quickly. You wouldn't want to miss the show."

"If I'm the main attraction, I think I'd love to miss it."

"Do you know what I am, Teacher?"

"No, but why don't we talk about it over a drink? I've been told I'm a good listener."

"My name is Jade, and your life belongs to me."

He shook his head and regretted it. "Why? Because I just happened to walk down the wrong alley?"

"Yes…" she hissed.

Max managed a weak laugh. "Then get on with it, lady, because I'm having a really bad day. These ropes are killing me and my head feels like it's going to explode."

"Let's dance then." Jade lifted her chin slightly. She was signaling to someone. A man who looked homeless was led out of the darkness by a tough-looking large man and left to stand before her. He was poorly dressed and unkempt. "What's your name?" she asked.

"They call me Rails," he said carefully.

"Well, Rails, you know the deal," she said to him. "Will you kill that man for one thousand dollars?" Jade pointed toward Max.

Max was really hoping he'd pass out now. Nothing that was going to happen at this point was going to be good. He struggled against the ropes, but there wasn't any give at all. Rails checked Max out and then turned back to Jade. "I'll do whoever you want for that kind of money."

"Good, but make it slow. We want to have some fun," she said. Rails nodded. The woman handed Rails a sword. Yes, he was having a really, really bad day. He tugged at the ropes frantically. He could think of worse ways to die, but not many.

Rails turned from her and took a couple steps toward him. The look on the man's face was set. Rails was going to kill him. Max gritted his teeth. "Shit. Oh, shit," he said.

Then Max saw Jade rise behind the man. He could swear her feet must have left the ground. She took Rails from behind in a violent embrace, pulling his head to the side to expose his neck. He dropped the sword as he struggled to escape, but he was no match for her. She smiled at Max, showing her teeth. Her canines grew into sharp fangs as he watched.

"Welcome to my world, Teacher," she said and then she plunged her fangs into the man's neck. Max watched in horror as Rails stopped struggling and Jade drank. Max's stomach was in knots, as he watched her and pulled against the ropes. She took her time, never taking her eyes off Max. When she was done, she dropped Rails to the ground. He wasn't dead. He started to crawl away from her.

Jade looked up at Max. She was licking the blood from her fangs.

"Why did you… do that?" Max asked, his voice breaking.

"We need to fake your death. Wouldn't want to have people snooping around looking for you. He just happens to fit the height, weight and age requirements. Are you really that concerned? He was ready to kill you without a thought for the amusement of others."

"He's desperate. This is insane. What's the matter with you people?"

"Well, that would fall into the category of us not really being people."

"So what? You're vampires?" Max laughed. The pain in his head was driving him crazy. "Well, Vampire Queen, no one has to die here. Just let him go. And let me and Crystal go, while you're at it."

"I am going to have fun with you, Teacher. And it will be such a tragedy when your house burns down, with that popular teacher burnt beyond recognition. There won't be enough left for the urn." Rails tried to stand. Two of her people pulled him out of sight. Max could hear others in the darkness and he knew they were finishing him off.

"I don't believe in vampires," Max said. A wave of dizziness swept over him. He was going to lose consciousness. That was one blessing.

"Really?"

As Max surrendered to the darkness, he knew one unfortunate thing. Rails was probably the lucky one.

# # #

Max woke up in a bed. He was naked. Someone had cleaned him up and, wherever he was, the air in the room smelled much better than where he'd been the night before. His head was still killing him, but the pounding had dulled.

He slowly sat up. His arms were heavily bruised where the ropes had held him. That alone was solid and unfortunate proof that the events he remembered weren't his imagination.

The sparsely furnished room he was in was not very large, but it had a bathroom. Max was guessing the door that might offer escape was locked.

"This really sucks," Max said. He couldn't stop himself from groaning at the unintentional joke.

He reached around and felt the back of his head. There was a pretty nasty scab where his head had met the brick building. He probably had a concussion, but that was the least of his worries at the moment.

Max carefully stood up. He went to the door, but it was locked as he had suspected. He saw that there were curtains, indicating a window. But when he pulled them back, there was nothing but a wall. Oh, well. Escaping was at the top of his list, right after peeing and splashing cold water on his face.

Max laughed at himself. His world suddenly had vampires in it and he still had to pee. He walked unsteadily to the toilet and took care of business. At the sink, he bent over as far as he could without feeling dizzy and splashed water on his face, cupping his hand to drink some of the water. He still had a bad taste in his mouth, so he drank a couple more scoops of water. He stood up to see his reflection in the mirror. He looked terrible. He had dark circles under his eyes, but no injuries to his face. He checked his teeth just for safe measure. At least he hadn't sprouted fangs while he was out.

Through the mirror, Max could see the door to the room open. Jade stepped into sight and looked at him. Suddenly in a blur she was standing behind him. "Feeling better?"

He turned too quickly. Just inches from him, Jade handed him a towel.

"What do you want?" Max didn't bother to hurry as he wrapped the towel around his waist. Max noticed that her skin was pink, not white like the night before.

"I thought you might want something to wear," Jade said as Crystal came through the door holding a pile of neatly folded clothes. Max looked over his shoulder to the mirror and saw all three of them, as if seeing them in the mirror discounted the entire vampire possibility. He felt unsteady and leaned against the sink for support.

"I thought vampires didn't reflect in mirrors."

"Just a silly rumor," Jade said.

"Do I have any choice in this?" Max asked.

"To the world, you're already dead."

"Jade, who am I going to tell? I'll get locked up if I start talking about vampires."

"Do you think this has something to do with your silence?" He could tell she was amused.

"Since I'm not a blood sucking creature of the night, I really don't have a clue what this is about."

"Well, the finding out is the fun part." Jade took a step closer to him. Despite himself, Max felt powerfully attracted to her. He wanted to run his fingers through her beautiful blonde hair and fall into those deep blue eyes. He turned away and looked into the mirror.

"I don't want to hurt anyone," Max said to her reflection in the mirror.

She pressed up against him and he was afraid she might take him right there. What scared him more was that a part of him wanted her to. He could feel her desire as though it was his own. "People hurt each other all the time, Teacher."

She released him. Max turned around to see that they had both gone. He walked unsteadily to the bed and got dressed as quickly as he could manage. They'd brought him jeans and a blue t-shirt that said, "Bite me" on the back, but no shoes or socks. At least everything fit. He was guessing it was morning and he'd end up as the main course when evening came. He had to find a way out before that or the only thing he'd be teaching in the future would be night school.

The door opened again, and Crystal entered carrying a bowl of soup with a spoon. The large guy he'd seen the night before stood in the door watching them and looking very angry.

"I thought you might be hungry," she said.

"Thanks," Max took the bowl and set it down on the dresser. His stomach was too queasy to eat. "I'll let it cool."

"I'm sorry I hurt you."

"It's okay. I guess you don't know your own strength… What's his problem?" Max asked about the big guy.

Crystal smiled easily. "That's George. I'm a newbie. He's watching me so I won't, you know, do anything. Jade has plans for you."

"How lucky I am," Max said. "I feel so comforted." Crystal was just a kid. Max couldn't believe any of it.

"Sorry you got caught up in this, Mr. Maguire. But it's not what you think."

"I think you're never going to graduate high school, and I'm in deep… trouble." Max had started to swear, but somehow he couldn't do it in front of her. It'd only been a couple days since she was one of his brightest students and he was her teacher.

"I've never felt anything like it. I know you can't understand that yet, but you will."

"These people are murderers." Max glanced at George, who was taking in the conversation.

"Then so am I, Mr. Maguire. When the hunger takes you, you'll do anything. It's so powerful, so amazing. Nothing else matters. Only what Jade wants and what I want."

She moved closer to him and Max pulled back. Dealing with Jade was one thing, but this was disturbing. Crystal looked back at George.

"They killed your grandmother."

"I know." Crystal looked away from him.

"How did this happen to you?"

"I was coming home from the library. I was so happy. I just found the perfect book on the French and Indian War." She smiled. "I was going to use it for that extra credit paper… It was late and I was walking home. I don't know why she chose me. I was so scared, but then…"

"What happened to your grandmother, Crystal?"

Confusion flashed over her face. She shook her head. "I was worried about Grams and Jade took care of her." She appeared so innocent and sweet one minute. Then in an instant something in her manner changed and she leveled a look at him that was frightening. "I gotta go."

She took a last glance at him and left quickly. So, that was it. Jade had turned Crystal into a vampire and then killed her grandmother so nobody would come searching for her. Max felt sick and not because of his head wound.

He should have stopped Crystal from leaving, but to tell her what? That it was going to be okay? That time would heal her? That she had the rest of her life to look forward to? As her teacher, he should have been able to protect her, to see she was in trouble. That was definitely one of his faults, believing he could fix any problem. Putting his nose in where it didn't belong. Well, his nose was going to get cut off this time. Max couldn't help Crystal. He couldn't even help himself.

He examined his brief knowledge of vampires. Max couldn't manage sunlight, at least from this room since it had no windows. Chopping off a vampire's head might work, but he didn't have anything to do that with and in his condition that would be quite a feat. Fire was a possibility, but even that would be difficult and it would be suicide. These vampires obviously didn't have any problems with crosses, but maybe a wooden stake through the heart would do the trick. The only problem was that there wasn't any wood in his room. The bed and the chair were metal and the dresser and the desk were made of some sort of plastic. And that was it for furniture. Of course, that probably meant that a wooden stake would be effective if he could get his hands on one. Either that or the vampire interior decorator must have believed wooden furniture was bad luck.

Max worked on the door for a while, hoping to figure out a way to open it. The door was made of steel, so he wasn't going to be able to break through it. Max used the soup spoon to fight with the hinges for a time, but they wouldn't budge.

The next possibility would be to go through the wall itself. The spoon was helpful in scraping off the paint, but the walls had been enforced with steel also. Max figured that the room had specifically been set up to hold a vampire, or perhaps one in training since they seemed to have great physical strength judging by Crystal. Logically, if the room could hold a vampire, he didn't have much of a chance of getting out with brute strength, especially in his condition.

Still, he had to try. The floor was his next target. Under the tile floor, Max found cement. It was possible to break through cement, but not without a lot of noise. Worse, he could barely stand up, let alone pound away at a cement floor. Finally, Max managed to get on top of the dresser to take a shot at the ceiling. But like the walls, a coat of paint concealed steel. He got down and sat on the bed. There had to be a way out.

Maybe he could electrocute them. A puddle of water just inside the door and a live wire might do that. He'd seen that in a movie once. Of course, he didn't know much about electricity. Max realized he was hungry. He got up and washed his spoon. It was pretty bent up, but would do the trick. The chicken noodle soup was cold, but still tasted good and he ate it all.

He never wore a watch, so he had no idea how much time he had left before she came for him. There was no frame of reference, except that his headache was coming back with a vengeance. Where would he get a live wire from? The light sources were all from the ceiling. He'd have to get enough wire to reach the floor. There weren't any outlets.

"Fuck!" Max grabbed the bowl and threw it across the room. He tried to grab the chair, but he had to catch the edge of the bed to keep from falling. He was simply too hurt to have the fit he wanted to have.

Max didn't have a chance. It served him right for not paying attention in history teacher school when they went through the "How to Escape from Blood Sucking Vampires" class. Too bad he didn't believe in vampires back then. Maybe he could have studied up and been more prepared. Bummer.

Max laid back on the bed. It was just a guess, but he probably wasn't going to escape in the next few minutes. If only his head would stop hurting he might be able to figure a way out. He closed his eyes and escaped the pain the only way he could.

# # #

Max woke up with a start. He felt terrible. He wasn't sure how long he'd been sleeping, but he had to use the toilet, so chances were it had been a while. He relieved himself and then stared at his reflection in the mirror.

He was a condemned man. After Jade finished with him, he'd never be a teacher again. Never buy groceries or grade papers or pay bills. If the myth about vampires and the sun was true, he'd never see the sun again. Would there even be anything left of him when the deed was done? Would he just end up being one of Jade's minions with no concept that killing was wrong?

Max studied his face. What was she going to take away from him? As Max looked at the mirror it struck him. The mirror was made of glass. If he could break it, he might be able to make a weapon. He'd probably end up getting cut himself, but at least he'd have a chance.

Max grabbed a towel and wrapped it around his hand. It was going to hurt for him to hit the glass hard enough to break it and he'd be lucky if it didn't make him pass out again. Max looked at the door. He didn't have any choices.

He took a breath and pulled his arm back. With every ounce of strength he could manage, he punched the mirror.

To the sound of breaking glass, Max screamed "Oh, shit!" as he crumbled to the floor.

He laid there for a while before he could open his eyes again. The pain was nearly blinding and it took him a few moments to focus on the small bits of broken glass next to him. None of them were big enough to do any damage. Max freed his hand from the towel and reached up to grab the sink. Slowly he pulled himself to his feet.

The mirror was bent at odd angles and radiated out from a central point like a freakish spider web and dozens of Max Maguires stared back at him. In the sink were several pieces of glass. Max put his weight on the edge of the sink and picked up the one piece of glass that just might save his life. It was about eight inches long and came to a point. Max laughed and tears ran down his face. He actually had a chance.

He took a deep breath and wiped his face with his hand. Something told him he didn't have much time. Max eased himself down to sit on the toilet and he grabbed a washcloth. He carefully wrapped it around the larger end of the glass. Now he had a knife. Even if he couldn't cut Jade's head off, he could at least do some damage.

Max left the bathroom and shut the door so no one would see the broken mirror. He sat on the chair and looked at his makeshift weapon. The knife was too large to fit in his pocket, so he carefully tucked it in the back of his pants. Then he practiced pulling it out and holding it threateningly. He managed to cut himself once, but after several tries he could do it pretty smoothly.

He sat back to wait and applied pressure to the small cut on the palm of his hand. Max had a feeling she'd be able to smell the blood. It didn't take long for the cut to stop bleeding. Max practiced pulling the knife out a couple more times. He focused on his breathing. His life depended on him being ready.

The funny thing was that if Jade only had planned to kill

him, like she had Rails, Max could have come to terms with that. But she wanted to make him into something terrible. Something evil, and he couldn't let that happen. If he couldn't stop her, he'd use the blade on himself.

Max jumped when he heard the door open. It was Jade. She was ivory white and he knew that was a bad thing. She was wearing a very tight black dress, and he was pretty sure, nothing else. Max stood up.

"I don't suppose we could talk about this?" Max asked. She came to him slowly, like a tiger stalking its prey. Max glanced at the closed door.

"It's not locked and I do like a good chase." She was so close he could feel her cool skin caress him. He felt the glass knife press into his back.

Max stepped to the side a few inches. "I still don't believe in vampires."

"I see."

"Please, don't do this to me." Max knew he was breaking his rule about begging, but he'd never tried it with a she-demon before.

"Do you think you could ever just go back to your safe little world, Teacher? If you're not one of us, you would be fighting against us." Max closed his eyes for a moment. She touched his chest and a shiver ran through him. "But that's not why we're here. I'm going to make you one of my children because I want to, because I can."

Her voice reverberated through him. It was all he could do to keep standing. He tried to avoid looking into her eyes, but she was so intoxicating. He couldn't identify her perfume. It was light musk with just a touch of something else. He continued to try to inch away from her, until he found himself backed up to the wall next to the bed. He hadn't seen her take a step, but she was right there, slightly touching him. There were simply no more options. He pushed the desk to the side and slid past her so his back was to the door.

"I really don't want to be a vampire."

She stood only inches from him. He could feel his body responding to her. "Then leave. Or try to."

Max reached back and put his hand around the knife. He'd have to make the cut deep, right across her lovely neck and then maybe he'd have a chance to run for it. Maybe vampires weren't as resilient as the propaganda.

He played the movement in his mind, taking measure of how far he'd need to step back to gather momentum and speed for the cut, making it into a calculation.

Max smiled at her. "I think I would like to leave."

Jade laughed. He took one step straight back and swung the knife toward her. But Jade wasn't there. She was suddenly just out of his reach, still laughing.

"That's a nice toy. Didn't your mother ever teach you not to play with sharp objects?"

Max stepped back a couple more steps. He was breathing hard and he felt unsteady. The knife was still in his hand, a jagged edge digging into his thumb. "I guess I missed that lecture."

He backed up another step, but she was suddenly gone. She was behind him blocking his way to the door. Max spun around.

"I just want to leave," he said.

"You know that's not going to happen."

Max nodded. He glanced at the knife in his hand. "No. I guess not." He felt so weak, so tired. He made up his mind. There was nothing else to do. With a swift move, Max drove the blade up to his own neck. But before the sharp edge of the glass could strike home she was there, holding his wrist. Blood dripped from the wound in his thumb. She suddenly seemed a little sad.

"That's not going to happen either. I don't want you to die. I want you to become part of my family."

Jade took his makeshift knife away from him and held his wrist. He tried to get away from her, but she pulled his hand toward her mouth. Her eyes never left his as she took his thumb between her lips and began to suck. Max felt as if an electric current ran through his body emanating from her mouth, and he could feel her intense pleasure at the taste of his blood. He could actually sense what she was feeling.

She released his hand and Max watched as the cut healed. "How…"

"See, it's not so horrible. I'm going to make you one of the most powerful creatures on earth." He stumbled back nearly falling. When she had been sucking his blood, it was as if he had a direct connection to her. When she let go of him, that connection was severed.

Max turned away from her. What the hell was she doing to him? He had to get away from her, but as he took a step he felt her hand in his. She was gently pulling him to the bed. Max wanted to get away. He really did. He reminded himself how evil she was. And none of that seemed to matter as he followed her. Through her touch, Max could feel her power, her desire, her hunger.

Jade pushed Max down on the bed. Her eyes captured him and his plans to escape vanished. His body betrayed him and Max's growing desire pushed away the nagging thoughts about what he knew she was.

She pulled off her dress. She wasn't wearing anything underneath. He studied her body for a moment and she was so perfect… captivating deep blue eyes, curls of cascading blonde hair cupped her beautiful breasts, legs long enough to wrap around him and never let go. She reached down to unbutton his shirt, but he stopped her and unbuttoned it himself.

As Jade unzipped Max's pants, he knew it was wrong. He knew she was evil and that she would take away everything that was precious to him. But then she started to touch him.

She straddled him and bent down kissing him with a hunger he'd never known before. Her desire welled up in him until it was his own. She kissed his neck, and Max gasped fearing what would happen next. He could feel her fangs brush against his skin. The part of him that could still rebel wanted to push her away, to make her stop.

Until she began to work her lips and tongue down his body as her hand reached down to caress his hard cock with her fingers, until his desire matched hers, until his body was in unison with hers. As his desire rose, he realized she was the woman of his nightmares. A woman who couldn't be resisted, who took away any choice he had ever had about what was right and what was wrong.

Suddenly she rose up and eased his cock inside her. It'd been a long time since he'd had sex without a condom. He'd almost forgotten how it felt. He was surrounded by her coolness and the sensation was beyond anything he could remember. So much for safe sex.

Then she started to move and all he could think about was getting deeper into her, touching her, kissing her.

She bent down to kiss him and then smiled and started kissing his neck. Max didn't want her to stop. Let her take his blood, his life. He didn't care. She lightly scraped her fangs over his neck and teased him for what seemed like an endless amount of time. "Oh, god…"

When she finally bit him, the pain was startling for a moment and then all he felt was exquisite pleasure. He couldn't help but laugh as she drank from him and fucked him. He didn't want her to stop. All she had to do was take it all, then he'd never have to worry about anything ever again.

As Max was about to come, she pulled her hips away from him, prolonging the sex but continuing to drink from him. He tried to get back inside her, but she wouldn't let him. Then, when she knew the timing was right, she started again taking him to the brink and then pulling back.

Max could feel himself getting weaker and he knew she was killing him. When he could stand no more, he felt Jade's passion unleash and a wave of climax shook through them both. Finally, release.

Max was so weak he could barely move. He was dying.

Jade pulled back to look at him with her beautiful blue eyes as she wiped his blood from her mouth. A strand of her hair had turned crimson with his blood. She'd grown pink and warm.

Jade used her fingernail to make a small cut at the base of her neck and her blood began to flow. She kissed him, and Max could taste a hint of his own blood in her mouth. "No, please, I don't want to…"

She smiled. "But you will." She tilted her head so he could drink from her, pulling his head to her neck. As his lips tasted her blood, he was surprised by how sweet it was. He tried to pull away, but she held him firmly. At first he refused to drink, but there was something about the way the blood tasted, something that created a whole new desire in him. Suddenly a powerful urge took over him, some strange overwhelming craving he could only identify as hunger and he couldn't stop himself. As he began to drink, her blood flowed into him giving him a feeling of power he'd never felt before. He wrapped his arm around her waist and pulled her tight against his body. He didn't ever want to stop.

She let him drink for a long time. When she finally started to pull away from him, Max held her tighter. She easily broke his grasp and stood up. Max reached for her, but she put her hand on his chest and pushed him back down on the bed.

"You're very tasty, Teacher. The next few hours are going to hurt like hell, but you'll feel better by sundown."

Jade picked up her dress and left the room naked. He had to go after her. Max tried to stand up, but something was wrong. Suddenly his skin felt like it was on fire. Agony swept over him. He fell off the bed and tried to crawl to the door, but waves of pain shook through him.

Her blood was killing him. Then Max realized it was worse than that because he was already dead.

## Chapter 3

Max never slept that night. He managed to crawl back into the bed, but eventually a strange paralysis set in and all he could do was wait and feel the agonizing assault her blood mounted on his living cells. His body was the battleground for a war, a war he was destined to lose.

In his mind, Max visualized his human blood cells facing off against a superior invading force. Since he suddenly did care whether he lived or died, something that had happened as soon as Jade left him, he determined to battle the invaders. He couldn't speak or scream, so he fought against them the best he could, taking on each wave of the assault. After hours, as he hunkered down in the foxhole in his mind, he amused himself by imagining his human cells with army hats and rifles. He led the charge as the next wave hit, but he couldn't win the battle. As the darkness crept into him he knew the war was lost as well.

Jade's blood was transforming him. Changing him into something horrible. When he was a kid, he'd discovered there were monsters in the world, monsters with human faces. A long time ago, he'd glimpsed that dark place himself and it had taken him years to find the light. Now he was becoming one of the monsters.

When he found his voice again, he let out a long agonizing scream. Finally, it all stopped and Max realized that the blinders of human existence had been removed from him. He could see everything in the darkness. He sensed that the sun was dipping below the horizon. He heard movement in the building and traffic from a street nearby. More importantly he smelled the vampire that guarded his door and several others, not far away. But the smell that brought him to full attention was something different. He didn't know what it was right away, but it didn't take long for him to realize it was a person who wasn't a vampire. A woman. She was in the next room and she was frightened. He could feel her fear.

The paralysis left him slowly as a new sensation hit him. It felt like something crawling around his gut, something deep and primal. It was more powerful than what he'd experienced with Jade. It was hunger unlike anything Max had ever felt before. He tried to push it away.

Max became aware of his body and he realized he was covered with some sort of residue. He scraped some of it off his arm and studied the pasty stuff. Was this the stuff that made him alive? Just expel it, get it out of there and suddenly, instant vampire.

He sat up easily, no pain at all. He reached back and found that his head was healed, although there were still some clumps of dried blood in his hair. It was as though he'd never been hurt. The bruises on his arms were gone. Nothing bothered him. Nothing except the hunger that was building inside him.

Max told the hunger to go away. He tried to force it out of him. He wanted to push it down and pee it right out of his body. But there was the woman. He went to the wall next to the bed and touched it gently. She was on the other side. He could hear her crying. Just a steel wall away.

Max realized that the residue on him was sticky and smelled sour. He suddenly felt he had to get it off, so he hit the shower. He turned hot water on and let it stream over him. He'd expected to turn on the cold water, but the hot water didn't seem to bother him. In fact, it made the residue come off without scrubbing. At first he wondered if the water wasn't as hot as he thought it was, but the bathroom was full of steam. How was it that the water wasn't burning him? His skin should be red where it washed over him, but instead it was white. Ivory white, as if all the pigment had left his skin.

Max turned off the shower and grabbed a towel. So, that was it. Game over. So much for the battle. Of course, he'd forgotten about the fangs. He could feel them in his mouth, long and sharp. He reached up and touched one of them. It sliced his finger open. Max examined the blood that oozed out of the cut. He licked it and then put his finger in his mouth and began to suck. When he pulled his finger away, he watched as the cut healed.

He considered that there must be some sort of healing properties in vampire saliva. That made sense as far as helping a predator conceal its existence. If people kept showing up in morgues with bite marks and drained of blood, the living would have known about them a long time ago. However, it also made sense if the vampire's bite wasn't meant to kill. That was the possibility he'd really like to consider.

He stood up to look at his new fangs, and dozens of Vampire Max's stared at him from the fragmented mirror. He looked the same, but different somehow. The same messy brown hair, the same jaw line, and the same Max. But there was something different as well. Ivory white skin, fangs, and the look of a predator.

He left the bathroom shaking his head. It was just not a real thing. None of this could be possible. He couldn't possibly be dead. Or was it undead? Vampires couldn't really exist. But his gut told him otherwise.

Someone had been in his room. They had cleaned up, collected the errant bowl and spoon, and left him fresh clothing, but with shoes this time. He dressed and thought about the woman on the other side of the wall. Max knew what they were doing. She was to be his first meal. They knew he'd know she was there, so close and yet in a place he couldn't possibly get to. They'd just let vampire nature take its course until the hunger drove him mad. He could feel it affecting him already. It nagged at him like an itch he couldn't get to. He could see the logic of the situation so clearly, and that was the problem. The logic was crazy.

He could sense her moving around. She was probably in a room similar to his. She was terrified, and something about that pleased the hunger inside him very much. And she had her period. Max threw his head back and laughed. "You guys are so subtle! That's it then. Anything to make Max a vampire!"

He put his hands on his head and grabbed at his hair. The hunger was starting to overwhelm him. He took deep breaths. He tried to remember stuff he'd learned in a Yoga class a couple years earlier. Meditation, non-violence, oh yeah. That was going to work for him. He'd just say a mantra. An insane cackle slipped from his lips.

Max shook his head. He had to get control of this. If he didn't, then Jade won and… then… the woman was just too close. The scent of her blood was too strong. How could he regain control with her right there? If only he could just stop everything for a few minutes, he could figure it out. This was all Jade's fault. She'd done this to him. If he could just rip out her heart, everything would be okay.

"You think you can make me your god damn little pet, Jade!"

Max threw himself on the door. He railed at it, pounding the door as hard as he could manage. When he saw that his blows had put dents in the steel, he hit it even harder. He pulled at the door handle, using every bit of new strength he had to pull it open. It wouldn't budge. They should have left him the fucking spoon.

Max grabbed the dresser and ripped it apart in moments. He picked up the chair and used it as a battering ram against the wall. The hunger crept at the edges of his sanity, taking him closer to the edge. It cheered him on, telling him to get out of the room and kill them all.

"You bitch, you think you can destroy my life! You have no right! I'm going to fucking kill you all!"

Max threw himself at the walls, the ceiling, the floor. Suddenly he stopped. The woman was being moved. He felt them bringing her closer to him. Max knew the woman was what his hunger really wanted. Jade was there with her right outside his door. He could hear the woman begging them to stop, to let her go. Max could have told her that the begging thing never worked.

He waited, drunk with her scent. He pounded the door once. What were they waiting for? But, of course, they weren't going to open the door until he moved away from it. Logically, Max knew when they opened the door he'd have a chance to escape. He could kill them all, burn down their building and then do the right thing by getting a nice suntan. He could rip Jade's head off and set it on that throne of hers. He could rid the world of monsters like him.

But the hunger didn't care about revenge or making the world a better place. It wanted the woman. If Max tried to escape, he probably wouldn't be able to have her. Of course, even though he knew there were other people that would make a perfectly good meal, he wanted this woman.

Max paced like a wild beast. Jade undoubtedly had to be careful with newbies like him because the hunger made them insane. Max giggled. Or maybe it was always going to be like this. In crystal clear insanity, Max and his hunger came to terms. The hunger would get the woman and Max would get to kill them all later. If immortality really was one of the perks, he'd have an eternity to get even.

Max sat in the corner where the bed had been before he'd overturned it. He put his arms around his knees and rocked. A moment later the door opened and the woman's scent overpowered him. It was all he could do to keep from attacking. No, he knew he had to be good, or Jade would make him suffer and take her away from him.

"Well, Teacher, you've been busy," Jade said.

"Jade, I'm going to fucking rip your heart out," Max said with a laugh. But all he could look at was the woman next to her. The woman had long dark hair and a sweet face. She was being held by a lady vampire Max hadn't seen before. George was there too.

"I've got a little birthday present for you."

"You're so thoughtful. How did you know what I wanted?

You even wrapped her up for me."

Max was ready to pounce. Maybe he could get Jade and the woman. That would be like winning the Daily Double or a triple point score in Scrabble.

"Her name is Michelle. You'll like her. She teaches high school too." Jade pulled the struggling woman into the room. She was crying as she fell to her knees.

"Really. You planning another barbecue?" Max growled.

"Have fun."

"Jade, I am going to kill you."

"You already tried once."

"If at first Max doesn't succeed…"

"That will be something for me to look forward to."

As Jade left and the door shut, Max said to himself, "Yes, it will."

Like a cornered animal, the woman scrambled away from him as far as she possibly could. Max knew he was the animal and she was his prey. Her eyes were wide in terror. The last sliver of Max's sanity stopped him from pouncing.

"You know what I am, Michelle?"

"Oh, god, please…"

"Do you know!"

"Yes. Please don't hurt me. Please… please… I'm getting married next month. Don't hurt me."

"Congratulations… well, maybe that's premature."

"Oh, god!" Michelle leaped up and ran towards the bathroom. Max simply thought about her and suddenly he had his hands around her waist. He didn't even remember moving his feet, but he had her. She was fighting him and he just held her until she stopped. He pushed her against the wall and then, quite gently, touched her face and hair. He could feel her fear draining out of her body.

"What's happening to me?" she asked softly.

"I don't know." Max kissed her and she responded. He really didn't want to hurt her. But the hunger inside him took over, and as his fangs found their mark. Max knew Michelle would never make that wedding date.

# # #

Max woke up, but his eyes weren't ready to focus. He felt so good. He hadn't felt this good in a long time. He arched his back in a nice long stretch. Was it time to get to school? It wouldn't do for the teacher to be late.

Grim reality startled him as his memory returned. The woman, Michelle, was lying next to him on a mattress that now lay on the floor.

"Oh, no. No." He had to be able to fix her somehow. She couldn't be dead. He couldn't have done this. He shook her to wake her up, but her body was cold. Suddenly he couldn't catch his breath.

"I… I'm… I didn't mean it… No… This isn't happening. I didn't do this." Max shook his head. "No, this wasn't me. Jade did this. It wasn't me!" He turned away from her and began pounding his fist against the wall. In a frenzy he finally hit the wall so hard he fell back onto the bed. His hand was bleeding. He watched it heal. So it wasn't just his saliva that had healing abilities.

How could he have destroyed her so easily? Jade had turned him into a fucking monster. Was this it now? His life would depend on the death of other people?

Max looked at Michelle. She was dead, of course. He ran his fingers through her hair and caressed her. She was cool to his touch. He traced the features of her face. She appeared to be sleeping. He had to remember her. Tears came easily to him, as he mourned her death and his life. As he reached to wipe his face, he almost expected his tears to be red. As if he was crying her blood, that would somehow be so right. But his tears were clear.

"I'm sorry." Max held her and rocked her for a long time. She didn't deserve to die like this. No one deserved to die like this.

Eventually, they came and got him. Another change of clothes gave him a chance to get out of the bloody and wrinkled shirt and into an outfit that was pretty nice. The dark blue dress shirt and black slacks fit him perfectly. Only the new dress shoes were uncomfortable, even though they were the right size. He missed his boots.

As he was led down the corridor, surrounded by three guards, Max realized he was in a large house with wonderful architectural details and lots of modern, expensive furniture. He noticed that none of it was made of wood.

They took him down to the basement, and Max knew he was in the same room he'd been in earlier. The basement was full of smells that now seemed to very much appeal to the creature inside him. The lighting hadn't changed, but he could see everything now. The area Max had been in before was the center to an arena. Rows of seats in three sections rose up to surround the arena, which Max figured might hold forty people. Jade's throne completed the circle. The basement had lots of little nooks and crannies. Just beyond the arena, there were a couple sofas and some chairs and several doors that might lead to separate rooms. There was a large container at the other end of the basement. From the smell, Max knew it was full of acid. What better way to get rid of those pesky bodies.

Several vampires were milling around, chatting. It was just one great big party. Max could sense two non-vampires nearby. No doubt, Jade had them in mind for the evening's entertainment. His guards left him and went to stand near the exit. After all, he was surrounded by vampires. Where was he going to go?

Max could see that the others were glancing his way. He must be the talk of the party. George walked up to him. He looked really angry and Max thought he was going to get hit. Then the guy smiled and stuck out his hand.

"Hi there, Teach. Welcome. I'm George."

Max reluctantly accepted his handshake. "Hi, George." This was too weird. Max was in the middle of a vampire mixer. What was he supposed to do? Make small talk like,

"So, you kill anybody interesting lately?"

"Just want to let you know, you did just fine. Jade was real happy."

"Thanks, I think," Max said.

"She likes you a lot. Not many newbies strike her fancy. Just don't piss her off, and you'll be fine." George looked around to make sure no one was nearby, and then he bent down closer to Max. "Just so you know, it's not going to last with her, but while you're the flavor of the month… enjoy."

"So you and Jade…"

"Oh, no," he shook his head and seemed embarrassed. "She likes you handsome guys. But I see pretty much everything that goes on."

"Say, George, that thing that happened last night, that doesn't happen all the time, does it?"

"No. That's the transformation. The hunger is just a bitch. It'll be easier from now on. The main thing is don't let it go too long before you take care of business."

"I'll remember that."

"Look, buddy, I've been there. I mean, I was an accountant before… all this."

"You were an accountant?"

"I know. Hard to imagine. I look like a bouncer. That's why Jade made me, if you know what I mean? Cause I look like a tough son of a bitch. But that's how it goes."

"Let me guess. You were in the wrong place at the wrong time."

"You got it, Teach. Fate's a bitch. Cool thing was, she let me do my boss. Now that was sweet."

"Yeah?" Max was in hell. There was no doubt about it.

"Look, if you got someone from the previous life, you know, wife, mother-in-law, mistress, girlfriend, or heck, even the principle of that school of yours, just say the word."

"Well, that's something to consider."

"It's really not such a bad gig. You keep Jade happy and you can do anything you want."

"Say, George, can you do this blood drinking thing without… I don't know… killing anyone?"

"Now Teach," George said sternly. "Don't go there. If you show any reluctance that way, Jade will make you do things you don't want to do. Just trust me. Be a good boy and she'll take care of you."

Max nodded. Yeah, all he needed to do was be a good little minion, just like George. Well, Max didn't do minion well.

George continued to talk and it wasn't long before others came to welcome him to the "family." He met Mitch, Wanda, Rachel and several others. Max nodded and listened. They were all too happy to fill him in on the house rules, which largely consisted of "Don't piss off Jade."

When he asked about specifics on Jade, he was met with silence and then the subject was quickly changed. Max listened, speaking rarely as they launched into a variety of topics that included how George really became a vampire, the best way to select a victim and cover up the deed and who Sonny's real father was on General Hospital.

When Crystal and a tall severe looking woman entered, George lowered his voice.

"That's Veronica, Jade's number one. Get ready for the show. Jade likes to do it when there's a newbie like you."

Everyone snapped to attention and all conversations stopped. Max thought everyone would make their way to the seats, and while a few did, most stood in a circle around the arena just outside the lit area. Max decided to stay near George since he was willing to fill him in on what was going on, so he took a place in the circle. Veronica and Crystal stood on either side of the throne and everyone waited. Max could feel something in the air, something that made the hair stand up on the back of his neck. A breeze blew by them. A fine white smoke circled the open area and then slowly floated to the throne. The smoke took the shape of a woman, and then blew away leaving Jade behind. Max wondered if the nifty special effects were really on his account. She cocked her head and surveyed the troops. It was absolutely silent.

Max saw that Jade was wearing the same dress she had worn with him. Somehow, he didn't think that was an accident. He knew that the dress was for him. So, in a way, even though she could do anything she wanted with him, she was still seducing him. Still wanting him to want her. And it worked to some extent. Max felt like he had a split personality. His body wanted her, his mind wanted her dead.

"Who will fight for me today?" she asked.

A male and a female vampire entered the arena from opposite sides of the throne. They were both wearing beautifully embroidered gold and green robes. They stopped to stand directly in front of Jade, with only a couple feet separating them.

"I, Maria, will fight for you," the woman said.

"I, Eric, will fight for you," the man said.

Crystal and Veronica stepped forward to take the robes. Underneath the robes, both vampires were bare-chested and wore only tight gold short shorts that left nothing to the imagination. They had impressive bodies, but Max attention was focused on Maria, who had an innocent looking face and a body to die for. She was so feminine and petite, Max couldn't imagine what kind of a match she'd be for Eric.

He was sure the "fight" wasn't going to be arm wrestling. Veronica and Crystal had taken the robes somewhere and returned with a weapon for each warrior. It was an odd looking thing that was about six feet high, with a sickle on one end and a staff on the other. The sickle had a large curved blade. The other end was encased in steel with a wooden end extending the last 12 inches that tapered off to a sharp point. The weapon obviously was perfect for fighting and killing a vampire. The sickle end could take a head off, while the staff could block a blow from either side and the wooden end would work nicely as a stake. The weapon would have been heavy to a normal human, but for a vampire it shouldn't be a problem. Max hoped he was about to get a lesson in how to kill a vampire.

"Do not disappoint me," Jade told her warriors.

The fighters took their weapons and bowed to Jade.

"Begin."

The man and woman walked to opposite sides of the arena and bowed to each other. Max could sense their excitement rise as they stared at one another. In practiced motions, each twirled the weapon impossibly fast as they began to circle one another. They both stopped suddenly and for a beat, nothing happened.

Then they flew at each other, their weapons spinning. In a violent clash they spun in the air, their lances meeting three times before they landed. Instantly they were back at each other, on the ground this time, as the warriors guided their weapons to strike and react to their opponent's tactics. Sickle met staff, staff met staff, sickle met sickle. It was a furious battle and the combatants seemed equally matched. Even though the man was larger than Maria, she made up for his size by being the more aggressive of the two.

Maria went after Eric with a series of blows until he was slightly off balance. Then she drove the sickle towards his feet, but Eric was suddenly gone. He had leapt up and came down, using his free hand to backhand her across the mouth. The blow drove her back and Eric moved the sickle side of his weapon into position to take her head, but Maria had the angle and took it. She stabbed the wooden point of her staff into his thigh. Eric shrieked as he fell backwards. But he wasn't done yet. He used his arms to flip himself back out of range and came down on his feet. There was a hole in his thigh where she'd stabbed him, but he pulled himself up straight, his hard eyes meeting hers ready for her attack.

Maria flew at him again, her sickle in position to plunge it in his heart. Eric held his ground until the last minute and then stepped out of her way, bringing his sickle around to bury it into her back. Maria lost her weapon and was on the ground, unable to stand. She was trying to reach back to remove the blade, which was deeply embedded in her back, but she couldn't reach it. Eric retrieved Maria's weapon and stood over her, the blade in position to take her head. Maria stopped struggling and simply looked up at him. She didn't beg or cry. She just waited.

Eric turned toward Jade, but she was suddenly standing beside him so that both of her warriors could see her. Eric waited her command. "You've fought well, Eric." The vampire seemed to glow with pride. Jade studied Maria, who awaited her fate. "You also fought well, Maria. You didn't win, but you risked everything. I will spare your life this time."

Max expected Maria to show some sort of relief, but she simply gave a nod. Eric lowered Maria's weapon and bowed to Jade. She walked slowly back to her throne and sat. Eric carefully pulled the blade out of Maria's back. Except for one slight gasp, she made no sound. She remained facing down and Eric gently picked her up, one hand under her arms, the other under her thighs. He took her out of the arena.

"That was a good one," George said.

"They both seem like excellent fighters," Max said.

"Oh, yeah. I mean they're not as skilled as Veronica, but they're good."

There was some chatter in the audience and Max tried to hear what people were saying, but it was difficult to make out. He could hear the whispering, but not make out the words. Veronica picked up the weapons and Crystal cleaned up Maria's blood. When they were finished they returned to their posts at Jade's side. She seemed in no hurry. After a couple minutes passed, Jade sat up straight and everyone stopped talking.

"Rachel." All eyes went to one woman. It was someone Max had met yet earlier. She looked around and was obviously nervous. Quickly she stepped into the light and went before Jade.

"You've been careless. Police have pegged one of your kills as a homicide."

"Oh, I'm sorry, Jade. I… It won't happen again."

"It's unfortunate, because it's happened before, as you know."

"That was a long time ago. I was new…"

"You're not new anymore."

"Maybe it wasn't me…"

"You know what happens when one of us threatens exposure."

"But Jade, really, I won't let it happen again. Please…"

"Rachel, on your knees."

Rachel's eyes got large. Jade pulled a sword from the side of the throne. She rose and walked down the steps toward Rachel.

"Jade, please…"

"On your knees!"

Rachel shook her head and backed away. "Please!" In a panic she was looking for somewhere to run.

"Let Rachel's death be a warning," Jade spoke to those in the circle.

As if Jade had transported herself, she suddenly held Rachel by the throat and lifted her off the ground. Rachel was struggling and fighting against her. Jade dropped her and the woman fell to her knees.

Jade caressed her cheek and stared into the terrified woman's eyes. "It's okay. You'll have no more worries." Rachel was shaking as Jade raised the blade and swiftly brought it down to chop off her head. Max watched the woman's head roll to within a few inches of him. Rachel's eyes stared at him. But then Rachel's body and head evaporated into dust. George was standing next to Max, and he looked even grimmer.

Jade returned to her throne and put the bloody sword on the arm rest.

"Any more business that has to be taken care of today?"

she asked calmly. There was silence. "Good… Teacher."

Max realized she was summoning him. He hesitated for only a moment before going before her. She probably wasn't going to chop off his head, at least not yet.

"I'm pleased with your progress. Do you still want to kill me?"

Max smiled. "Oh, yeah." Jade smiled back at him.

"Good."

She looked to the side and lifted her chin. Through the darkness, he could see that one of the captives was being brought in. A poorly dressed man struggled against his guard and was dumped next to Max. "What's the matter with you people? I got my rights. What the hell is going on here?"

"Teacher, you're looking a bit white. Go ahead, have a bite." Max glanced at the man and then back at her.

"What! Oh, shit! You people are some kind of cult." The man took off and ran into the arms of waiting vampires who threw him back into the circle. Max watched as he tried several times to get away, until he was left crying on the floor. "You all crazy."

"What will it be?" Jade asked. "Take him right here, right now, without the benefit of bloodlust, or maybe you'd like a different test."

Max didn't move. He wasn't ready for this. The memory of Michelle dead in his arms overwhelmed him.

"I see," Jade said. "Let me give you this little incentive. He's a drug dealer. In fact, he's a drug dealer from your old neighborhood."

"I am not," the man yelled. "Ain't no drug dealer. That's just lies."

"Of course, he's a user too. Right, Darren? That's why he hasn't done too well for himself."

"You people are crazy… Look, I can set you up. Really. You want some good shit. I'm the man. You don't have to be doing nothing to someone who's going to be a really good source for you. I can help you out. Really." The man started to babble and cry. Max could sense the man's fear and he felt the vampire rising inside him. It was excited.

"So you went out to find the scum of the earth from my own neighborhood… Why? So I'd drink him and not feel guilty?" Max asked.

"I thought it might make the whole… thing a bit easier. It's not easy joining the ranks."

Max laughed. "You got that right." Suddenly, she was there in front of him. "Stop doing that," he said.

"Here's your choice, Teacher. You take him. You don't have to finish him off. The others will do that."

"Or what?"

"Or we'll do something else. For example, maybe your mother would like to visit us here. Does she still live in Joliet? What was the name of that road? Prairie, maybe, no it was Richmond Street. Yes, that's right."

Max closed his eyes. They knew where his mother lived. Of course, Jade used past life entanglements to force her "children" to cooperate if she needed to. Doesn't every good tyrannical ruler?

"Don't… Jade…"

"And after that, if you still won't cooperate, Crystal knows who some of your students were. We'll bring them in one by one until this little problem's solved."

"Stop!" Max yelled at her. His voice went down to a whisper. "Just stop."

"This is your life now. You have to accept that," she said gently.

Max shook his head. How could he do this?

"You have to drink," she said. "If you don't you'll suffer from bloodlust again, and believe me, you'll take whoever you can. This man is a bad man. If you don't take him, do you think I'll let him go? He's dead already. Nothing is going to save his life. What will it be, Max?" He noticed she used his name for the first time.

"All very logical arguments for murder." The man was

crying. Max shook his head and went to him. He offered a hand to the drug dealer. "Look, sir, it's okay. It's just a bad joke. She didn't mean it. Really."

"A joke?" He was crying.

"Yeah."

"It's not very funny."

"I know. You know how rich people are." The man took his hand and Max pulled him up. "Come on. Let's get this fellow a drink."

"Okay, I'd like a drink."

"Sure you would," Max glared at Jade as he put his arm on the man's shoulder, making sure Darren was a few inches in front of him. The vampire inside him surged up and Max didn't stop it this time. In a swift motion, Max took him from behind and pulled his head to the side so his neck was exposed. He bit down quickly and tasted the man's blood. Darren struggled, but only for a few moments. As Max drank, his hunger drove him. Blood was the ultimate drug and it felt so good. He could have drained the man. The blood's power flowed through him and he found it difficult to stop. He forced himself to pull away and eased Darren to the ground. Max ran his hand across his mouth.

"Good," Jade said. "Very good. Shall we?" she motioned to the stairs.

Max studied his victim. The man was barely breathing. At least he was completely out of it. Someone pulled him into the darkness and Max watched as Darren was surrounded.

Max took a breath and nodded to Jade. As he followed her up the stairs, he could feel the man's blood flowing through him. He tried to think of the drug dealer being drained in the basement. He'd done a terrible thing. Still, the high was so intoxicating, so powerful.

Jade wasn't worried about him escaping anymore. She'd played her cards. She had his mother. That card trumped them all. Max followed her like a good little minion. When they got to her room it was enormous and very modern looking, done in black, red and white. Like the rest of the house it looked like something out of Better Homes and Gardens. Of course, there wasn't anything made of wood in it and there weren't any windows.

The biggest surprise was a large screen TV. Jade grabbed the remote.

"Want to watch some Colbert, honey?" Max asked as he sat on the bed.

"Actually, I'll never get over Carson dying. I really should have made him a vampire when I had the chance. He had a night job, after all." She smiled at him, and Max couldn't help smiling back. She looked so stunning, so perfect, so human. Max closed his eyes and remembered the little fact that she'd just taken a woman's head off and forced him to participate in another murder.

"No, I thought we'd watch something else. How about the news reports on the poor teacher who burned up in his house?" she asked.

Jade flicked on the TV. She found the news report and hit play. He sat on the bed and watched in silence as the story played out. There it was. A popular teacher dies tragically when his house burns down. People were interviewed. What a horrible loss. Strangers and his students and friends were crying. There was a brief shot of his mother walking to a candlelight service. At the end of it, he laid back on the bed.

"You're dead to them. You can't ever go back to their world. You can't ever truly walk among the living again. If you ever did see your mother or any of those students of yours, the only thing you'd want from them would be their blood."

"Jade, what do you want? You've got me. You win."

"I have your body. Now I just need your soul."

Max became aware of her next to him. What power did she have that her presence created this kind of desire in him when he knew she was a monster? She kissed him and he pulled her to him. It wasn't like before. It was much more powerful this time.

Sex as a vampire, with a vampire, provided many blessings including enhanced senses, amazing strength and increased stamina. Better yet, because they could both feel what was happening in the other's body, the climax was beyond anything he'd ever experienced when he was alive.

Max explored her body in a way he'd never explored a woman's body before. When Jade finally sunk her fangs into his neck and he into hers exquisite pleasure and agony mingled together. He let his mind go and forgot how very much he hated her.

# # #

Max watched her sleep. She was so still. He didn't know why she was different than the other vampires. He could sense they were all afraid of her. If it had been possible, the others would have ganged up and taken her out. That hadn't happened for a reason.

After Max had killed Michelle, he knew his conscience was still intact. His mind hadn't changed. He still knew right from wrong. The biggest change had been that the hunger had the ability to control him. He'd been told he could avoid that from happening if he kept the hunger in check by never letting it get out of hand. His first order of business was to find out how he could do that in his present environment.

He'd made a pledge over Michelle's body. No matter what it took, he'd destroy Jade and the others. To do that, he'd have to sit back for a while until he wasn't the focus of Jade's attention. He'd watch, listen and learn. He'd find out what her weaknesses were and when the time was right, he'd kill the bitch and everyone who followed her.

Max would wait as long as it took. If he had to kill during that time, then that was the price the human race would have to pay. It couldn't be helped. If he got himself killed right now, how many more people would Jade and her gang destroy over time? How many lives had they taken already? If Max could take her down, the net gain in human lives would be immeasurable. It was war, and that was something Max knew all about. When he was finished with them, if he was still walking on the earth, he'd even take care of himself too.

Jade had no idea who he really was. Of course, she didn't care. But what she didn't know just might get her killed. Michelle wasn't the first person he'd killed. She wasn't even the tenth. He had killed several people while he was in the army with Special Forces. But Max had been in dark places long before Jade or the Army had ever gotten their hands on him. He'd do whatever it took to protect the people he loved. Max had discovered that on his 15th birthday, the day he killed his father.

## CHAPTER 4

Max woke up to find himself alone with the full understanding that he was still in Hell. He felt the urge to pee and was grateful for the familiar feeling. But when he looked in the toilet bowl and saw the pink water, he felt sick. Max got in the shower and turned the hot water on full blast. He let it flow over him, praying the scalding water would wash away the evil that he could feel raising up inside him.

When Max finally got out, he watched as steam rose from his body. He laid back on the bed and let the air dry him. The hunger was already beginning to pulse through him and he knew what that meant. It would get worse, like needing a fix, until every thought he had was about getting that fix.

It was late afternoon. He could feel the sun in the sky. Max didn't know what he was supposed to do next. Probably get dressed and go down and mingle with the rest of the good little vampires.

Instead, he curled up in a ball and thought about his family, friends and students. They believed he was dead. His mother would be devastated. Others, like his brother, his uncle and his close friends would be terribly sad. It would be hard on some of his students too.

Max wondered where they would bury Rails? In Chicago? He hoped not. He would rather have been buried on his uncle's ranch. But that would be a long way from his mother. Besides, it wasn't him anyway. Another man filled his grave.

Max mourned the loss of his life. He could never go back. He'd never taste his mother's spaghetti, or be a teacher, or ride a horse at full gallop in the early morning grass on his uncle's ranch. He'd never fall in love, or have a family, or see his brother's newborn twin babies. He was dead to the world. The term undead perfectly suited him.

It hurt too much to think about the people he loved. Max got up and went to the bathroom mirror. The monster looked back at him. He found a toothbrush and brushed thoroughly. There might be hell to pay if he got a cavity. He found a brush and ran it through his hair. He laughed at himself. He was a vampire and he was worried about how his hair looked.

Max found some clothes that fit him in the closet and something else that sparked his attention. His boots. They had vanished after his run in with the building, but there they were waiting for him. His wallet was inside one of them. Nothing in it had been touched. Now his possessions were the only things he had left from his past life. He put on his boots and was comforted by their perfect fit. He tucked the wallet in his pocket.

There was a tap at the door and George poked his head in.

"You okay, Teach?"

"I have no idea." George came into the room and shut the door.

He looked as sympathetic as he could manage. "I know it's pretty weird, but you'll learn. You're going to see. Things will be okay. You're stronger, faster and better than you ever were when you were alive. And let me tell you, you can have any woman you want, as long as she won't be missed. If you know what I mean. Any woman."

Somehow, Max wasn't comforted. "I feel like I should be reading 'The Complete Idiot's Guide to Being a Vampire.' What are the rules? What am I supposed to do?"

George nodded. "Okay, the simple basics. You're immortal, but you can die by sun, fire or, of course the part you already saw, head removal. A wooden stake will do the trick, but it has to be directly through the heart."

"You guys seemed to have no problem with crosses."

"Nah, crosses and holy water, religious stuff like that, doesn't do anything to us. Garlic doesn't bother us either. And the having to be invited in thing, not true."

"So, why aren't we roaming around cemeteries and sleeping in coffins?" Max asked.

George laughed. "It's not like that. That's not exactly Jade's style."

"Can I turn into smoke? Or a bat or something? What's that all about?" Max had considered it might be a good way to escape when the time was right.

"No. Jade's special. She can do things we can't. She's a lot stronger than the rest of us too."

"What makes her different?"

"Don't ask too many questions, Teach, if you like your head."

Max thought about that one. "Okay… Where are we?"

"About half an hour north of the city. Not too far away from Chicago, but not too close either. It's a pretty nice estate. Far away enough from other houses, you don't have to worry about neighbors. There's a pool if you want to go swimming."

"It's a little early in the year for swimming."

"Temperature doesn't really bother us much." Max considered his long hot showers.

"Any other rules?" Max asked.

"Just the one you already know." Max nodded. He remembered well the "Don't piss off Jade" mantra.

"I already tried to kill her. What's it take to piss her off?"

"You didn't know any better then. Now you do," George said.

"Are you so sure?"

"Look, give the vampire thing a shot. You can always piss her off later and get yourself killed."

"Well, that's good to know."

"Let's go. Don't want to keep her waiting when she's ready to go."

"Okay "

"Just one thing," George said.

"Yeah?"

"You know, your hair's a little goofy in the right side." George pointed above Max's ear.

"What? Are all the other vampires going to make fun of me?" Max looked in the mirror and patted down the stay hairs.

Laughter rippled through George. "You're a funny guy. Come on, you want to look good for her… Oh, another thing. You can walk around inside during daylight, but don't let the sun touch you."

After hair styling tips, George managed to give Max a couple more "oh and another things" before they made it downstairs. "Don't eat solid food. Don't leave the house without permission."

George deposited Max in an old fashioned library with wall-to-wall books. Max looked through the shelves. It was largely made up of very old, very rare books, and included some nice volumes of classic literature. The Vampire Queen was well read.

The sun had just set and when she entered the room, Max was caught again by how beautiful Jade was. She was wearing a tight gold blouse with a short black skirt. She was, of course, dressed to kill.

She studied Max for a moment, appraising his choice of wardrobe and then nodded. She came up to him and whispered in his ear, "You look good enough to eat." It was as if an electrical charge ran through him straight to his groin.

"Come on, Teacher. We've got places to go, people to kill." Her smile was stunning, her words as sharp as her fangs. The hunger was pounding through him and he had no choice. He followed her reluctantly. He felt like a school kid who was told he had to go to the principal's office.

Outside for the first time, Max got a good look at the estate. Even in the dark he could see it was enormous. He suddenly realized how much better he could see at night. The perfectly manicured lawn seemed to go on forever. Nope, no problem worrying about the neighbors. The house was actually a Tutor-style mansion and appeared to have lots of windows he hadn't remembered seeing on the inside. He looked close at one as he went by and realized that the windows and curtains were real, but the interior was a very good painting that would have fooled nearly anyone.

Jade led him to a waiting black limo. The driver opened the door for them. He was one of the living dressed in a chauffeur's outfit. Jade slid in and Max sat next to her.

As the limo left the property, Max realized the estate must be worth a fortune. He smiled when it struck him he had to die to get a glimpse of true wealth. Jade caught his smile and gave him one of her own.

"You're wondering, what have I got myself into? More than you could ever imagine. Even now, you're thinking how do I get myself out of this? Have you figured out the answer yet?"

"No, but it doesn't stop me from wanting to know."

"So, before, when you were just one of the sheep walking around in daylight, would your life have been easier if you'd known who really shot Kennedy or what happened to the lost city of Atlantis or what killed the dinosaurs?"

"Yes. Do you know any of the answers to those questions? Especially the Kennedy one?" Max asked.

"The rumor is it was a lone gunman."

"I don't believe in rumors."

"Or vampires?" she asked.

"The next thing you'll tell me is that there are werewolves too."

"Actually, they are a distant cousin."

Max did a double take checking to make sure she was just kidding. "So you sit on your throne and rule your universe… it can't be very much fun after a certain point. I mean what challenges do you have left to conquer?"

"You'd be surprised. I guess that will be another mystery. But then there are always more mysteries to solve, aren't there. You never really can get all the answers."

"Let's see… How old are you? Where do vampires come

from? Why don't we hang out in coffins? Why are you different? George says I'm not supposed to ask that one."

She nodded, taking him in. "You do like to live dangerously."

"I thought I wasn't really alive," Max said.

"Life is relative, isn't it? For example, your mother's life. I suspect you cherish it. That you think the world would be a lesser place without it. Kill tonight, for me and for her. It has to look like an accident or it has to be someone who won't be missed. You can choose your own victim. Witnesses are not an option. It's easy, really. All you have to do is kill and do it well."

Max laughed and shook his head. "So that's all I have to do." Irony dripped from every word.

"You are going to be interesting to have around, Teacher. Until I get tired of you."

Max took the hint. He shut up and sat back as they drove to the city in silence. As the view went from suburban to city, he pondered over his situation and the creature beside him. Had Jade given this kind of attention to Crystal. He cringed thinking about Crystal's introduction into the world of vampires. How many people had this bright, special girl had to kill, maybe even enjoyed killing since Jade had decided she'd make a good addition to the family. He suppressed a desire to shudder at the thought. The Crystal he knew was gone. It made him so sad. He would have given his life for her or any of his students. Well, maybe he had.

The creature within him reared up with a hunger he never could have imagined in life. Max could smell the limo driver and part of him wanted to rip through the car and take the man. He'd become an animal. No, Jade had made him an animal.

Max had decided if he had to kill people, he'd set his sights on the evil ones. Jade told him to tell the driver where he wanted to go, so Max told him to head over to Broadway. The driver stopped the limo and they got out. Jade waited for him to take the lead so he did. Max decided to stick to the alleys and it didn't take long for him to see someone he knew.

The man's name was Jimmie Large and they had a history. Jimmie was a pencil thin slob of a guy, a small time former gang banger who liked to terrorize people for the fun of it. He would be the perfect victim.

Jimmie was sitting in his car with the door open talking on his cell phone. Max scanned the alley for witnesses. With his increased senses he knew there was no one. Jimmie hung up when he saw them coming and got out of his car. He recognized Max and smiled big. "Hey, Maxie, you're all grown up."

"Hi Jimmie," Max said walking toward him. Jade was a couple steps behind him.

"Hello, pretty lady."

Max smiled at Jimmie. His teeth were normal. He hadn't brought them out yet even though he could feel the hunger wanting him to. "Jimmie, I need to get hooked up. Can I get a name?"

Jimmie looked at him curiously. "Thought you went off to become a good guy. Wasn't you a teacher, last I heard?"

"Things change. Just need a little home protection," Max said.

"I know what you mean. Maybe I can help. There'll be a little finder's fee, of course."

Max nodded. That was understood. Max checked the alley one more time. "Of course."

"Thought you might have some bad feelings about last time," Jimmie said.

"Time heals."

"So it does. I got a guy who can help ya." Jimmie turned around to grab a notebook. In an instant Max had him, fangs ready, the man squirming in his arms.

"Thanks, but I've got everything I need right here. Guess I still have some of those bad feelings, Jimmie." Max held him for a moment, savoring Jimmie's fear.

"Maxie, what you doing?"

"I'm taking out the trash, Jimmie."

For such a thin guy, Jimmie was strong and he fought Max with everything he had. The creature inside Max loved the battle of wills and he let the monster overwhelm him and have what it wanted most. It took Jimmie a long time before he finally surrendered.

After Max was done, Jimmie was still alive. Max watched as the wound on his neck healed. Jimmie's breathing was ragged. His blood flowed through Max and he savored the feeling.

"Think anyone will miss you, Jimmie?" Max asked.

"Please, Max, please don't kill me," Jimmie begged.

Max put his hand over Jimmie's mouth and nose to suffocate him. Jimmie stared up at him, pleading for him to stop. Max watched as the life went out of his eyes. He was high from his feeding and from the power he had over life and death. The insanity of evil edged at him for a moment before he pushed it away. It would look like Jimmie had a heart attack and no one would care enough to question it.

"You knew him," Jade said as they left the scene of the crime.

"A long time ago."

"Revenge, Max?"

"Why not?" As they walked away Max realized he'd exposed something about himself. Jade now knew he had a history of being something other than a high school teacher. She didn't ask him any other questions, but Max would have to be more careful.

The blood acted like a fix in his system and he felt wonderful. He followed Jade as she took the lead and found a young prostitute who was hooking in an area she shouldn't have been. Max would have killed Jade right on the spot if he could have figured out a way. The hooker was just a kid, no older than Crystal.

She was perfectly happy to follow Jade and Max back to the limo. She thought it was her lucky day. That they were a rich couple trying to get their kicks in the bad part of town. Max didn't want to get into the limo, however Jade gave him a look that told him he didn't have a choice. Max wasn't going to make it if Jade kept throwing victims in his face that were young enough to be his students.

"What's your name, little one?" Jade asked.

"Honey. I'm actually an actress, you know. I'm just putting together some cash to go to LA." She was too fresh faced, too bright eyed. She hadn't been doing this for very long.

"Shut up. Come here." Honey looked nervous as she sat between Max and Jade. Max got up and moved to the seat across from them. Jade gave him another look. She kissed the girl, but she was watching Max. He looked out the window. The fresh blood coursing through him made him euphoric, but he couldn't stand what was about to happen.

Honey, which Max knew was not her real name, fell under Jade's spell. Jade pulled down Honey's top and began to kiss her breasts. Honey laid her head back against the seat enraptured. Max knew she didn't care if she lived or died right at that moment and he couldn't stand it anymore. He hit the intercom. "Driver, stop the car." The car slowed down, but Max opened the door before it stopped. He jumped out and slammed the door hard.

They were still in the city. He wanted to run, to run far and fast and never stop. Just run until the sun took him and then it would all be done with. Except, it wouldn't be done. Jade and her people were preying on the living world and someone had to stop them. There wouldn't be an escape for him. Besides, Jade knew where his mother lived. So he sat on a bench and waited for her to finish.

He'd been in the Army and he understood that innocents paid the price far too often, but Max couldn't watch the kid get murdered. Not like this. Jimmie deserved what he got and somehow when evil destroys evil it can be justified. But to destroy a runaway simply because she was trying to survive on the street, that was something else. Max knew he was blowing his chance to stop Jade, but what else could he do?

Jade opened the door and stepped out of the limo. Max couldn't read her expression.

"You left the party," she said.

"Look if you're going to kill me, get it over with. I'm not going to watch you do that to a kid."

"Such passion for someone who's going to be dead in a year or two anyway. What am I going to do with you?" She seemed amused. "She's still alive. I could make her one of us. Would that please you?"

Max wanted to ram his head through a wall. Another vampire equaled more dead people. "No. No, it wouldn't."

"You're leaving me out of options."

"I'll give you an option. Let her go. Who is she going to tell? She probably doesn't even have a clue what happened to her. Come on, Jade. Show a little sympathy for a lesser being."

Max could tell she was high from the blood. "Oh, Max, I'm going to enjoy turning you bad. There you are, so concerned that the poor little hooker might die. I'll tell you what. You get one 'Get Out Alive' free card. Do not pass go. Do not collect $200. You get to give life to one of the sheep. But buyer beware, someone better may come along later, someone worth saving, and you'll have used up your only card."

Max turned away from her. She'd probably find someone he cared about next. So that was her path to claiming his soul. Max didn't want to play this game.

"Let her go," he said.

"Then you win… this time." Jade stepped back toward the limo.

He followed her into the car and Max checked the girl. She was out of it, but he could sense she would be okay. Jade hadn't taken too much, no doubt expecting Max to join in. He carefully pulled her clothes back into place so she was covered.

They drove for a few minutes and then Max told the driver to stop. Honey was trying to come around.

"Well, give her some money," Max told Jade. She pulled money from her purse and handed him $100. "Come on. Give it up." She smiled and handed Max two $500 bills. Max stuffed the money in Honey's tiny purse. Lucky for him Jade was feeling good from her meal.

Max checked to make sure no one was around and then picked up Honey. Her weight was nothing to him. He got her out of the limo and sat her down carefully on a bus stop bench. She opened her eyes and smiled when she saw him. "That must have been some great shit. I am really dizzy."

"Your payment is in your purse."

She checked it and smiled. "Any time, Mister. Wow."

Max positioned himself so he was facing Honey with his back to the limo. "I'm not going to lecture you about getting out of this business. I know that won't do any good. What I will tell you is that you could have died tonight."

Honey stared at him, confused. "You mean the drugs?"

"Drugs… running into the wrong people… You could have died," Max said as he brought his fangs out so she could see them and her eyes went wide. "The streets are dangerous, more dangerous than you could imagine. Use that money to find a different line of work or at least relocate, because next time you might not be so lucky."

Max could sense the fear rise up in her. "I'll call an Uber for you," he said. He pulled his fangs back and returned to the limo. Max gave her one last look as he got into the limo and sat opposite Jade. Without asking he picked up Jade's purse and found her phone. He ordered an Uber for the girl.

Max watched the city go by as they drove, but he became aware that Jade was staring at him. He returned her gaze. At first, she made no movement and her expression held no clue, but Max knew what she wanted. Slowly, she reached across to him and looped two fingers around his belt. She pulled him to her side of the limo.

Jade pushed him down on the seat and laid on top of him. Max knew that at least this was one thing he could do with no problem at all. He started to rise up to kiss her, but she pushed him back down. She ripped open his shirt and the buttons went flying. She ran her fingers through the hair on his chest. He moved his hands up her body and, then with one quick movement, ripped her blouse down the center. She looked very pleased with him. His body was so glad she didn't like to wear underwear.

Max kicked off his boots. Jade unzipped his pants and then pulled them off him. She touched him, moving her hands down his chest, stopping just short of his cock. Then she laid on top of him and kissed him, much more gently than he expected. Max held her, loving the way her body felt against his. He ran his hand through her hair and down to the small of her back. Her skin was so smooth. He wanted to feel her touch between his legs. But she pulled up, and with a smile her fangs came out. Max knew what was coming next. She ran her tongue over his neck and she watched him watch her as she worked her way down to his chest. She scraped her fangs over his nipple and he felt a sharp sting as she drew blood. She licked it and then watched the small cut heal. Her lips and tongue continued down his body until Max could barely stand it.

When she got to his stomach, she looked up at him playfully. Then she bit down hard. "Oh, god!" Max said. The sharp pain gave way to pleasure as she drank from him. Then she ran her hand between his legs and her fingers teased the shaft of his cock. The intense pleasure of her touch and her bite were just about to make him cum. He wasn't quite ready for that yet. Max ran his fingers through her hair and then suddenly yanked her head back. His blood dripped from her fangs onto his stomach.

With one quick motion, Max twisted around until Jade was the one on the bottom and he was straddling her. It was his turn. She had lots of wonderful places he couldn't wait to bite and he was going to find them all. If he was trapped in Hell, at least he was going to have a hell of a good time.

## CHAPTER 5

When they got back to the estate, Jade left the limo without saying a word. She didn't have a stitch on. Max had to admire that, in a megalomaniac, Machiavellian tyrant like Jade. Not many others would have been able to pull it off so beautifully. He, on the other hand, put on his pants, boots and what was left of his shirt. He was smeared with dried blood everywhere, but he expected that was an occupational hazard. A swim would do the trick.

Max found George watching the tube and was told he could find swimming trunks in the room off the pool. Max knew he was a mess, but George was obviously used to it and he barely glanced at him.

As he walked through the beautiful mansion, he passed several vampires who, now that their murderous activities were done for the night were relaxing watching TV, reading, playing cards, or talking.

The room he was looking for was empty of vampires. Max riffled through a drawer of swimwear and found trunks that fit, along with a new shirt. He threw the old shirt in the trash and decided to take a shower first. He was beginning to realize no matter how many showers he took he'd never feel clean again. He remembered Shakespeare's Lady Macbeth who couldn't get the blood off her hands.

It was a couple hours until dawn, so he had plenty of time. He was coming down from his high and feeling a bit melancholy. That was the way it worked. High as Mount Kilimanjaro for a few hours. Then the fix started to wear off and suddenly life wasn't so rosy.

Max put on the trunks and shirt. He never had felt comfortable running around with just swimming trunks on. He piled up the rest of his stuff and took it with him. He wasn't taking any chances on losing his boots again.

As he opened the door, he saw her. Crystal was leaning up

against the building, starring at the stars. Max didn't move for a moment. He wasn't sure he wanted to talk to her. What would he say? But she sensed him and caught him looking at her.

"Hi Mr. Maguire."

"Hi Crystal." Max put his things on a pool chair. He wished he had pants on.

"It's a nice night for a swim."

"I thought it might be." Silence fell between them and Max leaned up against the building a few feet from her.

Her expression had been contemplative before, but she suddenly looked as if she might cry. Crystal turned her face away from him.

"I'm sorry," she said. "I know this isn't what you wanted."

He was caught by surprise. She was apologizing for getting him involved. "It's okay," he said in a whisper only she could have heard. She caught control of her emotions and then gave him a smile.

"I don't mind the killing. I really don't. It's afterward when I'm alone just before dawn, like now. Even though there are so many people around, it just hurts and I start thinking about before. In class, you were always talking about the future. Pretty weird for a history teacher, but I liked it. Do you remember asking me what career I wanted to have?"

"Yes."

"I wanted to be an astronomer. I never told you that, though. I couldn't imagine anything better than studying the stars."

Max followed her gaze to the night sky. "I considered that for awhile, too."

"I thought what could be better than discovering another planet with intelligent life or maybe just a new moon for Jupiter. Something miraculous and amazing." Crystal turned toward him. "That's not going to happen. And my grandmother's dead... The part that's tough is I don't feel bad... Why don't I feel bad?"

"I don't know," Max said.

"That's what hurts, that I should feel something. It's like whatever made me care is just missing. But you do feel bad about the killing. I can tell. So can Jade. She's going to take that away from you, you know."

"She's going to try."

"She'll win. She'll just keep after you until you don't have anything left, until she owns you… Grams is at peace, finally. You see, the only thing I feel bad about is you. I see what you're going through, even right now, I can feel it. And it makes me realize everything is wrong that I've done… When she's done with you, she'll kill you. At least that's what the others say." Max looked away from her. "But we're all in love with her, you know. So maybe they're lying or hoping they'll get a chance to take your place. I'm not sure. I just know I'll do anything for her… Anything… Being with her is the only time I feel alive, except when I'm hunting," she said.

"You deserve more."

"See, I've gone off and disappointed you. That's the way it is, Mr. Maguire. But you know the real tragedy?"

"What?"

"I'm never going to look older than 17," Crystal smiled.

"Well, I'm never going to look younger than 33. Seventeen isn't so bad."

"A lot of the girls at school thought you were pretty cute considering how old you are. A lot thought you were kind of weird too, but you had your fans."

"Oh." Max didn't know what to say.

"Now I've made you uncomfortable too. Disappointed and uncomfortable. See, you are different than me."

"I'm not disappointed in you, Crystal."

"Yes you are."

"It's not your fault," Max said.

She smiled. "It's funny, but I barely remember being the other Crystal. It seems very long ago."

"That it does."

"The other funny thing is that we both probably would have longer lives if we'd never run into Jade."

"You call this living," he said.

"Well, it's something. I don't know what." She pushed herself away from the wall and walked by him toward the poolroom.

"Crystal…" She turned back toward him. "I'm sorry too."

"I'm living in a mansion, Jade has big plans you can't even imagine and I'm never going to grow old or get sick." She looked wistful as she disappeared through the door.

Max was sorry for her.

He pulled off his shirt and dove into the pool. Max had always been a pretty good swimmer, and there had been a time in high school he'd considered going out for the swim team. But that was a long, long time ago.

As Max cut through the water, swimming back and forth, flipping to push off the wall at the end of each lap, he drove himself as far as he could physically. It amused him to think that he could win the Olympics with the speed he was doing the laps in. He wasn't tired, so he pushed himself even harder. Too bad he wasn't in an ocean. What would happen to a vampire who just kept swimming? Could he have survived if he'd let himself sink to the safety of the ocean floor where the sun couldn't reach? Would he just be able to swim until he reached the other side of the ocean? He wondered. Maybe he'd find out one day.

He focused on the position of his hands and the length of his kick and his breathing, even though he realized he probably didn't have to worry about the breathing. He went faster and faster until suddenly his thoughts crystallized and he thought about the day his life changed. Not the day Jade took him. No, he thought about his 15th birthday.

As his body cut through the water, the memory flowed over him and he knew there was no escaping it. It was why he couldn't join the swim team back then. You can't go swimming if your body is covered with bruises. Then everyone would know.

His father had beaten his mother as long as he could remember. At some point, Max realized that if he provoked his father, he could take the beating for her. The bastard was usually angry when he got drunk, so any punching bag would do. His mother, frail and terrified from years of abuse, begged Max to stop putting himself in her place, but he couldn't watch her get hurt.

It's possible to get used to anything if it happens often enough. Max didn't care about the beatings. They didn't hurt that bad. And even though his father was a drunk, the man usually managed to avoid hitting him in places that would show, so he didn't have to miss too much school.

Of course, there had been plenty of signs of abuse to the outside world, but no one was paying attention. Max had ended up in the emergency ward several times with broken bones. His father had broken his arm, his collar bone, and three ribs. All the while, during the hospital visits dear old Dad would berate Max in front of the doctors and nurses for being clumsy. Max just took all the abuse his father threw at him, because if he wasn't after Max, he'd be after his mother or his younger brother, Richie.

At some point while his father was beating him, Max realized he had the ability to let his mind take him somewhere else. History ended up being a great place for him to escape. He discovered the library and read every history book he could. When his father would start, Max would just stand there while the man hurled painful words and fists at him. In his mind, Max was somewhere else. He visited the Roman Empire, the Civil War and set foot on the moon with Neal Armstrong. It was like Max was watching the beatings unattached to his body.

The first time the old man went after Richie, Max began to think about killing his father. Richie was a slight, sickly kid, and Max couldn't bear to see him get hit. Max thought about trying to get a gun somehow. His uncle had taught him how to shoot when he was a kid. He considered other ways he might kill his father too, but it scared him to think about it. Not that his father might die, but that he'd try to kill him and fail. Then his father would kill him and there would be no one to protect his mother or Richie. He wasn't afraid to die, but his mother and Richie depended on him.

Even though it had been almost 20 years, that one day had changed his life and still stood in his mind clearly, as he lengthened his stroke to push himself even faster through the water. He could relive every second of it. His birthday had started out so great. He had a good day at school and his best friend had given him an imitation Civil War dollar bill as a present. But after school, he'd gotten something way better from Melissa Sue Lipton. When he finally got home, late, he didn't even care what his father did to him. Melissa Sue had let him get to second base and that was worth all the beatings he'd ever taken put together.

When he walked in the door he heard glass breaking upstairs. The old man had already started, and it was probably because Max was late. He took the stairs and found his mother crouched in a doorway, her left eye nearly swollen shut and blood running from her mouth. It was way worse this time. Worse than he'd ever seen it. Horrified, Max realized that his father was after Richie now. The noise was coming from their room.

"He lost his job. Max, he's going to kill Richie," his mother cried.

Max ran to the room and saw his father push Richie into a wall. Richie was a bleeding, swollen mess. Max knew his father wasn't holding anything back this time. "Stop it you bastard! Don't you dare touch him!" Max yelled.

Deliberately, Max's father turned to him. "So you finally decided to come home."

"Leave him alone! You want to kill someone? I'm right here," Max said.

"You think you can just come and go as you please? You

little prick." Max knew he had to take this downstairs, away from his mother and Richie. His father started toward him and Max backed up to the stairs.

His father stormed him and threw him against the wall. Max recovered himself and stood up to face him defiantly. "Go ahead. But you do it right this time, asshole. Just kill me and the cops will take you away and you'll never bother them again."

His father punched him in the stomach and then threw him against the wall a second time. Max tried to catch his breath. In that moment, Max realized his father's back was to the stairs. One good push and the old man would go down. Just one push and he'd never be able to terrorize them again.

"You're nothing. You'll never be anything. Nothing but a waste of my money," his father yelled as he smacked him hard across the face.

Max heard his mother cry out, but he was only focused on one thing… his father. Max felt no fear. "You're evil. You're not ever going to hurt them again!"

"Evil?! You little bastard! This time I am going to kill you." As his father pounded away, Max contemplated how hard he'd have to shove him to knock him over.

As Max's father pulled back his fist, Max moved forward using all his strength to shove the man back. It was like watching everything happen in slow motion as his father, so full of rage and surprise, teetered on the edge of the steps. His arm was pulled back ready to smash Max's face in, and he had no way to catch his fall. He went down the stairs hard, tumbling in a horrible ballet, his neck snapping as he reached the bottom.

Max was swimming too fast. He lost his rhythm and banged his head full force into the side of the pool. The pain flashed through his body. If he'd been alive, the blow would have killed him. It took him a moment to recover, and when he became aware of himself again he was looking up toward the surface watching the stream of blood that flowed from his head into the water. Max let himself sink down. He didn't have any great desire to breathe or to move at all.

The police ruled his father's death an accident. They had been no stranger to his house. All it took was one sniff of the alcohol on his father's breath and a look at the condition of the members of the family, and the authorities took care of the rest.

Max stayed with his family for a few months after that, but his mother had been watching that day and she knew what he had done. He'd killed his father, deliberately. Max didn't think she was sad her husband was gone, but the knowledge between them ate away at him until he had to leave.

Max hit the streets and learned to survive by his wits. He pulled some jobs, did other things he was less proud of, and felt his rage grow each day. One day some dirtbag called him a name and Max nearly killed him. As the crumbled man lay on the ground, Max stood over him and caught his own reflection in a window. The fury in his eyes was his father's. He realized he was becoming his father and he ran, trying to make the truth go away. He thought about killing himself, doing whatever it took to rid the world of the evil he was becoming. Just like his old man.

While Max was contemplating his suicide, something strange happened. He got busted for beating up that guy and got offered a choice. The guy had vanished right after they arrested Max. No doubt helping the police was not on the top of his list of priorities. But the police piled up weapons and drug charges, so it ended up that Max was looking at some time. He was only 17, so the public defender got his mother involved. He knew the judge was trying to get him straightened out, and he could tell by the look in his mother's eyes that she was part of the plot. She didn't want him to end up killing himself on the streets. So, the choice was jail time or the Army.

The Army would have never been part of Max's plans, but he signed up because his mother wanted him to. To his surprise he didn't mind it after he got past basic training. He didn't even realize that one of the Army's plans was to teach him to kill. He could have told them he'd already learned that one.

What Max finally figured out during his tour was that some people destroyed society and some protected it. Max had figured out a way to protect his mother and brother at an early age. His father was a destroyer. Max decided that when it came to protecting the precious things in life, those who would destroy forfeited their right to live.

In the Army, the rules were a little different, but the idea was the same.

Max watched the red stream of blood billow out in the water. He pushed himself off the bottom of the pool and broke the surface. He took in a long deep breath, but didn't feel winded at all. He swam to the side and pulled himself out of the water. The sun would be up soon.

Max had learned his lessons well. He was a protector. It was nothing he chose, just part of who he was. And he wasn't about to let becoming a vampire change that in him.

As a teacher, he tried to protect kids when he could, but usually his hands had been tied. He could always spot the signs of abuse, but few people in the system really wanted to deal with the truth.

Maybe it was meant to happen this way. He loved being a teacher, but he'd never quite escaped the darkness that had held him for so long. Now, in undeath, or whatever the hell state he was in, he had a new mission. He would be the self-appointed protector of the human race against Jade and their kind. He'd find a way to stop them. Whatever it took.

## CHAPTER 6

After another night of incredible sex, Max woke up with a start. Jade was gone. He could feel the sun high in the sky and knew that it was about noon. Much as he would have liked to stay in bed and sulk, it was time to play the game. He resolved to embrace his inner vampire and settle in for the long haul.

So his first order of business was to begin to fit in. That, and to find out more about the weapons he'd seen in the arena. The weapons held all sorts of promise when it came to killing vampires, since they were obviously designed for that purpose. Max had no idea how long it might take him to master the thing, but there were other possibilities. As far as he could tell, the wood in the weapon was the only wood in the house.

Max took a shower and dressed quickly. He wanted to do some subtle reconnaissance, so he took his time walking down the hallway, straining to hear what might be going on behind all the closed doors. He could hear far more than he would have been able to as a human, but there just wasn't much going on in the rooms. Most of the vampires were still sleeping, some alone, some in pairs either with a human or another vampire.

He had discovered that his ability to sense things increased dramatically when he focused on one direction, much like a search light in the dark. Max could reach out with his senses in any direction he wanted to, but like a beam of light he could use his sensing radar in only a small area with his senses fading along the edges into a kind of darkness. It was a good superpower, but a limited one. He needed to constantly sweep an area to really know what was going on.

As Max stood at the top of the stairway, he forgot about eavesdropping and found himself overwhelmed by the grandeur of the place. The marble stairway was... elegant.

That was really the only word that described it. It was the type of stairway the very rich might enjoy making an entrance from. It curved around and spilled out into the room with a matching marble floor. While everything about the house had an old fashioned feel to it, the furniture was modern. The mix of old and new shouldn't have worked, but it did and to a stunning effect.

Max made his own entrance down the stairway, but no one was around to appreciate it. He went from room to room, exploring. There was a family room, an enormous dinning room, Jade's study, and several rooms that seemed to have no purpose at all. The back area of the house had a game room, the poolroom and an exercise room. The weirdest part was that, except a picture window in the foyer, there were no windows, even though there were curtains where the windows should be. There were even hidden lighting fixtures that simulated light coming into the house from the outside, so the illusion of windows was nearly perfect. Nearly perfect, like something was just a bit off.

Max scouted through the rooms until he ended up in the kitchen. He checked out the cabinet drawers and found some knives, but nothing big enough to do serious damage. He opened some cabinets, but most were empty. There were a few cans of food – for the captives, he assumed – kitchenware and plates, but not much else. His search hadn't yielded anything beyond the fact that Jade had a really good decorator.

He went to the refrigerator and hesitated for a moment. It occurred to him there might be something inside he wouldn't want to see. He pulled the door open quickly and let out a breath when all he found was a couple of six packs of beer, some bottled water and some sodas. He laughed at himself. He'd almost expected to find a decapitated head staring at him.

He grabbed a beer and sat down at the kitchen table. Max couldn't remember any rules about not drinking, so he'd take a couple sips and find out how the beer felt about him becoming a vampire. He hoped it'd be okay. He really liked beer.

Max popped the top of the bottle of Coors and took a sip. It tasted a little weird, but he didn't feel sick or anything. He took a full drink and decided it wasn't bad at all.

He took stock of his situation. Max was sitting in a mansion, drinking a beer and had just enjoyed a couple of nights filled with the best sex he'd ever had. Only one problem. He was a vampire. He really was a vampire. It was crazy, insane, nuts.

Max took another drink of beer and clicked one of his fangs on the bottle. He hadn't realized they were out. He thought about making them go away and they did. He felt his teeth to make sure they were normal again. In a way, the fangs coming out were like a vampire's version of an erection. Max laughed. In fact, the darn things seemed to have a mind of their own and would pop out at the strangest times. Yep, they were just a sign that a vampire was ready, willing and able. Well, he was all those things and he had hours to kill before he fed. He took another drink of his beer. Somehow, he just knew that beer wasn't going to satisfy his thirst.

At the edges of his awareness, Max felt the house begin to stir. He decided before he began tripping over other vamps, he should check out the basement to see if he might accidentally run across one of those bizarre weapons. He was about to head off to the basement entrance when he realized the door he was looking at led to a stairway that went down. He reached out with this senses and, almost as if he was physically walking down the stairs, found his way to the basement. It was a back entrance he hadn't noticed before.

Max got up and went to the door. He touched the door handle and was surprised when it opened. The stairs were a stark contrast to the ones he'd taken from the upstairs. They were small, poorly lit and obviously meant for servants. Max bounded down the cement steps, knowing exactly what to expect and that no one was waiting for him at the bottom. The stairway ended in a pitch black corner of the basement, close to the acid vat.

Even though he couldn't sense any of the humans he had last night, he went to the area they'd been kept in. Since the scent of human had lingered he had no trouble finding the room. It must have been designed to be a laundry room. The door to the room was open, Max assumed because there was no need to shut it. The room had a sofa, a couple chairs and a cot. There was also a toilet in the corner.

Max went into the room and closed the door. Through the small window in the door he could see what was going on in the arena. Max shook his head. Had Jade designed the set up so whoever was in the room could see their fate? In a way it was her own little death camp, a holding place where people were brought to die.

Max's hatred for her flared. How many people had spent their last hours in her dungeon? How many lives had she destroyed? How many monsters like him had she set loose on the world?

Max realized he wasn't alone. Someone else was in the basement. He left Jade's little dungeon and followed his senses to the arena. Maria sat on the edge of the throne platform with one of the weird weapons in her lap. She was wearing a halter top and shorts, which made her vastly overdressed as opposed to her outfit she'd worn the night before. She smiled at him.

"It took you awhile to sense me. You'll get better at it with practice," she said. Max realized she had a very slight Mexican accent.

"I hope so… Good fight last night. I was impressed."

"I lost."

"I was still impressed," Max said. "How's your back?"

"It's healed. If he'd gotten me with the wooden end, I'd still be hurting. But wounds from steel heal right up if you're well fed."

Max nodded, trying to push that disturbing thought out of his mind.

"Then the man you were fighting, Eric… you got him in the leg with the wood."

A smile dusted her lips. "He's limping, but he'll be okay in another day."

"You're very good with that. It must take a lot of practice."

"The Saracian Lance?" Maria held it up with both hands. "Yes, it takes some practice."

"I've never seen anything like it," Max said.

"They are cool, aren't they? When I'm in sync with the lance, there's nothing better. I feel like I can do anything."

Max wanted to ask her if she was forced or if she volunteered for Jade's little shows, but the timing didn't feel right for a personal question like that. "Very cool indeed."

"Want to give it a go?" She smiled the way a woman smiles when she knows she's got the upper hand.

Max laughed. "What the hell. I'm guessing if you kill me right now, Jade wouldn't be too happy. So what's the worst?"

"Maybe a good ass kicking."

"Sure. I haven't had my ass kicked by a woman since yesterday. Let's go."

Maria nodded and jumped off the platform. She threw her weapon to him and he surprised himself by catching it gracefully. "Give me a minute."

Max looked at the beautiful weapon in his hand. As a history buff, weapons had always fascinated him. However, he hadn't seen anything quite like this one. With the weapon in his hands, he almost forgot to pay attention when Maria left the arena. He wanted to find out where the weapons where kept and he reached out with his senses to follow her. There was a small room, and Max felt Maria enter it. He couldn't quite tell how she gained entrance. It was undoubtedly locked. He could sense weapons in the room, maybe even some guns, but he'd stretched his ability about as far as he could and it all seemed fuzzy. He felt her pick out another lance and then he let his focus fall way so he could examine the weapon in his hands.

The lance was as tall as he was, and even with his vampire strength he felt some weight to it. The weapon was obviously made by a craftsman and had ornate designs imprinted into the steel. The large curved blade was incredibly sharp and went from point to thick center to narrowing down to a thinner blade at the hand guard. It would have made a fine weapon all on its own, but instead the sickle's metal grip extended down about two feet. Max examined the wood at the end of the lance. He had considered that it might be possible to actually break the wooden stake off for later use, but as he examined it he realized the wood had a steel shaft in the center of it. The point of the stake had a steel tip for better piercing. Since stealing part of the weapon wasn't going to work, he'd just have to learn how to use the damn thing.

Max realized Maria was watching him, so he looked up and smiled. She was a pretty, delicate looking woman, and if he hadn't seen her in action the night before he wouldn't have believed she could handle herself the way she had. The only reason she lost the fight was because she'd made a mistake. He watched her twirl the lance in an orchestrated dance-like motion. Yep, he was definitely in for an ass kicking.

Max held up his forefinger. "Just a minute." Max laid the Saracian Lance on the ground and took off his boots, throwing them to the side of the arena. He'd never been great at hand to hand combat, but he did a quick stretch on his neck, arms and legs. His body felt ready to go, despite, or maybe because of, the hunger.

Max picked up the lance again and realized how good the perfectly balanced weapon felt in his hands. He experimented moving the lance, like a really long baton. Maria watched him, amused.

Max shrugged his shoulders. "Okay, just do me a favor."

"What's that?"

"Be gentle."

Her smile got bigger. "No promises."

In a practiced motion, Maria swung the lance around so it rested along the length of her shoulder, with the blade part curving up around the back of her head. She bowed gracefully. Max kept both hands on the shaft of the lance and bowed awkwardly. Maria placed her arms out to her sides as though she was going to embrace him. While she wasn't even holding onto the weapon, her arm was wrapped around the lance's shaft and Max could tell that from this position she was ready to use either end. He wasn't about to try and copy her moves, so he braced himself.

"Well, Teacher, go for it," she said.

"Call me Max."

"Okay. Max, go for it."

Max shrugged and hanging onto the weapon with both hands, swung the lance's blade toward her head. Only she was gone in a blur and he felt her behind him. Max was committed to his swinging motion, which left his back exposed. The sudden stinging sensation in his butt didn't surprise him, but his body's decision to jump at the stabbing pain left him in a heap on the floor. Maria had stabbed him in the right butt cheek with the blade and it hurt like hell.

"Well, that was fun," Maria said laughing.

Max got up. The pain was nearly gone and he knew it was beginning to heal already. She must have just nicked him. This little lesson was going to be hell on clothing. "So are you just going to poke me with that thing, or are you going to show me how to use it?"

Maria took a deep breath. "All right, but I may still poke you now and then."

"And, no doubt, you'll enjoy it," Max said. She laughed easily. She was the first vampire he'd met that he liked.

For the next hour, Maria worked with Max on how to

move the lance and they did some gentle sparring. Well, mostly gentle. True to her word, she did poke him a couple of times. It didn't take long before Max was beginning to feel like the weapon had real possibilities. He wasn't interested in joining Jade's arena of fun and games, but as far as he could tell, it was the only weapon in the house he had a shot at getting his hands on.

Beyond that Max began to feel some of his new-found strength. He could jump much higher, run faster, maybe even leap tall buildings in a single bound. His body didn't have human limitations anymore and his little workout with Maria gave him some insight into his situation. If only all the other vampires didn't have superpowers too.

Maria also offered possibilities. She was a patient teacher. She seemed much more straightforward than the other vampires he'd met. He couldn't be sure, but he sensed she might have the potential to be an ally. Of course, he'd always been a bad judge of character. He'd have to tread carefully.

"Swing through the target," Maria said, as she guided the sweep of his arm. Max practiced a couple times.

"It's like swinging a tennis racket," he said.

Maria smiled. "Not quite. But you're doing better."

She looked off in the direction of the main stairway, the smile fading from her face. Max knew it was Eric before he saw him.

"So, you're giving the history teacher a lesson," said Eric, his voice dripping with sarcasm. He limped into sight. "Why bother? He'll be history in a couple weeks." He stared at Max intensely.

"Well, that's two weeks more than you'll have in Jade's bed," Max snapped back. He just couldn't stop the alpha male in him from rearing up. Eric's nostrils flared and anger danced across his face.

"Eric," Maria said softly, placing a hand on his chest. He took a breath and stepped back.

"Good boy," Max said.

"I could take your head before you'd even have time to miss it," he said.

"Probably, but then you'd have plenty of time to regret it when Jade found out." Max smiled broadly at him. The bastard couldn't do anything to him, but even if he could have it wouldn't do to show Eric any weakness. Max knew exactly how this game was played. He'd learned that on the streets of Chicago.

"Eric, he's not worth it," a voice said from the darkness. It was Veronica. "He's just a plaything for her. He's nothing." Eric tore his eyes away from Max and nodded to her. He retreated to stand next to Maria.

Max wanted to come back with some snappy comeback to Veronica's dismissal of him, but he fell silent. His mission was to fit in, not to antagonize the Queen Bitch's First Lieutenant. The harsh-looking woman regarded him for only a moment before scrunching her face as though she had bit down on a lemon.

Then something interesting happened. Veronica turned toward Eric and just dismissed Max, as if he wasn't there. "Eric, you are being sent to New York. We lost another house last night and Jade's furious. There's a leak and you need to plug it. Our enemies have been chipping away at us for far too long. Put a stop to it."

"Of course," Eric said. "When does she want me to leave?"

"Tonight."

"I'll prepare to leave immediately."

Eric shot a glance back at Max and stalked off.

"Maria, Jade wants to see you," Veronica said.

"I'll put these away first," she said.

"I'll put them away. See to Jade at once."

"Yes, Veronica." She nodded and left.

Max was suddenly very aware that they were alone. In truth, Veronica scared him way more than Eric. He watched as she picked up the weapons.

"Don't come down here again without an escort," Veronica said without looking at him.

"All right," Max said. He didn't wait for any other commands. Instead he put on his boots and went the way of Eric and Maria, bounding up the stairs as quickly as he could. That was one bad ass vampire he didn't want to be alone with for any length of time.

# # #

By the time Max got back upstairs the house had come to life. There was someone in most every room, reading, playing games, watching TV or just hanging out and talking. Max wandered from room to room, trying to catch all the bits of information he could. He heard several references to "Jade's enemies" or "our enemies" and the term "war" more than once. Max wondered if it was some kind of turf war with different factions of vampires. It was certainly something he wanted to find out more about.

However, no matter where he went, he felt uncomfortable. The others looked at him oddly or stopped talking when he entered a room. Max finally settled in the kitchen, which was thankfully vacant of vampires. And at least it felt familiar.

Max picked up a newspaper along his travels and sat down to read it. Unfortunately the paper only offered him a slight distraction. Somehow the latest information on the stock market, the outbreak of a new Covid strand and a win by the Bears didn't hold the same interest for him it would have only a couple of days earlier.

He found himself falling into thoughts of the past as melancholy memories washed over him. His family, his friends, the kids at school, Crystal's loss of a normal life, it all took hold of him while the hunger began to pound through him. The hunger that would only be satisfied at the cost of another life. Max studied the kitchen door. Presumably it led outdoors. At least that was implied by the fake light coming through the fake window in the door. What would happen if he just opened the door and took a walk in the sun? Would the sun set him on fire or turn him into dust in an instant? How long would it hurt before he wouldn't care anymore? He wondered.

He could feel the sun just outside the door. Waiting for him. Waiting to embrace him and end the insanity. Or maybe it was all an elaborate joke. Maybe his buddies were waiting for him on the other side of the door, waiting for a big laugh at how they got him with the biggest practical joke in the history of the world. That had to be it. Vampires couldn't really exist. Max ran his tongue over his fangs. Nope. Vampires couldn't possibly exist.

Max suddenly felt her. Jade was standing only a few feet from him. She seemed positively overdressed in her t-shirt and jeans. The clothes didn't quite look right on her. She looked so much better naked.

"Curious about the sun?" she asked.

"It's not the sun. It's just a lighting fixture that simulates the sun."

"But the sun rests right outside this door." Jade walked up to the door and pressed her body against it. "Can't you feel it?"

"Yes."

"Do you want to walk out into it?" she asked.

"I don't know. Maybe."

Jade turned around to face him and leaned against the door.

"It'd be so much easier, wouldn't it?"

"Absolutely."

She smiled easily at him. "Can I show you something?"

Max laughed. "Yet another offer I can't refuse."

Jade walked past him and then turned back and held out her hand. Max got up and put his hand in hers. She led and he followed. She glanced back at him with such a magnificent smile, a lover promising sweet and loving things. He wanted to forget about the evil buried beneath her surface. He wanted her to let him forget.

She led him to the foyer, with its grand stairway. She pulled him into an embrace and he looked down into her eyes. Max held her around the waist and he couldn't have refused her anything at that moment. She reached up and ran her fingers through his hair. Jade kissed him so tenderly and softly, he didn't want the kiss to stop. Ever. But she pulled away and wistfully went to the big window. Max knew this was the only window in the house that was real. A steel covering was lowered from some hidden place in the wall each morning before sunrise. For the first time, Max noticed that one tiny sliver of light escaped through the side of the covering. It was about half an inch around and the beam was strong, as if the sun was in just the right position to give it its maximum strength.

The beam was between Max and Jade.

"Jade, what..." he started.

She slowly shook her head and put her finger up to her lips signaling him to be silent.

She held her hand out and waited for Max to take it. Now Max understood. It was another lesson. Max smiled and took her hand. Jade let the light slide over her hand as she pulled Max's hand toward it. She stopped and held her hand steady in the beam with Max's hand less than an inch away from the light. He'd almost expected her hand to burst out into flames, but there was no change in the appearance of the skin or sign that she was suffering any kind of discomfort.

However, somehow Max knew when she began to tug on his hand he was going to have a different reaction to the tiny spot of sunlight. As his hand entered the light, he instantly felt a burning sensation. He flinched, trying to pull his hand away, but she held onto him keeping his hand steady. Finally, she stopped, the beam immediately began burning through his forearm like acid. Max felt the flesh begin to burn and burst into flames catching his shirt on fire. Teeth clinched, Max refused to scream as the fire danced over his skin.

He let his mind go someplace, as he'd learned all those

years ago to do. It was Japan this time during the 1600s when peace was established under the Tokugawa shoguns after constant warfare. He could barely feel the pain.

Max knew when some evil son of a bitch wanted to hurt you, you just couldn't let them win. He unclenched his teeth and let his eyes bore into hers.

Suddenly she released him and Max stumbled back, falling to his knees. He smothered the flames with his good arm and ripped off the shirt, which managed to take some skin with it. Even though the fire was out, his skin still felt like it was burning. Worse yet, he had a hole in his arm where the light had been concentrated. If he'd been human, he probably would have lost his arm.

"You done?" Max asked, his voice rough and angry.

Jade walked through the light and stood before him. She gently touched his face, running her fingers along his cheek, caressing him. He knew she could feel his pain. She leaned into him, and let her lips brush his, at first so lightly he could barely feel her and then slowly the kiss grew deep and passionate. When she finally pulled away from him, Max thought maybe it was the best kiss he'd ever had.

"Do you still want to go outside?"

Max cradled his damaged arm. He looked at the beam of light and back to her.

She nodded and walked away. Max sat back on his ankles. A tidal wave of pain took him. When Max's vision cleared he realized he had an audience. Several vampires were watching, and maybe they had been there through the entire show. Max stumbled to his feet and staggered to the stairs. He pulled himself up along the banister, but lost his footing and slipped down a couple steps before he could catch himself. Max felt like he was going to pass out, but suddenly George was there picking him up and helping him to Jade's room.

"It's okay, Teach. You're going to be okay."

George laid Max on the bed and took a long look at his

arm.

"It's going to take a couple days to heal. The pain will go away in a few hours."

"Thanks George."

"You just stay here. You're going to need a meal and you're going to be worthless for hunting tonight. I'll talk to Jade and see what she wants me to do."

Max didn't even want to think what "meal" would be provided. As another wave of pain hit, hunger took hold of him and Max passed out.

Max faded in and out of consciousness for hours, as the pain from his arm and the demands from his hunger took turns pounding through him like two enormous drums vying for attention. When he felt the sun leave the sky, the hunger reared up.

He tried to sit up, but his body started to shake. He felt like to was going to die, even though he knew that a vampire wouldn't die from a little sunburn. But he didn't have any control over his body and every time he moved or touched his arm, pain seared through him. Eventually he stopped trying to get up or move and decided to wait it out. Someone would have to come for him eventually. And suddenly there she was, Jade, looking down on him like an angel… or at least an angel from Hell.

"What's wrong with me?" Max asked.

"It's sun poisoning. You'll feel better after a good meal."

He closed his eyes as his body began to shake again. Max knew that she could bring him one of his former students at that moment and he'd kill them. His body would take over, the desire ripping right through his heart, and he'd drink dry anyone she brought to him. And just as Max was focusing every ounce of his being on hating her, Jade sat down on the bed next to him and pulled him into her arms. Tenderly, almost lovingly, she rocked him like a mother would a sick child.

"It's going to be okay. Drink me, Max," she said.

Max looked up at her surprised. Jade laughed.

She leaned down to kiss him on the forehead and then turned her head to the side, exposing her neck for him. Max's body took over and in an instant he wrapped his hands around her and crushed her into his body, his fangs sinking into her neck. His mind went blank as he drank her deep and hard, extreme pain mingling with intense pleasure driving his senses to places he'd never been before. Better yet, he could feel her pleasure in his act.

When his mind came back to him, Max kept waiting for her to push him away, but she didn't. When he finally stopped, he laid back wiping the blood from his mouth. She watched him with her deep blue eyes, like a curious cat wondering what he might do next. She'd gone from being pink and warm to pale and cool.

"Do you feel better?" she asked.

Max nodded. "Thank you." He realized it was a kind of twisted logic that would have him thank her for helping him considering she hurt him in the first place. Regardless he'd go with it. He had to make Jade believe she owned him body and soul, and there was no time to start like the present.

He was still in some pain, but Max felt much, much better. He rolled over to look at her, resting his head on his good arm. "You're beautiful."

"And you're an idiot."

"Okay," he said.

"When I was holding your hand, you could have twisted out of the sun. You could have screamed, begged me to stop. Any number of things. But you didn't. You just endured the pain. Why?"

"If I had done those things, would you have stopped sooner?"

"Probably not," Jade said.

"Maybe I was trying to impress you."

"I don't think so."

"And what do you think?"

"I think… you weren't going to let me beat you."

"You've already beaten me," Max said as he played with her long, blonde hair rubbing a strand over his lips.

Jade laughed and shook her head. "Not yet. But I will. Time is on my side… Do you want to continue with lessons on the Saracian Lance?"

"Sure. Why not?"

" 'Why' is more like it."

"I don't think learning how to handle myself in this environment will hurt me."

"It might not help you either… You're a very interesting former human. Not always too bright though."

"Somehow I don't think being bright is a requirement for this job." Max let his eyes run down the length of her body. She was wearing the t-shirt and jeans from earlier. He really wanted to take them off.

Jade touched his chest and Max could feel her flowing through him like an electric current. "I suppose not." Jade pushed him onto his back and Max stopped talking. He didn't want to think anymore. He just wanted to let the feeling of her power wash through him. At that moment he didn't even have the energy to hate her.

## CHAPTER 7

Max felt like he was in the middle of a twisted reality show and he was waiting to see if he got voted off the planet by the television viewing audience. For the next few days he set about fitting in to his new environment. He smiled easily, made jokes and let his obsession with Jade show. When he got the chance, he worked out with Maria learning all he could about the lance. What he hid from all of them was the growing darkness he felt with each life he had to take.

Jade hadn't come up with any new tests for him, so he began to relax a little. For her part, she teased, threatened and sparred with him often, but she was preoccupied with other things she didn't bother to share with him, like the war everybody and nobody talked about. That was fine by him. He was sure his time would come, but he was happy to wait and focus on his education. Since his own primary agenda was to destroy Jade, he took in all that he could by listening, watching and learning. It was Vampire 101.

Vampires had two primary types of attacks on their victims. The first was the seductive attack that George called the Loving Embrace. It was clear to Max that vampires produced something to attract their prey, maybe a chemical reaction or a scent. Whatever it was it seemed to kick in when the victim was touched. Max remembered his experience with Jade. He felt her power from a distance, but he wasn't lost until she touched him. Whatever it was, it was so powerful the victim completely lost the desire for self-preservation. If someone could have figured out a way to bottle it without having to deal with the vampire thing, they would have made a fortune.

The second was the violent terrorize-the-victim-as-much-as-you-can attack George liked to call The Takedown. After Michelle, Max had enough of killing women and he didn't feel comfortable lovingly embracing guys, so he stuck to the takedown and took out whatever evil he could find on the streets. The problem was that the hunger seemed to feed on fear as much as it did on his victim's blood. Worse yet, it made him enjoy the hunt and the kill. Max would do what he had to to stop Jade and the others, but it was disturbing for him to get pleasure from it.

Being a vampire would have been the greatest gift in the world if it weren't for the evil serial killer part. Max was stronger, he could heal within moments, and his senses were completely in tune with his environment. He felt like Superman until the vamp took over. For every benefit there was a seriously demented drawback. Killing was the primary one. Still there were other more personal drawbacks. Max really missed the sun. He had been a morning person and there was something about watching the sun come up that had thrilled him as he waited for his day to start. Worse than that, he couldn't feel his heart pounding. For the others, that seemed to cement that they were neither alive nor quite dead.

Max wasn't so sure. He had another theory. It had occurred to him that vampires might be another species that evolved when the human race had become too clever and eliminated the threat of their natural predators. Perhaps vampires were simply nature's way of trying to keep the human population from getting out of hand. Still for Max, it was easier to deal with what had happened to him if there was some scientific explanation. He decided it was best to keep his thoughts to himself on his theories.

George was Max's source of free-flowing, mostly useless information. Max managed to catch George alone in the kitchen having a beer after the big guy had his daily dose of 'Judge Judy.' It was a perfect time to pin him down on some things.

"Come on, George, tell me." Max grabbed a chair and straddled it backwards, resting his arms on the chair's back.

"Teach, that's like asking where do babies come from."

"Well, there's an answer to that one, isn't there. You and I both know that Jade is different than us. I can't turn into smoke. If you can, you're holding out on me, big guy. She's like ten times stronger than us. Jade made us, but who the heck made her?"

"If she knows, she wouldn't bother telling me. I like you, Teach, but you have to stop asking these questions. I'll tell you this much. I figure whoever made Jade was a demon, maybe even Lucifer himself. Even Jade may not know the answers."

"So your theory is that we're evil because someone, a long time ago, was damned."

"Maybe. The truth is, it doesn't matter. Killing is in our nature. What do you think the purpose of that hunger that scratches at your gut is? It makes us what we are, and what happened a hundred or a thousand or ten thousand years ago doesn't matter one damn bit to you or me… You want to play some cards?"

"Sure." George pulled a deck out of one of the kitchen drawers. He liked to play Gin.

"You're a good kid. Don't let these things bother you."

Max nodded. "George, do you ever miss your family? Your old life?"

"Yeah, sure. I check in on them once and awhile. The kids are in college now, but the wife still lives in the old house."

"You didn't stop loving them then?"

"I love them enough to let them live their lives. But if Jade locked me in a room with my wife, I'd give her my loving embrace because that's the nature of things."

Max and George played cards in silence. Max had been thinking a lot about his family and the kids at the high school. His family was in pain, and now he was causing that pain for other families. Even the most evil son of a bitch had a mother.

He couldn't help but run the video of the fire over and over again in his mind, remembering that brief glimpse of his mother. But if he had died in a fire, it would be over and he'd be at rest. He envied Rails.

# # #

Max quickly settled into the routine. Sleep til 2 in the afternoon, hang around for cards or to watch the tube or videos on the net, take in Jade's show in the arena if she felt like having one, a bit of bloodletting for dinner, and sex with Jade. The usual stuff.

There were 12 vampires living in the house under Jade's control, including Max. However, he knew there were other vampires out there too. Sometimes vampires would come to meet with Jade or to fight in the arena. They didn't mingle with the house vampires much so Max didn't get much info from them. Beyond that there were those long angry phone conversations Jade would have. Max knew she was keeping him in the dark about certain things. Conversations would stop when he entered a room. Looks between her and some selected members of the family and odd word choices were clues to Max that there was something larger at stake than Jade's little kingdom. Max mulled over what Jade must be fighting against. Perhaps some of the living were fighting back, or maybe Jade had an old enemy. He liked that thought a lot.

It'd been a little over a week since his transformation, but Max realized he had to settle in for the long haul. He'd wait as long as it took to find the answers. He still needed more information, but at some point the time would be right and he'd strike. Until then he would be a shining example vampirism.

Max had discovered it was great fun to play with his food. He was hunting with George when he ran across a former gang banger turned hit man who liked to call himself Jack King. Max remembered him from his time on the streets and killing King seemed like a really good idea once the hunger set in. Max's conscious found the game appalling, but the hunger driving him just ate it up.

Max saw King coming out of a restaurant and recognized

92

him right away. He was wearing a trench coat, making him look like a black mobster. King was headed down the street, probably to his car. Max started shadowing him, while George hung back a bit to let Max do his thing. King spotted his tail almost instantly. He was a pro and he knew he was in trouble. The area was too populated for Max to take him right there, but a good chase would add some spice to the game.

King dropped his keys and Max knew he was checking him out, sizing up the situation. His gun was probably out, waiting. Max had never been shot before, but hey, why not? It wasn't like it was going to kill him.

King stood and walked between the cars lined up along the street. Max followed him. King wasn't afraid yet. He still felt he had control of the situation. He turned toward a car, as if to open the door, but Max saw the gun in his hand. He was about ten feet away when King turned and pointed the gun at him. It was a .45 and had a silencer on it. Max was glad of that. It wouldn't do to wake the neighbors.

"Do you want something from me?" King asked, ready for a fight

Max smiled and walked a little closer. He held his hands out to show he wasn't holding a weapon. "Yes, I do. Are you going to shoot me? I don't have a gun."

"That depends on what you want. Who sent you?"

"Jimmie Large. I thought we might have a little chat." Max leaned up against the trunk of King's car.

"Jimmie's dead."

"I know."

"He died of a heart attack."

"Really? I thought I killed him," Max said. King looked surprised. He caught site of George lurking in the dark, and took a long breath.

"No loss, either way."

"No, it wasn't," Max said.

"What do you want?"

"A little conversation. Maybe a bite later."

"I just ate."

Max turned to face him and smiled. He brought his fangs out. "Funny, I haven't."

King looked horrified. He was expecting a hit, not a horror movie. He raised his gun and pulled the trigger three times. The bullets hit Max in the chest and tore through his body. Max heard them hit the pavement behind him. It hurt like hell for a moment and Max staggered back a bit. He looked down and watched the bullet wounds heal. He touched one of the holes in his shirt.

"Ouch, that hurt… You ruined a perfectly good shirt."

"It's a vest. It's got to be a vest."

King took aim at his head, but Max wasn't ready to let his brain be turned into Swiss cheese, even if it would probably heal. He thought about King and he suddenly had him by the throat. He took King's gun and put it in his pocket, and then released him.

"I'd hate to have you mess up my hair," Max said.

King fell back, terrified. The hunger inside Max was so happy. The man scrambled back. "What are you?"

"You know what I am." Max saw him reach for his ankle, no doubt headed for another weapon. "You shoot me again and I'm really going to get pissed off… You don't want that."

King pushed himself up and ran. He was headed toward a busy restaurant, so Max got in front of him and forced him to run down an alley. Max laughed. He toyed with King, finally forcing him to run into an abandoned warehouse that would be perfect for Max's little game of cat and mouse.

The interior of the warehouse was set up like a maze and King, breathing raggedly, ran from room to room, looking for an escape. But Max was right there with him, making noise to force him back to the center of the building or showing his face just for a moment so King could take a shot at him. When he was finally out of bullets, Max figured he must have gone through a couple clips. King sunk to the ground, out of breath.

Max walked up to him and took King's second gun away, pocketing it with the other one. Max squatted down and looked at the desperate man.

"I've killed lots of people. I never tortured them unless there was a reason," King said as he grasped for air.

"How many people have you killed, King?"

"Twenty seven."

"Well, you've got me beat... Here's the thing. Do you remember a kid named Stinger?"

King closed his eyes. He did remember.

"What number was he on your list?" Max asked.

"I don't remember."

"Yes you do." Max slapped him on the back of the head.

"It was a long time ago!"

"What number?"

King looked defiant. "He was number seven."

"Lucky number seven... Well, Stinger was a friend of mine," Max said. "You killed him because he made a mistake and robbed the wrong establishment. He was sixteen."

"Who wasn't sixteen back then. It was gang stuff. I was doing what I was told to do. If I hadn't done him, it would have been someone else," King said.

"Yeah, I know. Nothing personal. Right? Well, it was personal to me and it pissed me off. But I couldn't do anything about it back then. If you'd just shot him, that would have been one thing, but you ripped his guts out and cut his head off."

King pulled a knife from somewhere and was going to cut his own throat. Max took the knife away from him and pocketed that too.

"That would be a waste of perfectly good blood..." Max said.

"So do it already!"

"You see, I'm really not angry anymore about it. I had issues for a long time. Stinger was my best friend on the street. But you get past that stuff. The problem is, I've got to drink someone. I'm really hungry. So I can drink just anyone or I can drink someone who's really bad. You sense my dilemma. I'm conflicted about it, but it occurs to me I might as well go for the bad guys, have a meal and clean up the streets at the same time," Max said.

King tried to get up, but Max put his foot down on the man's back and pinned him to the floor.

"Am I going to turn into what you are?" King asked.

"No. That would just defeat the purpose of cleaning up the streets, don't you think? But I'll promise you this. You will go to hell, right where you belong."

"Then I'll meet you there!" he screamed.

"No doubt, but not for a long, long time."

"What are you waiting for?" King screamed.

"Actually, the vampire in me just really gets off on your fear. It's kind of a bonus."

Max took his foot off King's back and let him scramble up. Then Max took him from behind and bit down hard. His hunger was at such a heightened peak, the blood had never tasted so sweet to him, so wonderfully powerful. King struggled for a couple minutes before he surrendered to Max's embrace. Max couldn't seem to quench his hunger and he didn't want to let go of his prey. At some point, Max could feel King's heartbeat slowing down. He was dying. Max couldn't stop. He had to keep drinking. When King's heart finally gave out, Max let him drop to the ground.

He was glad. King was evil and deserved to die. Just call him Judge Max. Maybe he could have his own TV show, deal out justice, and drink the people who lost their cases. As his blood high began to take effect, Max felt like he *could* do anything. He jumped up and swung from the rafters that were two stories above him. He loved testing his physical abilities.

George was there, looking out a window. Max reached out with his senses. George was watching a couple making out.

Max pushed himself to see how fast he could run, how high he could jump. As Max began to test himself physically, he suddenly sensed the presence of someone else. A boy was hiding by King's body under a table. How did he miss him? Jade's rule was no witnesses.

He must have been too wrapped up in the bloodlust. The kid was maybe 9 or 10. Max went back to the room and stood near King's body. He could make out the boy clearly in the dark shadows. Max sensed the fear in him. He'd been careless and if George sensed the kid it was going to be bad. He might be able to take George, but probably not. Max didn't have the experience or George's bulk.

The kid realized he'd been made and started to move. Max shook his head and motioned for him to stay put. He threw King's body over his shoulder and went to meet George. The big guy was still caught up in the show outside.

George had already called for the limo and it showed up right as Max got to the door. He waited a moment as the couple outside took off after seeing the limo's headlights. The driver popped the trunk and Max reached out with all his senses to check the area. No one was around except the kid. Max put King's body in the trunk and closed it. George was already in the limo waiting.

"What did it feel like to get shot?" George asked.

"It hurt for a moment and then nothing."

"You're not afraid to die, are you? I mean, I know you're afraid of other things. You're afraid Jade's going to hurt someone you cared about in your past life. You don't much like killing until the hunger hits you. I also think you're afraid the vampire will take over permanently. But if you had to fight to save you own life, I don't think you'd do it. Why is that, Teach?"

"What's to save, George?"

George looked at him curiously. "You get to spend time in Jade's bed. That should be worth hanging around."

"She only wants me for my fangs," Max said.

George shook his head and laughed. "What do you have to lose by staying around?"

Max stared out the window as the city went by. "It's what they have to lose. The people like your kids or my students. You going to tell me they don't deserve better?"

"You're going after the scum. In fact, you've been working pretty hard to make the streets a safer place."

"Yeah, George. I'm a real good guy."

"Maybe too good. What about the kid back there? You know Jade's rules."

Max nodded. He hadn't really believed George had missed the kid. "I'm not killing a kid… You've got my life in your hands."

"I don't want your life, Teach. Self-preservation is what makes us kill and it keeps us alive in Jade's house. You're not going to last very long without it."

"I refuse to kill a kid."

George considered him and then nodded. "I'm not going to protect you."

"I'm not asking you to."

"But I won't say anything either."

"Okay… Thanks."

"Don't thank me yet. I'm just full of self-preservation," George said.

Max smiled.

They continued to chat during the ride. Max liked George. He would have been a great guy if he wasn't such a literal lady-killer. Max figured George actually didn't like the killing part either. He just liked having sex with pretty girls and drinking their blood. The killing was just a necessary thing… And he hadn't gone after the kid when he could have.

Max was really going to hate having to kill George when it came down to it. But it wasn't like George was going to change. Max realized what he needed to do was take out the entire lot of them. He might be able to manage a stake through the heart for Jade while she slept, but it would be tricky. She had incredible senses.

Max had considered starting a fire, but their sense of smell was so good it would be put out before the fire could take hold. Maybe a gasoline fire would work, still gas had a very strong smell and unless there was some reason for gas in the house, someone would notice before any real damage could be done. A bomb would work if it were set off during the day, to prevent escape. The problem was getting the materials for an effective bomb, one big enough to do damage. Max had gotten some basic experience with bombs during his time with Special Forces, but it hadn't been his specialty.

Max went round and round thinking about it, but the answer didn't come to him. The only thing he could do was wait for the right timing and be ready when that one special moment came. Max realized that if he could, he'd take care of all of them. The priority, however, had to be killing Jade. In the mean time, Max had no problem having great sex and plotting Jade's destruction at the same time. Some things were worth the wait.

## CHAPTER 8

Doing whatever it took proved to be much harder than Max ever imagined. Another week had passed and he realized he was doing a really poor job of being a shining example of vampirism. He couldn't hide his reluctance to kill people who didn't deserve it. When it came time to gang drain some poor shmoe from the arena, Max vanished to hide in a room upstairs until it was over, even though the smell of blood tore him apart. He held out until later when he could go after someone who did deserve it. He had discovered that if he fed well the night before, he had a small amount of control over himself the next day.

Fortunately he managed to keep Jade entertained in other ways. There was nothing like vampire sex and feeling exactly what your partner felt. What more could a guy ask for… except maybe a girl who didn't define the term "evil dead"?

It was also fortunate for him that she was preoccupied with other things. She stayed locked in her office often into the morning. A variety of people and vampires came for meetings, she took conference calls and video meetings, and the walls of her office were covered with surveillance maps. On the way to the bedroom, he'd heard more than one heated conversation coming from behind the door of her office. Something serious was going on and it put her in a bad mood. Max often avoided her until after she'd fed. That always put her in a better, more amorous frame of mind.

Every night Jade would go hunting by herself. Max caught her watching him while he was out more than once as she checked on his progress. He knew that acquiring his soul was still on her "to do" list and that he'd have to make a decision. Give her at least a piece of it or refuse and risk being killed.

George had been right about one thing. Max didn't care if Jade killed him. His father had beaten the fear of death out of him at an early age. When the moment came, he'd welcome the end of his existence because his struggle would be over. Still, this wasn't just about protecting the handful of people Max cared about. As much as he didn't want to see his mother or students get hurt, the price Jade exacted on the rest of the human race was far too costly.

Max knew he was headed for a train wreck. One that would happen sooner, more likely than later.

Max was in the living room catching a pre-season baseball game with George and a couple of the guys. The Cubs were playing the Cardinals. George was from Missouri and everyone else was from the Chicago area, so they were naturally involved in a spirited discussion. It was a late afternoon and no one was going anywhere for a while.

"After last season you're going to tell me they suck?" Max asked.

"Of course. They had their ticket to the World Series and they blew it." George countered.

"George! They made it to the playoffs…"

Crystal came down the stairs. "Mr. Maguire, Jade wants you in her office."

Max looked up surprised and then moved like he had a purpose. He had a bad feeling.

The door was open and Max saw Veronica working behind Jade's desk on the computer. Jade stood over her shoulder watching the screen. She looked up at him. He couldn't read her expression.

"Hi," Max said.

"Storm clouds are coming my way," she said. Max instinctively glanced at the curtains, even though the windows were blocked. He knew Jade wasn't talking about the weather anyway. "I've been thinking about you." Max realized this was a not a good thing.

"About what?"

"Tonight, I want you to go out by yourself. George will give you the keys to one of the cars."

"Really?"

"I think it's time."

"Okay. Good." Max waited but Jade's attention had shifted back to the monitor.

As he turned to leave she spoke softly. "When you go, bring me some take out. I won't get a chance to go out later. Something tasty, young, pretty… female."

Max didn't turn back. He left and went to her bedroom. He laid back on the bed, knowing he had come to his crossroad. He was to go out and bring back a young woman for execution. Do not pass go. Do not collect $200. Whoever Max brought back, their death would be on him, totally and completely. And just to insure he was tortured fully enough, she'd given him some time to think about it.

Max decided to take a shower. As the scalding hot water ran over him he realized no matter how much soap and water he used, he'd never be able to get the blood off his hands.

# # #

The afternoon seemed to stretch on. He went downstairs to try and pass the time. Both George and Crystal had tried to talk to him, but he made an excuse and went to a different room. Max was actually grateful when it finally came time for the arena.

Jade had made a new vampire who, from what Max could tell, had roughly his same vampire experience. He was a good-looking college kid named Steve, and Max wondered if that would be the end of his and Jade's great romance. Perhaps this test with the "take out" was to see whether or not Max kept his head.

Max was actually grateful not to be the new kid on the block anymore. George acted as the welcome wagon, just like he had for Max. Max hung back, away from the new guy and the others.

Steve had that deer-caught-in-head-lights look to him. When Veronica came in, they gathered round for the show. It was a new guy, so Jade did the smoke thing again. It did

102

make for a pretty impressive show. Max wondered if he'd have to find a different bed to sleep in. Of course, if he didn't have a head, that part wouldn't matter much.

"Peach," Jade commanded.

A very nervous woman Max didn't know well stepped into the light. Peach went before Jade. She was terrified.

Jade stood up and pulled out her sword. Peach started to cry.

"How long have I allowed you to live, Peach?"

"Please, Jade, please, I'll do whatever you want."

"On your knees."

She fell to her knees. She burst into tears. "I'm so sorry. Please, what have I done?"

Jade circled her and raised the sword. "Why nothing. You just really annoy me." She lowered the sword slightly. "I'll tell you what, Peach. Stop crying and pull yourself together."

In an instant, Peach managed to calm herself down and put a look of resolve on her face. Jade began to bring down the blade, but stopped it just before it touched Peach's neck. Max could see a slight crack in Peach's determination, but she recovered nicely. Jade laughed. She let the sword drop to her side and patted Peach on the head like she were a dog. "Good girl. Now get back where you belong."

"Thank you, Jade." Jade nodded. Peach got up quickly and turned to get back in her place.

"One thing…" Peach turned, waiting. "You know I hear everything. When you listen to music, I listen to music. Do you think I like country music?"

"No. I won't…"

"It might be wise, not to listen to music at all for awhile. Just a suggestion."

"Of course." Peach scampered back into her place.

Jade went back to her throne. Max was surprised. He thought Peach was history.

"Teacher."

Max smiled and went before her. Maybe he was going to

lose his head after all. Jade still had the sword in her hand.

"Yes," he said.

"Are you going to take care of my request?"

"Your wish is my command." He even bowed slightly to make his point.

"Good." Her look told him everything he needed to know. She lifted her chin slightly and he knew he was being dismissed. Once he was back in his place she called the next contestant. "College boy."

Steve looked nervous, but he went before her. "Yes, Miss Jade."

Jade tapped the sword on the arm of the throne. "What will you do for me?"

"Anything," he said without hesitation.

"Good. We need to fake your death." Veronica was bringing in a man who was struggling hard. He had a vague resemblance to Steve. "Poor Wilson here is a visitor to our fair city."

"Let me go! What the hell is going on here?" Veronica pushed him into the arena. Wilson caught his footing and kept from falling, but when he looked around the look on his face told Max the guy knew he was in deep shit. Steve watched Wilson, a look of hunger written all over him.

"Wilson, what do you think of Chicago?"

"What do you people want?"

"How does it stack up to New York?"

Wilson's eyes darted back and forth. He was looking for a way out. "It's just great. Can I go now?"

"Not quite yet."

"You know people are waiting for me. You can't just kidnap someone," he said.

"But you told our sweet Crystal here that you were exploring America and that you were completely on your own."

"I was lying. It was just something to tell a cute girl."

"At this point, it doesn't really matter... Steve, he's all

yours."

Steve grinned broadly and Wilson did a melt down as he saw the fangs come out. Wilson didn't even have time to run before Steve was on him. Steve was like an animal and he literally ripped the man's throat out. Max was both horrified and strangely thrilled at the same time. His own bloodlust kicked in with a vengeance and it took every ounce of will he had to keep from joining Steve.

Jade laughed. "College boy, you're certainly going to have to work on technique a little bit, but I can see you're not having any trouble with the concept… George, find College Boy a room after he's done." She left. Max didn't know whether or not he should be relieved that Steve hadn't replaced him yet.

The scent of Wilson's blood washed over him, so he got out of the house. George had given him keys to a red Jaguar and Max couldn't help but admire it for a few moments before hopping behind the wheel to take it out for a spin. It felt good to be back behind the wheel of a car. And what a car it was.

Max opened the windows and laughed. It was just too cool. It was a guy's dream. Here he was tooling around in the Jag with the wind racing through his hair, he had super powers and he could have any woman he wanted. Definitely a guy's dream. So why wasn't he happy?

"Oh, yeah, I'm a fucking serial killer," he yelled out the window.

Max calmed himself down. George had warned him not to get stopped by the police, so Max followed the speed limit and drove like a good ordinary living citizen of the world. All the way into the heart of the city he considered his lack of options.

The hunger was kicking in strongly by the time he parked the car and went on the prowl. Max needed to take care of himself before he worried about getting Jade what she wanted. He had found a good candidate on a previous hunt.

The guy was a nasty pimp who liked to beat up his girls. Max caught him in his apartment while his girls were out and did his business quickly, making it look like a fall in the bathtub. Most accidents did happen in the home, after all.

With his hunger satisfied, it was easier for him to think. Escape occurred to Max, but letting Jade live didn't seem to be an option. Refusing to do what she asked was another option, but it seemed a sure path to his destruction and to the letting Jade live problem.

Max's mission to stamp out evil on the streets had given him a reason to continue. However, the only evil woman Max had ever met was Jade. Even during his time on the streets he couldn't think of any woman that deserved what Jade had in store. He met women who were mean or selfish or conniving or cold, but mostly on the street he'd met women who were just trying to survive.

It was early yet, so he had plenty of time. Max kept to the shadows as he surveyed street after street, alley after alley, looking for a victim. As he considered the women who crossed his path, he wondered how he was going to decide whose life had the least amount of value. The homeless were in abundance and several hookers looked like possibilities, but how could he choose to end some poor girl's life? As he searched the city, he tried to consider the bigger picture. Funny, but he couldn't help but realize that whatever girl he chose wouldn't have a bigger picture. She would be dinner and her body would be put in acid to dissolve. No one would ever know what happened to her and someone, somewhere would be devastated when she came up missing.

As the night wore on, Max realized that there was no way for him to choose. Whether it be God or chance or fate, he'd let a higher power decide. Whatever girl he found at 2 a.m. that fit the bill and fell in the "wouldn't be missed category" would be the sacrifice.

Max had about 15 minutes before his deadline, so he sat on a box in an alley, closed his eyes and took in the city with his senses. Even in the middle of the night the city felt alive with sounds, smells and emotions. Traffic went by, people made love and Chicago became a living, breathing thing to him. At some point, he became aware of a woman. Even though she was over a block away he could feel her intense sadness.

He went to find her. She was sitting in the loading dock of a warehouse, back in the depths of the shadows. She was crying softly, overwhelmed by despair. The woman was young, but not a kid. She wasn't pretty, but it was because the street had taken that away from her. She wore the mismatched uniform of the homeless. Max saw that it was exactly 2 a.m.

He left to retrieve the car. He couldn't drag her several blocks without being seen and she wasn't going anywhere. As he drove back, the fancy Jag seemed more like a hearse than his dream car. He pulled into the area slowly, checking for witnesses. It wouldn't do to be spotted. Just to be careful, he parked in the shadows a couple buildings down and scanned the area.

When he approached the woman, she looked up, pain written in every feature of her face.

"What's the matter?" he asked as he stooped down.

"Why is it so hard?" she asked.

"I don't know."

"I just want it not to be so hard. You know… I want it to stop. I just want everything to stop."

"I'm sorry."

"Are you going to hurt me?" she asked.

"Yeah."

She dropped her head and started crying again. In another life, he would have tried to save her. She would have meant something to him simply because she crossed his path. Now, in this life, he would be her executioner for the same reason. Simply because she crossed his path.

"Take my hand and I promise the pain will stop."   She

looked up at him and nodded. Slowly she reached out and took his hand, accepting whatever fate he had in store for her. Max watched as his touch made the pain and anguish go away, while her dread filled him up. She looked surprised.

"How did you that? Am I dead?"

"What's your name?" Max asked.

"I don't remember... Amanda, maybe."

"Come on, Amanda."

"Are you going to take me to heaven?"

Her words vibrated through him. Where Max was taking her, it didn't have anything at all to do with heaven. He led her to the car. She was reluctant to let go of his hand, but he pulled it away and opened the door for her. Amanda couldn't take her eyes off him.

Max started to go to the driver's side when he spotted an old wooden table sitting by a garage dumpster. He considered it for a moment. He left Amanda, and with one punch, he reduced the table to pieces. One particular piece looked a whole lot like a wooden stake. It was long and one thick end narrowed down to a sharp point. He sniffed the wood but even he couldn't smell anything. It would fit perfectly in his boot. He thought about Jade. Would she sense or smell it? Maybe tonight was the only chance he'd have, if College Boy Steve became the new flavor of the month. He probably wouldn't be able to save Amanda, but maybe he could save others. He tucked the stake in his boot. It was worth the risk.

Max got into the car and drove out of the area quickly. After Amanda lost physical contact with him, Max could feel her pain returning. She touched him on the arm and Max watched as her pain vanished once again. Slowly, she leaned her head up against his shoulder and closed her eyes.

Max closed the windows because he knew she'd be cold, but once he did the hunger took in her scent. It'd had been several hours since he'd fed.

"What kind of angel are you?" she asked.

"I'm not an angel."
"What then?"
"I'm a vampire," Max said.
"Are you going to kill me tonight?"
"Yes."
She was quiet for a moment. "Good."

## CHAPTER 9

Jade was laying on the bed naked when they came in and Max could sense her impatience. He was holding Amanda's hand and the girl didn't look at anything except him.

"Not so pretty, but acceptable. She stinks of the streets. Give her a shower," Jade said.

Max nodded. He took Amanda into the bathroom and turned on the shower, making sure it wasn't too hot. Amanda started taking off her clothes. Max looked into her eyes and caressed her cheek with his hand.

"Come on," he said.

She stepped into the shower and the water and soap washed the street away. She was too thin and it was obvious she didn't eat regularly. Her breasts were a little small and her hips a little too large, but to him she was lovely. He turned his back to avoid watching her. He didn't want to get aroused. His hunger wouldn't be denied her blood. Killing her would be one thing, but the other would be too much like rape. It wasn't right. It was a line he wouldn't cross.

When he glanced back to see how she was doing, she was staring at him, tears streaming down her face. Amanda knew what was coming and she really didn't want to die. She just wanted the pain to stop.

Max handed her a towel and she stepped out of the shower. She dried herself and used the towel to get the excess water out of her hair. She dropped the towel and put her arms around him. She kissed him softly, but Max stepped away from her.

"I'm sorry," Max said.

"Please…"

"Go to her." Max motioned toward the bedroom.

"I don't want her."

"You will."

Reluctantly, Amanda walked into the bedroom.

"Come here, little sheep," Jade said. Amanda did as she was told.

Max watched from the door of the bathroom, his arms crossed.

Jade took Amanda in her arms and kissed her. Jade suddenly had Amanda's total attention and Jade delighted in the girl's touch.

"You managed to find one that wants to die. How did you do that, Teacher?"

"Just lucky I guess."

"I have a feeling you're going to get lucky tonight."

Lucky was exactly what Max was hoping for. He could feel the wooden stake in his boot. The feel of it comforted him. He wondered what would happen when he plunged it into her heart. Would she dissolve into dust or would something different happen?

Jade was exploring Amanda's body and Max could sense the girl's desire build. He decided to keep his clothes on and, for once, not fight the vampire within him. If he could focus on the girl's blood and Jade's death, he might just have a chance.

Jade had stopped and she was starring at him. "Are you waiting for an invitation?"

Max smiled. "Just enjoying the view."

Jade pulled Amanda into a sitting position, and sat behind her so they were both facing him. Jade wrapped her arms around the girl, sliding one hand between her legs and the other across her breasts. Amanda threw her head back on Jade's shoulder, lost in the vampire's touch. "How's the view now?"

"Even better." Max pulled his shirt off. Well, at least he'd keep his pants on and definitely his boots. He focused on the hunger. He realized for the first time that with the living it was more about the hunger, and with another vampire, it was more about the sex. He could feed from either, but the hunger didn't want Amanda's body. It wanted her blood.

Max went to them. He sat on the bed in front of Amanda and ran his fingers through her hair. She looked at him with such longing. He buried his head in her neck and breathed deeply. She cried out when he sunk his fangs into her neck, then she gasped as Jade dug in on the other side. As they both drank from her, Max could feel the desire from both women. But with two vampires taking her life's blood, Amanda began to fade quickly.

Max stopped himself. Suddenly he was behind Jade, pulling her away from Amanda. Amanda laid back. He watched as the wounds on her throat healed.

"Don't kill her yet," Max said.

"No, not yet. I want to watch you with her."

Max twisted around to face Jade. He pulled her to him. "I don't want to be with her. I want you." Max pushed her back, kissing her, unable to ignore his sexual desire any longer. He unzipped his pants and pushed them down to his knees. The ever-present feeling of the wooden stake in his boot only made him want her more. Maybe it would be the last time. That was just fine by him. With his blood lust satisfied, there was only one more thing he needed to do before he killed Jade and saved the girl. Fuck Jade with a vengeance.

He knew Jade could feel his desire building, and she got caught up in it. He bit her breast and then teased her nipples with his fangs and tongue. She bit his arm and wouldn't let him get between her legs. Max managed to kick his pants off of one leg, along with the unimportant boot. Jade twisted away from him. As Max tackled her, they tumbled to the floor and he ended up on top. He pulled her legs apart and forced himself deep inside her. She slapped him and he slapped her back. As Max began to move inside her, Jade threw her head back and laughed.

"Better watch out, Teacher, or you're going to become a bad boy." Jade wrapped her arms around him and she began to move with him. Max drove his fangs into her neck, and he felt the sharp pain in his own neck. He knew it was so right that he should kill her this way… or die trying.

He sensed she was close to climax and he moved faster, thrusting deeper into her and she matched his intensity. He could feel what she felt and when she climaxed he let his moment of release finally come. He eased himself down on top of her. He actually felt slightly winded, but he suspected it was more because he thought he should be than that he actually was. He didn't want to move. He actually loved being inside her and he wasn't quite ready to kill her yet.

She kissed him as tenderly as any woman ever had. He looked into her eyes. How was it possible for this beautiful creature to be so thoroughly evil? How was it possible?

Max sat up and straddled her. He played with her right nipple while his free hand retrieved the stake from his boot. He bent down to take her right nipple between his lips and he could feel her pleasure. She threw her head back and closed her eyes.

Max sat back up and quickly raised the stake and drove it down. He suddenly felt himself spinning around, as he was slammed into the floor. She was now straddling him. The stake was still in his hand, but she had his wrist pinned to the floor. She looked disappointed. He'd been caught and there was no way he could take her one on one.

"You're probably beginning to think this was a mistake. It wasn't a very good attempt. Not that it matters, but it was a really stupid thing to do. The sex was inspired though, I'll give you that."

"Thanks for the critique," he said.

She took the stake away from him. It was now pointing toward his chest. As she raised the stake over her head, Max got ready to die. Someone else would just have to save the world. In a quick motion, Jade thrust the stake into his chest, just missing his heart.

"Shit! Oh God!" Intense pain radiated through him in every direction. It wasn't like the bullets that only hurt for a moment. Instead it was as if she'd driven a burning hot poker into him. Max tried to pull it out, but Jade pushed it in deeper.

"FYI, God has nothing to do with this. Additionally, a wooden stake in your body will hurt like hell and take a while to heal once it comes out... You really should have listened to George. I think you broke the number one rule."

Jade got off of him and Max ripped the stake out of his chest. Max cried out again. "Shit. It hurts." The bloody stake was in his hand but he couldn't even sit up, let alone go after her. She took it away from him.

"Poor baby. Want a Band-Aid?"

She grabbed him and with a flick of her wrist, threw him across the room into the wall. Max crashed into the dresser on the way to the floor. His head pounded for a moment before he became aware that he was flying across the room again. When another wall stopped his flight, he didn't even try to get up. Every single part of his body hurt, even the parts that were busy trying to heal themselves. The funny thing was that the hole in his chest still hurt like a son of a bitch. It felt more like burning needles now, and it took him a moment to realize the pain was coming from splinters.

Max turned over onto his back. She was standing over him, the stake still in her hand.

"Just do it."

"Do you really think I'm going to make it easy for you? Just let you off the hook with a quick jab to the heart?" She laughed. "I don't think so."

"What the hell do you want from me?"

"Well to be fair, you did say you were going to try and kill me right from the beginning, didn't you?"

"I'm never going to be one of you!"

"But Max, you *are* one of us." Jade pulled Amanda out of bed and to her feet. The girl was conscious, but confused. "You brought her to me. You picked out one of the sheep and you knew she would be slated for death. Her life is on you."

Jade grabbed Amanda by the chin and in a quick motion

broke her neck. Then she let Amanda's body fall on top of him. Max couldn't get out of the way and the girl's dead eyes starred at him accusingly.

"Take out the garbage." Jade grabbed a robe and opened the door to leave. She turned back to him, and the slight smile that crossed her lips chilled him. "Teacher, how many students did you have?"

Jade closed the door and left him with Amanda's corpse. Her body was too warm. She couldn't possibly be dead. Max gently laid her on the floor. He was horrified when her head rolled to an odd, unnatural angle. Holding his hand over the hole in his chest Max tried to sit up, but it was agony. He realized he was bleeding badly. He had to get the splinters out.

Max stumbled to the bathroom and into the shower. He turned on the faucet and tried to wash out the wound. He got a few of them out, but he couldn't get to the deeper ones. Pain radiated through him. Max managed to stand. He needed to find something he could dig with. He pulled open the medicine chest and knocked several things into the sink before he found the metal finger nail file. It had a pointed end that would work.

He fell back into the shower and started to dig into the wound. "Shit!" Blinding pain struck as he scrapped away at the inside of the open wound. He was able to get most of it out, but there were still two or three small pieces deep inside him. Those pieces were burning him alive. Max screamed as he went after them digging out chunks of his own flesh. As he pulled out the last piece of wood, he fell back and let the water wash over him. The hole in his chest was bigger than it had been and it still hurt intensely, but at least the pain was duller. He waited to see if it would heal. While the bleeding slowed considerably, the hole didn't appear to be in any hurry to disappear.

Max closed his eyes and began to cry. The worst thing had happened and Jade was going to torture him at the expense of those he cared about. He cried for Amanda. He cried for his mother. He cried for his students and for every person he'd killed in his life and death. Every person except the first one.

He wasn't sure how much time passed, but Max could tell that the sun had come up. It was daytime. He still was in severe pain, but he could move again. As he got out of the shower, he realized the hole was finally beginning to heal, but very slowly. From the doorway, Max studied Amanda's body. How many people had she been discarded by in her life? How many had let her down before she had the misfortune to run into him?

Max sat down next to her and carefully moved her head so she didn't look broken. What would he do? Another pledge over another unfortunately young woman? He traced her face with his fingers taking in the memory of her. She deserved a better fate.

He dressed. The wound looked a bit better, but it still was bleeding. He took a sheet from the bed and wrapped Amanda and her clothes in it. He lifted her weight easily and took her downstairs. George and Peach stopped talking when they saw him and they both starred at him. He could sense their anxiety. They knew he'd broken the golden rule.

"Hi George, Peach." Max said. He could feel their eyes follow him as he passed them. What disturbed him even more was that their judgment of him had absolutely nothing to do with the fact that he was holding a dead body.

The basement was empty and Max set Amanda next to the acid vat. The vat was several feet wide and round. The only opening was on the top and it was just big enough to fit a large body through. Max unlatched the door and pulled it open. The stench hit him full force. He unwrapped Amanda and took one last look. "I'm really sorry," he told her. "You didn't deserve this."

Max carefully lowered her into the acid and watched as she sunk below the liquid. He was supposed to throw her clothes in too, but instead he went through her pockets. He wanted to find out who she really was. Maybe someday he could let her family know that she was gone.

Amanda had an odd assortment of stuff that included the practical and the bizarre. She had tissues, a toothbrush and other useful items, along with a doorknob and a refrigerator magnet in the image of a watermelon. Max lowered her clothes into the vat. He picked up her shoes and tossed one in. He was about ready to toss the other when he saw something. He pulled out an old driver's license that was wedged into the sole of the shoe. There she was smiling and pretty, an Amanda from a lifetime before. Her name was Amanda Markinson. "What happened to you, Amanda?"

Max put her driver's license in his wallet and threw the shoe into the acid. He quickly shut and latched the door to the vat. He walked toward the arena and sat down on one of the sofas. His shirt had a bloody stain and he pulled it up to check the wound. He still had a hole in his chest and it still hurt like hell, but he knew it was the least of his worries.

He laid his head back. He'd wait. He had nowhere else to go. Max let his mind travel back in time until he stood next to the great explorers, Lewis and Clark and explored a new world with them. But at the edge of his thoughts sat something dark which refused to let him submerge himself in his fantasy. It was always almost out of sight, in the corner of his eye. He knew what it was, of course. The vampire didn't have to show itself for him to know what it was or that it was hungry again.

He sensed someone watching him. It was Crystal. She sat next to him on the couch.

"She wants to see you in her office," Crystal said. She looked so incredibly sad.

"Don't be sad. Remember, this stuff doesn't bother you."

"Why did you do it? She is everything. How could you betray her?"

Max sat up. "What is the matter with you? She doesn't care

about you or me or any other creature on this planet. She allows us to stay in her world because it entertains her. She is an evil cold-blooded killer, and because it gives her amusement, she makes other cold-blooded killers share her hell. She takes life indiscriminately and she destroys everything she comes into contact with. It's wrong, Crystal. It's wrong. I'm just sorry I wasn't a better assassin."

"How can you say that after what she's given us?" Crystal was crying.

"She gave us nothing. We're trapped between life and death… We're puppets," Max laughed. "And she's pulling the strings."

"You're wrong!" Crystal got up and ran to the door. She looked back at him.

"Really, we'll you better watch out. I think you're feeling something. Better watch out or you might end up just like me."

She disappeared up the stairs. Max stood up. It was time to face the music. Maybe Peach would let him borrow one of her country western CDs. At least he had his boots on. A cowboy should die with his boots on. Too bad he didn't have his hat.

By the time Max got to the main floor, he realized something else was going on that had nothing to do with him. There was a new energy in the house that was more like anticipation and nervousness. No one even bothered to look at him accusingly.

When he got to her office, the door was open and Max entered slowly. Jade was sitting behind her enormous desk yelling at someone on phone. The stake she'd taken from him was next to her stapler.

"I don't give a shit. You take care of that bitch!" she said with venom in her voice. She paused for a moment to listen.

"Really. Well, let's put it this way. If you can't take care of our little problem, you'll get a glimpse of what sunlight looks like again." She slammed her cell down on the desk and unbridled rage played across her face. Then she looked up at Max and took a breath.

"You wanted to see me," he said softly.

"What exactly were your plans after you'd taken me out?"

"I figured I could burn down the house."

"Take out the entire nest all at once. Is that it?"

"Yes."

"You would have died too."

"Then the world would have been a better place all the way around."

"No more games then?"

"I have a hole in my chest and I'm afraid I just don't want to play anymore."

She laughed. "What a pleasure it will be to dissect you. And just in case you're feeling suicidal, remember that if I don't feel satisfaction, someone else will pay. In fact, a lot of people will pay. Do you understand?"

"Yes. You want to torture me until you get bored. I've got it."

"I'm in a war and as much as it would give me great pleasure to torment you for the next twenty or thirty years, I don't have time to deal with you right now. We'll have to get to it later. If you give me any more trouble I won't just kill your mother, I'll make her one of us. Got it?"

"Yes."

"Good. Then you get a reprieve for the moment, if you behave yourself. We're leaving. We have to move quickly tonight. Help George and the others pack up what you can, while I get the new location set up."

"All right."

She studied him for a moment. "Did you actually think you were going to beat me?"

"I don't know. You pushed me too far… "

In an instant, Jade was in front of him. He pulled back slightly and she pushed him hard and pinned him to the wall. Then she kissed him. He couldn't stop his body from responding to her. Once she had his total attention, she drew back. "I haven't even started to push you." She let him go and went back to her desk. Max nodded and turned to leave. He glanced back and saw that unreadable expression she used so often. No, she definitely wasn't done with him yet.

By the time Max got back to the living room, everybody was moving.

Max caught George going by. "What do you need me to do?" Max asked.

"You fucked up, you know that."

"So I've heard." George looked grimmer than Max had ever seen him. The big guy only nodded. He was holding some sort of odd-looking gun and several pencils. Something else was definitely going on. George was obviously nervous and managed to drop the pencils. As Max bent down to pick them up, he realized they weren't pencils, so he pocketed one and handed the rest to George.

"Thanks. There are two suitcases in Jade's closet. Fill them up with whatever's in the dresser and closet. And you best grab a few changes of clothes."

"Think I'll need them?" Max asked with a smile.

"You really fucked up."

"What's going on, George?"

"It's bad, Teach, really bad."

As Max started up the stairs he noticed that several of the others had those odd looking guns either tucked in their pants or in a specially made shoulder holster.

Max went to Jade's room and shut the door. No one would come in except Jade without knocking first. He pulled out the pencil thing he'd lifted from George and examined it. No. It wasn't a pencil at all. It was more like a short wooden arrow. It was about six inches long and had a steel tip for piercing. A shell was attached to the end. This was a bullet of some kind and could only have one purpose, to kill a vampire.

Max knew his weapons, and the gun he'd seen had a short

double barrel, with a revolver long enough to hold the arrow-bullets. He was guessing it could fire about 10 rounds. The problem was a gun like that would probably be pretty heavy, but that wouldn't be a challenge for a vampire.

All that meant was that someone had designed a gun with the specific purpose of killing another vampire. It'd be effective on humans too, but there'd be no reason to have something like that unless there was a use for it.

Max put the arrow-bullet back in his pocket. He already knew first hand what effect wood had on a vampire's body. Maybe it would come in handy later. Of course, if Jade caught him with another wooden stake she'd probably change her mind about that reprieve. Maybe that would be a good thing. He packed quickly. It didn't take long.

Downstairs, everyone was running around, unorganized and nervous. It occurred to Max that it might be a great time to escape, if he'd wanted to. No one was really keeping an eye on him. But with all the commotion, he might get another opportunity to take them out. He couldn't destroy Jade or the others from a distance.

After the suitcases were packed and in the car, George sent Max up to help Peach with Jade's office. Jade was gone and Max suspected she'd taken Crystal and Veronica, since he hadn't seen either of them for a while. Peach had a couple of boxes ready, so Max took them downstairs.

Max set them down and caught George. "Should I put these in the van or the car?"

"The van."

Max ran out to the van and put the boxes in the back. Taking off occurred to him briefly, but then he returned to the house.

On his way to the stairs, George caught him again. "Are you almost finished up there?"

"There's a bit more."

"Hurry up, we're just waiting for Jade to call with a location."

"What is going on here, George?"

"Don't worry about it. It will be okay." George put his hand on Max's shoulder and gave him a smile. Then Max saw something through the open door. As George turned, an arrow-bullet struck him in the chest.

"Oh, shit," George said as he grabbed his chest and dissolved into dust. Another arrow hit Steve the college boy square in the back, and Steve followed George into the dust.

Max hit the ground. He looked up to see the attackers storming the house. For some reason, he wasn't at all surprised that they were vampires.

## CHAPTER 10

Searing pain took hold of him and he realized he'd been hit. One of the arrow-bullet things was sticking out of his leg. It hurt like hell, but probably not as badly as the one poor George had taken. Max had to get to cover so he pulled himself behind a couch. It wasn't much, but it would have to do. He pulled the arrow out of his leg and the pain calmed. He put it in his pocket. Might as well start a collection.

If Max could get to the basement, there was a back way out. It might be under attack too, but he'd take his chances. Until he found out more about the attackers, it was in his best interest to avoid capture or worse. The attacking force hadn't gotten very far into the house before some of Jade's gang started returning fire and everyone had taken cover.

Arrows were flying through the air and when one missed his head by inches, Max knew he'd better get to safer ground. An arrow through his head might not be fatal, but it would be darned unattractive.

Keeping low, Army style, he scrambled into the next room where the arrow traffic was a little less overwhelming. He would have loved to pick up George's gun along the way, but it had gone the way of George.

The battle in the living room was wearing down. The superior forces were the attackers, no doubt about that. Max had seen at least two more of Jade's people go down. That was four that he knew about. At the most, there might be four or five of them left.

Max kept low until he got to the basement door. He reached out to turn the doorknob. An arrow pinned his hand to the door and pain shot up his arm. Someone threw him back against the door and put a gun to his chest. The guy was even bigger than George, and far uglier looking.

Max raised his free hand. "I give up."

The guy literally growled at him. He pulled the arrow out

of Max's hand and pushed him back toward the living room. Max grabbed his hand. This wood thing was really starting to annoy him. He now had three holes in his body and none of them were healing very fast.

"Hands behind your head," the ugly guy ordered. Max did as he was told.

The guy had hold of the back of Max's shirt, and shoved him when Max hesitated about going back into the danger zone. The battle was over and Peach and a guy named Jackson were on their knees, with their ankles crossed and their hands behind their heads. Max was thrown next to them and he assumed the position without being told to. Each captive had their own personal guard with a gun pointed inches from their back. One twitchy finger and Max was going to find out personally what the dust business felt like.

The attackers were all wearing headsets and their guns were similar to the ones he'd seen on George and Veronica. From a military standpoint, there were only eight of them, but they were well organized and trained for this. They were all wearing similar fatigues made of black.

"All clear," the ugly guy said. The troops were waiting patiently for orders. Several of them looked up as a woman walked into the room. Max was surprised, but not because she was lovely with chestnut colored hair and stunning green eyes. She moved like Jade, in a catlike way that was… unusual. She was dressed like the rest, but the fatigues look much better on her. She had one of the guns tucked into the back of her pants. It was obvious she was in charge.

"The good news is we got her office."

"She must have had some warning," the ugly guy asked.

"Without a doubt."

"There was one captive. She was shaken up, but she's fine. She's been given a sedative and is being dropped off at the hospital."

"Good. Tank, who do we have here?"

"I haven't interrogated them yet," Tank said. "Those two

I've seen before. But this one's new." He nodded toward Max for his last comment.

She glanced at Max and then went on to the first in the line. "Jackson Stevens. It's been a while," she said.

"Look Chase, she captured me. Thank god you found me… I wasn't with her. Really."

"Okay, Jackson." Chase nodded to Jackson's guard and he was dust in an instant.

Peach was next to Max and she freaked a bit. Chase moved on to her next.

"What's you name?"

"Peach," she said with a quivering lip.

"How long have you been with Jade?"

"I don't know."

"She's been around at least a couple years," Tank said. "Conversion isn't likely."

"We'll give her a chance anyway. Send her to Detroit though."

"Thank you."

"Don't thank me yet." Her guard pulled her up and took her outside.

Chase turned her attention to Max. "You look familiar."

"He's that teacher that was supposed to have died in a fire a couple weeks ago," a tall woman said who was looking out the door.

"I remember seeing the report."

"My name is Max Maguire."

"You're looking surprisingly healthy for a burned up corpse."

"I work out. Stay in shape. Only eat the right people. You know how it is."

"You're funny. And you're not scared of us. Why aren't you afraid of dying, Mr. Maguire? You didn't even blink when we took out poor Jackson."

"What's conversion?"

Chase stooped down and looked Max in the eyes. "Maybe

you'll get a chance to find out. How many people have you killed?"

"In my life or just since I died?"

"Give me both numbers."

"I was in the Army and had 9 kills. Since Jade, another 14." Max decided not to mention his father. Some things were private.

"How long have you been with her?"

"Almost three weeks."

Chase nodded. "You could have killed far more people."

"It seemed like enough."

"Why?"

"Because that's all I had to kill to survive and to get Jade off my back."

Chase laughed. "A real vampire with a conscience… What do you think, should we give him a shot, Tank?"

"No." Chase looked at Tank sternly. "He stinks of her."

"Yes, he does."

"If you're planning on killing her, then I'm on your side. I have no loyalty toward her, if that's what you're worried about," Max said.

"Was it unpleasant?" Chase asked. A slight smile crossed her lips.

"Actually, yeah."

"I'll bet. So, why should we take a chance on you, Mr. Maguire? It seems like a lot of trouble considering I'll probably just have to kill you later anyway."

"Why is it that since I became immortal, everyone is threatening to kill me?"

"I'd say that's ironic."

"The reason I have no loyalty toward Jade is that she a demon bitch from hell who likes to kill and force others to kill because she thinks it's fun. She plays with people's lives and destroys anyone who crosses her path. Somehow, when she threatened to force me to kill my mother and then my students one by one, it put a damper on our relationship."

"Good answer." She pointed to the wet blood on his shirt. "What's this?"

Max slowly moved his hands to open the top couple buttons on his shirt.

She examined the hole in his chest. "That's too big to be from one of our bolts."

"No, that's a lesson for trying to kill her. She kind of got pissed off about that."

"I look forward to hearing about it, Mr. Maguire… we'll take him with us."

"To the high-rise?"

"Yes," she said. Tank growled again, but in a very low tone. "Box up her office and anything else you can find."

Suddenly Chase whirled around. "Everyone out! Now!" she screamed. "There's a bomb!"

Chase pushed Tank through the door and grabbed Max by his shirt and tossed him through the broken window. He was only beginning to comprehend the fact that he was flying threw the air when the house exploded.

Max hit the ground hard and debris rained down on him. He realized his pants were on fire and he rolled around to put them out. By the time he knew he was okay, Tank had a gun pointed at his chest.

Max could see that the flames had engulfed the entryway and part of the upstairs was missing. Tank put his foot on Max's stomach to make sure he didn't go anywhere. But Max's attention was on the house. He saw no sign of Chase. A couple of vampires were thrown out of the house through the window like Max had been. Their clothing was on fire and others ran to help them out.

But Chase hadn't made it out. The fire raged and the others seemed in shock. Max saw something through the flames. Someone else came flying through the window. He was badly burned. Then Chase leapt from the fire holding another vampire. She landed on her feet and rolled the horribly burned vampire around to put out the flames. Chase wasn't even singed. Her clothing had been nearly burned off, but she was completely unharmed.

The others stared at her. They weren't expecting this either. She was different than them. Different like Jade.

"Get to the vans now!" she commanded. "We don't have any time before the authorities get here."

Tank grabbed Max and lifted him to his feet. Max ran with him to the vans everyone was headed toward and Tank pushed him into one of them. Tank was right there with him and the gun was still pointed at Max's chest.

"Wait," Max said. "There are two boxes of her office stuff in the van over there, and two suitcases of Jade's personal things in the car next to it." Tank and Chase looked at each other.

"Hold on," Chase said as she leaped out of the van.

"It might be another trap," Tank yelled after her.

A moment later she was at the back door with the boxes and suitcases. She threw herself in the van, pulling the doors closed and they took off.

Chase brushed by him and hopped into the passenger seat of the van.

"Thank you, Mr. Maguire."

Chase was on the radio immediately.

"How's it look, Terry?" She waited for the reply.

"Phillip and Latrise are going to be okay. Looks like we lost Jenna, unless she's with you."

"No, she's not." There was silence for a moment as she considered the news. She looked upset. She shook her head and gave both instructions to the drivers. Chase stared out the window, and suddenly looked alert.

"Stop," she told the driver. "Tank, open the door." Tank didn't want to take his eyes off Max, but he reluctantly glanced away to open the side door as the van stopped.

"What is it?"

"Just wait."

Out of the darkness someone flew into the van. It was one

of Chase's people, an oriental woman with short black hair. She didn't say anything, but quickly moved to the back of the van.

Chase turned and smiled. "Missed you."

The woman smiled back, but then settled in for the drive.

Chase spoke over the radio. "Terry, Jenna's okay. She's with us."

"That was close," the man on the other end of the radio responded. Chase nodded, but didn't reply. She suddenly realized what state her clothes were in. Max watched as Chase pulled off her ruined top and grabbed a spare one from a pile of stuff next to him. She smiled at him when she saw him looking.

"Tank, give Mr. Maguire a good night kiss." As Max looked at Tank, confusion creased his brow. Tank opened up a box and pulled a dart gun out. He leveled the gun at Max.

"Good night, Irene," Tank said as he shot Max.

Max pulled the small dart out of his stomach. "My name's not… Irene." Then the lights went out.

## CHAPTER 11

Max woke up to find himself in a cage. It was large, probably 10x10 and was at least 7 foot high. He was laying in an easy chair, and had a small table sitting next to him. The only other thing in the cage was a portable toilet in the corner. He suddenly grabbed his chest to check where the hole had been, but his chest was smooth with no sign of damage. Enough time must have passed for it to heal.

He felt a bit groggy as he sat the chair up. He checked his pockets to find he still had his wallet, but his arrow stash was missing. His cage was located in the corner of a large room with wall-to-wall windows on two sides, and they seemed to be in a high-rise office building. From the view, Max was guessing they weren't in Chicago anymore. It looked more like New York City. Max didn't have to guess at the room's purpose. It was a war room. Computers lined the walls, papers covered a large table in the center of the room and people were running around with purpose in their stride and determination on their faces. These people had a mission.

The bigger surprise was that the vampires were working along side the living. The people had no fear, and appeared to be working efficiently. Max realized his fangs were showing and he pulled them into his mouth. His hunger was at the forefront of his thoughts when Tank turned and saw he was awake. He turned away to talk to a young male vampire with shoulder length hair and a mustache, who looked at Max and then left the room.

Max thought Tank would come over to talk to him, but he didn't look back his way. Max sat back in his chair. They'd have to deal with him at some point. A few minutes later, the male vampire came back into the room carrying a large plastic glass. Max didn't have to guess the contents. He could smell the blood.

"Here you go. Looks like you need a hit." The vampire

reached through the bars and sat the glass on the table next to Max.

"Thanks."

"Sure. My name is Terry. We'll bring you more in a bit," Terry said as he left. So much for small talk.

Max picked it up. It was warm. He hadn't ever tried to drink blood from a glass before and his fangs seemed to get in the way of the plastic. But he managed, and drank it in a couple gulps.

"It's a little easier when you're not so hungry," an attractive older woman vampire said in a sweet voice. "That way you can keep the fangs from coming out."

"I see."

"My name's Nadine. Welcome."

"Thanks. Where are we, Nadine?"

"We're in New York City. But that's all I'm supposed to tell you about location at this point."

"Well, I always wanted to visit New York City. It's great so far," Max said, motioning to the room.

"Oh, it actually is a wonderful city," she said.

Max took a good look at the view. It offered a spectacular look at the city at night.

"You got me on that one."

"What would you like me to call you?"

"Max is fine. It is a really great view," he said.

"My job is to make sure you have everything you need right now."

"Well, Nadine, I could use three or four more glasses."

"Don't worry. You'll be taken care of. I'll get you another glass to tide you over until Chase has time."

"What is conversion?"

"Chase will tell you all about it."

"What about them?" Max motioned toward the living workers.

"They're human," she said.

"Why aren't they afraid?"

"None of us would let anything happen to them. They know that."

"You might not hurt them. But why aren't they afraid of me?"

"Well, you're in a cage."

"I might get out."

She just smiled and shook her head. "They know you won't."

"I see… Who are you people?"

"Chase will fill you in."

"What exactly can you tell me, Nadine, besides the fact that I'm in New York City?"

"I'll just go get you that drink."

"Thanks," Max laughed. Nadine must have been the welcome wagon vampire, full of too much good will and no real information. He couldn't imagine her actually killing someone. Her disposition seemed too sunny.

Well, Max had found a world outside Jade's domain. They even might be interested in the same things he was. They'd fed him and stuffed him in a corner. He wasn't their top priority, that was for sure. Their experience with Jade's people must have made them cautious, but they were treating him well.

Max thought a lot about Jade. His self-appointed primary mission, to take out Jade and her crew, was looking up. Max certainly had a better shot with some help. But the hunger was banging away at him. It'd been too long since he'd fed and there were too many people walking around who would have made perfectly good happy meals.

Nadine got back with his drink and he downed it quickly.

"It doesn't take much of an edge off," Max said.

"Chase is going to be right along."

"Then I guess I just wait for Chase."

"Just holler if you need anything."

Max waited. He sat back in the chair. He wasn't tired, so he watched the staff run around. He didn't get much of a hint of what was going on. His hunger came to the forefront as he watched the clock and smelled the humans nearby. After an hour, Nadine brought him another glass without him asking. She knew what time it was too.

There were two human women and three human men waltzing around as if they didn't know how very dangerous he was. As if they weren't concerned at all. There was one woman with pretty brown hair Max particularly wanted. He could almost taste her, her scent was so strong and with each very dirty, nasty thought he had about her, about killing her, he hated himself. Still if he could find a way out of his cage, he'd take her. Right and wrong, even knowing how much he wanted to kill Jade, didn't matter.

Max was ready to leap out of the chair when Chase finally walked through the door. She went to Tank and gave him instructions. Then she talked to a couple other people. She didn't seem in a hurry to get to him. Max was ready to rip the cage apart. The living were just too close and the scent was overpowering.

Finally, she came to him. "How are you doing, Mr. Maguire?"

"I'm starving. But you know that," he snapped.

"Let's take care of your needs, and then we can get on with business."

Chase picked up something that looked like a remote control and punched a number pad. The door of the cage released. Max got up and walked out. The hunger inside him made it difficult for him to follow her. The living were so close. The girl was only a few feet away from him. He could take her and no one would be able to stop him, at least not before he could sink his fangs into her throat. Max paused, the hunger suffocating him. He pushed the overwhelming feeling away and focused on Chase. She led him to a bedroom and shut the door after he entered.

It was a nice room with a four-poster bed in the center and large windows. At any other time in his life, Max would have thought it was an odd place for a bedroom, in the middle of an office building.

"It must have been torture for you to walk through that room and not take one of them. Being surrounded by them for hours with only a few drops of blood to quench your thirst."

"Do you want me to go insane?" Anger was welling up in him.

"No, Mr. Maguire. I wanted to see what your level of control is. I'm actually very impressed."

"My level of control… Well, that's just great." Max laughed. "Will somebody please tell me the goddamn rules at the beginning of the game. No one's bothered to give me the fucking handbook! Why does everything have to be a test with you people?" Max yelled, letting the insanity bubble to the surface.

"Because you're not human anymore, Mr. Maguire. Jade's reasons are evil, ours aren't. And that will not be the only test you'll face during your stay with us."

Max giggled. "You're very beautiful."

"Okay, let's get you fed," she said.

"Well, bring 'em on."

"Today you get me."

"Really?" Max grinned broadly.

"Really. You're not ready to be turned loose on the human race."

"You are so right." Max stepped up to her. She smelled like flowers and something else he couldn't put his finger on, something familiar. He kissed her gently at first and then with a passion she seemed to return. But his hunger wasn't interested in her kisses. He ran his tongue over her neck and gently bit down. He wrapped his arms around her, pulling her tightly to him, and he drank.

# # #

Max was lying on the bed. He felt so good, so full. His hunger was satisfied as it seldom had been since he had become a vampire. It was a euphoric high that only happened after a deep, long feeding. Chase had let him drink all he wanted.

She was sitting on the bed a couple of feet away from him. She was definitely a little whiter than she had been before. They were both fully dressed. They hadn't had sex, even though Max would have really liked that. Except for that first long kiss, Max had behaved himself. He suddenly felt bad though, like he'd overstepped his bounds.

He looked at her. She was waiting for him to recover. Her rich brown hair seemed to be an entity all its own, as it danced and moved with her slightest movement. Max remembered how soft her hair had felt.

"Are you all right?" Max asked her softly.

"Do you mean, was it good for me?" She smiled easily.

"Don't make fun of me. I'm only three weeks old."

"I'm fine."

"Thank you… Are you going to tell me, 'Don't thank me yet?' "

"Don't thank me yet," she said.

Max sat up slowly. "What are you?"

"Why, I'm a vampire, Mr. Maguire."

"Call me Max… You're not like me. You're like Jade."

"Max…"

"You're different. But why?"

She hesitated. "I'm very old, Max. So is Jade. Time provides certain rewards."

"So what? After a hundred years you get a bonus, or something? Like an extra week's vacation? A hundred years and fire doesn't burn you anymore?"

"It's more like a thousand."

Max was shocked. He'd never imagined it was possible. Not really. Everyone in Jade's house had been pretty new as far as he could tell.

"A thousand years? Oh, my god."

"It's a long time to be alive," she said as she stood up.

"But what was it like? Where were you born?" Max stood.

"England."

"A thousand years… Did you see the plague, or maybe one of the wars? What was England like a thousand years ago?"

She hesitated. "It was muddy."

"It was muddy?" Max laughed. He wanted more. "This is amazing. You must have seen so much history. I can't even imagine. Please, you have to tell me more."

"Max… the history teacher in you is coming out."

"Sorry, I just… A thousand years… Wow."

"There are other things we need to talk about right now."

Max nodded. "Okay. You just blew me away. Assuming you let me live, you think we can talk about it later?"

Chase laughed. "Assuming that."

"Can you at least tell me, are we demons, or is this some kind of medical experiment gone awry, or I don't know… something else? I mean, what does it mean to be undead?"

She looked seriously amused. "Just because it's part of the myth, doesn't make it so."

"My heart doesn't beat anymore."

She touched his chest over his heart and he felt how calm and relaxed she was. He also felt her power. "Your heart beats, but very slowly. And you will age, but at slow pace. Like a day for a year."

"So we're not really the undead?"

"I've never quite been able to figure out what that's supposed to mean. If you get a clue, let me know. As far as your heart, I can slice open your chest so you can check it out, if you'd like." Max put his hand on his chest as if to protect it. The wooden stake experience was too fresh in his memory.

"That's okay. I'll take your word for it."

"I don't have all the answers. I don't think anyone still walking the earth does," she said. But she looked away quickly and Max realized she was lying to him. Years of teaching had provided him with a built-in lie detector. She might not have all the answers, but she knew more than she was telling him. He also knew that was probably the only thing she had lied to him about, up to that moment.

She got very serious. "We're in the middle of a war that we have a good chance of losing."

"If your goal is to stop Jade and her people, I want to join you. That's all I've wanted to do since this started."

"Stopping them is our primary mission, but whether or not you can join us is more complicated than that."

"You mean the conversion thing?"

"Yes. The biggest battle you're going to end up fighting for the rest of your life, will be against yourself."

"You mean the hunger," he said.

"It's a powerful enemy and until you get control of it, you won't be of help to anyone."

"Okay. Let's get on with it then. Conversion can't be any worse than everything else I've been through since Jade."

"It's not like that, Max. Conversion isn't a drug or some quick process we put you through. Conversion has to happen within you… up here," she said, as she pointed to her forehead. "We'll help you, but it's up to you in the end."

"So you guys are like Vampires Anonymous?" Max smiled at the thought.

"Not exactly. There won't be meetings or a big hug at the end. There's only one rule you have to live by from now on. Our job here is to protect the human race against our own kind. If you ever kill another human, you will be put to death. If you break that rule, you'll get no second chance. No excuse will provide salvation. No reason will justify your actions. There are no exceptions…. Do you understand?"

Max cleared his throat. "How do I stop… I just…" He struggled with his thoughts. It's what he wanted, but how was he supposed to manage it? "Will you teach me how?"

"We'll try," Chase said.

"Then I want to learn."

"Good."

Chase let Max take a shower and he was brought a fresh change of clothes. The pants were the same ones the vampire soldiers wore, but the shirt was bright orange. There was no way he was going to blend into a crowd. It was probably just to let him know he wasn't considered one of the good vampires just yet.

Max mulled over the situation. When the hunger overtook him, he had never had any real control. How exactly did these vampires operate? If it was possible for him not to ever have to kill another living person again, then he wanted to know how to do that. And if he couldn't manage it, then it was probably better that he get taken out like Jackson. There had been no cruelty in his death, but there had been no mercy either. He had been executed because he had broken the rule.

It was a good rule. Now all he had to do was figure out how to follow it. The relief was if he failed, he now knew there were others would who had taken on the mission he'd created for himself. He wasn't alone anymore.

# # #

Chase and the others sat him down at the big table and grilled him for the rest of the night. They'd been going through the boxes he'd helped them find. They wanted to know everything he knew about Jade and her set up. Max told them his story with as much detail as he could. He told them about the people he'd killed, including Amanda. He'd take responsibility for her, too.

They didn't seem too impressed that he'd focused on taking out bad people on the streets of Chicago, but they weren't judgmental either.

As morning approached, he was returned to his cage. He looked at the wall of windows suspiciously. There didn't seem to be any curtains.

"Don't worry," Chase said, as she set the lock. "The windows are specially made. The sun won't harm you."

"That is very cool," he said.

"It wouldn't be any fun having to live in darkness for the rest of your life, would it?"

"Chase… Whatever happens, thanks. I never wanted to hurt anyone. I really didn't."

"You'll get a chance to prove it."

Max nodded. He hesitated for a moment and then put his hands on the bars.

"If I don't make it, you will get her, won't you?"

Chase cocked her head. "That's one of the reasons I still walk the earth, Max."

He watched her leave. She'd said "one of the reasons." Max wondered what the other reasons were.

The room was empty except for Max and a couple of other vampires. The one called Terry was keeping a discreet eye on him, so Max figured he must be the guard. Max turned the big easy chair around so he could get a good view of sunrise. As he waited for daybreak he realized he had something that he hadn't had during the eternity since he became a vampire. He had hope. Max leaned the chair back and watched the sun come up. It was the most glorious sunrise he'd ever seen.

## CHAPTER 12

Max slept like the dead. It was around noon before he became aware that the war room was a beehive of activity, mostly non-vampire activity. It was strange to be around so many of the humans, and their scent woke up his hunger. Just three weeks before he'd been surrounded by 30 students every day.

He'd never been able to properly mourn the loss of his life. Everything he had was taken away the instant he went down that alley. But there was no way he could have known, and he would have tried to save Crystal even if he had. Incredible factors had come together to insure his present situation. Vampires did exist. One of his students had gotten involved. Max had jumped on his white horse to try and protect her, and promptly fallen right off it. Some hero he'd turned out to be. If only he could have saved Crystal, it would have been worth it.

If he believed in God it would have been easier too. But what kind of a god would make a creature like him, even if he was supposed to help save the human race? He didn't have an answer for that one either.

Max studied the activity of the war room and slowly his fellow vampires started showing up. Terry had been relieved some time during the morning, but he came back in with a drink for Max.

"Good afternoon," he said, as he sat the glass on Max's table. Max let it sit there. He wanted the blood, but he also wanted to talk to someone.

"Hi. Is it okay if we talk? You don't have to answer any of the questions. I'm just kind of bored."

Terry shrugged his shoulders and then grabbed a chair and pulled it up. "Sure."

"Does your group have a name?"

"Not really, but some of us call it The Corps. It's just a

joke, really. According to the rest of the world, we operate out of different companies. This one's a security company called *Nightwatch*."

"What about Jade's crew?"

"We call them The Bad Guys." Terry smiled.

"What about you? Who made you?"

"That's private. You survive and you get to know me, and you can ask that question. The thing is, you probably have a ten percent chance of survival. So, not many people here are going to invest any energy in getting to know you. Every time another one of us doesn't make it, it reminds us that we might not make it either. Sorry to be so blunt, but that's the way it is."

"Who knew immortality could be so short?" Max said. "It's okay. Ten percent… Those are really bad odds."

"We've got a pool going."

"Anyone bet on me to make it?"

"Only Chase, but she always bets on the new recruits," Terry said.

"What about you?"

"I've got you checking out on Sunday."

Max took a breath and nodded. "Do you win often?"

"Often enough."

"How long do I have to go before I've 'made it'?"

"That's the problem with betting that way. You never win, because failure is always an option," Terry said.

"Can I bet on myself?"

Terry laughed. "You'd never actually win any money."

"It's the principle of the thing. How much?" Max asked.

"Twenty."

Max took out his wallet and opened it, thumbing through the bills. "Here you go." Terry took the bill.

"You're a strange guy… Just so you know, the odds were five percent yesterday. Every day you make it, they get better."

Terry got up and left. Max drank the blood slowly. It was

still warm. He didn't have any illusions about where the blood came from. They'd nuked it in the microwave to warm it. Nobody was sitting around donating when the need came.

Ten percent. Well, Max wasn't going to worry about the odds. He'd just take it one day at a time.

# # #

Max needed something to do. He was going to go stir crazy and his hunger was driving him nuts. It was the overwhelming scent of the living. He was brought a drink every couple of hours, but it barely seemed to be helping.

When Chase finally showed up, he was ready to forget about the Conversion thing and take one of their arrow-bullet thingy bolts through the heart. The hunger was pushing him to think those really bad thoughts.

"Hello," Chase said as she let him out of his cage.

Max didn't walk out of his cage right away. He waited, and then stepped out. Chase watched him carefully, waiting to see what he'd do. There were two women, tasty human women, just a few feet away from him. They were so close. Max held on to the bars on his cage, unwilling to let go for fear he might attack. "Chase… "

"Come on, Max." He looked up and saw that all the vampires in the room were watching him. He wondered who had bet on him to fail that night. With all his strength, Max followed Chase to the bedroom.

Inside the room, it was better. The scent wasn't as strong. "Why is it so bad?"

"Humans bring out the bloodlust in us. It's like smelling popcorn in a movie theater. Suddenly you just have to have some."

Max was confused. "But I've been drinking the blood…"

"That's only a temporary fix. It's not in the right container for us. We use it to take the edge off, but that's all it can ever do. Something is missing from stored blood that can never satisfy our hunger."

Max felt like something was crawling around in his gut

and it wanted to rip him apart from the inside out. He leaned against the wall and bent over grasping his head. "Please help me," he begged.

"We are." There was a tap at the door and she went to open it. She let Nadine in. "Nadine will help you tonight. When I tell you to stop, you have to stop. Do you understand?"

Max nodded. Nadine sat on the bed and Max sat next to her. He sniffed her hair and pulled it away from her neck. "Thank you."

"It's okay, Max," Nadine said. Max pulled her to him and bit down.

He drank deeply. It seemed that he had just started when Chase told him to stop. He tried, but he couldn't pull away. All he wanted was the blood. She told him again, but he didn't want to stop. If he just kept going, she'd stake him and then he'd just be another victim of the ten percent odds. No surprise to anyone.

Chase grabbed hold of his hair and yanked his head back. Max licked his lips. Chase still had hold of his hair when she pulled him to his feet and shoved him into a wall. "I said stop," she said quietly. "You have to learn control."

Max bent over. The hunger raged through him. "Okay." He stood up. Both women were looking at him.

"Try again," Chase said.

Max went to Nadine again, happy to resume his meal. Again, just after he started, Chase told him to stop. The hunger drove him on. He didn't want to stop. Would a vampire die if they were drained? The hunger didn't want him to care.

This time she yelled at him. "Max, I said stop!"

But Max did care. He wasn't ready to give up living yet, not even as a vampire. He pushed himself away from Nadine, and fell to the floor. Max curled up in a ball and waited to see if the hunger would subside. Slowly, it did. When he could think again, he saw that both women were watching him, waiting.

Max sat up and leaned against the bed. "I'm sorry. I'll try harder next time."

Nadine smiled. "It's okay." She got up and left the room.

"I couldn't control it," Max said.

"But in the end, you did." Chase sat next to him on the floor. "How's the hunger?"

"Better. I feel much better."

"Good. It won't last, but you'll have a few hours before the battle starts again."

"How long before this gets easier?"

"It's never going to get easier. You'll just learn to control it," Chase said.

"How long?"

"That depends. Everyone's different. Probably two weeks, at least."

"Two weeks. It's going to be a really long two weeks," Max said.

"You have to figure out a way to deal with it."

"How do I do that?"

"That's the secret. It's different for everyone."

"Well, so much for ten percent. What do the odds go up to tomorrow? Fifteen percent?"

"You've been talking to Terry. Thirteen percent. But you know the odds don't mean anything. It's going to be hard. You're a drug addict, and it's a drug you can't exactly kick." Chase got up. She gave Max her hand and she pulled him up.

"So, does that make you my sponsor?" Max asked. He was starting to feel very good.

"Don't push it."

"Well, I mean you bet on me to make it. That's got to count for something." He was flirting with her a bit, but he couldn't help himself.

"You are definitely feeling better… Come on. We have some more questions for you," she said.

"I love questions. Can I ask some too? Like did you ever meet Henry the Eighth or Queen Elizabeth? Was there ever really a Robin Hood?"

"Max… "

"Oh, come on. Throw me just a little history bone. You'll probably stake me tomorrow and then I'll never know. It would be such a shame to die without ever knowing."

"Tomorrow, I'll answer two questions about English history if you make it into this room. That's it."

"How about three?"

Chase shook her head and walked out the door. Max followed her like a puppy. He was definitely doing way better.

# # #

That night they only questioned him for a few minutes. He was allowed to take a shower and move around for a bit with two guards flagging him. Tank watched him carefully. The ugly guy wasn't taking any chances and he didn't like Max at all.

Far too quickly for him, Max was put back into his cage and pretty much forgotten about. Max was sitting there listening in on a conversation Chase and Tank were having across the room, when he noticed the vampire named Jenna glancing up at him and then sketching. As he studied her it struck him that she had the most soulful eyes he'd ever seen. Her short black hair was tucked back with a baseball cap and she was wearing the black fatigues. She was focusing intently on what she was doing. Max watched her for a while, watching him. She was drawing his picture, which seemed like the strangest thing in the world.

She didn't say anything, so he finally smiled and waved.

She smiled briefly and then went back to her work.

"Hello," Max said. "Miss?"

She was ignoring him, so he spoke louder, but she didn't even look up.

"She can't talk or hear, Max," said Terry. "Her name is Jenna."

Jenna looked up and realized they were talking about her.

"Can she read lips?"

"Yes, and she signs," Terry said as he went back to what he was doing.

"Hi," Max said.

Jenna waved and mouthed the word "hi."

"Can I see what you're doing?"

Jenna smiled and shook her head. She seemed shy.

"Are you drawing me?"

She nodded. She signed and mouthed, "It's not done yet."

Max nodded. He had had a couple of deaf kids in his classes at different points and he'd taken a sign language class years before. But he only remembered the alphabet. He clumsily signed, spelling out the words, "What's it for?"

Jenna laughed silently. She stood up and picked up a large book from a shelf behind her. She handed it to him through the bars and then went back to her work.

The book had a leather cover and was a large loose-leaf notebook. On the cover, written in red paint that dripped to simulate blood, it read "The Corps: The Few, The Pail, The Undead." Max laughed.

Max opened the book and saw that it was in different sections, including The Corps, The Damned, The Recruits, The Wars, The Others and The Dead. As Max looked through the book, he saw that it was full of ink drawings, each one carefully protected with a plastic covering. Some of the drawings were on old paper, from parchment paper to most likely whatever paper was available. A couple of the early drawings looked like they might be done on silk. It was a vampire history of the past and the present.

The drawings were beautiful, and they seemed to have been done by the same artist, although the style had changed over the years. Max looked up at Jenna. She must have been very old. Max studied each page. The first section was The Corps, and Chase's picture was in the front. At the bottom of the picture, was simply the name Chase. No last name. She'd been captured perfectly, and she hadn't changed. Tank's picture was next. Jenna had made him look almost good. The caption on his drawing read Michael "Tank" Drake with the dates 1492 – 1527. Max looked through the pictures. All the vampires he'd seen with The Corps were in the book.

In The Damned section, Jade's picture was first. Her drawing simply had the name Jade under it. Veronica was in there, but Crystal wasn't. Except for Veronica, Maria, and Jade, Max didn't recognize any of the other pictures. The Recruits section was undoubtedly where Max's picture would go when it was finished. There were several pictures there, but no one Max recognized.

The Wars section was amazing. It must have been based on many different battles, and it showed what a soldier in The Corps might have seen over endless battles. The truly interesting thing was that the battles had taken place over time. The manner of dress was different. Swords were used in some pictures, and crossbows and then guns in the newer pictures. Each battle was labeled with a year and a place.

Max figured The Others section, which was filled with faces he'd never seen, was a sort of 'None of the Above' and featured vampires that didn't fit into any category.

The largest section was The Dead. That was split in two sections, Our Dead and Their Dead. In the Our Dead section, every picture had a name and three dates. Max decided they were Date of Birth, Date of Transformation and Date of Death.

In Their Dead, the very first picture he saw was of Peach. So, she hadn't made it after all. He wasn't terribly surprised. Max saw George's picture and stopped. It was a great likeness of him. Out of all of Jade's people, Max kind of missed George. He'd been a ruthless killer, but a heck of a nice guy otherwise.

As Max flipped through The Dead section, he couldn't help but be amazed. The war between The Corps and The Damned had been going on for centuries. Max looked up at Jenna. She was staring at him.

"How did you know what George looked like?" Max asked.

She dug around in a pile on the table and found what must have been a surveillance photo with George and some of Jade's people and held it up so he could see.

"Some I do from memory, but photos help now when we have them," she signed and said silently. "Many of our kind have never been captured over time."

"Wow," Max said. She had seen so much and expressed herself the only way she could.

Max dug back into the book. No one wanted to answer his questions. Well, he'd just use Jenna's history book to learn from. He had lots of time to kill.

The next day, Jenna showed Max the picture she'd drawn. She'd originally used pencil to sketch it out and then ink to finish. He didn't like pictures of himself, but she'd done a great job. He said and signed, "Thank you." He watched as she scanned it into the computer and then put the original in plastic. Jenna took great care to page through the book and placed his picture it at the beginning of The Recruits section.

# # #

It was early in the day and Max still felt pretty good. He listened to every conversation that went on, but didn't get much new info. They all left when they started talking about the super secret stuff.

They had a line on some of Jade's people, but they were suspicious of it. Max watched the world go by outside the windows. When he was let out of his cage he could see the busy little ants as they went to work, drove their cars, had dinner, lived life, and most of them didn't have a clue what horrors awaited for them if they happened down the wrong alley. If they were lucky, they'd never find out.

Max had studied Jenna's book intently. He learned some things, but few of his questions had been answered. No one except Chase and Nadine really talked to him. However, Terry did occasionally chat a bit. He couldn't blame them.

He watched the humans and wondered about them. What they did wasn't exactly the kind of job you saw listed on CraigsList. Undoubtedly, they'd discovered the truth about vampires and been offered a way to help in the war. Jade had been right about that. Once a living person knew vampires existed, you couldn't exactly go back to your nice cozy home and forget about it.

Max discovered that there was an entire network of humans that worked with Chase. They offered tips, information and support. They also made sure she had a blood supply to keep the troops in line. Max wondered if the Corps ever did win the war, would the humans give her a medal or a stake? Keeping vampires around wasn't really in their best interest, even if those vampires had fought the good fight.

As the day wore on, he was feeling lonely and bored. Max studied the various humans and made up stories in his mind about how they might have come to this place in their lives. One of them named Sheila, was of particular interest to Max. She was girl-next-door pretty and the type of woman he was always attracted to. She had a sweet laugh and a slight touch of sadness in her eyes. Chase caught him looking at her, and he looked away feeling guilty. He wasn't even thinking about her blood. Other things were on his mind.

Max got up and started to pace. He needed something to keep him busy. He put his hands on the bars and leaned forward, so he face was resting between the bars. "Hello. Terry. Chase. Anyone. Can I please have something to do? Or maybe a TV? Or a book? Or something? Please…"

Terry looked up and nodded. He went to one of the bookshelves and picked a book out for him. Terry gave him a quick smile and handed Max the book. As Terry walked away, Max realized he'd been given a copy of *Dracula*. It had obviously been read many times before.

"Terry, you think this is funny, don't you. I don't think it's funny… Okay, it's a little funny." Max sat down. He never had read the book, but he'd seen the latest movie, which was terrible. He sat his chair back. Well, why not?

# # #

With the odds being what they were, the fact that they wasted any time at all on Max was amazing to him. Of course, they needed to replace soldiers lost in battle, but recruiting from the enemy camp seemed like a challenge.

Max wondered if Chase used living volunteers to create her own recruits, ones she could train properly. He suspected there'd be a better chance of success if a recruit was trained right from the beginning. But somehow he couldn't see Chase taking a chance on turning something evil loose onto the human race. She had a reverence for the living, a respect. For her to take a living person and turn them into a vampire, it would go against everything she seemed to be fighting for.

In fact, Chase cherished human life more than any living person he'd ever known. He could see it in the way she dealt with the humans and the way she worried about casualties. The cause she was fighting for was only about them. The Corps was just a necessary evil, a tool to insure the survival of the human race.

Recruiting Jade's people was probably just a necessary evil too. Why waste them if they could be turned?

Max took everything in. It bothered him that he couldn't be part of the action when they mobilized. He wanted to help them. The problem was that he could barely help himself when the hunger took over. He had his own battle to win.

Every day it seemed to get harder for him to control the hunger. He was able to stop when she told him to, eventually, but each day it was more difficult to take that step out of his cage and get past the humans. He'd be fine until late afternoon, until the scent of the living began to overwhelm him.

Day nine, the war inside his body raged to a new height. Insanity was in full force. Max decided he wanted Chase to kill him. He couldn't stand the pain any longer and he had to make it stop. Let him just be another failure. He decided to exercise, but he suddenly couldn't stop himself from throwing himself against the bars. He wanted a human, not a vampire. And they were all around him, just waiting for his loving embrace. All he had to do was get out of the fucking cage.

Max grabbed the bars at the top of his cage and swung a few times with his knees bent. Then he lifted his legs through the bars until he was hanging by his knees. He made himself swing widely back and forth. He was having a running conversation with himself, but no one was much paying attention to him. He yelled at them but they didn't look at him. He could see them saying to the humans, just ignore the crazy vampire in the corner.

"…Next on our tour of the Living Dead Zoo, we have Vampire Orlicus or Batman. Be sure not to feed the animals. Keep your hands away from the cage. The Batman might be dangerous," Max fell to the floor and rolled around, hysterical laughter overtaking him. He started humming the theme to the TV show Batman. "Why don't you guys just get me a used car salesman? Nobody'd miss one of those. Or a politician? I've got the munchies. Or how about a lawyer. Yeah. What do you call 500 lawyers at the bottom of the ocean? A good start. I dated a lawyer once and she was very tasty… On second thought, lawyers probably don't actually have any blood in them, so maybe they'd make a terrible meal."

Chase entered the room. "There's my girl," Max said.

"He's been like this for a couple hours," Tank said to Chase.

Max scrambled up and grabbed the bars. "Chase, I'm a bad boy. Thinking really bad, bad thoughts."

"Hi, Max," Chase said. Max wondered why she looked so sad. "Tank, clear everyone out of here."

"Don't make them go away. Not that. I want them to stay. Really, Chase, I've been thinking… let's open up a fast food vampire joint, like McVampires. Yeah! It would be the talk of the undead. We could make a fortune. We could specialize in the McCheerleader Burger. I'll take two to go. Hold the catsup." He laughed at his own joke.

Max saw everyone leaving. "Don't go. No. Don't leave. Chase… I'll be a good boy." Chase waited until everyone was gone.

"What will it be, Max?" she asked.

"What do you want from me? Should I just apologize for being what I am?" He threw himself against the bars. He couldn't figure out why she looked so sad? "I am so fucking tired of you people. Oops… that's right! You're not people."

"Do you want to die?"

"Yes," he hissed.

"If you can't get this under control now, you never will," Chase said.

"Why do you care? Save it for the recruits that are worth it. Just do it. Kill me. END IT NOW!" he demanded.

"You can fight this thing, Max. But you have to want to."

Max fell to the ground. His body felt like it was coming apart. Why did it have to hurt so bad? "I don't. Put the wounded animal out of its misery. Just kill me."

Chase sat on the other side of the bars. "What happened to you to make you not want to live? You are strong enough to do this. But you have to want to survive. We're trying to protect your world, Max. A world you lived in up until a few weeks ago. You can be part of what we're trying to do. Isn't that worth living for? Isn't it worth it to take down Jade? People you care about still live in that world, Max. If there aren't people like us, who will protect them from Jade?"

"I don't know," his voice was a whisper.

"Do you care?"

"We're just sharks, Chase. Sharks with big teeth." His eyes were wide.

"I need you Max. You can help us beat her."

He started giggling. "I just wanted to be one of the fucking sheep. Just be a history teacher until I become a fat old man who retires at 65 with legions of former students out making the world safe because they know all about the French and Indian War."

"Reel it in, Max. Pull yourself together."

Max put his head between his legs and took deep breaths. Listen to Chase and then he'd get to feed the hunger. Just listen to her. Then at least she'd open the door.

"Okay. Max's going to be a good boy now… Let's do it."

"Do you really want to die today?"

He tilted his head and studied her for a moment. Max laughed. "Those who are about to die salute you, General Chase," he said with a salute.

"Max…"

He stopped laughing. Pull it in. Listen to Chase. Pull it in. Stop. Pull it in. "No… I don't want to die today."

"Good. Make it to the bedroom and we'll talk about the Civil War."

"The Civil War… "

"You don't want to die before you find out about the Civil War, do you?"

Max giggled, and then clarity came over him. "If I can't make it, do me fast. Just get it over with."

"That I promise."

The human named Sheila came into the room. Max smiled at her. She looked like lunch to him. She wasn't scared. Probably knew Chase wouldn't let anything happen to her.

"Let the games begin," Max said, as he stood up. Chase was at the door to the cage and she was holding the remote. She unlocked the cage. The sound was so sweet.

"What's it going to be? Life or death, Max?" Max stepped out of his prison. Sheila was five steps from him. She smelled so, so good. If he just thought about her hard enough, he'd be there. Chase wouldn't be able to stop him from getting to her and taking a little nip. He took a step. All he had to do was sink his fangs into her neck. Then that would be it. It'd be over. He'd be just like his old man. The destroyer.

Max thought hard about the bedroom. Suddenly he was there, alone. Chase came in behind him. "Good."

Max fell on the bed and waited. He'd made it one more day. Time to chow down on another vampire. That he could handle.

Sheila entered the room. "What are you doing?" Max asked Chase.

"This is one of your biggest tests."

"Is this like the final?" he smiled weakly.

"More like a mid-term."

Max thought about Sheila and he was holding her. He took in her scent. Sheila looked up at him. He knew she could feel his power. She wanted him to take her.

"You know when to stop. No second chances," Chase said.

Max turned to look at Chase. So that was the game. Get him at his weakest and give him the most tempting bait.

Sheila was his. He kissed her and she returned his passion. Her heart began pounding more quickly and she began breathing harder. He touched her breast and she moaned. He knew what she wanted, but his hunger wanted something else. He ran his tongue over her neck and he bit her. She let out a tiny, sharp gasp. But then he could feel her desire and he felt himself become one with her, as he drank, satisfying the deepest part of himself. The hunger never wanted any woman more. It wanted to take everything from her, rip her apart, drink her down. The vampire wanted to take her life. To drink her dry... But something nagged at him. The part of him that wasn't his father and wasn't a vampire, told him to stop. Just pull up and stop.

With everything he had, every ounce of who Max Maguire had been, with every bit of him that had been a protector of life, that had been a teacher of children, he stopped and fell back away from her. Sheila looked weak, but Chase was there to help her into a chair.

Max's hunger wasn't satisfied. He held his stomach until the pain eased. By the time he could see straight again, Sheila was gone. Chase was waiting for him.

"Is she okay?" he asked.

"Yes, but you almost didn't make it," Chase said.

"How close did I come?"

"Close enough."

"I'm sorry."

"You didn't disappointment me, Max. You don't understand. Most recruits don't make it this far."

"So it's okay?"

"You did good. You found something inside yourself that helped you take control. Hold onto that."

Max shook his head and sat up. "This is not easy."

"No."

"I'm not done yet, am I?"

"No. But Terry is talking about selling tickets to the Max Maguire side show."

Max laughed. "Hey, what about my reward? The Civil War."

"That's really why you made it, isn't it. Just so you could play history teacher," Chase said with a smile.

"Absolutely."

"Okay. I'll tell you about the time I met General Ambrose Burnside."

"No way! Burnside? Sideburns are named after him."

"And he was a terrible general," she said.

"It was worse than that. He was considered the most incompetent military leader, not just for the Union, but… maybe of all time."

"Still, a genuinely nice man…"

Max smiled. He closed his eyes and listened to her tale. He did so love hearing her talk about the past. Chase had fed his body, now she was feeding his soul, something Jade had never managed.

He'd survived one more day. One more feeding. But

something bigger had happened. He'd gotten control of the vampire. The key to his survival as a vampire ended up being his father. After all these years… Now that was ironic. He'd have to decide how much he really wanted to live.

## CHAPTER 13

Once he related the vampire within him to his father, Max was able control the hunger. Becoming like his father had made him want to kill himself when he was younger. And now, not wanting to be like his father made him want to live.

His father had been a vampire in his own right. He had fed on their fear, he drank up the power he had over them like it was blood. He just used his fists rather than teeth. But all the time his father beat him, Max never let the old man have power over him. Not really. His father may have owned his body, but he'd never controlled Max's mind. Or Jade his soul. It was that part of him that no one could touch. The part that made him who he was.

If Max gave up and let the vampire take control, he was giving in to the monster. He was giving it power over him. And that was something he must never do. No matter how much it hurt. No matter what the hunger wanted. Because in the end, it was all he had of who he was. It was all he'd ever had.

After his test with Sheila, they had begun to trust Max. He began to trust himself, too. He felt better than he had since he'd followed Crystal down that alley.

He was thrilled when they gave him his own room. It was a floor above the war room. He was not at all unhappy to say goodbye to his cage. The room was vampire-escape-proof and he was still locked in when they didn't have someone to keep an eye on him, but it was way better. He even had his own TV, which at least occupied some of his time. He was finally able to indulge his History Channel addiction, that and find out if he'd win his bet with Terry about whether Nadine could name the capital of every state in the country. She did so, there went another twenty.

Still when he could, he usually hung around the war room and Terry and Nadine would give him something to do. Max made copies. He did some research on the net. He even made coffee for the humans.

It had been made clear to him how to behave with the humans. He couldn't touch them or get closer than an arm's reach to them. Getting too close would have an effect on them and would screw up their minds. Max understood the rules and followed them carefully.

But when the team mobilized, Max was put back into his room to wait. He hated that part. He knew he could help them, and he worried that one of them would get killed.

A couple of days after Max had been liberated from his cell, he walked into the war room to find another vampire in his cage. He was a scruffy looking kid with long dark hair, about 17. The kid was starting to have the vampire meltdown. He was throwing himself at the bars and screaming.

Terry was talking to a vampire named Shades when Max walked up to them. Shades, who always seemed to wear a different pair of sunglasses whether it was night or day.

"Hi, Max," Terry said.

"Hi," Max said grimly.

"Jade did him and then just threw him out on the street," Shades said. "She didn't tell him anything. Just threw him out."

"That is just evil," Max said.

"Evil deeds for an evil bitch," Shades said.

"Do you know anything about him yet?"

"No," Terry said. "Except that he calls himself Savior. We don't have a real name on him."

"He's like a wild animal," Shades said. "We figure he was on the streets for a couple of days. But why would she do that? Doesn't make a damn bit of sense."

"No, it doesn't. Has she done this before?" Max said.

"A couple of times," Terry said. "But suddenly in the last two weeks we've gotten three of them. Chase thinks Jade's trying to keep us busy because she's up to something."

"So, some poor kid loses his life. And god knows how much damage he did in the mean time."

"It's just not fair," Shades said.

"No, it's not," Max said.

"So, you guys want to get on the pool?" Terry asked.

"Sure," Shades said.

"Me, too," Max said.

"Anybody got Friday?" Shades asked.

"Father Frank," Terry said.

"Saturday?"

"That's free. What about you Max?"

"I'll go for the win."

Terry looked at him and shook his head. "Optimist. You really like wasting money." Max took his last twenty out of his wallet and gave it to him.

"If I was worried about money, I never would have become a teacher in the first place."

"You got a point."

Shades studied the kid for a moment and then glanced at Max. "You're going to be a bad influence on me, Max." Max looked at him curiously. "Change mine to win, too."

Shades pulled out his wallet and handed Terry a twenty. "Okay… to win. But you tell anyone how I bet, Terry, and I'm gonna tell you know who about that thing in that place that one time."

"You know you can't blackmail me. Not when I know about that other thing at the place with the tree," Terry said.

"Oh, man, you are not gonna bring that up again," Shades said. "That wasn't even me. It was Father Frank." Max felt like he was hearing them talk in some sort of secret code.

"Give me a break!" Terry laughed. "You think he's really going to care when he finds out what you did to his… "

Terry and Shades suddenly stopped talking and looked at Max. He got the feeling they thought he was getting too much information, even though he had no idea what the hell they were talking about.

"Hey, Max, can you get a drink for the kid?" Terry asked.

"Sure."

He went off to the kitchen. It looked like Max would never find out what Terry did in that place that one time or what Shades did in that other place with the tree, but he didn't think he really wanted to know.

He was surprised to find Eugene in the kitchen reading the paper and eating his lunch. The surprise was that it was the first time Max had been alone with a human since his days with Jade. He hesitated.

The old guy just looked up at him and smiled. "It's okay. They wouldn't have let you out if they thought you were going to hurt one of us."

Max nodded. "Thanks." He went to the fridge to get the blood. While Max was pouring the drink, he couldn't help but study Eugene. The elderly gentleman looked up.

"What is it, Max?"

"I'm sorry… Can I ask you a question?"

"You can always ask."

"Why are you here? I'm mean, why aren't you afraid of us?"

Eugene laughed and shook his head. "Sometimes I wonder myself."

"I just don't get it."

Eugene looked out the window and then considered Max for a moment.

"I sorry. I know I don't have a right to ask," Max said.

"It's okay. I'm an old man. You're not going to offend me. Actually, I want you to know, because if you do then you'll remember why you're fighting this war. Every one of us is here because we lost someone, either as a victim or a vampire. If your mother knew what had really happened to you, she'd be here too... especially if you were still out there killing." A shiver ran through Max as he thought about that possibility.

Eugene paused to look back out the window. "And it's

about them, Max. All the people out there who don't know and don't want to know. Who can blame them? No one should really have to live with this knowledge."

"How long has it been for you?" Max asked.

"Almost thirty years."

"Hummm... Bill Clinton was elected as President, the North American Free Trade Agreement was signed, and the US Supreme Court reaffirmed the right to abortion, I believe," Max said.

"Do you do that automatically?"

"Yep. History teacher. Can't help it."

Eugene laughed. "I remember. I read the newspaper every day until... I wasn't that much older than you are now. It's so funny how you vampires never change, never get older or get sick. Just poof and you're gone one day. If you live long enough, you're going to forget what it is like to be human. You're just going to be doing your vampire tricks and then all you'll have left to remind you is us."

"I won't forget."

"Maybe not. But in ten years or a hundred years, who knows?"

"Who did you lose?"

"My daughter. She was such a beautiful child. I still remember holding her when she was little. Do you have any children?"

"I was a teacher. But no. I never did. I guess I never will now."

"Well, you can't understand then what it's like to hold your own child. You want to keep them safe forever. You make that promise, which of course is a promise you can't keep. 'Cause they go off and grow up. Miranda came to New York to go to college, but I knew she really wanted to be an actress. You have no idea what it's like letting your child go off on their own..." Eugene stopped for a moment.

"About six months after she came here, she just disappeared. The police weren't any help. They just figured she'd run away or ran off with a boyfriend. No one would help us find her. My wife, Stella, was here too. I just started walking down every street looking for her. I lost my job. I wasn't there for Stella either."

"You don't have to tell me this," Max said.

"Yes I do… All I could think was that I had to find her. So I kept looking. I got a map and walked the streets until I was too tired to continue. Then the next day I'd start all over again. You see a lot of bad things when you walk through New York City like that. I even got mugged once. I thought I saw it all. The girls being used, the kids getting sucked into gangs. That is until one night, when I ran across a vampire after he killed someone. Blood was everywhere.

"He was going to come after me, but some people came along and he took off. I didn't want to think that it was real, but I knew what I saw. I saw the teeth, the face, I just knew. And I knew somehow in my heart that it had something to do with Miranda."

"It must have been hard to accept," Max said.

"No. Not at all. At least it was an answer. Somehow it was better than not knowing. I read up on vampires. I started reading the paper, looking for signs of people who were missing or who might be victims. I got holy water and wore a crucifix. And because I'm Jewish I wore a Star of David too, just to cover all the bases. I got a crossbow and started prowling the streets looking for others. I did the whole nine yards.

"Finally, I started finding them. I was still pretty young then and I managed to kill a couple of them. But the dead ones can't tell you anything and the live ones, well, they weren't so easy to catch. Crosses and holy water were no use, so the only thing I knew was that a wooden arrow through the heart would kill.

"I started trying to figure out what I'd do if I found her and she was one of them. I mean, what if she was killing people? I decided that if I found her like that, I'd have to kill her myself. It's not something a parent should ever be forced to think about."

Eugene looked out the window. It was a few moments before he could continue. Suddenly he looked back at Max and their eyes met.

"I found her. She was… feeding… The person was still alive. I yelled at her to stop and she did when she recognized me. There was blood all over her face and she had fangs. She smiled at me, like nothing was wrong. She said 'Daddy, come here. It's been so long.' I can tell you with absolute truth that I wanted to do nothing more than that.

"But part of me wanted to drive an arrow through her heart. She had become a demon and she wasn't my little girl anymore… I raised my crossbow and fired, but I missed her. Pulling that trigger was the worst moment of my life. In the blink of an eye she had me by the throat, and I closed my eyes thinking I was going to meet my maker. But then she screamed and I felt myself falling backwards. Another vampire had shot her with an arrow. It just missed her heart. She escaped."

"Was the other vampire Chase?"

"No. It was Nadine. She saved my life that night and the life of the guy Miranda was feeding on. I found out there were different kinds of vampires. When they told me about the war, I knew what I had to do. I had to join up. I never could stand to tell my wife what really happened to our daughter. Two years later she died of cancer, and I know that Miranda's disappearance caused it. That and my… preoccupation.

"I lost my family, Max. I lost everything. So when you ask why do I do it, I can only tell you I don't have any other choice.

"Every one of us has a story about the people we've lost. You think that what's happened to you is the worst thing you can imagine. You're wrong. The worst thing is knowing that it happened to someone you love and you can't do anything about it. That's truly the worst thing.

"So that's why we do it. That's why we feed you when you need it. That's why we work here to make sure that the bad vampires will lose. That's why every time a new one of you is captured, I pray you're going to make it. Because if you make it, maybe my daughter will make it too someday. I'm an old man, Max. And I'm not afraid of you because if I was there would be no hope."

"I'm sorry about your family."

"And I'm sorry about yours," Eugene said.

"I miss them."

"As long as you do, you'll know what you're fighting for." Eugene took a bite of his sandwich. Max nodded and warmed up the blood for the new vampire.

# # #

Max spent most of the next day working on the computer. He got to know a little bit more about the other humans who worked in the war room, but mostly he worked at keeping them at ease. He also tried to talk to Savior, but the kid wasn't being very communicative.

Max was watching Savior when Terry came up to him. The kid wasn't having an easy time of it.

"Max, Chase wants to see you in her office."

"Okay… Terry, give the kid a break if you can."

"You know how it is, Max." Terry shrugged his shoulders.

"Yeah."

Max went to Chase's office and she looked up as he walked in. "Hi Max… Put on your dancing shoes. We're going out."

"Out? You mean outside the building?"

"Yep." Max smiled widely. Then a concern came over him. "I don't have any money. I gave Terry my last twenty."

Chase laughed. "Don't worry about it. You won't need any. Still, I'll have Terry put you on the payroll."

"You've got a payroll?"

"Yes. And I pay taxes, too. How about that, Max? The

humans have to eat, and we all have to have someplace to live. Nightwatch and the other companies I own make a lot of money quite legitimately… I'll take you shopping so you can get some clothes of your own and then we'll get a bite." Max watched as the corners of her mouth worked their way into a beautiful smile at her own joke.

"What stores will be open? It's after ten."

"I have a special arrangement regarding nighttime hours with many establishments."

"I'll bet you do."

"Give me an hour."

"Great." Max felt excited. He started to leave, but a thought struck him. He turned slowly back to her. "What percent am I at? Right now." Chase tilted her head slightly. "I mean, how am I doing?"

"Fifty."

Max was disappointed. It was certainly better than ten percent, but he thought he was doing better.

"Don't get hung up on the odds, Max. It never gets better than eighty five percent. You've been doing great, but you're still a vampire. You can feel the hunger as it builds and you still have thoughts that make you dangerous."

"Well, at least I'm 50/50. Not the worst odds. I might bet those odds in poker." He smiled. "I'll be in my room."

Max thought about it. Well, he was half way there. Terry took Max back to his room to wait.

# # #

Max felt like a little kid, walking down the streets of New York City with Chase. It all seemed so much bigger when you looked up. Well, that's what he was, really. He was still a newbie. They went down several side streets until they came to a closed store front that looked like a classy establishment. Chase pressed a buzzer and the lights went on. After a moment a thin, young human named Nancy let them in.

When they got inside, Max realized that it was an enormous department store. They seemed to have everything. Chase led Max to the men's clothing section. Nancy had vanished so it was just the two of them.

Chase was happy to wait while he tried things on. Chase offered opinions and he thought she was enjoying his distress at what he wanted.

Chase laughed. "Max, everything you've tried on is black." He frowned. "Try some other colors."

He reluctantly tried on some more colorful things, but when he put on a black trench coat, he could see she was trying not to laugh.

"Let's call it vampire chic," Max said, as he spun around for her. "What all the cool vampires are wearing." Then Max saw what he really wanted. A cowboy hat. There was a western wear display. He tried one on with the trench coat and Chase laughed fully. Max tried on several and then found the one he wanted. It was black, of course. But before he settled on it, he had to give it the test. Holding it by the brim, he flipped the hat around once and landed perfectly on his head. It went just right with his boots.

"The vampire cowboy. You're going to start a trend," Chase said.

"Tell me if I look stupid. I mean that."

"You don't look stupid. Somehow on you it works, Max."

Max looked at her suspiciously. He found a dummy and put the outfit on it so he could see it. He liked it a lot.

He got a complete assortment of clothing, including underwear and shoes. Everything a fashionable vampire could want. When they were ready to leave, the human mysteriously reappeared. Chase gave her everything Max wasn't wearing to send off to headquarters. He let the woman take the trench coat. However, Max couldn't part with a black leather bomber jacket which he thought also went just fine with his cowboy hat. Reluctantly, he took off the hat and started to hand it to the girl.

"You're not going to wear it?" Chase asked.

"Cowboy hats in the big city stand out a little too much. I

just really want to have it, if it's okay."

"Well, why don't you wear it tonight, at least? Break it in."

Max regarded the hat and then put it back on. It felt good, a perfect fit. It wasn't a real cowboy hat. It was one of those city versions of a cowboy hat. But since he was a city version of a cowboy himself... He smiled at Chase. Why not?

Back on the street, Max felt good. The vampire cowboy. He kind of liked that. He did love reading about the old west.

They talked casually, as though they were two normal people on a date. They talked about everything except what was really on his mind. The hunger didn't overtake him the way it had in the past, but it was never very far away. Max knew he was headed to another test.

Chase led him to a club named "Night Life." There was a long line of people waiting to get in. Chase walked past them and the bouncer nodded and let them in. Inside the club was decorated with an odd mix of gothic and art deco. A laser beam light show covered the ceiling. The club was brimming with people and Max saw some vampires in the crowd.

"This is one of my clubs," Chase said as they made their way.

"How many do you have?" He realized he was shouting. The music was blasting.

"Five in New York." Chase wasn't shouting. Of course, she didn't have to. He could hear her just fine.

The scent of the living was incredible. In his other life the smell of sweat, perfume and alcohol would have made him sick. But it wasn't another life. He took it in. He felt the pounding of their heartbeats, of their blood pumping, and it surged through him. The vampire inside him reared up, making him take notice of the power he had over life and death. Max had to keep his teeth from coming out. They were ready and he knew he was looking pretty pale. Luckily, and probably by design, the club's lighting hid his lack of color.

They squeezed through the crowded aisles to a reserved table.

"Is this the final exam?"

A waitress came up with drinks for them. The glass of blood mixed with wine had a little umbrella in it. Max drank his. When he saw that Chase hadn't touched hers, he drank hers too.

"Here are the rules. You come here or to one of my other clubs for the time being. Anyone in here is fair game. We get a lot that come back and we have to be careful. The clubs are popular, so we can pick and choose who gets in. The bouncers don't let former partners back in until a month has passed for them. As you know, it's not an unpleasant experience for a partner if you do it right. Make up a name for yourself… Follow me."

Chase took him to the back to a door that said "Private." They stepped into a dimly lit room that had a couch and a second exit. "Every club has a couple of rooms like this. Use your senses to see if the room is occupied. Bring your partner here. Don't forget to lock the door. It wouldn't do to have an errant human stumble in. Your partner won't be able to see much, and won't really know what happening. After you're done, take them through that door. There's a lounge and they can rest there. They'll be a little dizzy. Leave them and get out of the club. Someone will bring them some OJ and call them a cab. It's best to find a partner who is on their own and not part of a group… Come on." She led him back to the table and they sat down.

"Max, look around. You have to learn who to take and who not to. We don't let former partners back in for a month, but there are other people you shouldn't feed on. Like people who are ill, or have a disease such as Aids or cancer. Feeding on them could make their condition worse. You have to be careful. Look around and tell me who's sick."

Max studied the crowd. "What am I looking for?"

"Take a look at the guy in the black." He reached out with

his senses and studied the tall fellow. Something about him was odd.

"What's wrong with him?"

"Often it's not possible to tell. It might be a cold, or Covid, or it might be Aids. Some cancers, we're able to smell."

Max nodded. He looked out at the dance floor again. Sure enough, a couple of other people didn't seem right to him.

Max turned to her. "The guy with the blue shirt and tan slacks. Also, the lady with the pink dress. Something seems off about them."

"Very good. What you're sensing has to do with their life force, Max. It's just weaker than it is with a healthy person. The point is not to hurt them, so we have to be careful."

"Okay."

Chase nodded. She motioned to someone and one of the waitresses came over and sat down at their table.

"Max, this is Carla. I want you to study her neck."

Max looked at Chase suspiciously and then smiled at the woman. "Hi," she said.

"Hi." Max nodded and then followed Chase's strange request. At first he didn't notice anything, but as he probed with his senses he could feel a disturbance of some sort. Something under the skin of her perfectly unblemished neck. She'd been bitten.

Max looked back to Chase. "She's been a partner."

"Which side?"

"My left."

"Good… Thanks, Carla." The waitress smiled and left them.

"Carla is one of our humans, and she was a partner five days ago. When a bite heals, there is still a disruption of the skin's cells that lasts for about 10 days. You can sense that. It's dangerous for them, just like it would be dangerous to donate blood too often. Like the Red Cross, we don't like to use a partner more than once a month. The bouncers are very good at making sure former partners don't get back in until a month has passed, but if someone does happen to slip in, it's up to you to make sure it's been at least 10 days."

"I'll be careful… You know, I've always been embarrassingly bad at picking up girls in bars."

"I guess you'll have to work on that. I'm sure the hat will help."

Max shook his head and Chase deserted him. It all made a lot of sense. The environment was controlled. No risk of witnesses. The "partners" were willing, for the most part. The members of the staff were there to keep things under control.

Max worked his way to the bar to scout out dinner. He could feel Chase nearby. He wasn't very far out of her sights.

The two ladies next to him started talking about him. He could hear their entire conversation. He got a critique on his outfit, which they thought was kind of sexy. It amused him to actually know what women were talking about in this kind of situation. He'd never been good at bars because he'd always felt out of his element, a little like he was a student back in high school.

As he watched the crowd, he found the woman he wanted. She had the girl-next-door thing going and wasn't wearing a lot of make up. She saw him looking at her and smiled shyly. He walked up to her, dodging people as he went.

"Hi," he said, giving her his killer smile.

"Hi," she said, looking away briefly. She must not have done this a lot either.

He took in her scent. "My name's Jack."

"I'm Sara," she shouted. He couldn't stop himself from looking away. He really hated bars. Max took a breath. Well, he really didn't have to follow the dating rules anymore. He took her hand, and she started to pull it away, but then stopped. She looked up into his eyes, fully. That vampire mojo was kicking in. "I… I like your hat." She was yelling to be heard over the pounding music.

"I could say, do you come here a lot, but that would be a

bad line," he yelled back. He moved closer to her so she could hear him.

"Yes, it would be."

"I have a table over here. Would you like to sit down?"

"Now that's a good line, cowboy." Still holding her hand, he took her to the table. Max never let go of her hand, and she didn't take her eyes off him. They tried to talk, but the music was overwhelming. Max smiled and nodded and talked, but his inner vampire was more concerned with the smell of the sweat and people, and especially the scent of Sara.

"Look, I'm really bad at this. Can we go somewhere?"

She looked a bit bashful. "Okay." He stood up and she followed him through the crowd.

Max led her to the room. No one was in it. Sara pulled back just a bit when she realized the room was so dark. "It's okay. A friend of mine owns the club," he told her. She stepped in and he locked the door. He led her to the couch and she sat down.

"I don't…" she began to say.

"…run off with strangers," he said.

"No. I don't understand," she said. Max took her in his arms. He nuzzled her neck and then kissed her very lightly.

"Do you want to leave?" he said.

She paused and then shook her head. "No." He was very gentle with her and careful. At first she held back, not understanding what she was feeling. But as he began to kiss her neck she surrendered to him, fully and completely.

She let out a slight gasp as he bit down, but then clutched him tightly. "Oh, god. Oh, god," she said. Max could have easily drained her. The hunger never stopped demanding more, but he pictured his father in his mind and then pulled away.

Max held her. "Please… Don't stop. Please…" she begged.

"I have to. It's okay." He lifted her easily and carried her into the next room. As he sat her down, their eyes locked.

She knew. Somehow, she knew.

"Don't go," she said. He bent down and kissed her.

"They'll call a cab for you." A waitress came in and handed Max a drink, but it wasn't for him. It was orange juice. She left quickly. "Here you go. Drink this. It will make you feel better."

She took the drink, but she looked so sad and confused. With her free hand, she reached up and touched her neck where he bit her, but the skin was smooth and unbroken.

"I want to be with you," she said.

"No, you don't. You wouldn't like my world," Max said. He went back to the dark room, got his hat and left. The waitress had already called a cab for Sara, so Max went outside. Chase was waiting for him. They started walking away from the club.

"I feel bad. She's a nice girl."

"And by tomorrow, she'll realize that she shouldn't be hanging out with dangerous types like you."

"It just seems wrong to take her blood. It's not like she had the power to say no."

"No. But you know it's not unpleasant. Nothing really happened. She met a strange guy in a cowboy hat, she necked for a while with him in a dark room, she wanted more, he stopped and she felt dizzy. That's it."

"And she knew what I was."

"They usually do on some basic level. That's why she's going to be really grateful tomorrow that nothing else happened."

"Man. What kind of a creature of the night am I going to make?"

"Next time, don't pick a woman you're attracted to. Forget those nice, sweet types. They are going to make you feel guilty. Pick a woman who's attracted to you. The pushy kind. Maybe someone who's a little drunk. The kind that hang out in clubs a lot. They're always too busy focusing on themselves to pay attention to what's really going on."

"I was never good in bars. I hate this. I want to go back to eating cheeseburgers and fries, big juicy thick steaks, my mother's spaghetti, and sausage and eggs in the morning."

"It's amazing you survived long enough to be turned into a vampire," Chase said.

Max laughed. The blood was beginning to make him high.

They talked and they walked just like normal people. Max almost forgot he wasn't just another member of the human race until they got to the high-rise and he realized that dawn would be coming in a couple of hours. Even though he still felt guilty about Sara, he didn't want the night to end. It had been a long time since he felt normal at all, and it had been a good night.

Max had no idea what the next day would bring, but he did know that as a vampire, he was doing okay.

Suddenly, Max noticed that Chase's focus was somewhere else. When they got up to the war room, all hell had broken loose and the team was mobilizing. They had a lead on another vampire who'd been thrown on the street with no knowledge of what she was, and the night was almost gone.

Max stood and watched as instructions were shouted and everyone moved as though their lives depended on how well they did their job. Everyone was going, except Nadine, Max and the new kid. Inside his gut, Max felt a longing to be a part of what they were doing.

As Chase followed her team out of the room, she shot back a quick smile at Max. At that moment, Max would have given anything to be at 85 percent.

## CHAPTER 14

The next night, Tank took him out to the club so Max could feed. It was pretty funny because the big guy did little but growl in a low tone the entire time. He reminded Max of Lurch from The Addams Family. Max had taken Chase's advice about the type of person to choose as his partner and he had felt much less guilty afterward.

After that, Chase and the significant members of the team left on a mission, and Max made himself as useful as he could in the war room. Terry was in charge and short-staffed, so Max helped out by occasionally watching the new vampire for a few minutes here and there when he needed help. Max thought it was pretty funny, because he still needed an escort to get to his room on the floor above.

Savior was a street kid who talked about himself in the third person. Max couldn't help but to be drawn to the kid. They just had too much in common, not the least of which was Jade. There was no doubt Savior had a God complex, but Max could see the signs of abuse.

Max also started to spend time with Jenna. He asked her to help him learn sign language better and she agreed. Jenna had lost her lover, Mason, a year before in a battle, and Max could tell the pain of his loss was still with her.

There was a quietness about her that went far beyond the fact that she couldn't speak. She was Japanese and Max knew she must have come from a time when women were subservient. He tried to look up her picture in The Corps book, but he couldn't find it.

Max asked her where her picture was.

"I never could quite capture myself," she signed. "Cameras are new to me. Pictures, video, all that just happened in my life. I'm still getting used to it."

"Why didn't anyone else draw your picture?" Max signed.

"The others have better things to do than draw pictures,"

she signed.

"Your pictures are important. They tell the story of what happened."

"It's a story no one wants to hear."

"I do."

She changed the subject and they went on to talk of other things. She often corrected his fingers and hands, making sure they were in the right position. She had such a sweet and gentle nature, Max realized he had a crush on her. Of course, Max had a crush on Chase too, but she seemed very illusive to him. Jenna didn't. Chase was a mystery, but all Jenna's secrets were right there in her eyes.

A couple days had passed since Max's big shopping spree. He woke up in the afternoon thinking about Jenna. He was considering asking her out, but he wasn't sure exactly what vampires did on a date. It was uncharted territory. It wasn't the first time he'd hit uncharted territory since he died, but women had always confused him and vampire women had the same mysterious ability to make him feel out of sorts.

As Max pondered the difference between vampire men and vampire women, he realized he was alone. Not just alone in the room, but alone for as far as he could sense. He couldn't find anyone, not a vampire or a human. Something was very wrong.

Max scrambled out of bed and used the call button by the door. He buzzed endlessly but nobody answered. It terrified Max to think that there was no one left to talk to him. Max sat down and concentrated. He reached out as far as he could but there was nothing. For all he knew the entire building might be empty.

Something had happened, something bad. But what? Did they have to evacuate and leave him behind for some reason? Were they all dead? Would he find a bunch of dust if he got out? What could have happened that would leave him as the only one left? Was it some strange test? Why leave him in a locked room he couldn't get out of and then get everyone out of the building? Had there been a zombie apocalypse? Was the building about to blow up?

It made no sense. None of it. Unless, maybe, the building had been attacked by Jade's forces. If the attacking force couldn't open his door, they might have moved on quickly, sweeping through killing everyone they could. Chase and the team were supposed to have gotten back the night before, but he hadn't sensed them come in. If there had been an attack, some of The Corps might have escaped, but they may not have been able to get to Max. He was a low priority to them. They might have had to leave him behind.

If there had been an attack, why hadn't Max sensed it or heard anything? And if humans had been killed, he would have smelled their dead bodies. Maybe Jade's forces had captured them and taken them to be interrogated and then become dinner. There was no way to know until he figured a way out of the room or someone opened the door. He thought about Chase, Jenna and the others. If there had been an attack… he didn't want to think about it.

Who would he have to face if he did have to wait for someone to open his door? If it was Jade, what could he do? Who would there be to stand up to Jade if Chase was gone? If Jade opened his door, she would probably torture and kill him. Then there'd be no one else to fight her. Maybe, if Jade went unchecked, the human race was doomed to become nothing more than the sheep she saw them as.

Max realized he was making himself crazy. He had to get out of the room and see for himself. Then if Jade did come back for him that night, he'd at least be able to make a run for it.

Max's room didn't have any windows. He felt déjà vu as he explored his prison to find a way out. The room had been reinforced, similar to the first room he'd tried so hard to get out of during his last moments as a human. The biggest difference was that The Corps didn't use steel. It was some sort of impenetrable plastic. Max went over the room completely, but couldn't find any means of escape. There were several small vents, but unless he suddenly figured out a way to turn into smoke, they weren't going to help him.

He spent several hours going over everything. When nightfall came, Max was no closer to getting out than he had been when he woke up. Max settled down to wait. He was starting to feel the bloodlust, but he shoved it down deep inside himself. He could see it all ending so badly. If Chase opened the door, he'd be okay. But if it was Jade, he was in trouble. More than likely she'd make his mother suffer for his sins. The other option was that no one would come for a long, long time. He'd starve, the insanity of hunger taking him over, but never killing him. Then when the door finally did open, he'd destroy whoever opened it. The destroyer, his father, was never far from him anymore. He waited deep inside Max with the hunger, waiting to take over. That scared Max most of all.

Max laid back on the bed. He waited. As the hunger began to attack him, he let his mind go to a better place. The hunger had his body, but it didn't control who he was. He created his own universe in his mind and traveled to the only place he'd ever truly felt safe, his uncle's ranch.

Max and his brother had spent a couple of summers there when he was a kid. He knew why his mother sent them to stay with her brother. She wanted to get them away from "him," to give them some time to just be kids. And it had worked while they were there.

His Uncle Jackson and Aunt Ruth were simple people. They'd never had any kids and they loved having Max and Richie around. That first summer had been the best time of his life. Richie was still too little to do a lot of things, but Max got to hang out with the cowboys and his uncle spent time teaching them how to hunt, fish and ride a horse. His most glorious day had been when his uncle gave him his own horse, a mare named Freedom. His summer had all been so wonderful, until he got home and saw the fractured look in his mother's eyes. No one had been around to protect her.

Max refused to go the next summer, but the summer after, she'd made them go again. This time Max was fully aware of what was happening in his absence, but at least it was Richie's turn to become a cowboy. Max was sullen most of the summer, but he did spend a lot of time learning to shoot. He'd gotten into hunting for a while, but the first time he killed a deer was the last time he'd killed an animal. His uncle had been so proud of him, but the buck hadn't done anything to Max and it disturbed him to realize he'd killed it. After that, he'd just practiced shooting at targets and thought about his father too much. When he got home, his mother's arm was in a sling. She told him she'd had an accident.

Max refused to go back after that, although his mother agreed to let Richie go for a couple of summers by himself. Max hadn't made it back to the ranch until after he got out of the Army. He'd had his share of killing, so he just hung out as a ranch hand for over a year. His Aunt Ruth had died of cancer a couple years before, and Max knew his uncle was lonely. He seemed happy to have Max around.

But something nagged at Max. As he sat on his uncle's porch watching the sun go down he decided it was time to start his life. He'd never had a plan before. He'd always just reacted to the situation he was in. However, at that moment Max realized what he wanted to do with his life. He wanted to be a teacher and to teach kids about the thing he loved most… history. Of course, he need to get his GED and go to college first, but the Army would help him pay for it and for the first time in his life he looked forward to the future.

His uncle listened to his plan and nodded when Max mentioned college. It was a nod of great approval. Max would be the first one from their family to make it past high school. That day on the porch with his uncle was the day Max's life had started.

Max reached out with his senses again. No one was around to open the door. As Max felt the sunrise and set again and again, he refused to feel anything. He pushed all thoughts of Jade far away. Max stopped himself from worrying about why this had happened.

Max pulled himself back into his mind and thought about his life as a human and his time with the Corps. However, suddenly he found himself at the ranch sitting at a table with his mother, Richie and Uncle Jackson. He was all grown up and they were laughing the way they did when they got together as adults.

"How big was that fish again, Max?" Uncle Jackson asked, teasing him.

Max held out his hands a foot apart and they all laughed at him.

Richie grabbed Max's hand and pulled his hands farther apart. "You sure it wasn't this big, Maxie?"

Max smacked his brother's hand.

"I don't suppose you'll be doing a lot of fishing, now that you're a vampire and all," his uncle said.

"I don't suppose I will," Max agreed. "I'm sorry about that, by the way."

"Oh, Max, you couldn't help it," Mom said. Her voice was so forgiving and full of love.

"I've done some terrible things," he said.

"But you got control of it, kiddo," Richie said. "That's the important thing."

"You think I died in a fire. How is that right? I should have…"

"What would you have done? Told us about the vampire thing? We wouldn't have the ability to understand," Mom said. "You've always done the right thing, Max."

"Not always," Max said.

"Always. You protected us. You loved us," she said.

"I still do."

"Whether I think you're alive or dead, I know that."

They dissolved and Max was in his room again. It was the fourth morning, and he realized something had changed in him. His senses went much further and he could sense movement on the street below. It was rush hour. He could feel the humans going about their business. He could hear the noise from the city so clearly.

Max sat up. He hadn't moved in days and it felt odd. His arms were whiter than he'd ever seen them, the color of fresh snow. He reached out with his new senses and explored the room again. He studied the walls with his mind. And there it was, so obviously there waiting for him to find. It was a flaw in the material that reinforced the walls. It was small, but he got up and examined it. He pounded at the wall until it cracked. Max beat at the small crack with a fury he hadn't let himself feel in years. He refused to stop, and finally the wall gave. He broke through the outside plaster easily.

He widened the hole so it was big enough for him to get through. Max pulled himself into the hallway. He looked through the rooms that were unlocked, but nothing was disturbed or strange. Nothing except the dust on the floor everywhere. Dust in piles. Max wondered if the piles had been anyone he knew. Max got to the elevator, but it wouldn't work for him. It had a security feature, and the proper code had to be punched into a keypad to make it work. However, the stairs wouldn't be a problem. They were locked but Max easily forced his way through.

He reached out, but felt no one in the war room. Still, he had to go and check it out. Down a flight, Max broke the stairway door and ran to the war room. It was empty, except for the dust piles. Some of the papers were disturbed. Max got a sick feeling in his gut. There weren't any humans. No blood. Nothing to tell him what really happened. The door to Savior's cage was closed, but the cage was empty. The computers were running. Reports that were four days old sat where they'd been left. But The Corps book was gone. Jenna would have never left it behind if she were going somewhere. But if she'd been killed, it would have still be there. Max felt relieved that the book was gone. Of course,

Jade could have taken it too, but…

Max felt something stir in the building. It was a human coming into the parking garage. A young woman. Max could hear the music she was listening to. Max ran to the stairway and then suddenly he was floors below in the garage. Sunlight spilled through the windows of the closed garage door. The rest of the garage was in darkness, but Max could see her clearly. She looked like a street person and was wearing headphones, listening to rap. The woman's scent brought out the demon in Max.

The hunger he'd denied for so long welled up trying to push Max out of the way. His teeth were ready. The creature he'd become wanted Max to take her. Max held himself back and closed his eyes. He made himself see his mother's face, her eyes so sad and old. If he took this human, he'd kill the woman. He wouldn't be able to stop himself.

Max opened his eyes and looked toward the windows and the sunlight streaming through the garage doors. He heard his mother saying, "You've always done the right thing." All he had to do was walk outside. Let the sun take him. It would hurt, but then all his pain would end. Max walked to the door that led outside. If he died, who would stop Jade? Maybe he was the only one left. Who would be left to protect the human race?

Max looked to the woman, so wrapped up in her own world she had no idea what kind of danger she was in. It wasn't right. No matter what. Not because of Chase's rule, but because Max just couldn't destroy another life. And he couldn't protect the human race alone. He wasn't strong enough. He could have fought with Chase against Jade forever, and killed vampires if he had to. But he'd destroyed too many human lives already.

Max reached out to take the doorknob. It turned so easily in his hand.

Suddenly he sensed movement. Someone had come into the building in the floor above. He reached out and knew it was Chase. She was alive. Max pulled his hand away from the door.

He thought about her and suddenly found himself on the main floor. She was waiting for him in the building manager's office near the elevators.

"Hi, Max," she said. She looked sad.

"Was that the final?" he asked.

"Yes."

"Did I pass then?"

"You passed."

"I thought you were dead!" he screamed. Max spun around and punched a whole in the wall. "I thought she won! I thought the war was over. Damn you!"

Max flew at her, grabbing her around the waist. They spun around in a violent dance, flying into the wall. He clung to her as they fell to the ground, and then pulled her tight as he sunk his fangs into her neck. She let him feed. He could feel her warmth enter him. She ran her fingers through his hair and she touched him tenderly.

He stopped when he could and pulled his mouth away from her neck. He didn't want to take anymore than he had to, but he couldn't let go of her. "I thought you were dead," he whispered.

Max pushed himself away from her and leaned against a desk. Chase was sitting against the wall, so they were facing each other. Max waited until the hunger began to subside. His skin was still white. One feeding wasn't going to get him back to normal.

"Why?" he asked.

"I had to know for sure. You had to think you were alone, and that no one would be around to help. I can't risk losing this war because I trusted the wrong person. Do you understand that?"

Max put his head in his hands. "Trust?" He laughed. "All I wanted to know was why. Not why did I have to go through another fucking test. Why am I a vampire? Where the hell did we come from? Why are you different? But you're not going to tell me. You've got some god damn little secret, and you know why we are what we are. Maybe you even know why vampires exist in the first place. You lied to me."

"That makes two of us," she said. He banged his head against the desk. "We're both liars. You're right. I do know more than I've told you. But let me ask you this. That secret do you guard so tightly, the thing that keeps you in control, why do you keep that secret? Why do you hold onto it?" Max didn't answer. "It's because you have to, you don't have a choice… and neither do I."

"So, we'll both just keep our dirty little secrets. Well, mine doesn't affect you," Max said angrily.

"Yes it does. Because if you join our battle we have to trust each other. I'm trusting that your secret has nothing to do with Jade. And you have to trust me too. That's why you had to go through this last test. If for just one moment you don't have enough control, or you begin go think that your life is more important than theirs, you belong to Jade again. And I'll never let that happen. You were a good man, Max. But I had to make sure that part of you is still alive."

"Did I get an A?" he asked, with too much anger in his voice.

"There's something else. Another result of this little test. Tell me about you senses. How did you get out of the room? How did you know about the woman in the basement? How did you know I was here?"

Max looked at her curiously. "Something happened to me."

"When you go through deep deprivation, you learn to extend yourself. It happens naturally, but not unless there's a reason for it to come out. It makes you more powerful and your abilities reach a height they can't otherwise… That's the other reason you had to go through this."

"I could feel it happening, but I didn't realize…"

"You're free, Max," she said softly.

"Free?"

"You can go. I would really like it if you join us, but you're under no obligation to. We need you, but I'm not going to force you to stay. If you're not a threat to humans, then you have same choice you did before all this happened. You can travel where you want to, do what you want, be whatever you want. I'll keep an eye on you, of course, just in case, but it's up to you how you live from now on."

Max stood up and put his hand out to help her up. "So, I'm not a prisoner anymore?"

"No." She took his hand and stood.

"Or a recruit?"

"No. If you join us you'll start slowly. You'll learn to shoot our weapons and a bit of hand-to-hand, but that will be a snap for you. You'll become a full member of the team."

"But I don't have to," he said. Max started laughing. His anger vanished.

"You're free."

"That is a truly beautiful word. FREE. That almost makes it worth it… Almost."

"Will you stay?"

Max thought for a few moments. "I'm really pissed off at you guys."

"I know."

"It's like chopping someone's arm off and then saying, 'Sorry, just had to make sure we trusted you.'"

"I know."

"I'm still really, really, really mad," Max said.

"But you're going to join us, aren't you?"

"Really mad."

"Max…"

"I want Tank to beg me."

"Tank doesn't beg," Chase said.

"You sure?"

"I'm sure."

"I'm pretty good with a rifle. I can take out a moving target at three quarters of a mile."

"That is pretty good. I knew you were a sniper with Special Forces, but the records we have didn't…"

"They wouldn't. I was a really good sniper."

"Three quarters of a mile?"

"Yeah. Do you think that might come in handy? Are you sure Tank wouldn't be willing to beg, just a little?"

"You need to feed again. The woman downstairs is Dixie. She's a volunteer. She's waiting for you."

"I'm still mad," Max said on his way out of the room. He stopped at the door. "Oh, yeah. There's a hole in my bedroom wall, kind of a big one. And I think some of the stairway doors are broken. Sorry about that."

After Max had a bite of Dixie, he went back to his room and crawled back through the hole. He was feeling very tired. He hadn't really slept in four days. He thought about the hole for a moment, but shrugged his shoulders. He'd been sleeping in a cage for weeks.

He fell into bed and reached out. A van was bringing Tank and the gang into the parking garage. It was one of their special vans, set up for moving them around during the day. Jenna was with them. Max was glad she was okay. A couple humans entered the building too.

Max was relieved. "Do not adjust your television set. This is only a test." No one was dead. He wasn't alone. Jade hadn't won. It was a horrible test. But still, he could feel the world moving and people walking and the wind blowing and… his heart beating. It was beating very slowly, about a minute a beat, as if he'd been slowed down somehow. How about that? He wasn't really undead after all.

## CHAPTER 15

Max had been sleeping soundly, when he found himself on the floor, fully alert.

Tank was standing over him, looking more angry than usual. Tank had thrown him out of bed. Max remembered the begging thing and smiled. Tank only got more pissed off.

"What?" Max yelled.

Max could tell it was all the big guy could do to keep from killing him. "Chase…"

"I don't want to hear about Chase," Max said as he got up off the floor and sat down on the bed. "Just ask me."

"Three quarters of a mile?" he asked. Max thought it was amazing how Tank could talk and growl at the same time.

"Yeah. Moving target. I'm over a mile with a stationary target. Of course, with wooden bolts you couldn't have the same kind of range. Probably."

"No."

"Look, you can either kill me, leave or ask me the damn question. What the hell did I ever do to you anyway?"

Tank nodded. "You were with her. You slept with her and you killed for her."

"Yes, I did."

"Why should I trust you?"

"Maybe because I got close enough to know what she is," Max said.

"I don't believe in maybes. I believe in what I see, and I believe you're dangerous. We're the last line of defense against Jade and her people, and why in the world should I take a chance on you?"

"Maybe because someone took a chance on you once, a long time ago. And maybe Jade took a lot away from you, too," Max said. He was just guessing.

Tank looked away and then slowly returned Max's stare. "She is a powerful force I can't afford to underestimate, ever."

"I can respect that."

Max and Tank fell silent, their eyes locked in understanding. Finally, Tank nodded. "All right then."

"You still have to ask me. I'm not even going to try if you're going to be my enemy."

Tanks low growl returned for a moment. "Will you join us?"

"See, it wasn't that hard. Yes." Tank seemed unsure how to react.

"Good."

"Good. Now go away so I can sleep… Please."

"You can come and go as you want to now. The code of the keypad is 8 1 5. It will operate the elevator too."

"Thanks."

Tank considered him sternly, but the anger was gone. He left abruptly. Max laughed. It must have taken everything the big vamp had to ask him.

# # #

Max woke up a couple of hours before sunrise and headed toward the club. It was odd going out by himself without a guard looking over his shoulder. As he roamed the streets of New York, he realized he really could go anywhere he wanted. He'd missed his freedom. Still, freedom was relative. While there was no doubt a part of him that wouldn't have minded falling through the cracks and vanishing, he'd never be truly free so long as Jade walked the earth. The truth was he would have joined the Corps whether Tank had asked him to or not. Whether he was a vampire or not. He would have joined the Corps for Crystal.

When he got to the club, it was packed. He took care of business quickly and then got back to the high-rise. He was looking pink again and feeling better.

He decided to go to the war room since he wasn't quite ready to go back to bed. Jenna was there working on her computer. She was wearing her black cap and looking so cute. She must have sensed him because she looked right at him. He was so glad to see her, he couldn't stop himself from smiling.

"Hi, Jenna. It's good to see you," Max said and signed. He wanted to add the word "alive" but didn't.

She gave him the sweetest smile. Yep, that crush he had on her wasn't going anywhere. "I'm glad the trials are over for you," she signed.

"Me too."

"Are you okay?" she asked.

"Yes. I'm feeling better."

She pointed toward the computer and nodded. "Later?" she signed.

"Okay," Max said. He reluctantly left her to her work.

Dixie, Max's last volunteer, walked by him and smiled. "Max."

"Hi, Dixie. Thanks for earlier."

"Always happy to take one for the team," she said, giving him a nod. She walked over to Eugene and they began going over some paperwork. It was the first time he'd seen her in the war room.

Max was about to hunt down Terry, when he walked in from the kitchen with a drink for Savior.

"Hi, Max," he said.

Max could tell Savior was having a rough time. He looked bad.

"Hi Terry. Sorry you lost your money."

"It's okay. Glad you made it, Max." Terry put out his hand and they shook hands. "There are worse ways to lose twenty bucks. Can't believe you got Tank to ask you? I wouldn't have bet on that happening."

"Me either."

"We're setting you up with a new identity, so you'll need to fill out a couple things."

"What do you want me to fill out?"

"Some forms. We're a corporation, Max. A pretty

successful one at that. Got to have something to fund the war drive. Your job description here is Special Consultant for our security company, Nightwatch. Your new name is Arnold Henderson."

"Arnold? Seriously? Arnold?"

The next thing Terry had Max do was the strangest thing he'd done since he became a vampire. He filled out employment forms, a W2 and some paperwork regarding a pension fund. Of course, he was also given a cheat sheet to make sure the info was accurate with the new identity he'd been given.

Max's death had been faked and now he was being resurrected as a guy named Arnold. He really hated that name.

# # #

Two days later, Max was working in the war room while the team was out. Savior was going through major withdrawal. He was throwing himself at the bars and swearing at everyone he saw. Max brought him a drink, and Savior tried to bite him when he attempted to hand him the glass. The blood ended up on the floor and Savior began licking it up.

"I am totally disgusted," Max told Terry as they watched the newbie. "Was I ever that bad?"

"Well, there was the embarrassing Batman incident, but we won't talk about that," Terry replied. Max nodded. He remembered all too well.

Savior looked up at them, wide eyed. "You think Savior can't hear you? Savior hears everything. He will strike you down, for he is all knowing, all seeing. Bow to the glory that is the Lord. I am the glory. I am the resurrection. Now open the motherfucking cage, you bastards, before I kill you all! I will smite you down with my wrath…" Savior babbled on in a continuous rant.

"I'll get some more blood," Max said.

"You do that. Don't put your hand in the cage again

though. Put it on the floor and scoot it to him."

"I have no problem with that. Any chance I could change that bet… Just kidding."

Max got the blood and realized he couldn't take his eyes off Savior. He was a wild animal and he was completely insane. It was close to daybreak and the team still wasn't back. Terry took a call from Chase and then called Max over.

"I've got a problem," Terry said. "They can't get back in time. I need you to help me feed him."

"Can you handle him?"

"Not a chance. Only Chase and Tank are strong enough."

"Well, you can't let him out, then."

"No, but I need a volunteer. There are four of us here, but I need the others, so you're it, buddy."

Max looked at the animal in the cage. "I'm not going in there with him."

"Don't worry. We're not opening the door. Just give him your wrist through the bars. I'll have a cattle prod, just in case he doesn't want to let go."

"Can't we just hit him with one of those tranquilizers? I'm all for helping the cause, but he's nuts."

"No, that stuff would knock him out for a couple days and Chase doesn't want that unless we have to do it."

The sun was coming up. Max rolled up his sleeve. "Thanks for thinking of me… It couldn't be an insane pretty girl. No. I have to get insane religious animal boy."

"Just give him enough to get him through. I'll get a human volunteer lined up for you afterward, so you'll be good."

Jenna came in with the cattle prod. She handed it to Terry.

Max saw that she had the tranquilizer gun ready, just in case things got out of hand with Savior. The two other vampires on duty came in as well.

Savior was watching them, waiting to pounce. Max sat down on the floor just out of reach and Savior was ready for him.

"… I shall deliver you from the evil that walks the

earth…"

"Oh, shut up," Max said as he stuck his hand out. Savior grabbed it and yanked hard to pull Max's entire arm into the cage. He sunk his fangs into Max's arm hard and drank. Max screamed at the pain. "Shit!"

Max felt like the kid was going to rip his arm out of his socket, and he had a feeling that would be a really bad thing even for a vampire. Savior drank like he was starving to death, which Max knew he felt like he was. He could feel Savior's insanity and thirst bubble up through him. When Max started to feel the effects of blood loss, he tried to pull his arm away, but Savior wasn't about to let go.

"Terry, can we get Jesus Christ off my arm before I rip his god damn head off?" Max yelled.

"Yeah, Max."

Savior bit down hard again for no good reason. Max reached through the bars with his other arm and grabbed Savior's hair to pull him off. Savior bit down again and Max lost his grip. Savior caught hold of both of Max's arms and tried to go for his neck right through the bars. Max used his foot to kick Savior in the chest, but just as Max was able to pull his arms free, the kid grabbed his leg and bit down right through his pants.

"Damn it!" Max yelled.

Terry managed to get the cattle prod through the bars around the commotion, but ended up zapping both Max and Savior. Max fell back, his body jerking a bit.

"Oh, shit. Sorry Max," Terry said. Max felt himself being pulled away. He really didn't like being a vampire anymore.

# # #

Max found himself in his bed, naked. Light spilled in from the bathroom. Someone had cleaned him up. He looked at his arm, but all the bites were healed. He was white and he had the hunger bad. Jenna was sitting in a chair watching him.

She stood up and looked at him. She signed, "Are you

okay?"

"Yes," he said. "Thanks. I could use that volunteer Terry talked about."

"May I be your volunteer?" she signed.

"But why? I can control the hunger."

"I know. You don't understand," she signed. "I would like to be with you, if you want me."

Max studied her in the darkness. He signed, "I do."

She smiled. He watched her take off her clothes and when she sat next to him, she was warm and beautiful. She was perfect to him, the way her hair framed the features of her delicate face, the way her small but full breasts fit exactly right on her slight frame, the way her legs seemed longer than they had a right be. Her smile let him know she wanted exactly what he did.

She reached down, running her fingers through his hair and then caressing his cheek. Jenna ran her hand down his body slowly, teasing him with the movement until her hand was between his legs stroking his cock. Her touch thrilled him.

Max reached up and touched her back in all the best places. He knew what she wanted because he wanted it too. She loved it when he played with her breasts. She arched her back as he raised up to take one of her nipples in his mouth and tease it, before moving on to the other one. Then he did lots of other fun things with his tongue only moments before she got her revenge with her own very experienced tongue.

Neither of them wanted to rush. Max took her in his arms and they kissed, deeply, fully, completely while their hands roamed over each other's bodies.

He pulled back to look at her and she nodded. Max's fangs were ready and he gently bit her neck as they both delighted in the pleasure he felt drinking from her. He pulled back just long enough for her to straddled him and guide his cock into her.

Max continued to drink and Jenna began to move her hips.

It took a few moments but soon their movements were in synch as though they'd been making love for centuries.

Making love, not fucking, Max though. It wasn't just sex.

Jenna shared her blood with him until they were the same temperature, and he released his bite so they could stare into each others eyes, the passion boiling up between them until they came within moments of each other. She was passionate and giving and nothing at all like Jade.

Max opened himself up in a way he never had before. She brought out a desire that was much deeper than anything Jade could have touched in him. She made love to him in a way that made him feel she wanted him and only him.

Later, Max watched her in the dark. She was sitting up in bed signing. He was lying down signing back to her and they were having an animated conversation. Jenna was much faster at signing than he was, and she laughed at him when he made mistakes. It was a wonderful silent laugh. Max loved watching her because she wasn't wearing anything and as she signed, her breasts moved in ways that reminded him how much he wanted to be inside her.

"You are not," he signed.

"Yes, I am." She touched his stomach.

"No. Can't you just do a picture of me in my hat?"

"But the Batman outfit suits you so much better." She smiled.

"I was insane at the time. It's not fair."

"You'll make a great Batman. Maybe you could star in the next movie."

Max started laughing. "Somehow I don't think so. Of course, then I'd be the first vampire Batman." Max caressed her thigh. "Tell me about you?"

"What would you like to know?"

"Where were you born?"

"Japan, but other than that I don't know. I was always deaf and mute, so I didn't understand much. My father was a fisherman and we were poor. My parents were angry for being cursed with such a child. I don't remember much from the time. I had no way to communicate with anyone. My mother beat me often."

"Did you hate her for treating you badly?"

"I had nothing to compare it with. I didn't know any other way to live."

"Who changed you?"

"Chase… But that wasn't her name then."

"Chase. I guess I'm surprised. Somehow, I can't see the Chase I know today making anyone into a vampire."

"She hasn't for a long time now, unless it's to save a life. Back then, times were different. Women had few choices. When I met Chase she dressed as a man and no one knew otherwise."

"Chase as a man?"

"She was very convincing. I was being sent somewhere. They didn't tell me where I was going, not that I would have understood, but I felt great shame, I remember. I was traveling with two men from the village and I was very scared. Chase came across to our campsite. She was dressed as a soldier and the men were frightened of her, too afraid to tell her she could not join us. She talked to me, but I couldn't understand her. The men said something and laughed. She looked very angry at them. In the night she took me away while they slept. I was very frightened, but then she touched my hand and the fear left me. She took me to a cave and deep inside she had created a home. She treated me kindly, as I had never been treated before. I didn't understand what had happened. I could have left the cave as she slept, but I didn't. It was much later when I found out she was a woman. She became my teacher and taught me how to read and write. Eventually she made me a vampire. I've been with her ever since that time."

"How long?"

"Nearly eight centuries. A long time."

"Wow... Did you ever regret it?"

"When Mason died, my heart broke. There have been others through time. It's hard to lose people."

"I know."

"You, Max, are a baby. You don't know."

"Then you can teach me."

Max pulled her on top of him. She stopped signing and used her hands for Max's favorite form of communication.

Maybe being a vampire wasn't so bad after all.

## CHAPTER 16

As dawn broke, Jenna fell asleep in his arms. Max watched her. She was just as silent in her sleep as she was when she was awake. She didn't make any tiny noises or fitfully move from side to side. Besides the warmth of her body, the only thing to signify that she was alive was an occasional breath.

He played with her soft, thick hair. He took a deep breath, loving the smell of her. She was so young looking, it was impossible she could be 800 years old. Well, Max always had liked older women. He smiled to himself and took another breath of her.

They were both children of abuse. They both had been saved by Chase. But the closeness he felt toward Jenna went much deeper. He'd entered a world of mystery and lies, but Jenna had a truth about her, an honesty.

He had had a couple of long-term relationships, and the women in his life always ended up telling him he had a fear of commitment. He accepted their judgment because he couldn't tell them about the darkness that lived within him. He'd always known there was no white picket fence in his future. How could there be? But now here was a woman who understood darkness, and his darkness didn't matter to her because she'd been there herself.

As Max burned the memory of her face into his mind, he realized she just might be the one woman he could give his soul to. He closed his eyes. It was too early for him to start thinking he might have a future. Still, if he did have one, he wouldn't hate it if Jenna were part of that future.

# # #

Max felt her stir and he woke instantly. Jenna was trying to sneak out of bed without waking him. He pulled her back into bed and kissed her stomach. She smiled and pushed him away. "I have to go to work," she mouthed.

"It's too early. Come back to bed."

"My shift starts at 11," she signed.

"You have lots of time," Max said, as he pulled her to him and put his hand between her legs. She wiggled away and got out of bed. Her hair was messed up and her face was full of sleep. She looked so lovely standing there without a stitch on.

"No, I don't. It's 10:30," she signed.

"It's not fair," Max groaned and turned away. She slapped him on the butt to get his attention and he turned back to her.

She signed, "I have to take a shower, but I don't have to take it alone." She smiled and ran into the bathroom. It took Max about three seconds to untangle himself from the sheets and get into the shower. She already had the water on. Max took her in his arms and kissed her deeply, desire overtaking them both. As water washed over their bodies, the steam began to rise. Max glanced down to discover she'd only turned on the hot water. He looked into her eyes and smiled. Yes, if he had a future, he definitely wanted her to be a part of it.

# # #

Max dozed til 1, and then lazily got dressed and made his way to the war room. Jenna was there, looking bright-eyed. She was drawing Savior's picture. Savior was quiet. He looked dejected. Max didn't have any hard feelings about being bitten. Fighting the vampire was something Max could understand all too well.

What Max really wanted to do was to give Jenna a kiss and maybe accidentally cop a feel, but he decided to behave himself. He was absolutely sure there was no way they were going to be able to hide the fact they'd been together. There wasn't any such thing as privacy amongst vampires. The senses were just too keen. Vampires were a randy lot and he could always tell who slept with whom. Terry and Nadine, Shades and just about every available female vampire he could find, Rhonda and a vampire named Christine. Everyone except Chase. She never had anyone else's scent on her that he could detect.

The rule seemed to be that no one said anything about the obvious. At least he could pretend to be professional about the work, even if he knew he wouldn't be able to focus on anything else but jumping Jenna the first opportunity he got.

Terry walked up to him. "Hey, Max. I'm really sorry about last night."

"It was a shocking experience, Terry," Max smiled. "Don't worry about it... It doesn't look like our boy is doing too well."

"He's having a hard time." Max studied Terry for a moment. Terry had seen it all many times before and he didn't think Savior was going to make it. Max realized that even he didn't think the kid was going to survive.

"Chase wants to see you now, and you're to report to Tank in the basement at 4."

"The basement?"

"It's one of our training facilities."

"Okay."

Terry looked at Max and then glanced at Jenna. A slight smile crossed his lips. No, no secrets among this bunch.

Max went to Chase's office. The door was open, so he just stood there until she looked up from her computer.

"Hello. Come in."

"Hi." Max sat down in the chair opposite her desk.

"A couple things… First, since you're joining us, we have to take precautions. Jade may find out you're with us. It's not beyond her to take revenge out on someone you care about, someone from your past. She thinks you're dead now, but that may change when you become an active part of our team."

"She'll go after my mother."

"We've already moved your mother."

"What? But how?"

"We went in as a large corporation buying the land for development, and made her a generous offer for her home. She just lost you, Max. She was happy to sell. She's with your uncle on his ranch. She's got a nice nest egg now and she can retire. We've covered her tracks, so Jade shouldn't be able to find her."

Max looked down. "Is she… okay?"

"I'm told she's better now that she's with your uncle."

Max put his head in his hands and nodded. "I didn't… Thanks… Thank you for taking care of her for me." He looked back up at her.

"Did you tell Jade anything about other members of your family?"

"No."

"Do any other members of your family live in the area?"

"No. My brother and his family live in Utah... But my students… she threatened them many times."

"I've beefed up security in the area, but I need a list of students who might be at risk so we can keep an eye on them. Max, I'm going to take care of this. It's what I do. Still, there are no guarantees."

"I know… I'll make the list," he said, sadness creeping into his voice.

"Understand that it's in my best interest to make sure you're not compromised."

"Thanks."

"You can still back out."

Max didn't say anything for a moment. "No, I can't… Jade said something to me before she made me. It was something like, 'If you're not one of us, you'll be fighting against us.' She was right. I can't go back. I have to fight against her. I don't want anyone I care about to get hurt because of me, but the truth is there's too much at stake. You've been fighting this war for a long time. For me this is all new. I may be deluded to think we can win."

"Maybe we both are." Max met her gaze and then nodded.

"I guess we deluded optimistic vampires need to stick together," she said with a smiled.

"I suppose we should… I'm in this for as long as it takes. I'll do what you need me to do."

"The cost may end up being pretty high, Max. Higher than you know."

"Well, I'll jump off that bridge when I get to it."

Chase nodded. "The other thing… I wanted to thank you for helping out with Savior last night."

"No problem. Do you think he's going to make it?"

"He's so young… I don't know, Max." Chase looked away. She wasn't as hard to read as Jade. She didn't think Savior would survive.

"Then I have a favor to ask you, if you're willing."

She looked at him curiously. "What?"

"Let me work with him in my spare time for at least a week, before you give him the life and death tests."

"What are you going to do?"

"I don't know, but I know kids and I'll bet this one hasn't had a single break in his entire life," Max said.

"It will still come down to whether or not he can find the strength to beat the vampire."

"I know. Can I have the week?"

"Yes. But if he doesn't make it, I don't want you to feel like you failed," Chase said.

"No guarantees on that one."

"You're never going to win the office pool this way." She smiled at him and Max nodded with a laugh.

"What can I say? I always go for the sucker bets," he said.

"I don't know. You bet on yourself."

"I had a vested interest in that one."

Max stood up to leave. "Max, welcome to the team."

"I'm sure I'll live to regret it."

"Quite possibly, Arnold," she said.

"Do not call me that. I'm already learning to regret that name."

Max turned to leave, but then he looked back. "I know I thanked you for saving my life, but you saved a lot more than my life that day. Jade wouldn't have let me die. She was forcing me to become a monster. So even if you won't answer my damn vampire questions, thanks for the rescue."

"You just keep asking those damn questions, Max. Maybe someday you'll get lucky and find out some of the answers."

"I hear vampires can live a very long time," he said.

"That's the rumor. And you're welcome."

"All I've got to do is live long enough. Someday has to happen sooner or later."

"Perhaps…"

"Hey, if I do something special during training, how about another Civil War fact?" Max asked.

"Max, we're fighting a war in this century."

"Yeah, but if I get staked tonight, I'll never know the cool things you could tell me. One more little bit of history."

"I'll tell you what. You get Savior in the room tonight, and I'll give you two… Deal?"

"Deal."

Max smiled. He might not find out where vampires came from, but he was darn well going to find out some very cool Civil War stuff.

He went back to the war room. Savior hadn't moved and he looked terrible. The kid was a mess and probably hadn't been out of the cage since he used Max as a meal. First thing on his road to saving Savior was to let him take a shower and get cleaned up.

Terry came up to Max. He was holding a thick manila envelope.

"Hey, Terry, I'm going to be spending some time with the kid."

Terry nodded. "It can't hurt."

"Can I take him to get cleaned up?"

"I'll check with Chase, but I don't see why not. It's still early. He should be pretty manageable… I've got some stuff for you."

Terry handed Max the envelope.

"What is it?"

"Phone, driver's license, birth certificate, stuff like that."

Max sat down at a desk and pulled out the contents of the envelope. There was a black cap engraved with the words "Nightwatch Security," like the one Jenna wore. There was also a bunch of life's little necessities. He checked out his new driver's license. They'd used his old picture.

And Max had a phone. He turned on his new iPhone.

"You can't call anyone except us on that," Terry said.

"What am I going to do? Call my mom and give her a heart attack? Don't worry. I know. Max is dead... Thanks, Terry."

Terry nodded. Max pulled out his wallet and put the new license over the old one. A couple other items from the envelope also caught his interest. An American Express Gold Card, a set of car keys and a checkbook. Max held them up.

"The credit card has a limit of $5,000 a month and the keys are for a BMW in the parking garage. It's now registered to your new identity. You've got a bank account with the bank across the street. You're now a real and living person, Arnold Henderson"

Max looked at the bankbook. It had a balance of $10,000.

"Who could have guessed that dying could be this profitable, and don't call me Arnold. Max was never this rich."

Terry laughed. "Why don't you get Savior a hit and I'll check with Chase about letting him out to get a shower."

"Will do." Max gathered up his stuff… how cool was it that he actually had stuff again… and put it back in the envelope. Everything except for the cap. Max looked over at Jenna, who as still concentrating deeply her drawing. Jenna's cap made her look so darn cute.

Max put his cap on backwards and went off to get Savior a drink. By the time he got back, Savior was alert. He could smell the blood. The kid glanced up at him, but didn't say anything.

"Hi, Savior."

Max handed him the glass and Savior took it, downing the contents. He waited for a few moments and then looked up at Max again.

"Savior thanks you."

"You're welcome."

"He's sorry he bit you." The kid set the glass on the small table.

"You bit me a bunch of times... It's not a problem."

"The devil got into him."

Max held up his arms. "It's okay. See, no bite marks. There wasn't any damage done." Chase and Terry came into the room.

"The damage is in here." The kid pointed toward his heart.

Terry nodded to Max.

"Look, I'm going to take you out to get cleaned up. Is that okay with you?"

Savior looked down at himself and realized he was a mess. "Savior is unclean. He's covered with the blood of Christ!" he screamed.

"Okay… So, do you want to get cleaned up?" Max asked.

The kid held his arms away from his body like he was afraid to touch himself and nodded. Chase had ushered out the two humans who had been in the room, making sure he had no temptation. Terry unlocked the cage and Savior just stared at them all in horror as he followed Max to the bedroom.

Savior retreated to the bathroom and Max closed the door so the kid could have some privacy. Life in a cage didn't offer a lot of that and Max remembered his long showers had given him a little time to do the things you just couldn't do in public, like cry, jerk off, whatever.

Max had grabbed his envelope on the way and he sat on the floor and started going through everything. Whoever put it together had thought of everything. There was even an "In Case of Emergency" card. Max put the credit card in his wallet and went through the other contents, taking out most of the Max Maguire stuff. The pictures of his family stayed, however.

He pulled out Amanda's old driver's license and a tidal wave of guilt flowed over him. He'd told Chase and Company about Amanda, but he couldn't quite part with the license or the happy image of her smiling at him. Chase had promised to try and find her family, but so far they had come up empty.

People like Amanda and Savior were the lost ones. The ones whose lives would never be celebrated and whose deaths would never be mourned. Their lives were wasted because of abuse or illness, and Max had known too many people like them. Well, Savior still had a chance and Max had a week to give him a reason to keep living. Nothing would ever make up for Amanda or Michelle or the rest of the damage he'd done, but at least it was a first step in the right direction.

Terry brought in a change of clothes for the kid, which seemed to brighten his spirit a bit.

Max returned Savior to his cage and the kid looked better, but he refused to talk. Someone had cleaned up the cage and it smelled lemon fresh. Max had a couple of minutes before his appointment with Tank, so he got Savior another drink and pulled up a chair. Max wasn't thinking about winning Civil War facts when he looked into Savior's devastated eyes.

"Here you go," Max said as he set the drink on the table.

Savior just stared at him and then slowly picked up the glass and drank. When he was done he put the glass back on the table.

"Savior's evil. You shouldn't be nice to him. He deserves to suffer," the kid said.

The humans were coming back into the room and Savior's eyes followed a fellow named Pete. Max had known Savior was gay pretty much from the beginning. A hungry vampire didn't have the luxury of hiding his sexual preference.

"The vampire is evil, but you have the ability to control it," Max said.

"Really?" Savior said with a challenge.

"Really."

"So tell me, how is Savior supposed to control his demon?"

"If Savior decided to talk to me himself, I might be able to help him find that one thing that will keep the demon in check."

"Will your 'one thing' get rid of the demon?" he challenged.

"No. But if you win the battle, you can lock the demon up and put it where it won't hurt anyone again."

Savior shook his head and laughed bitterly. "You don't know anything about me!"

Max smiled. It was the first time Savior had referred to himself in the first person.

"No. I only know about me." Max stood. It was time to go see Tank. "Before that cage was yours, it was mine."

Savior looked surprised.

"I've got to go, but I'll be back later," Max said.

# # #

Max arrived five minutes early to find Tank waiting for him. The basement was set up with a shooting range, a weapons area and a matted area Max assumed served for hand-to-hand training. Shades and Father Frank were sparring. Tank was cleaning one of the odd pistols Max had seen them all carrying. Tank didn't acknowledge Max in any way. Max watched the sparring while he waited. He could tell that Shades and Father Frank were pretty much pretending to spar, probably waiting to see what Max could do.

Tank finished cleaning the gun and put it back together. He regarded Max sternly and then handed him the gun.

The double-barreled revolver was much lighter than he'd expected considering the long cylinder capable of holding six-inch bolts. "Interesting… is it made of epoxy?"

"Yes."

Max had heard about epoxy guns, but hadn't held one before. Epoxy was a plastic that was as strong as metal, making for a nice lightweight gun.

"What's the range?" Max asked as he opened the cylinder. There were two rows of holes in the cylinder, one inside the other. With six holes on the outside, and four on the inside, the gun allowed for 10 rounds. The short barrel existed primarily to give the shooter a sight for accuracy.

"About 200 yards."

Max closed the cylinder and aimed the gun toward the target area.

"We have quick loaders for reloading. You get to practice with epoxy bolts." He looked at Max and smiled. It was almost scary seeing Tank smile. Well, epoxy bolts would make sure no one would turn to dust accidentally or on purpose.

Tank handed him a yellow box with no label. Inside were the bolts, or pencil shaped bolts, which looked similar in shape to the one's he'd seen at Jade's. There was a steel tip on the pointed end of the black epoxy arrow with a cap on the blunt end for the gunpowder.

"The weight's the same. The bolts, both the epoxy and the wooden, have a steel shaft inside," Tank said.

Max nodded and loaded the gun. It'd been twelve years since he'd held a gun and it he hated the fact that it felt so familiar… and so comfortable.

Tank walked with him to the firing range and handed him protective ear muffs. He put a pair on himself, while Max put up a new target sheet and hit the switch to send the target out. The target was the usual kind with an outline of a person, with a bull's-eye around the heart area.

"That's far enough for now," Tank said when the target got

to the 50 foot mark.

Max leveled the gun, cocked it and shot once. His bolt barely hit the target. He figured the gun had the kick of a 45. He adjusted his aim to the left a bit and fired again. This time he hit the shoulder. Max made one more adjustment and then fired the remaining eight bolts. He hit the switch to bring the target back. When Tank saw the target he just nodded. Max also had the attention of Shades and Father Frank. All the shots except one had hit the center circles, with most centering around the bull's-eye or where the heart would have been. The one errant one was up by the chin.

When Max took off the ear muffs he could hear the big guy grumbling. Shades and Father Frank went back to sparring. Max shrugged his shoulders. "It's been a while. I'll get better with a little practice." He handed Tank the gun. Tank turned away from him and walked back to the weapons area.

Tank put the weapon away and then leveled his gaze at Max. "How long has it been since you've handled a gun?"

"About twelve years or so."

Tank cleared his throat. He didn't look happy. "Let's see how you do with hand-to-hand." Tank started toward the area with the mats. Max followed him. The two sparring vampires stopped and relinquished the hand-to-hand area.

"Now that's another story. I wouldn't consider that one of my talents." Even though he'd spent a lot of time in the Army on it and some time with Maria and the Saracian Lance, hand-to-hand was different. He could handle himself, but probably not against Tank.

Max kicked off his boots. Tank purposefully removed his shoes and then his shirt. Somehow, Tank looked even bigger without his shirt on. His muscular chest and arms were enormous. Max took a breath and decided to keep his shirt on. There were some things a guy just shouldn't try and compete with.

Max faced off against Tank on the mat just knowing this

was going to hurt. Well, anything for the cause. The worst thing was that they had an audience. Shades and Father Frank weren't even pretending not to watch anymore. They were sitting on stools near the weapons area, beers in hand and waiting for the show.

Tank gave a small bow. "The main purpose of this right now is for you to discover your strengths and limitations. Your body has changed. You need to rely on your senses during battle. Your life will one day end up depending on it."

Max bowed. He got his body into a fighting stance, with his arms bent in front of him at chest level, his hands in fists.

"Go ahead. Attack me," Tank said.

Max took a swing, but he hit air. His arm was extended in a punch when a strong hand pushed him from behind, shoving him down into the mat, hard. Max hadn't even seen Tank move. He rolled over and pushed himself up.

"Again."

Max punched with the same result. Face kissing the mat. He rolled over again and got up again.

"Again."

Max wanted to complain, but he'd never do it to Tank. He punched again, but this time Tank deflected his punch and hit him square in the chest. Max flew back hitting the wall. His head and back ached for a minute.

"I didn't like that one. Can't we go back to the other one?" Max asked.

"Again."

Max sighed and got up. He'd taken some martial arts, and obviously it was time to switch tactics. He tried a leg sweep. Tank body slammed him and cracked a rib.

Max tried a scissor kick, and Tank flipped him up so Max went spinning through the air and landed hard outside the matted area.

He threw an upper cut and got tossed into the wall.

Max performed a perfect roundhouse kick, just barely missing Tank's chin. Tank grabbed his leg and lifted Max into a spin so he flew through the air before he slammed into the mat. Max just laid there a minute. His audience applauded. Slowly Max sat up. He looked over at Shades and Father Frank. They were holding up sheets of paper so he could see. Shade's paper had a large 5.6 written on it, while Father Frank had given him a 5.8. Max laughed. "Don't I get any extra points for style?"

"Those were style points," said Father Frank.

They were laughing, until Tank glared at them. They put their signs away and got quiet. Max got up. He tried a flying scissor kick, a punch to the groin, and even a left hook.

Max stopped for a minute. "Use your senses," Tank said.

Max nodded. He thought about Tank and flying at him, this time with an elbow punch. Tank knelt pushing Max up so he slammed into the wall. Pain shot through Max's arm. Max looked down to see his wrist is laying at an odd angle.

"Being a vampire doesn't keep you from breaking, it just helps you heal very fast," Tank said. "We have to set it quickly or it will heal at that angle… That was better."

"Shit. It hurts."

Tank took hold of Max's wrist and set the break. Max screamed. It felt like Tank was ripping his arm off. The terrible sound of bone scraping bone vibrated through him. "Oh, fuck!"

Tank grimaced. He was feeling everything Max was.

"Stop moving so it will heal properly or I'll have to rebreak it." Tank held Max's arm like a vise. Slowly the pain began to subside. "It will take another five minutes or so."

Max looked at his arm, which was turning a variety of colors as it went through the healing process.

"You may need to do this for someone else during battle. Just set the bone and keep it straight."

After a couple minutes Max could barely feel any pain. The break was nearly healed.

"Thanks," Max said.

"It won't be the only bone you'll break during training."

Three hours later, after not landing more than a couple of ineffective hits, Tank stopped suddenly. Max was sprawled on the mat, feeling pretty hungry and exhausted.

"Tomorrow," Tank said. Then he put on his shirt and left the basement with a surprised Max watching him as he left. Max laughed and fell back, staring at the ceiling. Father Frank was suddenly standing over him, offering him a hand up.

"Not bad, Maxie. You actually almost hit him a couple times." Shades was still sitting on the stool, laughing. Max took Father Frank's hand and let the thin man pull him up. Max put on his boots and joined his audience in the weapons area, as Shades got up and went around the counter.

There was a small mini-fridge under the counter and Shades opened it up and pulled out a beer. He handed one to Max. Max twisted the top off and took a drink. He was hoping they were about to do a little male bonding. Max needed all the friends he could get.

"So, was that the initiation?"

"Oh, goodness no, my boy. The initiation's going to hurt," Father Frank said.

Max winced. Shades shook his head, laughing.

"He really does hate me," Max said.

"Sure he does," Shades said. "It's his job to hate you… Still, you have a natural talent."

"Funny. That's what my CO said in the Army."

"You said that first day you had nine kills, but you were in Special Forces for nearly three years."

"After the first couple kills, my CO could tell it was hard on me. There wasn't a war going on. He was a smart man and he knew if he pushed me too hard, he'd lose me. I was the best they had, but he only used me when he needed that impossible shot, the one no one else could make. I did kill a lot of equipment and machinery, though. Some tires too. I excelled at that."

"What do you mean?" Father Frank asked.

"Often a well-placed shot can be more effective in stopping machinery than in killing one man. It can be a much more disruptive force," Max said.

"What about now? If you had trouble doing it then..."

"Yeah. Well, in the Army, half the time I had no clue why we were doing the things we were doing. We followed orders. I killed who I was told to kill. This is different. I know the enemy intimately and I know what the stakes are. I'm not going to kid you. I'm going to hate it. But I'll kill vampires for the good guys because every one I kill means less dead people in the world from that moment on. It means the world's a little safer for idiots like me who end up in the wrong alley at the wrong time."

Shades smiled. "You are one strange fellow, Max. Most men with a talent for death embrace it. You turn your back on that talent and then end up getting turned in a creature that's compelled to kill to survive. Then when you finally figure out how not to kill, you discover you must kill to save lives. I think your fate was sealed a long time ago."

"You right about that. My life is just full of irony these days." Max took another drink of his beer.

"So what does a soldier who doesn't like to kill end up doing while he's in the Army?" Father Frank asked.

"I did some teaching on the firing range. Also, did you know that you can never, ever get a gun clean enough? No matter how well it's cleaned, it's never cleaned well enough."

"Yes," Shades said.

"And the Army has a lot of guns that need to be cleaned."

"That's odd. So do we."

Max grimaced. "I was actually really bad at cleaning guns."

"You obviously didn't get enough practice. I think we can help you with that, Maxie," Father Frank said.

The two men smiled at him. The joke was on Max. He looked back at the racks of guns.

"Those are just the practice weapons," Shades said.

"I think we need to talk to Tank about a new job for Max," Father Frank said.

"Wait guys."

"Absolutely, guns should be cleaned by someone with experience. Don't you think?" Shades said.

"You are so right, my good fellow," Father Frank replied. The two men started walking to the door.

"Oh, come on. Guys."

They kept walking. "Yes, I think Max would do an excellent job in that department," Father Frank continued.

"Wait, guys…" Max watched them leave the room. He sighed. He looked at the half empty beer in his hand and downed the rest of it in a couple of drinks.

It was a good thing vampires lived a really long time. With the help of Tank, Father Frank and Shades he'd be lucky if he did anything more than get beat up and clean guns for, oh… maybe the next few decades.

# # #

After a cracked rib, a broken wrist and three hours of getting beat up by Tank, Max was more than ready to get away from the basement and get back to the war room. At least no one would hit him up there, although he was pretty sure Father Frank and Shades might come up with some more mischief.

Max really wanted to see Jenna. But first he needed to take a shower and change his clothes. When he got to his room he checked his arm, but it looked as if it had never been injured. He had to admit that was pretty cool. And all he had to do was drink human blood for the rest of his days.

It was the give and take of his new life. He'd drink blood because he had to. He had no choice on that one. He'd let Tank beat him up for a few hours every day if that meant he could join their team. He'd kill Jade's vampires because someone had to stop them. Someday, if he was blessed enough, he'd find Jade herself in his scope. And if he were really lucky, everyday he'd be able to make the world just a little bit better place than it had been the day before. That, and share Jenna's bed for another 800 or so of her years. Those were the perks.

It was the good mixed with the bad, the ebb and the flow of life… even vampire life. But first there was a kid a floor below him who Max strongly believed wasn't going to make it through conversion without some help. Max laughed at himself. A part of him still wanted to save the world one kid at a time. Some things never change.

## CHAPTER 17

Tank was in the war room by the time Max got there. He usually ignored Max, but this time he glanced up. It was the first time Tank had bothered to acknowledge his existence since he'd been captured. Max figured he must be making some progress with the big guy.

Savior was starting to go bonkers in the cage. He'd ripped off his shirt and was screeching a continuous sermon mixed with a fair amount of creative profanity. Terry caught Max's eye and pointed toward the kitchen, meaning get Savior a drink. Max felt like he needed a drink himself.

As he walked into the kitchen, Max picked up a familiar scent and smiled. Jenna was leaning against the counter drinking a glass of red wine mixed with blood. No one else was there. No one was headed their way. Jenna cocked her head when she saw him. Max walked up to her, and took the glass out of her hand and put it down on the counter.

She looked at him questioningly and then smiled. He took her cap off and set it next to the drink. Max took her in his arms and planted the deepest, longest kiss he could manage. He cupped her breast and ran his hand down the length of her. Very slowly he started to pull away, but then she pulled him into another deep, long kiss and he felt her hand between his legs. Reluctantly they separated. Jenna put her cap back on. "Tonight?" she signed.

Max nodded. "Absolutely," he signed and said back. He watched her leave the kitchen.

"Absolutely," he said to himself. Max looked down at the bulge in his pants and realized he wasn't going anywhere for few minutes. He was glad he was alone. The best thing he could do was to think of other things. Like the poor kid who was going insane in the other room. Max opened the fridge and got a bag of blood out. As he made the drink he tried to focus on Savior and nothing but Savior. A couple times he caught himself smiling as his thoughts drifted to Jenna, but he dragged his mind back to the subject at hand.

He felt Chase headed his way, so he put the glass in the microwave and hit the button. Max grabbed the newspaper that was sitting on the counter and sat down at the kitchen table. He pulled out the sports section and opened it up so it looked like he was reading it.

Chase walked in. "How was training?"

"Lots of fun. Tank got to beat me up and I got up close and personal with the cement walls, the very thin mats and I think with the ceiling once or twice. Tank and I bonded. At least my face bonded with his fist, his foot, his elbow. Probably even his knee."

She chuckled. "Well, he's impressed with your marksmanship abilities."

"Next time, could we do that for three hours?" Max asked.

"He's going to take you out to his farm next week for a couple of days so you can work with our rifles. Also, I think you're going to prefer your hand-to-hand training without quite so many walls around."

"Even more fun."

"How would you like to go out on your first mission?"

"Really?" Max said.

"As an observer, of course."

"Great. When?"

"Later tonight."

Max hesitated for a moment. "Okay."

Chase looked amused. "Don't worry, Max. Jenna's going with us. You won't miss anything." She left him with his mouth open.

"I… I knew that." Max called after her. Nope, no secrets at all.

Max's bulge problem was gone, so he nuked Savior's drink for a few more seconds and took it out to him. The kid was throwing himself at the bars, spewing a mouthful of obscenities at any target he could find. When he saw Max he calmed.

"There he is! The one who threatens to teach that pathetic creature Savior how to lock ME away! I am the glory, you motherfucker! I am the resurrection! I am the demon God!"

"No, you're just the vampire," Max said. "I'm afraid you've got to let Savior talk to me if you want this blood. Otherwise, you can both just stay locked in the cage." Max realized everyone was pretending to be busy, but they were all watching him. This time he didn't mind an audience.

Savior squatted down and tilted his head. "Savior's dead. I killed him." He laughed as though he'd said something hysterically funny.

"Well then, there's no reason to keep you around anymore is there. Or to feed you. That would just be a waste of good blood." Max said. He took a sip of the drink in his hand. He felt his own thirst rise up.

"Wait!" Savior said confused. "That's mine!"

"I don't think so. It's Savior's. But if he's dead, well. Look, we'll make this quick. We've got another vamp just waiting to take your place. It'll be a quick one in the heart. You know, over before you even have time to worry about it. Besides there's some good money riding on you not making it past tonight… Hey Terry! Who's got that bet?"

"Rhonda has him checking out tonight," Terry said without missing a beat.

"There you go. Of course, I'll lose my money, but you can't win them all."

"Wait… wait… " Savior ran his tongue over his fangs and then shook his head as if trying to clear it. "You can't just kill me."

"Well, technically you're dead already. At least that's the theory. So if Savior's gone, I'm afraid there's not really much left to save." Max pulled up a chair just out of reach of the cage and sipped the drink. He really could have downed the drink himself, but there was a kid to save. He reined in his own vampire.

The kid was wide eyed and banged his fist against the bars. "Okay, he's not dead."

"Then let me talk to him, and if I like what he tells me, you can both have this drink."

"God damn it, you fucking bastard!"

"I'm just getting thirstier sitting here waiting."

Savior looked at him as though he was going to kill him, and then sat on the chair and started crying.

"Savior, talk to me," Max said.

"It hurts."

"I know."

"Why does it hurt so much?" he asked.

Max remembered Amanda. She'd asked him the same question. "The vampire's trying to control you."

"Can you make it stop?"

"No. Only you can."

He looked into Max's eyes. "I don't know how."

"We'll help you and you'll learn. Just like I did. Just like they did."

Max stood up and held the glass just inside the bars. Savior jumped up and looked from Max to the glass. He reached up and snatched the glass away from him. Savior was trembling as he brought the drink up to his lips and downed the contents. He dropped the glass and crawled back into his chair, curling up in a ball. He began to weep.

Max walked over to Chase and Terry. "Can we get him into the room before he freaks again?"

"Sure," Chase said. "You take him in."

"Really?"

"You wanted to work with him."

"Okay. Who's the entrée tonight?"

"That would be Shades."

"Lucky guy. What do you want me to do?"

"He hasn't responded to anything we've done. Just make him stop when he needs to stop."

Pete and Sheila were working on computers.

"You know, he's got a thing for Pete."

Chase just looked at Max.

"And, of course, I know you know that already, but somehow it just had to come out of my mouth anyway," Max said. "Let's go then."

Chase and Max walked over to the cage.

"Savior, how about a real meal?" Max asked.

Savior looked up. His eyes were wild, his face tinted red from his tears. "Are you going to kill me?"

"Not if you can make it to the bedroom."

He was hunched over from the pain and his arms were wrapped around his stomach. "I don't want to die."

"Then listen to what I tell you. When you step out of the cage, focus on the room. Don't look around or think about anyone or anything else. Just think about the room. Think about wanting to be in the room. That's it. Just think about it and you'll be there. There's no other source of blood for you anywhere except in that room. You make it there, you get fed. Both of you."

Savior looked at him. He looked terrified and crazy. He was barely hanging on by a thread. "The room… Okay."

Max and Chase positioned themselves in case Savior tried to take off on them. Jenna was standing next to Pete. Chase wasn't taking any chances. She keyed the code for the cage door.

Savior was staring at Pete. He put his hand on the cage door to push it open, but slowly he swept the war room with his eyes. When he stopped he was staring at the open door to the bedroom. Savior pushed the door open and stepped out, never taking his eyes off the door. "The room," Savior said.

In an instant, Max saw a blur as Savior rushed toward the room and disappear inside. Max inhaled deeply. He looked at Chase and then smiled. He remembered their deal. Max followed Savior into the bedroom and closed the door. No sooner had the door closed than Savior grabbed him and tried to bite him. Max pushed him down.

"Cut it out. You'll get dinner, but I'm not it."

Savior jumped up and looked angry. "I know what you want."

Max laughed. "Sorry, kid, you're not my type."

He looked confused. "You want that Jap bitch. I can smell her on you."

"That better be the vampire talking, because if that's Savior, we're not going to be friends anymore."

"Friends… that what we are, Max?"

"We could end up being friends."

"You gonna save me?" Savior challenged.

"Don't know yet, but I'll give it a shot. I did bet on you to make it."

There was a tap at the door and Shades entered. "Here are the rules, kid," Shades said. "You try and kiss me or touch me anywhere except my wrist and I'll rip your heart out. Got it?"

Savior just fumed at both of them.

"Answer him," Max said. He gave Savior a little slap on the back of the head.

"Okay!"

"The other rule is that when I tell you to stop, you stop. Got it?" Max said.

He started to slap him on the head again, but Savior pulled away. "Fuck you!"

"Not likely," Max said. Savior tried to fly at him, but Max knocked him to the ground again. He started to get up, but Max pushed him back down and put his foot on Savior's chest, pinning him to the floor. "You've got two choices. You can live or you can die. The vampire is nothing but an animal. It wants food, nothing more. So make up your mind… Do you want to live?"

Savior snapped at him and tried to pull him off balance, but Max stood his ground. The kid struggled against Max trying to hit him and do anything that might break his hold. Max pressed down with his foot and waited until Savior stopped fighting him.

"I hate you," Savior said.

"Sometimes I hate me too… What's it going to be?"

"Let me up."

"Say it," Max said.

"Let me the fuck up!"

"Tell me if you want to live or die." Savior started struggling, but gave up and started crying. "All you've got to do is say it."

"I want to live," Savior said softly.

"Good." Max lifted his foot and put his hand out to help Savior up. The kid ignored him and got up on his own.

Shades held out his arm. Savior grabbed it and bite down hard. "You get one bite, kid. You bite me again and I'm gonna rip out one of your fangs. Ever see a vampire with only one fang? It's a sad, pathetic sight… Say Max, you're a Cubbie fan, aren't ya?"

"Yeah, sure. What about you?"

"Oh, hell no. I'm a Dodger fan. You people from Chicago are crazy. They don't call them the Heart-Break Cubs for nothing. I'm surprised you can even bear to watch another season start."

"Wait a minute. They didn't do badly last season."

"Only a Cubbie fan would be happy the way that season ended."

"You're killing me…"

And they talked about baseball and football while Savior drank all he could manage. Shades was so cool and calm and unconcerned that it made Max feel calm too. When enough time had passed, Shades motioned to Max, who nodded.

"Savior stop!" Max shouted. The kid had no intentions of stopping.

"I said stop!" Max said again.

"This is the last warning! Do you want to live? I said stop!" Max slapped him hard on the back of the head and Savior pulled away. Anger dripped through his body and he looked like a snake about to strike out at anything that moved. As the blood began to ease his hunger, his body went slack and he crawled away from them to the corner of the room. Savior curled up into a ball and rocked himself.

The two men watched him and waited until he calmed. Shades got up.

"Thanks, Shades."

"Anything for the cause. Good luck with him."

Shades left the room and Max sat in the chair and waited. Eventually, Savior sat up but avoided looking at Max, as if he was ashamed of what he'd done.

"Do you still hate me?" Max asked.

"Savior doesn't want to do this anymore."

Savior buried his head in his hands. He was crying. Max got up and sat next to him.

"I'm so scared," Savior said.

"I know." Max put his hand on Savior's shoulder. They sat that way for a long time, neither moving, neither saying a word. Max could sense Savior's fear and the longing he had for the pain to stop. It was at that moment, surrounded by Savior's hopeless despair that Max figured out the "one thing" that just might keep Savior alive.

## Chapter 18

Max felt like a kid as he sat in the back of the van with Jenna, Tank, Shades and Father Frank. Terry was driving and Chase sat in the passenger's seat. He guessed that compared with the rest of them, he *was* a kid. He couldn't help being excited. He was on his first mission with the team, even if he was only an observer.

He was now an official member of the Corps and had the uniform to prove it. All the clothing was black with no tags or markings of any kind. A black jacket would conceal weapons until they were ready to use them. No one had identification on them and the van was black and had removable magnetic signs on the sides for Forever Bloom Flowers. It was beat up just enough to blend in. However, inside the van was decked out with weapons and state-of-the-art equipment. The license plate was legal, but untraceable back to Nightwatch or the Corps. It reminded him of the more covert stuff he'd done in the Army.

Max had fed before they took off, so he was feeling very good. He wanted to bounce around. He wanted to talk, especially to Jenna. He wanted to ask lots of questions. But he held himself back. He had to keep that professional thing going, no matter how much he felt like the little kid who wanted to ask, "Are we there yet?"

One thing did weigh on Max's mind, however. Savior had looked so sad and pitiful when he put him back in the cage, Max didn't know if he'd have the time he needed to turn the kid around. He was starting to formulate a plan, but he had to keep Savior alive in the meantime. And that might not be an easy task.

Father Frank and Shades were chatting away and didn't seem nervous at all.

"You did not know Billy the Kid," Shades said. Max's ears perked up.

"I'm telling you I met the man," Father Frank replied.

"You are so full of shit."

"True enough my boy, but I still met him. He was an ugly son of a bitch and mean as a snake too."

"Next thing you tell me is that you were the one who killed him."

"No, but I drank whisky with him one night. He was an insecure little shit, but he had talent with a gun," Frank said. Then he looked over at Max. "Somewhat like our newest recruit… Ever thought about taking up gunslinging, Max?"

"Can't say that I have. What about you, back in those days?"

"Well, I was a vicious killer, trained well by you-know-who, but why bother with guns? I wore them, mind you. Had to back then or you might as well have a target on your back, even for an honorable-looking preacher man like myself. Getting shot isn't fatal, but it's hell on the clothes. Actually, gunslingers were good eatin' back in those days. They liked to camp out alone or in small groups. No one would ever miss them. They were like cockroaches and people were glad when they were gone." Max noticed that as he talked a southern accent started to creep into his voice.

"But Billy the Kid?" Shades asked. "So what now? Billy the Kid, Winston Churchill and Elvis? I don't buy it."

"When you hang around long enough, why not? At a certain point, you just know that some people aren't just famous, they're what history is about. It's not that hard, really. I'd just do a little bit of detective work and make my way into a position where I could have a drink with them. Not to hurt them, just to… see what they were like. In fact, I was probably the first celebrity stalker."

"Next you're going to be telling me you met the Queen of England…"

Max was about to ask what it was like to meet Churchill when he realized he was staring at Jenna. She smiled at him and then looked away. Shades and Father Franks argued on, but Max lost track of their conversation. Jenna made him forget about history. Instead all he wanted to do was make new history with her. He knew it was no time to think about sex. Still, he couldn't help but notice the beautiful curve of Jenna's neck, the way Jenna's t-shirt clung to her breasts, and the slight glances she threw his way. Well, she definitely took his mind off Churchill and Savior. Max felt that stirring below, so he closed his eyes and took a couple of deep breaths. He certainly didn't want to go there before his first mission. Better to keep his mind focused.

They'd been briefed before they left. Basically, they were getting reports about an abandoned house and strange people in the neighborhood. There had been a couple of odd deaths in the area and they were going to check it out. They were unlikely to find Jade in an abandoned building, but they might find other vampires there. Or it might be a trap.

Max realized he was tapping his fingers on his knee to some frantic internal melody. It was a sure sign of nerves and he stopped suddenly. Father Frank glanced at him and laughed.

"Five minutes," Chase said.

Tank nodded, and for the first time looked at Max. "Here's the rules," he said. "You stay in the van with Terry. Use your senses to follow the action. No weapons... yet. Terry will arm you if necessary, but if they get through the rest of us you're probably dead anyway. Got it?"

"Got it," Max nodded.

Shades handed Max a tiny headset, which looped around the back of one ear and curved half way down his jaw. Everyone was putting theirs on, so Max followed suit.

They were in a poor suburban area on the outskirts of New York. Litter lined the streets, but that's not why Max knew it was a bad neighborhood. The owners of the small houses encased in barred windows and security doors had tried to lock out the violence of their world. The area had the sad desolate feeling of hopelessness that often descends on the most crime-ridden areas. The drug dealers on the corner didn't add to the ambiance either.

As they drove on, the houses got a little bigger and better kept. The yards were larger and the feeling of the area wasn't so claustrophobic. It was amazing to Max how a few blocks could make such a difference in the way people lived. It was a lot like Chicago in that way.

They drove passed the two-story abandoned house with boarded-up windows and an unkempt yard. The house had once been quite nice, but it looked like it'd been years since someone had cared about it. There was an unusually large yard and trees offered the house some privacy. The cars in the driveway and the light sneaking between cracks in the boarded windows betrayed the fact that someone was indeed home.

They drove by and around the block, stopping to park along the road just on the other side of the tree line. No one in the house would see them. The streetlights around the home were out, so there was little visibility for anyone without vampire eyes. Without a word, the team quickly exited the van. They barely made a sound, with only the muffled noise of doors opening and closing to betray their arrival.

Max crawled up into the passenger's seat and waited. Terry had a gun out and ready. Chase and the team stood near the trees and were sizing up the situation.

"Five hostiles inside with two humans, two out back alone," Chase whispered through his headset. Max watched as Chase pointed to Jenna and Tank and then to the rear of the house. They were being sent to take out the bad guys in the back. He knew from experience, no one would talk at this stage unless they had to. Sound was always risky.

Jenna and Tank took off in a blur. Max did as Tank suggested and reached out with his senses to follow the action. They crouched by the tree line for a moment and then Chase motioned for them to go.

Chase, Shades and Father Frank were beginning their approach from the front. The action in the backyard was happening so fast, Max was having trouble keeping track of what was going on. One of the vamps when down immediately and vanished from Max's internal radar. The other had avoided a bolt to the heart and took off. Jenna was in pursuit, but Max lost her. He tried to find her again, but she was out of his range.

He looked at Terry, a worried expression on his face.

"She's okay, Max. She can take care of herself," he said.

Max nodded and got back to the action. The attack from the front had started and Max could sense the chaos in the house as the vampires dove for cover or tried to reach their weapons. Two were killed immediately, but the other three were putting up a fight. Then one of them dove through a side window, right through the wood covering it, and Max realized he was out of the house and headed for them. Max didn't have a weapon, but he wasn't about to be a sitting duck. Terry nodded at Max and they both opened their doors to get out of the van.

The vamp looked like a biker, defined by leather, tattoos and long hair. And he was really pissed. When the angry vampire saw them, he raised his gun and started shooting at them on the run. One of the bolts whizzed by Max's ear and he dove to the ground in a roll, coming up on his hands and knees. Terry started firing back, but the vamp was moving fast. They were trading shots, so Max pushed himself up and flew at the vampire, tackling him, the two rolling one over the other until they crashed into a tree.

Max was stunned for a moment, but so was his opponent. He saw the flash of the gun and he went for it, the two struggling over the weapon. The vampire smashed Max in the chest with his fist and sent him flying backwards. Ending up flat on his back, he rolled onto his knees just as the vampire got a shot off. Suddenly his lower back was on fire and Max realized he'd been shot. Now he was pissed. Terry was rounding the van. He took a shot, but missed the vampire. The bad guy was distracted for just a moment, and that's all Max needed. He scrambled onto his hands and knees. Ignoring the pain, Max launched himself at the vampire again, breaking the branch of a tree off along the way and knocking his opponent to the ground. Max drove the large end of the branch into the vampire's chest as the bad guy was raising the weapon to take another shot. The vamp stopped, a look of total surprise on his face. The branch with its leaves still intact stuck out of him as if the tree was growing right through him. And then he turned to dust.

Max's back hurt like hell and he fell to the ground on his side. Terry and Chase were suddenly standing over him.

"Death by maple. That's a first," said Terry.

Chase knelt by him and pulled out the bolt. The burning eased.

"Good job, Max."

"I'll really be happy when people quit shooting me."

"Then you picked the wrong profession," said Chase.

"Sure, now you tell me."

"Come on, Max," said Terry.

He helped Max up and into the back of the van. Max reached out with his senses again and could tell it was all over. They were in mop-up mode. Two of the vampires had been captured, Father Frank was putting a victim into one of the cars in front of the house, and Chase was headed back to oversee things. Jenna was back at the house and helping with the clean up. That was the most important thing. She must have gotten her vamp.

He was relieved she was okay. In the past he'd been worried about her going out on missions, but now the danger was much more real. He knew he was going to worry about Jenna when she was on missions. In fact, he was going to worry about her a lot.

# # #

No one said much on the trip back. Both captured vampires were out for the count with Tank's "Goodnight Irene" juice. They'd be questioned later. There wasn't much at the house, so they'd gotten out of there as soon as they could manage it. Father Frank took the victims to the hospital. He'd ditch the car and vanish like a Good Samaritan.

It might have been his imagination, but Max thought the members of the team looked at him a bit differently. Even Tank. Maybe with just a little bit more respect in their eyes. Worry crossed over Jenna's face when she saw him and she checked out his injury.

"Did all of it come out?" she signed.

Max nodded.

She bandaged the hole in his back with gauze and tape. It still hurt, but the pain wasn't too bad by the time they got to headquarters. And there was something about the worried look in her eyes that made him happy. She was as worried about him as he was about her.

Max was hoping they'd have time for that "date," but the team had other plans. They took the elevator up to the roof. Now Max knew he was part of the team. He'd heard about these little after-mission parties, but he'd never been invited before.

The elevators opened into a glass room, with enormous glass doors that led out to a patio area. There was a bar, with plenty of comfy looking chairs and couches. Outside on the patio was a small pool and outdoor furniture. A brass railing lined the edge of the roof.

Jenna took his hand and led him out to the patio. It took his breath away to see the incredible view of New York City. It was alive with lights and movement, even at 1 a.m. in the morning. It was amazing. But when he looked into Jenna's eyes, he was only interested in a view that included her in it.

"You worried me," she signed.

"I was worried about you, too," he signed back.

She looked away for a moment, but then back at him and smiled. She reached up and ran her fingers through his hair. "I'm glad you're okay," she mouthed.

Max took her in his arms and kissed her.

"Hey, Max. You guys can cuddle up later. Come and join the party," Shades said. Max reluctantly broke the kiss and Jenna followed his glance toward the party room. She smiled mischievously and pulled him toward the party.

"Max, Terry says it was a thing of beauty. The maple tree. Who would have thought we could add an entire new weapon to our arsenal. Jade will never feel safe again," Father Frank said.

"You said you weren't good with hand to hand, but you never said anything about hand to tree," Terry said.

"Getting shot provides inspiration," Max said.

"Hurts like a son of a bitch, doesn't it?" Shades said.

"You betcha."

"Well, I guess you're an official member of the team," said Chase. She looked at him with approval.

"Does that mean I'm done with training?"

"Not on your life. But you did good. Congratulations." She raised her drink and they all did. "You stopped one of the bad guys today, Max."

Congratulations rang out and glasses and bottles clicked together. Everyone was happy for him, everyone but Tank. He sat away from the others, arms folded over his chest. Max knew he still had a long way to go before the big vampire was going to trust him, but he wasn't going to let it dampen his mood.

They chatted, argued and bragged, and for the first time Max did feel like he was one of them. Chase stayed just long enough to be social. It probably wasn't easy being the boss and being chummy with the team. Tank vanished shortly after she left. But then Rhonda and Nadine, along with some other vampires Max had seen, came up and joined the party.

It was the first time Max had seen Terry and Nadine as a

couple, and even though there was an apparent physical age difference, they somehow looked very right together. Max's eyes fell on Jenna. Well, 800-years-old to his 33. Now that was an age difference. She caught him looking at her and laughed her silent, beautiful laugh. She signed to him, "I'll be back in a little bit."

Terry followed Max's gaze as he watched her exit.

"Oh, man," Max said.

"Yep, she's special."

"So, what's the bet?"

"All right. You and Father Frank take turns and the first one to toss three beer bottle caps into the glass wins. It's $5 a cap."

"I think I should get a handicap. He's had more practice than I have."

"How do you know that?" Father Frank asked.

"I strongly suspect you've had more practice at everything than I have," said Max.

"See, Max here knows the score. How about Father Frank tosses the bottle caps and Max just shoots the glass," Rhonda said.

"No. Then I'm going to need a handicap," Father Frank said.

Everyone was laughing, having a good time. Max realized he hadn't felt this level of camaraderie since the Army. It was going from a life and death situation, to playing with bottle caps. He had missed that. Maybe it was the only thing he'd missed since he left the Army.

And he'd been right. Even with the handicap of being two feet closer to the glass, Father Frank had still won the bet. There were plenty of other stupid bets and Max didn't win a one. That is until Jenna came back.

She'd taken longer than he'd expected and when the elevator doors finally opened he knew why. She was wearing a killer floor length red dress with a slight oriental look to it, that was slit up to her thigh. Max just stopped and stared, and then he realized everyone was staring. The dress looked like it had been made for her and she couldn't have looked more sexy if she'd been wearing nothing at all. She was breathtakingly beautiful, her makeup accenting every feature of her face.

Jenna saw him and smiled. She held her hand out to stop the elevator doors from closing and waited. She'd dressed up just for him and he knew it.

"Sorry friends. Looks like I have a date," Max said.

"You are one lucky vampire, Max," Shades said.

"Absolutely."

Max never took his eyes off her as he joined her in the elevator and the doors closed. The slight smell of musk mixed with her natural scent filled him up. He took her in, every bit of her and then took her in his arms and kissed her neck. He was surprised when she pulled back and shook her head.

"Not yet," she mouthed.

When the elevator doors opened to the floor his room was on, she cocked her head and smiled. She took his hand and led him to his room. Max kissed her hand and stepped in to kiss her on the mouth, but she pulled away. She signed, "Take a shower and get dressed. You're taking me dancing."

Max laughed. He leaned in towards her, breathing in her scent again. She pointed sternly to the shower.

Max raised his hands. "Okay, okay. I give up. Dancing it is," he said.

In record time, Max was showered, groomed and dressed. Jenna waited patiently. When he was done and dressed in fashionable black with his boots, he twirled around. "Is this okay?" he signed.

She looked at him critically for a moment and then signed, "Just one more thing." Jenna retrieved Max's cowboy hat out of the closet and placed it on his head. "Perfect."

Max took her in his arms and gently kissed her. If she wanted to go dancing, he'd take her dancing. At that moment he would have done anything for her.

Jenna had a limo waiting for them, and they went to one of Chase's clubs, "P5". Max never thought of himself as much of a dancer, but Jenna made him feel like he was. The girl could dance even though she couldn't hear the music, no doubt about it. She touched him and he knew that helped her feel the rhythm of the music.

They laughed, they signed, and Max tuned into her silent world as if the blaring noise and the other people didn't exist. He didn't want to think about anyone but her. Didn't want to be with anyone but her. But as dawn approached they reluctantly parted to "take care of business." Max had gotten better at picking up girls and it didn't take long before his vampire was satisfied and he was back in the limo with Jenna. Part of him wanted to rip her lovely dress right off her body, but the other part didn't want to rush it.

As they sat next to each other holding hands, the city flew by. The driver was taking them to Jenna's apartment which was in the expensive part of town on 5th Avenue.

Max became aware that they weren't just holding hands. Their fingers were playing over one another, moving, touching, caressing. It was an unconscious movement that surprised him when he became aware of it. As they forgot about the world outside, they looked into each others eyes and Max realized that they could become much more than just lovers.

No words were spoken or signed. They didn't have to be. No games had to be played. Neither of them had to guess how the other felt. They just knew it. It was the most astonishing moment of his life. As a human lust happened often, but he had hoped for love, never really believing it would happen. And then suddenly at the most unlikely moment in his life she was right in front of him, a woman who would have died centuries before he'd even been born if not for the insane existence of vampires. A woman he never would have met if he hadn't walked down the wrong alley.

As if they'd been together for a lifetime, their lips came together and they kissed, ever so slowly, ever so gently. Max wanted their wonderful date to last. He wanted to hold onto it because tomorrow everything might change and the world as they knew it might end. He took her in his arms and held her, the overpowering tide of their emotions intertwining until he didn't know where her feelings started and his ended. Max knew whatever time he had with Jenna would be enough, whether it was one more day or if he was lucky enough to get 800 years.

Somehow, almost magically, they found themselves in Jenna's apartment. She led him to her bedroom and Max knew he should comment about how nice her apartment was, but he couldn't focus on anything but her.

There was no rushing either of them. As he touched her, he could feel her pleasure. She unbuttoned his shirt, kissing his chest as she made her way down to the last button. When he looked down he saw that her lipstick had left a trail of kisses straight down to his belly button. On her knees, she looked up at him as she unbuckled his belt.

She stood up and turned so he could unzip her dress. She wasn't wearing a bra, so as the dress fell from her shoulders Max wrapped his arms round her chest and played with her nipples. Jenna threw her head back as the pleasure of his touch shot through both of them. He kissed her neck without any thought of biting her. She turned in his arms to face him and pushed his open shirt off his shoulders. For Max, getting undressed had never been so sexy.

She had not a stitch on above her waist, but her dress hung forward, caught on her hips. Max eased the dress loose and held it for her to step out of. He carefully folded it over the back of a chair and then they came together in a deep, full kiss. Suddenly there was nothing cautious or careful about their movements. They acted as one, pulling off the last of their clothes, falling onto the bed, touching, kissing, driving each other into a sexual frenzy that lasted until the sun rose and they fell into each other's arms.

As Max held her, they lay awake but still. All his problems and worries escaped him, forgotten in the afterglow. He let it be. The problems would come back soon enough. Until then so long as they didn't move, Max was at peace.

## CHAPTER 19

It was late in the afternoon by the time Max and Jenna got back to headquarters. His feelings of peace flew out the window as Jenna left to attend to her work and Max took a look at Savior.

He was a rambling mess, alternately screaming and muttering to himself. He'd lost touch with his surroundings completely and began running into the bars of the cage, as if he didn't see them at all.

"Then the devil came to him and said, 'If you are God's Son, tell these stones to turn into peanut butter and jelly sandwiches!'" Savior screeched. He cocked his head at Max's approach. "What do you think about that, Max?"

"I always figured God was responsible for the peanut butter and jelly sandwich," Max said.

"Oh, the devil was very clear on that one."

"You don't look so good, buddy."

"The demon scratches away inside." Savior held his stomach. His voice fell to a whisper. "Savior wasn't a bad person. He married people and blessed them and... helped people when he could. No, he wasn't a bad person."

Max pulled up a chair. "I don't think you're a bad person."

Savior smiled. "You have no idea what I've done."

"Probably some pretty nasty shit, just like me before I found out there were ways to control to monster inside."

"Savior's not like you."

"You mean because you lived on the street and did what you had to to survive? We're more alike than you know... I'll get you a drink."

Savior shook his head. "It just doesn't help. Bad thoughts come and the demon possesses this body. And then I... Savior..."

"It does sound pretty crowded in there... Look, I know you've got your troubles, but we're short staffed." Max watched as Savior's face got even sadder. Now it was time to drop the boom, Max's "one thing" to see if this kid could be saved. "And I just thought you might want to help us out. I mean, you can sit here and have a go at the demon, or you can help us get through a stack of status reports. It's nothing exciting, but we could use the manpower. Jade always seems to be one step ahead of us. If we're going to defeat her, it's going to be because people like you helped out." Confusion spread across Savior's face.

"You want Savior to help you defeat the Queen Devil?"

"Yes, I want you to help us. Do you know much about computers?"

"Savior… I spent a lot of time in the library using their computers."

Max slapped his hands together. "Great. Is it something you want to do? You don't have to," Max said.

Savior stared at Max and then tentatively nodded his head yes.

"Okay then. It would help out a lot."

"Okay."

"One thing. While you're out here, if the vampire gets too powerful for you, let me know. You don't want to hurt anybody."

"It's hard," Savior said weakly.

"I know, but you have to let me know when it starts to get bad. Otherwise we can't let you out. Can you do that?"

"I think so."

Max stuck out his hand to shake Savior's. "It's a deal." Savior looked at Max's hand like it was a foreign object. He probably had never shaken anyone's hand before. Savior took his hand carefully and let Max do the shaking. "I'll go clear it with Chase."

Max headed to Chase's office. Convincing Savior may have been the easy part, but if Chase didn't agree Max would just give Savior work to do in the cage.

He tapped on her open door. She looked up from her work.

"Are you nuts?"

Max didn't even bother to ask how she knew what he was up to.

"The kid needs a purpose or he's not going to make it."

"Max, I'm going to have to have three people in there to watch him or I'm going to have to take the humans out altogether."

"Isn't one kid's life worth putting a couple extra people on? He's someone who never had a purpose in life until he became preacher kid. And now that's been taken away from him."

"And you think having him go through our status reports will do it?" Chase asked skeptically.

"We all need to feel useful. What future can he see right now? What reason does he have to get through this hell?"

Chase shook her head. "You're going to drive me crazy."

"Well, if that's my purpose in life…" Max shrugged.

"We can start him tonight after I've had a chance to get a couple more people down here. In the mean time, there are some reports he can go through in his cage. Just ask Nadine where they are and what needs to be done."

"You got it, boss," he said.

"One other thing, Tank's away. You'll be training with Jenna in an hour."

"Jenna?"

"You might want to stop smiling. She's going to kick your ass."

"I can't wait."

# # #

Max got Savior set up with the printouts. After spending a couple minutes with Nadine to fill her in on his plan, she went to work on Savior, telling him what she wanted him to do. The kid still looked a little unsure, but Max was very sure that this was his best chance at survival. Pile him up with work and make him feel important.

Max headed down to the basement. Two of the three cells

were filled with unconscious vampires from the raid the night before. They were guarded by a tough looking lady vamp Max knew only as Samuels. Like Shades, she wore sunglasses all the time which made her seem mysterious to him. She nodded when he entered, but then went back to reading her phone.

Rhonda was sitting on a stool, drinking a beer in the weapon's area. Max decided to join her while he waited for Jenna and his latest ass kicking.

"How goes it with Saint Savior?" she asked.

"I put him to work."

"Really. Doing what?"

"Going over some reports." Max took a beer out of the mini-fridge and opened it.

"Hummm. Well, I think we're going to have to call you Saint Jude, the patron saint of lost causes."

"Sure. Turn me into a vampire and then make me a saint. What's next?" Max shrugged.

"Probably you getting beat up by Jenna. At least that's the show I came down to see."

"Anything I can do to entertain. But I'll have you know Father Frank gave me a 5.8."

Rhonda laughed. "That's pretty good for a first time with Tank… So what do you think about all this, Max?"

"I don't know. Since I'm certain this is all a nightmare and my reality doesn't have evil blood-sucking vampires in it, I'm pretty cool."

"I've been waiting to wake up for a long time myself," Rhonda said.

"The world is so much bigger than I thought it was."

"Yeah. That must have been a surprise for a history teacher who thought he knew it all."

"You have no idea," he said. They both took a drink from their beers.

"Oh, I think I understand. I was a cop before. A hotshot detective. I was going to clean up the streets. You think you know it all, but then you walk down the wrong street."

"Boy, do I know that feeling," Max said.

"My partner got killed and I… well, I'm here."

"Better here than with the bad guys."

"I miss my life, Max."

"Yeah, walking in the sunlight, hanging out with friends, and… "

"Food… "

"Oh, yeah. Food. Cheeseburgers…" he said.

"And French fries."

"And spaghetti."

"And brownies," Rhonda said.

"Ooh, brownies were good. And strawberry cheese cake."

"And chocolate cake."

"And banana splits," he said.

"And banana splits."

Max closed his eyes for a moment, remembering. When he looked at Rhonda, she was nodding. "But you can't beat the superpower thing," Max said. "Faster than a speeding bullet, more power than, well maybe not a locomotive, but a motorcycle, and able to leap over bad guys in a single bound. And the healing thing. That is very cool."

"It doesn't suck," Rhonda said, and they both smiled at her joke.

"How long has it been for you?"

"About ten years… We aren't any further ahead than we were back then. There's been a lot of loss. Us, them, the humans. I guess I'm getting tired, Max. There are always more of them and there doesn't seem to be an end to it," she said, glancing at the unconscious vampires.

"Maybe that'll change."

Rhonda smiled. "I hope so. I'll tell you what, why don't you show me this amazing gunslinging superpower of yours."

Max nodded and got a couple of guns while Rhonda procured some plastic bolts for them to play with. They took turns shooting at targets and, while she was pretty good with a gun herself, having been a cop, Max didn't miss the bull's-eye after the first round.

They were still shooting when Jenna arrived and she watched them for a while. Max felt her come in but since she didn't stop them he figured it would be a good time for him to impress her. He looked back at her and winked.

Jenna didn't look impressed. She signed, "Show off." Max shrugged his shoulders. She gave a nod toward the workout area. As he looked at her, all dressed in black in a sleeveless t-shirt and sweat pants, he realized he wouldn't want to have his ass kicked by anyone else.

"Well, Rhonda, it looks like it's time for my girlfriend to show me who wears the pants in this relationship."

"As if there was any doubt." Rhonda smiled and took the weapons, heading off to put them away.

Max nodded and met Jenna on the workout mat. She signed, "I'm sorry."

"It's okay," Max signed.

"You don't understand. I'm going to be harder on you than anyone else. Learning how to master your abilities may be the only thing that may save you in the battles ahead. I want to give you every advantage possible. Unfortunately, that means this is going to hurt."

"You only hurt the one you..." For some reason he couldn't quite say the word "love" yet.

Jenna smiled. "Then this is going to hurt a whole lot."

Max laughed. "All right. Let's go."

As Max and Jenna faced off, he quickly discovered a couple things. First, Jenna was a great fighter. He'd thought Tank was good, but she was amazing. She was completely in tune with her body and she had the ability to anticipate whatever he was planning. She looked like something out of a Matrix movie. He expected her to start running up the walls at any moment.

Second, this really was going to hurt. Max spent more time

in the air than on the ground after the first few minutes. And while the flying through the air part was a little disconcerting, it was the landing part that caused all the trouble.

By the time they were done, Max had only tapped Jenna a couple times. He had, however managed to break his right arm and a couple bones in his foot. Still he was beginning to understand how to move his body and use his strength and speed to his advantage. Beyond that bumping into Jenna once in a while was way better than bumping into Tank.

# # #

After two hours of working out with Jenna, Max went up to his room to take a shower. He didn't mind when Jenna followed him up and offered to kiss all his formerly injured parts. It took a good half hour longer than it should have for them to get back up to the war room, but no one complained. Once again, as soon as Jenna left to attend to her duties and Max saw Savior, the smile left his face.

Savior was still going over the reports in his cage, but he was struggling to stay in control. His hand shook as he tried to make notes and squirmed in his chair, unable to sit still. Max quickly went off to get him a drink.

As Max returned, Savior's head snapped up. He smelled the blood and the vampire inside was ready. Still somehow Savior managed to hang on enough to pull away from the stacks of reports so he wouldn't knock them over. By the time Max got to him he was shaking all over.

"Savior, buddy, here you go." Max held out the glass just inside the cage.

Savior looked at him, but didn't speak. With both hands he reached for the glass and waited until Max let go. He closed his eyes for a moment and then released the vampire and downed the contents of the glass. Savior crumbled to the floor and rocked. Max waited until he'd recovered enough to sit up.

Savior's eyes were filled with pain as he sought out Max.

Wanting to be at the same level as the kid, Max stooped down.

"Hi," Max said.

"I… I went through 23 pages." Savior raised his shaking hand and pointed at the table he'd been working at. "I made… some notes, some things that… seemed suspicious."

"Good." Max realized Savior, for the first time, was referring to himself in the first person.

"I think I'm going to take a break," Savior said, shaking.

"That's a good idea. I'll get you another drink. You've got a couple hours to go yet."

Savior pulled his hair away from his eyes and nodded, the struggle etched into his young face. He handed the glass back to Max. "Then I'll work for a couple more hours."

Max nodded and got the kid another drink.

# # #

A couple of days passed and Max managed to observe on two missions without getting shot or shoving a maple tree branch through anybody's chest. On one mission they found a gang of drug dealers, who may have come from the worst end of the human gene pool, but they weren't vampires. Still, Chase did some surveillance and contacted her friends at the police department with a bit of inside information. The other mission led to a couple of lady vamps who were pretending to be hookers. One was killed and the other captured.

On their latest mission, it was Chase, Terry, Latrise and a couple vamps he didn't know very well, Mitchell and Michael, friends who liked to call themselves M&M. Again, his job was to observe. He watched with regret as Jenna left with Father Frank and Shades on a separate investigative mission.

On his way to the latest mission, Max's mind was on Savior. The kid was doing better, and at feeding time he was able to hold himself together long enough to get into the bedroom and stopped the second time Max had told him to.

Savior was positively happy when he found out he got to

242

stay outside the cage to work. There wasn't any doubt as to why there were three additional vampires between him and the humans, but Savior didn't complain. Instead he got behind a computer and did everything Natalie told him to do. Based on his first couple of days work, Savior appeared to be doing a good job on top of it all. For the first time, Max had hope that Savior might just have a chance.

Jenna was Max's other distraction. As he watched the scenery go by outside the back window Max worried about Jenna, but he had a feeling Chase had separated them on purpose. He didn't have much doubt that Chase would prefer to have him focusing on the progression of the mission, rather than whether or not Jenna was safe. It was a smart move on her part, especially while he was still learning. Still worrying about Jenna was probably going to be part of his new existence.

Their mission was to investigate a tip that had a dry cleaner doubling as one of Jade's training facilities. Chase believed Jade had small training facilities all over the country. Each facility would train up to six vamps at a time in the fine art of hand to hand, firearms and for Jade's amusement, the Saracian Lance. Chase's people had been able to shut down a few of these facilities, but each was set up as an isolated cell that didn't know any information beyond what was going on with that particular cell.

It was astounding to Max that he'd learned far more about Jade's operation now that he was on the other side than he'd ever learned during his nights in her company. With Chase continually hitting her operation, it was no wonder she was so testy when it came to the mysterious "war" he heard about during his stay with her. No doubt if he survived her attentions, she would have eventually shipped him off to a training facility to become one of her soldiers.

The dry cleaners was located in the heart of a busy street, but it was after hours and there wasn't much traffic, pedestrian or otherwise. Rather than their black ops clothing, they were wearing street clothes so they could blend in if necessary. As the van stopped a couple blocks away from the target, Chase and the group casually got out and headed up the street. Everyone wore jackets so the weapons were concealed. To outsiders they looked like a group of friends headed off for an evening out.

Once again Terry and Max stayed behind, with Terry in the driver's seat and Max right behind him.

"Where would you set up, Max? As a sniper?"

Max didn't hesitate. He pointed to a tall apartment building that loomed several streets away from their position. "Right there on the roof."

"Why not one of the buildings across the street from the target?"

"First, it's too close. They'd be expecting trouble from across the street and they might be able to sense me. Second, the apartment building is large enough a stranger shouldn't attract suspicion. Third, I could make the shot."

"You do that automatically, don't you?"

"Yep. When the Army trains you, you stay trained. It actually was extremely disturbing to find myself thinking that way as I headed off to school not all that long ago."

"With all the school shootings these days, I don't think I'd mind you being a teacher if I had a student in school."

"Don't think I didn't contemplate that," Max said.

Terry joined Max in the back and pulled the curtain. Terry turned on the tracking equipment in the back. They were too far away to count on their internal radar. Terry and Max put on headsets and waited. The group wouldn't put their headsets on until they were far away from human eyes to avoid detection.

There was a crackle over the headset, which meant they were in position. Max watched the tracking screen and the five blips, which represented the tracking devices on their people. If a tracking device vanished, somebody was dust.

Suddenly the headset came to life.

"Terry, nobody's home. It's empty," said Chase. "I'm going to do a sweep to make sure there aren't any bombs before we head in."

"Roger," Terry said. He flipped the microphone away from his mouth so he could listen without being heard. "You asked me a question a while back, Max, and I'm going to give you an answer. I didn't know you before and sure wasn't going to trust you. But you've earned it."

Max pulled his microphone away from his mouth too. "I don't need you to tell me any secrets."

"Who makes us into what we are is personal, private. But I want you to know, 'cause it's not what you think. I've never met Jade and only seen her handiwork. There's been plenty of that. It was Chase who made me."

"Why? Was she…"

"What? An evil bitch like Jade? No. It was the 60s and I was enjoying free love and the Age of Aquarius, if you know what I mean. Sex, drugs, oh man, it was a great time. We were so young and stupid. AIDS didn't exist. We were going to save the world with love… all the while getting high and getting laid. There has never been anything like it before or since… I was at Woodstock." Terry smiled.

"Woodstock? Wow. I would have loved to have experienced that."

"It was grand and then it was over. And just as the world started crashing down on us I ran into one of her people, someone a lot like Savior. He was crazy and decided I was dinner. The bastard attacked and started ripping me to shreds. It was like being mauled by a lion and feeling yourself being eaten alive. I just kept thinking, 'I am so fucked.' And then he was gone and I knew I was dying. I remember seeing Chase standing over me and there was a light behind her, which made her look like she had a halo. I thought she was an angel," Terry said.

"Maybe she is."

"I don't know. Maybe. But what I do know is that she

saved my life by turning me into a vampire. That and she killed the bastard that attacked me."

"So she killed you to save you." A brush of amusement touched Max's lips and they both broke out laughing.

"Yeah, that's about right," Terry said.

"You've seen a lot of history."

"The kind they don't put in history books."

Chase's voice came over the headset. "We're going in."

Terry pulled his microphone back into place. "Roger."

Max could hear commotion as they broke the door and entered the building. A couple minutes passed and they were silent while they watched the team advance on the tracking monitor.

Mitchell's voice, "They were here, but they left in a hurry."

Latrise's voice, "Looks like we've got at least a couple dead vampires, based on the dust piles."

Chase's voice, "There's another one over here. Probably three. We've seen this before. They clear out and get rid of the one's that aren't performing well… Terry, we're secure here."

"Roger," he said. "Do you want us to help search the place?"

"No. Stay put for now," Chase said.

"Will do."

Suddenly Terry looked over Max's shoulder as if he was using x-ray vision to look through the wall of the van. Then Max sensed it too. It was vampire, not far from their position and it wasn't one of their vampires.

Terry handed Max a gun, a real gun with real wood and steel bolts, and grabbed one for himself. The vamp was on the move and Terry pulled open the back door and jumped out. Max followed him, tucking the gun inside his jacket. Only a handful of people were on the street, but they didn't need anyone calling the police.

"Chase, we've got company, but only one in sight," Terry

said.

Chase's voice, "I'm on my way."

The vampire saw them and ran, bolting into an alleyway. The vamp was small, maybe a boy or a small woman, but Max couldn't tell because they wore a hooded sweatshirt. Max and Terry ran into the alley, but the vamp was gone. Max let his sense sweep out and caught the scent inside one of the buildings. It was an old, abandoned store and Max, with Terry right behind him, ran toward the side door. Max put his weight on the door and it gave in. The place had been a clothing store, and was filled with racks, boxes and garbage.

The vampire was running, but not very fast. She – Max was sure it was a she at this point – didn't appear steady at all. Max thought it might be a trap, but he couldn't sense anyone else around. She tried to jump over a box, but her foot got caught and she went crashing to the ground. Max came to a skid to keep from running over her.

She rose up and hissed at them, the hood on her jacket falling back. In life, she'd been a young black teenager, maybe 16. But now she looked like an animal. Her eyes were wild, her hair was matted and her skin transparent, the veins underneath looking as if they were ready to pop right out of her body.

"Oops. Chase, we've got a zombie," Terry said.

## CHAPTER 20

"A what?" Max looked from the girl to Terry. She was on her hands and knees, but looked as if she might attack at any moment.

Terry started moving to the side and Max realized he was trying to give the girl as little room for escape as possible.

"Let me alone!" she yelled in a scratchy, rough voice. "I didn't do nothing to you." She was ready to run.

"Look, miss, we don't want to hurt you," Max said.

She laughed bitterly, and kept an eye on both of them. She still had an escape route behind her and Max saw her glance back. "You're like them."

"We're not…"

She sniffed the air. "Oh, but you are. You eat people."

"Max, she's been living on animal blood. This is what happens…" Terry said.

"You're just cannibals."

"We don't kill people," Max said. "We're not like them."

"But you have."

Max sensed Chase's presence, but she hung back and waited.

"I don't anymore. I know better know. We're fighting against those that do."

Confusion spread across the girl's face and she closed her eyes for a moment. "You're a liar. I smell people inside you! You can't make me be like you… you can't. I won't do it!" She started to scramble backwards. Instead of going after her, Max crouched down so he'd be less threatening.

"I'm not going to make you do anything to harm a human being. We don't have to kill to survive."

"Liar. Murderer," she started crying.

"I know it's not easy to trust one of us. But did any of those that did this to you ever stop to try and talk to you? If we were like them, we'd just kill you."

She shook her head and scooted back another step. "No… I… I don't believe you."

"At some point, you have to trust someone. If you run away from us, where are you going to go? Who else is going to be able to help you?"

She shook her head, anguish rising up through every pore of her body. She looked at Max and Terry, and off in the direction where Chase stood behind them.

Terry crouched down like Max. Her head snapped in his direction. "If you don't let us help you, eventually the vampire inside you will take over and you won't be able to do anything about it. You'll become the thing you've been fighting," Terry said.

Max stood very slowly. He held out his hand. "Please, let us help you."

She broke down crying, but then her eyes got hard. The girl twisted around and launched herself away from them at the only exit she had left, but Max was ready. He thought about her and suddenly found himself with his arms around her waist. She struggled, her body tense. He could feel her anger and confusion, but it drained into sorrow, her body surrendering to him. He eased her down to the ground and held her as a father might hold his suffering child, stroking her hair and rocking her. Max looked up at Terry, questioning.

Terry shook his head ever so slightly. Chase came out of the darkness. "We'll try, Max. We'll try," she said.

# # #

Max sat with the girl in his arms while Terry and Chase went to finish up at the dry cleaners. The girl cried a steady stream of tears. Since he knew she could feel what he was feeling, he focused on hope as his feeling of choice, praying he could transfer as much of that as possible to the girl.

"I'm Max. What's your name?" he asked after her tears had slowed.

She didn't answer at first. She looked up at him and their

eyes met. "Becca."

"Hi, Becca."

"Hi." She sniffed and looked at the shoulder she'd been crying on, and the wet spot on his t-shirt. "Your shirt's all wet."

"It's okay. It's just a shirt. It will dry."

She smiled, tears still in her eyes. Terry walked in and she sunk down as far as she could manage into Max's arms.

"We're almost ready. I'm going to pull the van up."

"Okay."

Terry walked out.

"Becca, we're going to take you to a place where you'll be safe."

"You promise?"

"I'm not going to lie to you. What you'll have to go through won't be easy. But as long as you don't try to harm a human, yeah, I promise you'll be safe."

Uncertainty took hold of her, but she nodded once. She let Max pull her up so that they were standing. He let go of her and took a couple steps toward the exit, holding out his hand to her. Becca looked at it and then back toward the exit which might offer escape. She hesitated, and then a resignation came over her. Accepting whatever fate he had in store for her, Becca took his hand. He remembered Amanda taking his hand in a similar fashion a thousand years before when Jade made him make that last terrible choice of victim. He forced those feelings away. He didn't want Becca to pick up on them. They walked out of the building, through the alley and toward the van.

Max was scanning the area to make sure the coast was clear of humans, but something else caught his attention. Someone was on the roof coming towards their position… in fact lots of someones and they were vampires.

Instantly Max's world went into slow motion. He heard the shot and saw a bolt racing toward the girl. Max pulled her out of the way, spinning them around, but he was moving in slow motion too. Pain ripped through his left shoulder as the bolt struck.

A volley of bolts rained down toward them. Max scooped the girl up with his good arm and raced toward the van, but he could only watch as Micheal took a hit in the chest and vanish into dust. It was a trap, but Max could sense Becca didn't know about it. She was as surprised as he was.

Chase grabbed Terry and threw him in front of the van to the safety of cover, taking a bolt to the stomach. She ripped the arrow out and raced through the open door of the dry cleaners, vanishing into the depths of the building. Max and the girl flew into the open door of the van and out of sight of the attackers. A couple of bolts pierced the side of the van, landing in the seat next to Max. Another killed Terry's state-of-the-art surveillance equipment and then the passenger window of the van shattered, showering glass everywhere.

Latrise was pinned down at the door of an office building one building down. Mitchell was hunkered down in front of the van with Terry, and everybody was shooting at everybody.

The bolt in Max's shoulder felt like it was going to burn his arm off. He ripped it out.

"Max, get in the driver's seat," Terry yelled. Max tucked a terrified Becca between two seats and jumped into the driver's seat. The van was running, so he threw it into gear and eased it forward trying to get his team to safety. Terry and Mitchell walked backwards, using the van for cover and taking shots when they could. Max saw Latrise race out toward the van, making a run for the open side door. Two arrows struck her, one in the leg and she went down. The next one took her heart and she turned to dust.

Max looked up at the roofs to the side of them and realized they were about to be surrounded. The bad guys were leaping from roof to roof to get ahead of them. They only had moments before any chance at escape was cut off.

"Terry, Mitchell, grab hold of the front. We gotta go!" Max

yelled. Both men grabbed the windshield wipers and jumped on the bumper and Max took off. Bolts rained down on them, several ripping through the van's exterior. One came through the back window and curtain, hitting Max's other shoulder from behind. He screamed and then saw Mitchell stick his head out to make a shot and take one through the throat. Mitchell lost his grip, but Terry grabbed him with one arm and hung on with the other.

Max gunned it, and they were a moment from getting away. Then the bad guys started aiming for the tires and the passenger side front and rear tires blew. The momentum the van had worked against them, and Max fought to keep control of the vehicle. He clipped a parked car on one side of the road and overcompensated sending the van into a mailbox on the other, launching it onto its side and crashing through the front window of a real estate office.

Moments passed. Max knew he was alive, but his right shoulder felt like it was on fire and lots of places on his body hurt. His leg was broken and God knows what else. When his head finally cleared he realized he was lying in a heap against the passenger side door, covered with glass and blood from the cuts which covered him. The van was on its side and every window was broken. Bolts were still flying, but the undercarriage of the van proved more impenetrable than the sides, roof and windows.

He looked out the front of the van into a nice cozy real estate office with several desks which, fortunately for the people who worked there, was closed for the night.

Max had lost track of Terry and Mitchell when he sideswiped the first car. For all he knew he ran over them and Max was all that was left, except for Chase, who no doubt was fighting her own battles considering the strength of Jade's forces.

Max tried to move his leg, but pain radiated through him. The bolts were continuing in force and they had to get moving if they were going to survive.

Max looked around for the girl. But suddenly she was right there looking at him with her blue tinged eyes, her nearly transparent skin exposing the oddly beautiful mosaic of her the veins, muscles, fat, and all the things that make people up on the inside.

"You've got to get out of here. They're going to overrun our position," Max said. He threw out his senses and knew several of the bad guys were headed their way. Max reached behind him to pull out the arrow, but it was wedged in too deep. He gritted his teeth and yelled at her. "Now! Move it. Run or they will get you."

She looked back and then shook her head. "Come on. I can carry you."

She jumped through the window and then pulled him out easily. His leg twisted, making him scream again, but the pain eased when she threw him over her shoulder and the leg straightened up. He couldn't imagine what someone looking on might think. She was tiny and he was six foot tall. His hands almost touched the floor behind her. Max had grabbed the gun with his one good hand and got ready to use it.

Becca jumped over a desk and headed to a hallway. They found an office, a bathroom and a closet, but no back door or any windows which might offer escape. She turned around so she was looking out at the main office. Max could feel the panic rising in her. She knew they were coming.

"We've got to go through the wall," Max barked. Becca looked back at his face and nodded. Becca took a delicate fist and smashed it into the wall. The dry wall gave way to a fist sized hole.

Then they both stopped, concentrating on what was happening outside their fortress. Max threw his radar out as far as it would go. The bolts slowed and finally stopped. Jade's forces were disappearing one by one.

"Put me down," Max said, his voice rough with pain. Becca set him down carefully, but pain shot up his leg. "Shit!"

Max managed to keep an eye on the very large hole the van had made in the front of the office. His leg was already starting to heal even though the bone wasn't set properly. His shoulder was another story.

"Help me." Max nodded moving forward and put his arm around her shoulder. She grabbed his waist and helped him walk into the office. Most of the vampires were gone. He sensed two close by, but they might be Terry and Mitchell. Besides that there were a few other scattered around, along with a couple humans who were tucked away from the action. Max had the gun ready as they peaked outside. Glass, debris, and bolts littered the street, with most of the bolts broken or sticking in something. The few cars along the curb were messed up and the van had taken out the mailbox, a lightpost and part of a building. It was going to be one hell of a clean-up job.

Max held his gun ready as they popped into the opening where the office window had once been. The two nearest vampires were across the street. He found his gun trained on Terry, who was leaning over a fallen Mitchell, he pulled the bolt out of his throat. Max pulled back his gun and looked for targets, but they were all gone… except one. Up on top of the roof across the street Chase came into view.

Max hadn't realized he still had his headset on until he heard her voice. "Get out of here. I'm going after the ones that escaped."

Then she was gone.

## CHAPTER 21

One thing about the Corps, they were always prepared. Before Max and Becca could reach him, Terry was on his cell phone calling in the clean-up crew. Max knew only that they were humans, cops and other city officials, who made sure any evidence of a vampire battle vanished. A couple of humans had witnessed some of the battle, but the rest had run. The witnesses would be interviewed by Corps people who could determine if they needed to be brought into the organization, their nice normal lives forever gone with the knowledge that vampires really did exist.

"Can you walk? I've got car a block over," Terry said.

"Yeah, but I've got a bolt in my shoulder."

"It's too deep for me to pull out easily. Can you hang on?"

Max nodded. The pain was incredible, every bit as intense as the vampire raging through his gut insisting he kill someone. He wanted to scream and yell and cry like a baby until someone pulled the fucking thing out of him. But the area was going to be swarming with people in a matter of moments. Crying like a baby would have to wait.

Max was a mess, but the cuts on his face had already healed. While Terry was helping Mitchell up, Max wiped his face with his ruined t-shirt and, with Becca's help, zipped up his tattered black bomber jacket, which would hide the evidence from human eyes. Becca pulled up her hood. From a distance they shouldn't be too conspicuous.

"Mitchell, you okay?" Max asked.

He nodded, but his head dropped. He knew what had happened to Michael.

"He can't talk yet," Terry said. Max could see the hole in Mitchell's throat.

They started off down the street, not too quickly. As they rounded the corner the first police car went speeding by. While they only had a block and a half walk, Max could feel his leg healing badly. That meant they were going to have to rebreak it, that and he'd have two more holes in his body for a couple of days. While the experience of getting shot had long since lost its appeal, he'd survived. Latrise and Shades were occasional lovers and Michael and Mitchell as M&M had been with the Corps for a very long time. There wouldn't be any celebration party after this mission.

# # #

Terry removed the bolt with pliers when they got to the car and Max managed to keep the crying to a minimum. Becca stayed close to him, but Max could feel her fear, that and the vampire fighting her for dominance.

The bone in Max's leg knitted together incorrectly, leaving him with a limp by the time they switched cars. Terry took his time and checked Becca for a tracking device. It took another hour of driving and another car switch before Terry felt comfortable about heading back to the headquarters.

Repairing the injuries took up any spare resources Max had, bringing his own vampire to the forefront. It rose up, reminding him that the animal within wanted to eat and it would be very happy to take any human that came along. The vampire was always right there threatening to turn him back into a monster who could kill women and children. He'd been able to control it by feeding well every day, and by remembering his father's face as he loomed over Max that last moment of his life. Max closed his eyes and saw the twisted anger and rage, the monster ready to go after any target that presented itself. As Terry pulled into the high-rise garage, Max opened his eyes with resolve. His fangs had come out. He pulled them back and pushed the vampire down. He wouldn't do it. He could never let his father win. He'd killed that fiend many years ago, and he wasn't about to let his father's rage take hold of him again.

Becca was hunched next to him, terrified, hiding under her hooded jacket. Terry had called her a zombie, a vampire who lived on animal blood. Max could feel that there was something different about her beyond the way she looked. She was struggling, much like Savior and Max himself had been, but it was different with her. She was almost like an animal in her movements, but when Max looked into her blue tinged eyes, he knew intelligence had never left her. She was in control of the vampire. Unfortunately, based on Chase's comment in the abandoned store, Becca's chances didn't sound good.

Max knew she could feel his struggle, so he reached deep to make the nasty feelings go away. Almost immediately, he sensed her calm somewhat. For whatever reason, she trusted him enough to go with them. She'd even risked her life to save his.

By the time they pulled into the parking garage, Max knew he'd fight for Becca the way he'd been fighting to save Savior. Max would do whatever he had to to keep the Amandas of the world from running into creatures like him. If he could, it was worth broken legs, getting shot and whatever else came his way.

Max got out of the car limping badly. Becca scooted out after him and stayed near.

Terry took a quick call and then walked over to Max.

"Chase beat us back. Max, go see Dr. Felton on the 12th floor. She'll take care of your leg," Terry said.

"Can we put Becca up in my room for the moment?" Max asked. He didn't want to see her end up in a cage.

Terry hesitated for a moment. "Sure."

Max touched the girl's shoulder and looked into her eyes. "Terry's going to take you to my room. There is a lock on the door, but I'll be up just as soon as they fix my leg. No one's going to hurt you. Right, Terry?"

"Right." Terry sounded convincing to both of them.

"I won't kill anyone for you," she said.

"The blood we drink comes from volunteers, partners. No one is killed or harmed. We're not like the others." Max let determination and hope flow through him giving her as much as he could manage.

Becca looked like she might pass out for a moment. "I don't know if I can do this."

"We'll help you."

# # #

Dr. Mary Felton turned out to be a long-legged human brunette. She was the kind of girl he would have gone for a million years ago when he still had a day job. She poked his leg for a bit and then nodded.

"This is going to hurt."

"Why do people keep telling me that?"

"This doesn't look like a simple break. I'll take an x-ray so I can spend a minimal amount of time inside fixing the damage, but there aren't any drugs I can give you which will ease the pain. The only other choice is to knock you out, but then you'll be out for days. The better choice is to get you fed, which should take some of the edge off. Lucky for you, recovery time is measured in minutes and not months."

"Damn, I was hoping to at least get a nice vacation out of this," Max said. The pretty lady doctor didn't smile.

"It's an operation without anesthesia. You'll have to be restrained. The pain will be extreme."

"Don't sugar coat it, Doc. Give it to me straight."

"Vampires are very hard to operate on. You heal almost instantly, but that can be a problem when we have to spend some time making repairs."

"Cool. Let the healing begin." Max gave her his most charming smile.

"And worse, if I touch you, I feel what you feel."

Max let his smile fade. "I'm sorry."

"I don't like vampires, Mr. Maguire. I'm here and I'll do the operation with the hopes that someday what I do will help you save human lives. Got it?"

"Yeah."

"Good. I'll have everyone I need here in about 15 minutes. We'll get that x-ray in a few minutes. Take off your pants, shoes and socks, please." She walked out without a glance back at him. Max couldn't blame her. If he was her, he wouldn't like vampires either.

Max was sitting in her office in his bloody t-shirt and underwear feeling pretty self-conscious when Jenna walked in. She looked at him sternly, but it didn't matter. There was a huge smile on his face.

"I thought you were going to stop getting shot," she signed. Jenna pulled at the neck of his t-shirt to get a look at his latest bolt holes. She started to sign again, but he pulled her close and kissed her.

"It's good to see you," he signed. She smiled until she felt his pain.

"You're hurt," she signed.

"It doesn't matter," he said, but then Max got serious. "There's a girl in my room. Terry called her a zombie."

"I heard," she signed.

Max was going to ask her about the odds of saving a zombie, but he decided against it. He didn't want to know the odds. "Can you check on her for me? Help her learn to trust us?"

She nodded. As Jenna was about to leave Max pulled her into another kiss.

Luckily for him, the doctor returned quickly otherwise she might have caught them in a really embarrassing situation. Dr. Felton quickly kicked Jenna out and went into gruesome detail telling him exactly what she was going to do and why it was going to hurt like hell. Something about strapping him down, slicing him open and then reslicing as she fought to keep the flesh from healing while she pieced together the bone fragments in his leg.

Max discovered the worse part about it all was she hadn't been exaggerating one bit.

# # #

A couple of hours after the most excruciatingly painful moments of his life, Max walked as though he'd never broken his leg. The good doctor had managed to feel his pain literally more than once during the operation, and Max gained a good amount of respect for the woman.

Terry had arranged a meal before and after the operation for him, so Max was in good shape by the time he finally sat down with Chase and the others for the debriefing.

"Something big is going down," Tank said. "Jade could have done more damage than she did."

"Two of our people were killed. That seems like a lot of damage to me," Max said.

"Of course, Max," Chase said. "But we've been doing this long enough, we know this could have been much worse. Even leaving the girl behind to distract us…"

"Becca," Max said.

"Becca… Something big is about to happen and I don't know what it is."

Jenna tapped the table lightly to get everyone's attention. "We should hit back to keep them busy. We should take out Newport before they can mount another attack," she signed.

"I agree," Eugene said.

"All right, but let's reexamine the reports. We're missing something. In the mean time, Tank you take Max out for a little target practice. Make sure he's ready." Max was pretty sure he knew what they wanted him to be ready for and it had to do with his shooting abilities.

Tank low growl said it all, about how he felt about the idea. He took a breath and then nodded.

"What about Becca?" Max asked.

"Well, we'll try to get her on human blood, but if she doesn't trust us it's going to be difficult… Talk to her before you go," Chase said.

"I'll get Savior to help me." Max started to get up and then realized everyone was staring at him. "What?"

Terry and Eugene were laughing. Tank growled. "If you can manage it, go for it Max," Chase said.

Max knew they thought he was crazy. But in fact St. Max,

the patron saint of lost vampire causes, had an idea.

# # #

Max found Savior at a computer, compiling reports for Nadine. The kid looked so relieved to see him.

"They said you were hurt."

"I'm fine. It was just a scratch."

"I… I can still smell your 'scratch.'"

Max smiled. Savior was no dummy. "Unfortunately, with wood and steel bolts, holes are part of the deal. It will heal in a couple of days."

"And others died."

Max nodded. "It's a war, Savior… How are you doing?"

"Better. Savior… I like having something to do. Nadine is nice. Tank…"

"I know." Max bent down and whispered, "He's not a happy fellow."

Savior laughed. It was probably the first time Max had seen the kid happy.

"Look, you've been a great help here." Max hesitated just a moment. "If you're willing, I could use help with something else. We still need the reports done, but I thought maybe…"

"I'll help you," he said. "I'll help you with anything, Max."

Max patted him on the shoulder. "Good."

After he was done filling in Savior, Max went to Chase's office. Savior was the easy part. The rest would be a bit more complicated.

She gave him that look, but didn't ask him if he was crazy this time.

Chase shook her head and then laughed. "Okay. Try it."

Max left before she changed her mind and ran off to gather up Savior.

As Max and Savior rode the elevator to Max's room where Becca was waiting, Max could sense Savior's uncertainty.

"Now remember, she needs your help. I'm going to be

gone for a couple days to do some training and it's going to be up to you to see her through. Her life is at stake, Savior."

Max put his hand on Savior's shoulder. He could sense the kid's resolve take hold. Of course, he hadn't told Savior about his trip to see Becca when he asked for her help. He'd told Becca he was working with a young man who he worried might not make it. It was all true, but his evil plan was to get both kids to help each other. And since Becca was straight and Savior was gay, he didn't have to worry about sex getting in the way.

Max keyed the code on Becca's door and ushered Savior in to the room.

Becca was sitting neatly on the bed, a full cup of blood before her on the dresser. She was still wearing the hooded sweatshirt and they couldn't see her face at first. Then she turned to look at them. Savior gasped slightly, but then he smiled.

"Wow," he said. "You look so cool."

"Do I? I can't stand to look at my reflection anymore."

"Why does she look like that, Max?"

"Becca's different."

"Because of the blood thing?"

"Yeah."

Savior turned to her. "Well, I think you look cool."

"Thanks," she said shyly.

"My name's Savior."

"Becca."

Well, that was it for the small talk. Silence took over the room.

Max went to the dresser and picked up the glass of blood. It was cold.

"I can't drink it," she said.

"I know. Let's all go on a little tour."

Eugene was waiting for them when Max opened the door. Max tagged along to protect Eugene if necessary, but Eugene was in fine form as he introduced the kids to some of the volunteers. Other vampires hung covertly in the background along the path.

Max had to admire Eugene and the others. Several of them reached out and shook Becca and Savior's hands. They were fearless. Max decided that the tour should be on every newbie's "to do" list.

Max also had to admire Becca. He could feel the battle that raged within her skin, and yet she was able to control the vampire.

After the tour, Max took them back to Max's room.

Becca looked terrified. Max could tell that despite meeting the volunteers and hearing their stories and despite meeting "the good guys," feeding felt wrong to her.

"Becca, you have to. If you don't the vampire will eventually destroy your mind and you'll be lost. Everything about who Becca is will be gone," Max said.

"Maybe you should kill me then."

"That would be a waste."

"Why am I different than you? Than him?" she nodded toward Savior. He stayed silently in the background.

"The truth is, you're a better person."

"What?"

Max pointed to her heart. "Every bit of who you are thinks that this is wrong."

"Don't you?"

Max wanted to laugh. He looked at this amazing young girl and realized he'd given in so easily with Jade. Becca was a thousand times better person than he'd ever been.

"Yes," Max said. "It took me a long time to come to terms with the vampire."

"Then why do it at all?"

Max was formulating an answer when Savior stepped forward. "Because the Devil Queen is killing people and making vampires who don't care about human life the way you do. Max told me if you don't drink, eventually the beast will consume your mind and then you'll be just like I was when they found me. You'll be just like her. You'll be an instrument of evil and who you were will be gone forever. If you die, if Max dies and the others, there will be no one around to protect the human race."

Becca started crying. "I can't…"

Max stepped back as Savior sat down next to her. "Becca, you're the best of us. Don't you see?"

Savior put his arm around her and she leaned against him, crying silently. "Why didn't God just let me die?"

"He has plans for us," Savior said quietly.

It took another hour, but eventually Becca fed from Savior. Of course, then Savior needed a meal, but Max had it all worked out. As dawn approached, Max sat Becca down with Savior to work on the reports. Becca had a chance, Savior had a new mission and Max had hope that his "lost causes" might not be lost after all.

## Chapter 22

Max woke up the next day with Jenna curled up in his arms, surrounded in blankets in her big comfy bed. He breathed in her scent, his mind completely blank of any thoughts except how good she felt.

She stirred slightly, rubbing against parts of him that were so happy for the movement. Her eyes fluttered open and looked directly into his. A sleepy smile spread across her face. Without a sound her lips captured his name perfectly. "Max."

"Good morning," he said. Their lips met and Max's tongue entered her mouth. He explored the soft insides of her mouth, their tongues sliding back and forth against each other.

Max pulled away and looked at her. There was no question what she wanted. He could feel her desire. Max ran his hand across her breasts. Jenna arched her back, but she never took her eyes off him. Max kissed her again, almost chastely.

But then Max licked her neck. He used his nice normal teeth to capture her earlobe and sent shivers down her body.

Jenna's fingers outlined his thigh in a caress. As Max's tongue worked his way down her body, he could feel the pleasure she felt. Max was more than ready, but he took his time. It was his erection and he was going to hold on it for as long as he could manage.

Max teased each of her nipples into an erection of their own, one by one. The only sound she made was the occasional gasp as his tongue hit its mark and her body trembled beneath him.

Max put his hand between her legs and Jenna's back arched again as he licked her stomach. Max's finger found just the spot that made Jenna's breathing quicken. Max scooted down and let his tongue do things for her that a finger never could quite as well.

She was close, but neither of them were ready for the moment to end. Jenna grabbed a handful of Max's hair yanked his head up. Max smiled hungrily at her and she laughed. Then she gave him her own hungry look. Jenna sat up and pushed Max down on the bed.

She got on top of him and for the first time touched his cock. The pleasure rode through both of them. Jenna's expert hands knew exactly what to do with a cock after 800 years of practice.

It occurred to Max that sex with a vampire was the ultimate form of masturbation, except with four hands and all the sensitive parts that two bodies could offer.

Max's breathing became ragged as she took him to the edge and then back again. Jenna's mouth found his and they kissed. As Jenna eased onto him and his cock entered her, her tongue entered his mouth. At first the movement was slow and easy, their tongues caressing, their hips moving in unison.

It was a kiss never-ending, every bit as exciting as what was going on between their legs. Tongues, lips, flesh came together in the most exquisite dance. Their slow and lingering movements gave way to the heat of desire.

Max and Jenna rolled as one, first so Max was on top and then again and again trading positions, but never losing contact. As their kiss deepened, so did the urgency they felt between their legs. They were pounding, pulsating, moving as one being. Intense pressure radiated through Max. Their lips separated as Jenna gasped and the orgasm took them both. Waves of pleasure rushed through them as they struggled to catch their breath.

Max looked into her eyes and pushed deeper into her. Jenna lips rushed back to his, their tongues again intertwining. After it was over, Max thought only one thing as he eventually drifted off to sleep. He wanted the kiss to last forever.

# # #

Max wasn't quite awake when the call came that brought reality back to the forefront of his mind. They were at Jenna's place and Chase needed them to come in right away.

Max jumped in the shower, ready to hurry, but Jenna joined him with a look that told him they were going to take a few minutes for themselves before they faced the real world again.

The limo was waiting in the parking garage. The driver was human and the windows were tinted, so the sun wasn't an issue.

Despite the early hour, by the time they got to the war room it was hopping. It looked like just about everyone was there, running back and forth, consulting others, looking at reports, working on computers, making phone calls, and then heading back to their work stations or offices. The air was charged and Max knew something big was about to happen.

Max was scheduled to head off with Tank that afternoon to train for a couple of days, but Chase caught them as they entered and pulled them into her office.

"We've got a major break," Chase said, signing along with her words. "Jenna, work with Terry. We're going to go in an hour. I don't want to take any chances with this one."

Jenna nodded and left.

"Am I still going with Tank?" Max asked.

"Let me ask you this, Max. If I put you on the roof of a building, can you hit a target with one of our rifles?"

Max let out a hard breath. "I don't know. I've been practicing, but we don't have any distance here. There's no wind."

"Max, if I put you on a roof, can you hit what I need you to hit?" she asked again. Max had never seen Chase so determined.

"You think Jade might be here?"

She didn't answer.

Max closed his eyes, thought about her question and slowly nodded. "I'll need six rifles and someone to reload…

I'll hit what you want me to hit."

"You're not going to be able to tell the difference between human and vampire from that distance. I'll spot them for you."

"Okay."

"You've got one hour."

Max looked at his watch and nodded. He headed back to the war room. Savior and Becca were sitting side by side at computers intensely working. Max thought she looked better, but she'd lost none of her skin's transparency despite a meal of Savior.

"Hi," he said as he approached them.

"Max, they may have spotted Jade," Savior said.

"Yeah, I know."

"Are you going out with them?" Becca asked.

"Yes."

Concern filled her face. Savior looked away.

"Are you two okay?" Max asked.

"Becca's great with computers," Savior said. She smiled shyly.

"I've got to run. You two do whatever Nadine tells you to do."

Becca nodded. "Max…"

"Yeah?"

She hesitated. "Don't get yourself killed. Okay?"

Max smiled. "I'll do my best."

He trotted off. He'd be far from the action. It would be nice at least not to get shot for a change, especially since he was still had two holes from the last tango with the bad guys. And then there was that powerful memory of the operation and being sliced open again and again as his leg was reset.

Nadine was in her office. She looked up from her work and smiled that sweet smile at him. "Hi, Max."

"Hi. How are Savior and Becca doing?"

"Well enough I'm not giving them busy work any more."

"I have to go…"

"Yeah, I know."

"I just want to get a couple of volunteers lined up."

"Don't worry, Max. I'll take care of your kids."

Max smiled and nodded. "Thanks."

Max's kids. He didn't mind at all having kids to worry about again. Still, it was a world of difference between working with Savior and Becca and sitting on top of a building with a rifle. He hadn't thought much about what they wanted him to do. He'd been avoiding the subject.

Max pushed the thought out of his mind and found Jenna in Terry's office. He wanted to fill her in on the new plans. She nodded and signed, "Are you sure you want to do this?"

"No." Then he shrugged and gave her a quick hard kiss, before pulling away to head up to the armory on the 25th floor.

Max had to pass the inspection of three nasty-looking vampire guards before he was allowed to have his way with the weapons. He pulled one of the special rifles off the rack and admired it. It was finely crafted. A true thing of beauty. The rifle was made of epoxy, like the guns, and he could fire multiple rounds, in this case three, before having to reload. When Max realized he was caressing the weapon, he laughed. How could something meant to kill look so beautiful to him? Max shook his head and filled two duffel bags up with weapons and ammo. Then he went down the basement for some quick practice.

# # #

They were headed to Brooklyn, and each moment that passed blackened Max's mood. Everyone seemed a bit more subdued than usual, even Chase. There was no excitement bouncing through him. No distracting thoughts about Jenna, no interest in Shades and Father Frank's conversations about the past, no obsessive worry about the Saviors of the world. He was headed to someplace where he was expected to kill one or more someones. It didn't matter if they were blood sucking vampires. These days some of his favorite people in the world were blood sucking vampires. Those someones he caught in his sights would be dead when he was done.

Max checked the weapons during the drive. They were in perfect condition, clean and well-maintained. As Max explored every inch of every one of the weapons and ammo, thoughts of his last mission in the Army flooded back. He'd nailed a guard, some nobody who was just doing his job who happened to be in their way. Max killed the man because he was told to. Did the guard have a wife and children? Was he a good man? Was the world really a better place without him?

Now he was headed in a direction which, if he was successful, would cause more deaths. Being a sniper wasn't anything at all like sticking someone in the chest with a maple tree branch. That was a life and death struggle. This, on the other hand, was murder. Murder with a purpose… perhaps, but murder none the less. He was going to sit on a building's roof, point his weapon, pull the trigger and send someone to Hell. It had always felt like a cowardly way to commit murder to him.

Emotions swirled through him. Maybe he'd get a shot at Jade. Stop all the madness. Kill the bitch and save the world. Maybe.

Or maybe he'd just nail a kid like Savior, like Becca, like Crystal. Some poor kid who just went down the wrong alley and ended up in a Hell that would never end.

"Max," Shades said, breaking Max out of his no-win conversation with himself.

"Yeah."

"You okay?"

"Sure," Max lied.

"I got to admit, I'm glad you're going to be up on that roof covering our butts."

Max nodded, but he knew his mood was spreading out to the others like a virus. Or maybe he gave himself too much credit. Maybe it was just the thought of taking out Jade, a target that had driven them on through history.

They pulled into the area by 2 in the afternoon. Another van was coming at the area from a different direction so escape routes would be covered. Getting in position would be more challenging, considering the pesky sun and all.

They parked at a convenience store half a mile away, and Chase sent in a couple of human volunteers to do preliminary recon with a van that would relay the info to both teams. By the time they arrived, information streamed into the van's computers and they had a three dimensional view of the area. The thermal told them there were indeed vampires in the building in question. A lot of them. The initial count looked to be 25 vampires, with four humans mixed in.

"Terry, pull up the 3D," Chase said. "Where do you want to set up, Max?"

Max studied the schematic. The vampire nest was in a small two story office building. The heat signatures had most of the vamps in the northeast corner of the building on the second floor, but spread out in different rooms by one or two with the odd human mixed in.

"It depends on what you want me to hit. Since you're going in on the first floor, I'm assuming, you'll probably want me to hit here in the central area."

"Yes."

"After that I'll get who I can get and cover the exits. Is there a basement?"

"Not on the building plans," Terry said.

"There will certainly be a basement if Jade's involved in this location at all, one that wouldn't show up on the plans. And it will probably have an exit to one of these other buildings nearby… Have Nadine run a search and see if she's found any connections between this building and anything else in the area."

"Okay," Terry said.

Chase looked at Max and then studied the schematic again.

"Yes, hit the common area and take out whoever you can. Then get anyone you can on the second floor. Then cover the exits. I'll have to take the basement out as an option."

"What's the building made of?" Max asked.

"I'm still checking," Terry said. "It's not brick or stone."

"That's good. I may be able to shoot right through the walls."

"Here's some video that just came in of the area."

They plotted and planned and Max got himself as prepared as he could. He found the perfect building which would let him cover the area. It was far away enough that the normal vamps wouldn't sense him, but Jade was another story. There was a good chance Jade would pick him up.

Max, Terry and Chase worked out the best option. "Wouldn't it be better to use a human sniper?" Max asked. It'd seemed like an innocent question. "You could hit the during the day."

Chase's eyes hardened. He'd never seen that look on her before.

"No, it wouldn't be better." She bristled and he knew he'd hit a chord and ruffled the one vampire he thought couldn't be ruffled. Chase seemed to lose focus for a moment. "I'll be back in a moment. I have to check on something."

Terry watched her leave and then turned back toward Max. "We don't do that, Max. We use human volunteers to help us out, but we never let them fight our battles."

"But it's their world too. Their battle. They have the most to lose," Max said. "And there are snipers out there who'd be happy for the fight."

"She won't cross that line. If she did, so would Jade. Then it would all-out war."

"You mean not this nice little civilized one we've got going?" Max asked.

Terry nodded. "That's exactly what I mean."

In a way, Max was surprised Jade hadn't resorted to something more drastic. However, in some ways he suspected Jade needed Chase. Tormenting lesser beings like himself could only entertain her so long. Chase presented a challenge that most likely made her world a more interesting place.

Max realized they were right. If Chase changed the rules of the game, Jade wouldn't hesitate to take them to the next level.

Chase was back moments later with a plan as though Max had never asked that unsavory question.

# # #

They were moments from sunset. Everyone in the truck was silent. Max's guns and ammo were in place, taken earlier by a human team which included Dixie, the woman who'd both tempted and helped Max on his final. Rhonda stood next to Max. She'd been brought in to load his weapons and to help him out if things got hairy for the team. They were dressed in coveralls for Rosenberg's Heating and Cooling to give them a cover for being in the building.

They watched Terry who was orchestrating the mission. He looked at his watch. Terry slowly opened the door, peaked out and then nodded. Max pushed the door open and Rhonda followed him through.

They casually made their way up the street one block and entered the building. Max held the door open for someone who was trying to juggle the door and their laundry. Their number one goal was to get to the roof as quickly as possible while not doing anything that would seem suspicious to the building's tenants.

Max smiled at the woman with the laundry, and then entered the building. His sense of dread increased with each step he took. He really didn't want to kill anybody. Jade's words, "Kill for me," rung through him. He kept telling himself that this was different. Somehow it just had to be different.

They found the elevator and hit the button to the top floor. Rhonda read his mood, just like Jenna had.

"Wouldn't it be cool if she wandered right into the path of your rifle, Max?"

"Sure. That would be cool," he said unenthusiastically.

"You're going to save lives today."

"I'm going to take lives today. Maybe I'll save a couple today. Hopefully I'll save a whole lot tomorrow." Their eyes locked. She'd been a cop. She understood and let him fall back into his funk. He'd do his job and that was really all that mattered.

They hit the top floor and found the stairs that led to the roof. They were both putting on their headsets when they reached the roof. The guns were waiting for him. Max took a quick look, before grabbing a rifle and getting into position.

"In position," Max said into his headpiece.

"Any movement?" Chase asked.

Max looked through the scope.

"No. It's dark. I can't see light coming from the building," he said.

"Hold. I'm moving out."

The building was larger than he'd anticipated, but he had a good view of the main entrance and several of the windows. There also wasn't much cover around any of the exits, so he'd have a good shot at anyone exiting the building. Chase was right. He wouldn't be able to tell who was who a vampire and she'd need to direct him with his targets.

It was an older building and the windows were large. The building was serviceable, but it wasn't the kind of place Jade would want to spend too much time in. However, there were loading docks and other buildings were near, which would offer escape for Jade.

Max could see Chase walking in the direction of the building. He threw his focus on the building again. He didn't want to risk losing Jade because he was distracted. He checked the wind and distance, studying to see if he was missing any variables.

"She's not here," Chase said over his earpiece. She

couldn't hide the disappointment from her voice. Rhonda and Max looked at each other. They both knew what that meant. "If she was here, she's gone. But we do have a nest of them and they're not moving. They don't know we're here yet. It's on to Plan B, boys and girls… Hit it, Terry."

Max could see the only couple of human volunteers left in the area, ushering the few humans on the street away from the scene. Their badges even looked official and their cover story sounded plausible. The truck was launching forward to get the team in position.

"Max, we'll be ready in three. Right now I've got two targets and a civilian in the common area close to Window A," Chase said.

"Keep me away from the civilian on this first shot."

"The first two on your left are targets. Civilian on your right," Chase said.

"I'll aim high," Max said.

"In position," Terry said.

"Thirty seconds."

Max checked the wind one more time and lined up his shot. He wasn't likely to hit a heart from this range anyway without at least being able to see what he was shooting at, but he might get a head. Hopefully a vampire's head. And he'd break the window, which would offer him up any target that didn't move quickly enough.

"Ten seconds," Chase said.

Max took a deep breath and focused. His mind went blank as the thought about nothing but his target. The big mirrored window, Window A, near the front door seemed enormous to him.

"No change in target position, Blue. Go!"

Max squeezed the trigger and the rifle kicked to the right.

The window shattered and a very surprised male vampire looked at out the window. Max adjusted his aim and fired again. This time he hit the heart dead center. The shot knocked the vampire off his feet and he vanished into dust.

Then all hell broke loose.

## CHAPTER 23

Time slowed for Max. In an instant he took in what was happening in and around the building. The two teams moved in from different directions. Through the broken window, Max could see a man and woman near where the vampire had been taken out. The woman was screaming and the man was moving.

"The woman's the civilian, Blue," Chase's voice spat over the radio. Max already had the man in his sights. He pulled the trigger and a second vampire turned to dust.

Max handed his empty rifle to Rhonda and took the next one. The woman beyond the broken window screamed again and then ducked behind a desk.

Radio chatter exploded as the team entered the building from two different directions. Max lined up to take his next shot.

"Blue, Window F. No civilians."

He was ready and he targeted his first shot up for the center of a window on the second floor. The shot shattered the window, but missed the four vampires inside. Max took out one that was headed for a door. His next shot just missed the heart of an older female vampire, but she crumpled onto the ground in pain.

Max handed off the rifle to Rhonda, who handed him back the first weapon. He knew what to expect with this rifle now. The other two vampires had ducked out of the way, while the female Max had injured ripped at the arrow in her chest.

One of the two in hiding was behind a sofa. He was trying to inch the sofa closer to the door. He raised his head just enough and Max nailed him in the forehead. Not lethal, but he'd have one heck of a headache. The other vampire in the room, a big burly guy, ran toward the door when Max made the head shot. Max felt like he had all the time in the world. The guy's chest looked enormous to him. Max pulled the trigger and the vamp became dust.

"Window F, two dust, two injured."

Max spotted a thin woman running from the building. "We've got a runner on the Northwest side."

Max lined up his shot. A moment passed. "Vampire. Take her out," Terry said.

Max pulled the trigger and she was history. Max switched rifles again.

"Blue, we're pinned down near Window G. There is one human inside." Max took out the window to the surprise of those inside.

A man in a suit and two women in dresses were holding weapons and using a teenage boy as cover.

"I'm going to guess the people with guns are the bad guys," he said.

Max nailed the woman holding the kid. The surprised boy fell forward. The suit twirled around gun in hand, but he couldn't find a target. Max pulled the trigger and hit him in the throat. Someone from inside took out the other woman and Shades ran in and pulled the terrified boy to safety. Max switched rifles again.

A window broke on the first floor and two people jumped through and ran for their lives. "Two more runners."

"Vampires," Chase said.

"I'm going to take out their legs."

Two more shots and the vamps were on the ground. One in a Dodger's jacket grabbed the arrow in his leg and pulled it out. He got up and tried to run again. Max hit the other leg.

He handed his rifle to Rhonda and grabbed the reloaded one. The determined guy in the Dodger's jacket tried to run again, so Max hit him in the head this time. Even that didn't stop him, but it did slow him down.

Meanwhile, according to the radio chatter, the teams were still facing pockets of trouble inside the building. But Max suspected it wasn't in a location where he could be of help.

"It looks like we lost a couple through the basement,"

Chase said. "Blue, keep an eye out for anyone that looks out of place in the area."

Rhonda saw them first. "I've got eyes on a couple three blocks south of you."

"Rover One, check it out."

Max watched the couple as they moved quickly down the street. They did look out of place. He looked back to find his Dodgers fan making a bit too much progress and he hit him again. The guy was making Max go through a lot of trouble to keep him alive.

A van appeared from the outer perimeter and headed toward the couple. They ducked in to a dark area between two buildings. Suddenly they began running. "Rover One, they're on the run. Do you have a reading yet? At least one of them has to be human. They're not moving fast enough to both be vampires."

Static spit through the headset. "Yeah, Blue, a human and a vamp."

"Red, they're at the edge of my range. They're going to be in the wind."

"Go for the legs, Blue. Stop them."

Max hit the man and he went down. The redheaded woman pulled out a gun, but couldn't find a target. She ran, a gun in one hand and something else in the other. It was a cell phone. She was trying make a call.

Max glanced back at the man. He was crumbled over in pain and he was bleeding.

Time slowed again for Max and he zeroed in on his target. If the woman got a signal and managed to get a message to Jade, there would be hell to pay one way or another. The redhead lurched forward in an impossible burst of speed, but her angle was off and she had to slow to avoid hitting a wall. She knew she was being hunted. Max's target looked enormous to him. Max pulled the trigger.

The redhead pitched forward as the arrow struck her in the back. He missed her heart. She screamed trying to get to the arrow buried deep in her back. The woman rolled over and focused on the phone. She was trying to make the call. Max aimed and pulled the trigger again. He didn't miss this time.

"Rover One, the human is down but alive. The vamp is dust, but her cell phone isn't. One more block north of your location."

Max's attention snapped back to the building. The Dodgers fan had given up, but the woman next to him was trying her own slow escape. She didn't get far before Tank grabbed her and dragged the two of them back toward the building. They were in mop-up mode.

"Building's secure," Chase said. "We lose anybody?" No one replied with the knowledge of a fallen comrade. "Good. We've got four humans, 12 captives. Give me a count-down."

"One dead," Terry said.

"Two," Tank said.

"Two," Mitchell said.

"One," Shades said.

"Scratch," said the other members of the team including Rhonda, just to signify they were still alive.

"Blue?" Chase asked.

"Seven."

There was a pause. Max knew what it meant. It was the "holy shit pause." They'd look at him different now. He remembered that look from his days in the Army.

"That gives us our count… Let's wrap this up. Blue, stay put for a bit. Keep your eyes open."

"Roger that," Max said.

He kept his position and his rifle ready. Rhonda sat up, the tension draining from her body. She pulled the mic away from her mouth.

"Good shooting, Blue."

Max didn't respond.

"Shit, Max. Seven?"

He nodded.

"Don't you get it?" She said. "This could turn the tide of the war for us. We didn't lose anybody. All the humans will get out alive and we took out a facility with twenty five vamps, capturing almost half of them. Even without Jade, this was a good day."

Max didn't respond. He was too busy reliving the deaths of each and every vampire he'd murdered since the mission began.

# # #

Despite the fact that Jade had been MIA the team's mood had changed as they returned to the high-rise. They were animated in a way Max had never seen them before, with a couple of exceptions. Tank wasn't in the van. He was headed back with the prisoners in the truck. One of the exceptions was Chase, who couldn't hide her disappointment at the loss of Jade. And then there was Max, who sat in the corner and accepted the congratulations and pats on the back graciously enough, but none of the joy rubbed off of him.

Their success insured Max's new place in the team. The problem was that Max had to reconcile what they needed from him with the Max he desperately wanted to be. No matter how hard he tried, the mission kept running through his mind, over and over again. He saw each of his unsuspecting victims as they dusted into nothingness, one after the other.

Max said little and eventually let his mind wander into Shades and Father Frank's discussion of whether it was harder to kill vampires today or in the good old days before high powered weapons.

But he never got far away from the oppressive thoughts. How could he do such terrible things and then go curl up with Jenna as if nothing had happened? How could he save Savior if he couldn't save himself? Max had no allusions that he would ever make it to heaven when all was said and done, but had he been so evil in his life that his only purpose would be to become the instrument of death and destruction?

Killing evil was one thing. Most of those he'd killed on the mission never knew they had a choice.

He'd started to make a life for himself since he'd come to the Corps. He'd carved out his own little family. Okay, they were vampires, but they were the good guys. Unfortunately, they were also at war. He'd tried hard to forget about what was really at stake. He just wanted to fall in love, to be a teacher again who wanted to save kids nobody else cared about. He wanted to be human again with Jenna.

As they switched vehicles, Max knew he was going to have to come to terms with what Chase and the Corps needed from him. Too many lives counted on him. Somewhere within himself he was going to have to find young Max again, Max The Protector, who was willing to kill to save those he loved.

## CHAPTER 24

Once they returned to the high-rise, Max went back to his room. Jenna was out on her own mission and he just wanted to be alone. He stripped off his clothes and turned on the shower. As the scalding water and steam rolled over him, Max let his mind go blank. He wanted to pound his fists against the walls, to cry, to scream, to feel the horror of what he'd done, but he only felt numb.

Max laid down on the bed wet and watched the steam rise off him. He stared at the ceiling and he thought about Jade. If she'd walked into his sights would he have been able to kill her with a shot? What was she doing in New York, if she really was in New York at all?

She'd be furious when she found out about the attack. He remembered the fury he'd witnessed first-hand at the Corps attacks, and he suspected previous loses would be nothing compared to the nest they'd taken down today.

Max was laying there letting it all hang out when a vampire knocked on his door. At first he thought it might be Jenna, but then he smelled Chase. He looked down at his way too casual attire and decided he'd better put some pants on.

"Just a minute, Chase," Max said through the door. He grabbed a pair of sweat pants out of the dresser and a t-shirt and put them on. His hair was wet and he didn't have any shoes on, but he was presentable enough.

Max opened the door and Chase smiled, "Hi, Max."

"Hi." When she didn't say anything further, Max realized she wanted to come in. He stepped out of the way and let her pass.

"I wanted to talk to you," she said.

"I'm sorry we didn't get Jade."

She studied him for a moment. Then Chase laughed and shook her head, her long brown hair coming to life with the movement. "Max, this isn't the first time we've been this close. Like the time we got you. It's a disappointment, but… this isn't about Jade. Well, it is in the way that just about everything we do is about Jade. But no. This is about you."

"Me?"

"I'm sorry." Chase looked at him so sincerely and filled with so much concern that he took a step back. She was sorry for asking him to become a sniper again. Max just nodded and he looked at the floor.

"It's okay," he said.

"No, it's not." Chase touched his arm, the first time she'd ever touched him except when he had fed from her. He could feel her compassion. He knew she could also feel every twisted emotion that filled him. Max pulled away. He didn't want to share.

"Look, I'll do what I have to do."

"When I see what you've done with Savior, when I see the potential… I don't want to ask you to do this, Max."

Max turned away. "You don't have to ask, Chase… I hate it. I hate all of it. Every bit of it. I hate the killing. I hate that part of me likes it because I'm so damn good at it. Killing shouldn't ever be… easy."

"I know," Chase said.

He turned toward her and their eyes met. "But it's not about me," Max said. "It's not even about Jade. It's about the four humans we saved today and all those that are saved tomorrow and the day after and the day after that because we took 25 vampires out of play… So I'll do this, and I'll hate it. And maybe I won't be able to do it very long. I don't know. But I'll do it as long as I can."

"Okay."

Max nodded. "Okay, then."

Silence settled through the room like a wet fog. Chase started to leave, but then turned back towards him.

"I'm going to be interviewing those we captured. Would you like to join me?"

Max shook his head. "No." He knew most of them wouldn't make it and he didn't want to see their faces up close. "But, if he's a candidate for conversion, the guy in the Dodgers jacket, I'd like to work with him."

To her credit, Chase didn't ask why. "I'll let you know after I talk to him."

Max nodded. "When she finds out that you're using a sniper, she'll get one of her own."

"I know," Chase said. "But how much damage can we do before that happens?"

Damage… Max didn't want to think about it.

Chase opened the door and turned to him. "We're going to hold a memorial for Michael and Latrise tonight."

"I'll be there."

Max knew he had to check on Savior and Becca, but he just couldn't move. He'd defeated his vampire only to find himself back in another war, in another situation he had no control over. He really was a monster, a weapon, a necessary evil.

Max laid back on the bed. He felt Jenna approaching his room and heard her enter. Even though the room was dark he could see her clearly. She looked so concerned.

"I'm glad you're okay," she signed.

"You, too," he signed back.

She wrapped her arms around him and they just laid there. Max just wanted to lay with Jenna. If only everything would just stop. If only.

# # #

It was a couple of hours before Max and Jenna stirred. No passionate sex or deep meaningful talks. They just laid in each other's arms until Jenna's emotions eased Max out of his depression. He did have to admit it was a bonus being able to communicate without a word, just being able to feel what your partner feels. Chalk that up in the pro column when it came to being a vamp.

Eventually Max was able to get up and head back to the

war room as Jenna headed off to her own duties. She had an office a few floors below and she like to work from there.

Savior and Becca were talking like normal teens when he arrived and he took that as a big improvement.

"No, I hate it. How can you even like that?" Becca said.

"It's great music," Savior argued. "It makes me feel like it's going to rip my head apart."

"Why do you want your head ripped apart?" she asked, shaking her head.

"Hey guys, how are you doing?" Max asked.

Becca actually smiled. "Hey, Max. He wants to listen to crazy music and it hurts my ears."

"Mine, too," Max agreed.

"I think we found something. Becca found it actually," said Savior. "It's a pattern. I don't know if anybody's noticed it yet."

"What kind of a pattern?" Max asked.

Becca pulled a chart up on the computer. "So people can try to make things look random, but it's not that easy because humans and... well vampires, naturally follow patterns even if they don't realize it."

She started pointing to some numbers in the chart which told Max absolutely nothing. He wasn't a math guy.

"Okay."

"See here?" Savior held up a printed sheet with more charts.

"Why don't you break it down and pretend I know nothing about math and charts," Max said.

Becca smiled. "Okay, so let's say you want to buy property in an area. And you want to do it randomly so no one knows where you're buying the property."

"Yeah."

"But you always have a specific criteria that you use to choose your property... So by running real estate records of properties that have been purchased, and running an algorithm on those properties you can narrow down which ones might be purchased by a certain person."

"Like Jade," Max said.

"Like Jade," Savior said.

"So how many properties are we talking about?"

"Over the last year, maybe 40 fit the criteria in this area?" said Becca.

"40?" Max asked.

"Well, actually 42," Becca replied. "42 that we should investigate."

"Have you told anyone this yet?"

"They've all been busy," Savior said.

"Let's go talk to Chase," Max said.

# # #

Minutes later Max and the kids were sitting in front of Chase's desk and laying out the discovery.

"So you're telling me we can find Jade's properties, her training centers," Chase said.

"Well, where they might be. There's ways to narrow it down more, especially if we go over the buyers' financials and where the money is coming from and like that. We've just been going over this year's data. We think she could have a couple hundred places altogether in the country. Maybe more," said Becca.

"Tell me again."

"Okay, we run the real estate records against an algorithm I wrote looking for houses with a certain number of bathrooms and bedrooms and an attached garage and other stuff," Becca said. "Based on info from other locations you've already found of what kind of place she needs, big enough to have several people who can't walk to an exterior garage during the day and need a large enough town near by for... people who won't be missed. The things you'd need with six or seven vampires. Assuming it's not a big place like the one you just raided. They have to take lots of showers for obvious reasons, so they need a lot of bathrooms. They need space to keep humans, so basement or garage space. Not a lot of big windows. I just added in all the things I thought they might need based on the places you've already raided.

”On the other end we can dig into buyers' financials, who's paid cash, all that stuff,” she continued. “I'd need help with that part. It's a little beyond my hacker skills at this point. We come up with that list. Once we put the lists together we should have a pretty good picture.”

“We've been trying to trace her financials for a long time,” Chase said.

“But you're not combining it with the real estate. Even if she's using fake names there's going to be connections when you put the two things together,” Savior added.

“So right now, even without all the financial info, you think we can narrow down your 42 or do we need to check all these places out?” Chase asked.

“You're probably going to want to check them out just to make sure at some point, but we can narrow it down by digging into the financials,” Becca said.

“And if we add in a place like the one I was kept at that's a little bigger and fancier, it might be a place a certain vampire queen might be at,” Max added.

“And I had an idea,” Savior added. “While you're probably going to want to check out all the locations, we can do the initial sweeps with silent drones.”

“We tried drones at one point, but they weren't quiet enough,” Chase said.

“How long ago was that?” Max asked. Chase cocked her head but didn't reply.

“They're super quiet now. A friend of mine used to buzz apartments... well, not buzz but fly around apartments, you know to watch girls, and he showed me how they worked. It was pretty cool,” he said sheepishly.

Chase both looked at the trio, mouth opened. Chase closed her mouth and nodded.

“That's amazing work, Savior, Becca. Thank you.”

Becca smiled and then looked away embarrassed. Savior,

however, was positively brimming with pride.

"Thanks Max. Have Natalie set these two up with anything they need and find Becca some assistants to help her. Let's narrow this down... and let's get some of these silent drones so we can run some tests."

"Sure," Max said. He smiled at Chase as they left her office. Max stayed. He didn't say anything right away.

"Max?"

"How did Dodgers Jacket do?"

"Haven't made a decision yet," Chase said. "Why didn't we think of that? Why did it take a couple kids to come up with this?"

Max smiled. "Chase, most of your most trusted people were born before computers were invented. The world has changed and you're not that comfortable using humans. It might be wise to get some computer savvy humans on the payroll. Just saying."

Chase nodded. Max looked in the direction the kids had gone and then to Chase.

"Something else," Max said. "Look, I know we're in a war. I'll do anything I can to help you win. But I'd like to see about getting some longer term holding situations. We can save more of them if we give them time... I want to save more of them. Help me save more of them, Chase. Please." Max was begging breaking his number one rule.

Chase looked away for a moment and then nodded slowly. "I'll think about it, okay?"

"Look, what the kids just gave us may change of the tide of this thing. And that wouldn't have happened if we didn't give them time," Max said.

"I'll think about it. Seriously. I will... As well as updating my mindset about this brave new world of yours."

Max took a deep breath and nodded, then followed the kids. Maybe he could make this work.

# # #

It turned out Becca was great when it came to computers,

and Savior was clever in his own right. They fed off each other, acting like kids one moment and melding minds brilliantly the next. Nadine brought in other computer people and some hackers to help them sort things out. It didn't take long before the new team, led by two teenage vampires, came up with 16 locations that were probables, or for Savior to help Chase figure out which drones had infrared and were silent enough to scout a vampire house.

A few tests buzzing headquarters, with Chase listening, pinned down just how close the drones could get without being heard or seen by Jade or other vampires.

Max's kids, as they were often called, did good. Getting control of their inner vampires did pose some challenges, especially for Savior, but they supported each other in that too.

He began to believe the kids might actually make it. Becca's skin was starting to become less transparent and Savior rarely talked about himself in the third person.

It was a full war room. Chase was buzzing around checking in with everyone, Eugene was having an in-depth conversation with Terry, and Father Frank was making some sort of bet with Shades about something Max couldn't identify.

Max was working with the kids, going over some of the reports they had generated, when Rhonda came into the war room and walked up to talk to him.

"Hey, Max."

"Hey, Rhonda," he said, looking up.

She hesitated looking a little nervous.

"What's up?" he asked finally.

"So... I was thinking... maybe it wouldn't hurt to have another sniper, if you were willing to train me."

He crossed his arms and nodded. She was kind of perfect. She was an ex-cop, familiar with weapons, steady under pressure.

"I think that's a..." he paused for great effect.

"Hummmm... Yep. That's a great idea. I love it. I'll ask Chase, but I'd love to train you."

"Cool," she said, nodding and smiling, the tension leaving her. "I just want to do more."

"Cool!" Max agreed.

"Thanks Max," Rhonda said as she turned to head back toward the door. She stopped. "Oops! Got to ask Terry something," as she headed toward him.

Max went back to his report. Teaching others would only be a good thing in the long run. While the darkness was still nagging at him, he was starting to feel much better, at least until a shell shattered their big, beautiful sun-protected window and an explosion took out half the war room.

## CHAPTER 25

Max saw the shell coming and threw the kids to the ground, covering them with his body when the explosion hit. As he was moving, he saw a chunk of glass slice through Rhonda's neck and she was dust. Pain shot through his back and neck. He and the kids were just out of the sun, but his back was riddled with dozens of glass shards.

The vampires struck by the sun began to catch fire and scream. Chase was there in a moment and started throwing them into the shade. Terry and Shades were on fire as they flew by his head, striking the wall. The sun didn't seem to affect Chase at all. After she got the vampires out of the sun, she started rescue operations for the humans.

Eugene was badly injured, his leg bent at a strange angle. He was still alive, though. Several other humans were also injured or dead. The smell of blood hit Max hard, as he knew it must have every other vampire in the room.

Savior and Becca were wide-eyed and in shock. Max pulled them up and pushed them away from the window.

"Nadine, kill the servers. Hit the alarm," Chase ordered. "Everyone, they're going to hit us from below. Get out of here. Anyone who can move, grab someone who needs help and get them through the escape doors. Everyone, be ready to fight. Get down the stairs and out the escape tunnels. We only have minutes until we burn the building."

Nadine and anyone who was mobile, moved with a purpose.

"What escape doors?" Max asked.

Nadine grabbed him and pushed the others toward the door of the room. Max knew every good vampire den had an escape plan and a way out, but no one had filled him in on where theirs was. Injured vampires grabbed injured humans or more injured vampires and hauled them out. Everyone who could move moved, escaping the war room, but there were at least a couple of humans who were dead.

Savior stopped and started to go back. "Wait. We have printouts that they can't get. They'll know what we're doing."

Nadine pushed him back. "There won't be any printouts left. The building's going to burn."

The kids hesitated for moment, but then moved quickly and helped injured humans.

Max and Chase were the last out the door when a second shell came through the open window and exploded, throwing them through the door and to the ground.

Chase was up in an instant and grabbed Max pulling him onto his feet, his back still riddled with glass. "Max, get them out!" she yelled.

Half a hallway down, Nadine tilted a painting that cracked open a secret escape door. She pushed the door open and rushed in and humans and vampires followed her. Max followed the kids and the humans they carried through door. He looked back but Chase wasn't there. Nadine pulled him away from the door and hit a small button on the wall which closed the entrance. Max suspected the painting would straighten as if it had never been tilted, and the opening would become invisible.

He looked over his shoulder and saw the stairway descending down, with the some of the survivors running or stumbling downward.

Nadine was operating a keypad next to the closed door. She punched in a code and a loud alarm pummeled his ears. Her fingers danced over the keypad, which Max assumed would take care of the local computer servers. He knew there were backups far, far way and safe from the invasion.

Nadine yelled, "We've got 12 minutes." She stopped for a moment and found a small painted arrow on the wall. She pulled back her arm and rammed her fist into the wall, which gave way to a compartment. Inside were three guns and phones. She handed Max one of the guns and yelled, "Move!". Then she fled down the stairs following the others.

Max yelled over the alarm to the kids, "Follow her." Becca and Savior looked terrified, but nodded and followed the others with their human cargo. Savior's fangs were showing but he was holding it together.

Max followed the others down a couple flights and saw another hidden entrance that was open. He looked through the door but there wasn't anyone in the hall. Next to the button which closed the door there another small arrow mark on the wall. Max punched a hole through the wall with his fist and inside the cubbyhole were three more loaded hand guns and cell phones. He tucked two of the guns into the back of his pants and one into his sock, pulling his pants over the bulge. He put the cell phones in his pocket with his own phone.

Max looked through the open door and slid out into the bright light of the hallway that was steps from his room. He shut the entrance and went to his room. The siren was still blaring so he didn't have to worry about being quiet.

He knew it was stupid, but wasn't ready to leave his boots and Amanda's driver's license to get burned up. Max hit the code on his door and ran inside. He quickly grabbed the necessities, along with his new identity package, and threw them and the extra cell phones in a backpack from his closet. He was really, really glad he had guns as thoughts of Jade flashed through his mind.

Max reached out with his senses and carefully pulled his door open going into the hallway. He knew he didn't have much time, but he needed to see if Jenna was still in her office a couple floors below. He hadn't run across any dust piles so far, but he didn't have any illusions about everyone besides Rhonda and the dead humans from the war room making it out alive. The attack was so sudden, they were bound to lose more people. He pushed thoughts of Rhonda and the others away. He just hoped Jenna hadn't been caught in this.

Max grabbed his own phone out of his pocket. "Where are

you," he texted. Just then the siren stopped. Someone had figured out how to turn it off stop it.

He waited for a moment and then headed back to the escape door, and went through, closing the door behind him. He realized he was holding his breath and he forced himself to breathe.

"Safe, but I couldn't get my book," Jenna texted back. Relief spread through him.

"Stay safe," he texted. He stopped for a moment. "I love you. I'll get out if I can." He put his phone back in his pocket. He hadn't told her he loved her before. It was just like him to wait until he might die to express some big romantic gesture.

Max ran down two more flights of stairs. A wave of pain ran through him and he suddenly stopped and reached back touching his neck. He still had shards of glass sticking out of him. Well, he had less than 10 minutes before the building became a fireball, so the glass wasn't coming out anytime soon.

He stopped on Jenna's floor and went through the door. Max reached out with his senses again. There wasn't anyone ahead of him. He could get to her office and get the book. It was too important to leave to fall into the hands of Jade or get burned up.

He sprinted down the hall towards the office, but stopped suddenly when he saw a body. It was Sheila, the human volunteer who vampire Max had wanted so badly in the beginning. She was dead. He closed his eyes and shook his head. He wanted to take her body and put it somewhere safe so her family could bury her. He wanted to go back in time and save her, but there wasn't anything he could do for her or her family.

Max ran past her to Jenna's office and punched in the code when he got there. He was relieved to see the book sitting on the desk, right where he'd seen it many times before. It was open to his picture. Max slammed the book shut and stuffed it in his backpack. When he put the heavier backpack on right over the embedded glass in his back he couldn't help but wince as pain shot through him.

As he headed out he sensed movement. He couldn't tell who it was, but he did sense another human and a vampire moving slowly. He could hear a woman crying and realized she was being dragged in the direction of the elevator.

Max readied his gun and eased toward them.

"Shut up, bitch," a large vampire who looked like a lawyer ordered. He even had a suit on. Lawyer vamp hadn't sensed him yet, so Max rushed the guy. Max shot him between the eyes and then through the heart. The vampire dropped the woman he was holding by the arm and vanished into dust.

The injured woman looked up at him. It was Dr. Felton. She'd been shot with a bolt in the collarbone, which stuck halfway out of her.

"Oh, Doc, you're okay." Max looked around the area for a moment to make sure they weren't in danger and then looked back at her. "Let me get this out. It's going to hurt."

"No. Just leave it. It's better if you leave it," she said, breathing hard. "Besides, I think you've got your own problems."

Max looked back. "That will wait too. We don't have time," he said.

The elevator's ding announced its arrival forcing Max to move. He scooped up the good doctor. She cried out as he ran toward the escape door.

"Shit! They're coming," he said.

Max could sense there were a lot of bad guys heading toward them. He zoomed, moving vampire-fast for the escape door. He triggered the painting. As the door opened with a swoosh, he carried the doctor through the opening and slammed the button shutting the secret door. He and Dr. Felton paused, waiting to see if the bad guys would figure out where they'd gone. He was sure the walls were soundproof and vampire sensing proof, but Jade's gang would figure it out if they had time.

"Thanks, Max," she whispered weakly.

"I'm glad I found you," he nodded, still holding her. "We've got to hurry."

She started crying softly. They went down a flight of stairs when he ran into Terry, whose burns looked nasty. He was carrying boxes.

"Terry, you okay."

"Sure," he looked at Max's back. "You?"

"Peachy... Can you take the doc down? I want to check to see if anyone else needs me."

"You trying to get yourself killed?" Terry asked.

"Yep, you discovered my secret plan... Not everybody made it out. You know the building's about to go."

Max handed off Dr. Felton and the backpack to Terry. "Jenna's book is in here," Max said.

Terry nodded. "You've got about 5 minutes," he said as he took her and the rest of his cargo down the stairs.

Max watched them descend for a moment and then started hitting the code on the keypad he'd seen Nadine use. The door cracked open and he let his senses spread out.

Several vampires headed right toward him.

Max was about to close the open escape door when the bad guys stopped advancing and a battle broke out. He could hear gunfire and he knew it wasn't good. He took a few steps out the door and toward the battle. Someone needed help, but which side of the battle was he going to come in on?

As he got closer he realized it was probably one of the Corps and a bunch of the bad guys who had that person pinned down. Then he heard a voice he recognized.

"Come on, Tank. Just give up. Jade really wants to get reacquainted," Veronica said.

"Fuck," Max said silently. If they had Tank pinned down, that was a very bad thing and he only had minutes. Max slowly let out a breath and headed toward two of the scariest vampires he knew, Tank and Veronica.

As Max got closer he realized that Tank was running out of ammo. The bad guys were shooting a lot more bolts than Tank was. He also realized that Tank was probably injured because he smelled blood.

Veronica and the other minions would sense Max coming, but he knew the layout of the floor. Max figured Tank was in a small kitchen and they were outside the room. They wanted him alive, which was the only reason they hadn't rushed him. Plus he might be able to take Veronica in a fight.

If Max came up through the hall they'd just send a couple of guys after him and keep the others on Tank. However, if he came up on the other side of the kitchen, he could go through the wall which he doubted was reinforced and maybe get to Tank that way. That was by far the better option. They'd sense him heading away from them and focus on Tank. Hopefully the big guy wouldn't run out of bolts before Max's plan played out.

He headed away from the fight and found the storage closet he knew was on the other side of the kitchen. Max quietly pulled a shelving unit way from the wall and let his senses roll out. He felt Tank. He was pretty sure Tank would know he was coming. He'd be going through a cabinet under the sink in the kitchen, but that would give him a little bit of cover.

It wasn't going to take Veronica long to figure out what he was doing, and he really didn't have time to waste. Chances were by the time he got Tank out, Jade's vamps would be on him from the closet door. But he had to try.

Max checked for studs in the wall and then slammed his fist into the wall, which shattered. Pain radiated through him from his fist and his back. He widened the hole and then pushed his way into the cabinet in the kitchen. A bolt whizzed by his head.

Tank had several bolts in him, but he wasn't surprised to see Max. The big guy was even less happy than usual. Tank crawled to him and took another bolt in the back. Max went back through the hole in the wall and pulled Tank through.

"Happy to see me?" Max wise cracked.

Tank just growled.

Max handed Tank one of his fresh guns from his waistband, and lifted him over his shoulders, the glass in Max's back slamming deeper into him. He ripped the door open just as two of the bad guys were headed toward them. Max sprinted with Tank in the other direction. Tank shot at the men, which slowed the bad guys down for a moment.

Max vampire-flew toward the escape door as Tank shot back at them. If they could just buy a few seconds they could disappear.

"Keep shooting, big guy!" Max yelled. He knew it must have been a hysterical sight with Max holding a huge guy like Tank over his shoulders while he was shooting, and him running like a bat out of hell. He sped as fast as he could and slid to stop, throwing Tank to the ground with a thud so he could get the escape door open. The big guy only grunted when he hit the floor. The bad guys were right behind them.

Max fired a couple of shots in the direction of their pursuers and then cracked the escape door open. Max pulled open the door and threw Tank inside, with the big guy landing with a thud and a grunt. Max ran in after him, slamming the opening and hitting the button. Max grabbed Tank again and pulled him to his feet as they hit the stairs down. Max had his gun ready and was hoping the vampire-proof walls would work. Tank was in rough shape, but he controlled his breathing and pulled his gun up ready to shoot anyone following them.

"Thanks," Tank grunted.

"Be careful. Before you know it you're actually going to start trusting me," Max said.

They were halfway down the flight of stairs when the opening behind them blew apart. The bad guys had found their escape door.

"We found them," one of the bad guys yelled and bolts

flew toward Max and Tank. "There are hidden stairs. Looks like it runs through the building."

They only had moments before the building would be engulfed in flames, so there was no time to do anything other than move. Max really hoped Veronica would hang around to get an early start on burning in hell along with all her friends. If Max and Tank didn't make it, he really, really hoped that.

By the time they hit the first level, two bad vampires had busted through the escape door and were on them, tackling Max and Tank and sending them flying and hitting the ground hard. The only good thing was that they really didn't want to kill Tank, which gave Max the advantage. He had no problem with killing them.

One of the vamps, who looked like a lady librarian, slammed Tank to the ground as he started to get up and pushed one of the bolts deeper into him.

The other vampire, a wiry tough looking man, aimed his gun at Max and fired. Luckily, Max was moving and the bolt missed him. Max was able to pull his own gun up and hit wiry vamp in the gut, only inches from his heart. The vampire was stunned for a moment and Max shot him again, not missing his heart this time.

As the lady vampire started to turn her attention toward Max, Tank pulled out one of the bolts sticking out his leg and stabbed her through the heart with it. Dust to dust, two less bad vampires in the world.

Max was breathing hard, "Good job."

Tank just grunted as he struggled to get up. Max pulled him onto his shoulders and hit the stairs again. He heard movement above them and he knew it was more of Jade's minions headed toward them and the others.

When they hit bottom level, below the building, they saw Nadine holding open a door.

"They're coming!" Max yelled.

Max looked up and saw Jade. He paused for just a split second. There she was. Terrifyingly beautiful, the embodiment of evil, but she had a slight look of surprise written across her face.

"It's going to go now. Hurry!" Nadine said, ready to slam the door.

Then Max heard the scariest thing he'd had ever heard. "Teacher," Jade's voice floated down, almost caressing him.

Max and Tank flew through the open door.

"Close it!" Tank yelled. Nadine slammed the door shut and threw a medal bar over the door.

Nadine and Max with Tank on his shoulders ran. They had to get away from the building. Whatever was going to happen with the building might bring it down.

Max heard a loud bang on the metal door, and then a couple more. At that moment they heard an enormous clap as the building ignited and a cloud of heat engulfed Nadine, Tank and Max.

They ran to safety until the corridor widened until it was large enough to fit a couple of cars. When they'd cleared the building they saw a couple more vampires with guns.

Max sat Tank down gently, but the glass in his back managed to cut both of them.

"Was that..." Nadine started.

"Yes. It was Jade," Max said. Tank looked at him and then nodded.

"Do you think she's dead?" she asked.

"No," Tank growled. "Chase?"

"I didn't see her. I'm sure she's out though," Nadine said.

Max nodded. This was bad, really bad. Jade could turn into smoke, so she was certainly just fine. As for Chase, Max hoped she'd survived too. Even if they hadn't gotten her, they'd gotten so close.

He'd never been down in the area before. It was a dank looking place, poorly lit and damp. "Where is everyone?"

We have cars up ahead and drivers to get us out of here... Jenna's safe."

"She texted me."

"Rhonda... " Max said. "Sheila didn't make it either. There were at least a couple more."

"While I was waiting for you, I heard about others too," Nadine said.

Max felt bone tired. He knew the glass in his back was embedded with the skin healing around it. Humans and vampires he knew and cared about were dead. Chase was missing. Even the one bright spot, that they may have killed Jade, didn't make him feel good. It was a really bad day.

## CHAPTER 26

After Max made it to one of the waiting cars, he laid down on his stomach, taking up the full back seat. One look at his back and no one begrudged him the space. He grabbed his phone out of his pocket and rested on his elbows so he could text Jenna.

He was about to punch in his text when he saw she had texted him back. "I love you too." Max stopped for a moment as emotion took hold him. He breathed in deeply and then closed his eyes. He nodded to himself. As horrible as things had gone, she was safe and she loved him.

He texted, "I'm safe. I'm on my way." Before he could hit the send button, Nadine opened the door by his head. "Max, I need your phone. We can't take a chance. I'm sorry."

Max nodded and handed her the phone. Nadine shut his door as he laid his head down and rested. Thoughts of Jenna drifted through him. Now if he could only get the damn glass out of his back.

# # #

They rode for what seemed like a long time. He, of course, couldn't see where they were going. Beyond the fact he was on his stomach, all but the front windows were darkly tinted. Max knew the drivers were being cautious, making sure they weren't being followed so they didn't take a straight route.

When the car finally stopped, Max waited until someone opened the door. It was Shades who offered him a hand. Max took his hand and was helped to his feet.

Shades had a serious case of sunburn, which Max knew from his own sun-poisoning experience would take a while to heal. Still, Shades didn't look in too much pain, so maybe sunburn and sun-poisoning was different or perhaps Jade hadn't shared the secrets of treating it with him.

"You okay?" Max asked.

"Hurts like hell but it will heal," he said.

"Is Jenna here?" Max asked.

"Yeah, she knows you're here," Terry said as he came up next to them. Max nodded, relief filling him. He noted Terry's burns didn't look much better than Shades.

"You guys look like hell... Chase?"

"Look who's talking. No word yet," Terry said.

Max looked around. They were in an airplane hanger that was teeming with humans and vampires. There was a small plane nearby and several cars. One corner was filled with cots, patients and bodies.

Savior and Becca ran up to him. "Max, are you okay?" Savior asked, about to hug him. Then he saw Max's back. "You're hurt."

"We were so worried," Becca added.

"It's okay. I'll be fine. You guys did great. Are you all right?"

They nodded.

"Come on, Max. We got to get the glass out of you," Shades said.

"Excellent plan," Max said, as he followed Shades. "Hey, guys," Max said, looking back at the kids. "Let me get this taken care of." Like sad puppies they nodded. "Terry, have we started a list of survivors and such?" Max avoided saying "the dead."

"Just getting started on that, Max."

"Have the kids help you... Okay guys?"

"Sure, Max," Becca said. Savior nodded and they went off with Terry. Max watched them for a moment. He was so glad they were okay.

As Max got closer to the triage area, he saw that Tank had his own cot and was getting the bolts pulled out of him with pliers. As usual the only sound Tank made was the low grumble that was uniquely his.

When Max found an empty cot he unbuttoned his shirt and started to pull it off. Pain shot through his back as the shirt caught the some of the glass in his back and ripped it out. There was a lot more of that to come he knew. Max pulled off his pants, which also had plenty of glass shards. He stripped down to his underwear and socks. There wasn't room for privacy. He twisted around and began pulling out the glass he could get to. It stung like hell because the skin around the glass that was half sticking out of him had healed.

Shades came up. "I got you, Max."

"Thanks..." He was about to lay down but then he saw Jenna. She broke out into a smile, but then looked away. When she looked back at him there were tears in her eyes. She wiped them away and came to him.

Max suddenly forgot all about his back as he took her in his arms and kissed her deeply. As Jenna reach up to stroke his neck she pulled her hand back.

"You're hurt," she signed.

"Suddenly I feel much better," he signed back with a smile.

"Max, come on. Let's get that shit out of you," Shades said.

Max reluctantly let go of Jenna and laid down on the cot on his stomach, but didn't take his eyes off her. Yeah, he was definitely in love. He realized he was smiling.

Jenna stroked his hair and then bent down to look him in the eyes. "Thanks for saving my book," she signed. "You shouldn't have, but thank you." She kissed him on the forehead. "I've got work to do."

"I know," he said, not bothering to sign. She read his lips and smiled. He watched as she walked away.

"Okay, Max, I'm going to get what I can see out first," Shades said. Max looked at him. Shades was holding his own set of pliers.

"Goody," Max said. He heard another set of footsteps and looked up to see Dr. Foster. She had a sling on binding one of her arms and looked in rough shape.

"Shades, if you can be my hands, I'll help so we can get

everything out."

"You okay, Doc?" Max asked.

"I'm alive," she said. "And this will hurt, Max."

Max laughed. It wasn't the first time she'd told him that. He closed his eyes as Shades did surgery on him under the direction of the good doctor.

Max realized saying it was going to hurt was an understatement. A really big one. Another surgery. No anesthetic.

Shades pulled out what he could, but the skin had healed around the glass so that when the pieces were pulled out they made fresh wounds. Max was not as stoic as Tank and felt his skin being sliced open with each piece that came out.

After Shades and Dr. Foster got the visible pieces out they had to go for the ones that were buried under healed skin. The only way to find those was to push down on the skin and wait til Max felt them. There were a lot of "Shit!", "Fuck!", and angry "There!", along with whatever other nasty language Max could think up. Then Shades had to dig the pieces out with a scalpel and tweezers. More colorful language ensued. It was even less fun than when Max's broken leg healed and had to be reset.

Max didn't approve of crying like a baby any more than he approved of begging, but he wasn't feeling very manly by the time they were finished.

Dr. Foster put her hand on his shoulder. "So we've gotten everything out we can at this point. There's going to be some small ones we missed. We'll have to get those when they bother you," she said.

"Okay. Can't wait," he said. "That was not fun. Thanks Shades, Dr. Foster."

"It was fun for me," Shades said with an evil smile, as he walked away.

Dr. Foster used a paper towel and alcohol to wipe down Max's injured back to clean up the dried blood. His back was healed again by the time she was done. Max sat up and grabbed the fresh clothes Terry had dropped off for him, along with his boots.

"If you feel some little ones in there let me know. Have Jenna give you a back rub and then mark with a Sharpie any rough spots."

"Okay, Doctor... Thanks," he said.

She stopped and considered him for a moment.

"Look Max, you saved me. I mean, I'd be dead... Thank you."

"It's okay. I'm glad..." he said.

"I mean it. You shouldn't have risked it, but you saved me and you saved Tank..." She stopped and shook her head, putting her hands on her forehead. "I don't know why you didn't get out when everyone else did."

"Chase didn't."

"Let's hope she's okay. Why she hasn't called yet?" she asked.

"She might not want to risk making that call."

Dr. Foster nodded. "Yeah... Yeah."

"Doctor, Jade was there. I don't know, but she might have gotten caught in the fire."

She started breathing hard and didn't know where to look. "I guess we can hope."

"Yeah, we can hope," he said.

Max hopped off the cot. Most of the cots were empty. A couple had bodies with sheets pulled over them. Tank was gone. "You need to lay down," he said. Max realized the living humans were gone. "Where did..."

"They were sent to a private clinic Chase owns. Obviously healing will take time. We can't exactly send them to the regular hospital. If Jade found them, it wouldn't be good."

"What about Eugene?"

"He's been taken with the other humans. He'll live, but I don't know if he'll walk again."

Max nodded. "Lay down. You've done what you can. Maybe you should go to that clinic too and get your shoulder looked after."

"I will. I just want to make sure no one else needs me."

"Then lay down. It looks like you've helped everyone you can help at this point, Doc."

She was trembling and slowly nodded. Max took her hand and felt a horrible mix of pain and fear. He closed his eyes and forced himself to feel calm, sending it to her. After a few moments her fear eased.

She looked up at him, surprised.

"Better than when you accidentally touched me during the last surgery, isn't it?" Max smiled.

She nodded, a slight smile creasing her lips. Max led her to a cot and continued to hold her hand as she laid down. She nodded and closed her eyes. He finally released her hand and watched her for a second before heading to the bustling area across the hanger that Max figured was the new war room.

As Max came up to Nadine he asked, "Chase?"

"No, Max, we haven't heard anything from her."

"Do you think..."

"I don't know."

"And how many..." Max started to ask.

Terry walked up holding clip board. "Some people might have made it out. The vamps couldn't have escaped with the sun, but maybe they weren't in the building. We know a few that died for sure, so everyone else is classified as missing."

"Sheila and Rhonda are dead," Max said grimly.

Terry nodded. "Nadine told me."

"How many are dead and missing?"

"Not counting Chase, 5 dead humans, 7 vampires including Rhonda. Missing 5 humans and 8 vampires. 25 total."

Max gasped. "Twenty-five... That's how many we got of hers... How did they find us, especially during the day... They had to be using humans."

"Yeah... Tank's asking for you. He's in charge until we hear from Chase."

Max nodded and headed toward the big guy, who was at a computer.

Tank looked up as Max approached and nodded curtly at him.

"Tank, you okay?"

"I'm filled with holes," he growled. Max knew from first hand experience that Tank wouldn't heal for a couple days. "Thank you. I hadn't thought about going through the wall."

"No problem. You were kind of busy."

Tank looked back at the computer screen and then glanced back up to Max.

"Did Chase say anything to you?"

"No, just to get everyone out I could," Max said. "Do you maybe think she's..."

"She wouldn't let Jade take her. And she wouldn't call, at least not from her cell phone. She might be leading them away from us. She might be dead."

Max closed his eyes. If Chase was dead they'd all be dead eventually. An involuntary tremble ran through him.

"What do you need me to do?"

"I know your kids came up with a way to hunt down Jade's houses."

"Yeah. If we have server access, we can pull up the info."

"Becca's already working on that... Can you help them? We need to hit back as soon as we can. If we strike back, it should buy us time to get our people to safety."

"Will do," Max said. "We lost the drones."

"Savior's working on getting replacements."

Max looked in the direction of "his" kids. He liked having kids again. He really hoped he could keep them safe and far, far away from the Queen Vampire Bitch.

"Hey Max," Tank said. "Jenna's over there. Take a minute."

Max took a breath and nodded. "Thanks."

Jenna was working on her own computer and she looked up as he approached. Without a word he took her hand and led her away from the busy area. He was about to stop when she started pulling him to a door with the word "Office" on it. Max smiled. He wouldn't mind at all having a little privacy.

She opened the door to a small office with a couch. Perfect, thought Max.

After they went into the room he closed the door. Despite all the horrible things that had happened that day, Max couldn't stop smiling. She was the most beautiful thing he'd ever seen, even in just a plain black t-shirt and pants. On her it was stunning. She was smiling back as she pulled a strand of hair behind her ear, her delicate features looking so perfect.

"I love you," she signed.

"I love you back," he said.

She put her arms around him and they held each other for a moment. Love rippled through them. He'd never felt anything like it. He'd been in lust before, but not love, not really.

They kissed gently at first and then passion took hold. Max kicked off his boots and pulled his clothes off while she did the same. In seconds they were both naked, except for their socks.

Max ran his hands over her breasts and she touched him in all the right places. Jenna took Max's erect cock in her hands and moved her fingers up and down the shaft. Max lifted her left breast up and took her nipple in his mouth, running his tongue along it. He felt her pleasure along with his own. Max moved on to the other nipple and Jenna threw her head back but never making a sound.

Being a vampire there never any question about if your partner was ready or what she wanted. Max lifted Jenna up and they laid back on the couch. She spread her legs ready for him. Max entered her and excitement rippled through them both.

They both began to move, adjusting for each other's

pleasure. Slight movements this way or that intensified the feeling between them until Max didn't know where his pleasure ended and hers began. They moved in unison as though they'd been making love for years, decades, centuries.

Each touch was a promise, each kiss filled with passion, each thrust into her electric as joy overtook them. Max forced himself to slow slightly so he could hold out a little longer while Jenna's body caught up with his. He wanted them to come together, or as close as they could manage.

Max pushed into her deeper. As he got closer he couldn't hold out any longer. With his last few thrusts, he knew Jenna was so close. When he came, she was only moments behind him. Their pleasure mixed together in the ultimate shared experience.

Finally they laid together still, connected, their bodies one. Max pulled back just enough to look at Jenna. He loved her. They came together in a kiss, gentle, hungry, perfect.

They laid together for a while, longer than they should have, Max knew. The world was falling apart just outside the door that separated them from the rest of the hanger. Terrible things had happened, people he liked had died, maybe one or both of the most powerful creatures on the planet were dead, and for just those few moments Max didn't care.

After Jenna gave Max his glass-seeking back rub and used a Sharpie to mark places that still hurt, Max and Jenna tried to sneak out of the office. Still, it wasn't like every vampire in the building didn't have the senses to know what they were up to. He didn't care.

What he did care about was the growing hole he felt in his gut about who they'd lost. Rhonda could have made a difference in the war and maybe been a replacement for Max if he got killed or couldn't do be their sniper anymore. Some of the other vamps and humans, like Sheila, he didn't know well, but he knew them well enough to be very sad they were gone.

After Max went to the men's room to clean up, he saw Dr. Foster, who was still hanging around and she did much more minor surgery on him to get out some of the hidden glass slivers.

After thanking the Doctor once again he joined the kids to try and pin down some of Jade's locations.

Becca was running one of her algorithms, while Savior and Max went through charts that were being spit out by the printer. They'd lost some of the work from earlier in the day, but they were caught up and starting to make progress, especially after some of the computer people showed up to help.

Max was deeply engrossed in his work when his head suddenly snapped to his left. A human was passing by him a little too closely and the smell overwhelmed him.

Savior noticed. "Whoa, Max. You're white," he said.

Max nodded. "Yeah. Having to heal takes it out of ya. Well... Let me check with Terry."

Avoiding any human close encounters, Max made his way toward Terry, who was working with Nadine.

"Hey, Terry," he said.

"Hey, Max," Terry said as he looked up. "Oh... Volunteers are on the way. It will be a bit though. There's blood in the frig."

Max nodded and headed off to a little kitchen area. He poured himself a drink and nuked it in the microwave.

As Max drank his blood he contemplated Chase, Jade, the dead, the missing, and how long he thought it might be before he'd get to have sex with Jenna again. He felt the blood ease his hunger. He was preparing a second drink when one of the garage-type doors opened.

A car pulled up which Max sensed had humans in it. The volunteers had arrived. He was more than a little happy about that. What he was drinking only just eased his blood lust. He still downed a second drink so he'd stay in control. He didn't want to hurt anyone.

As the humans started to get out of the car, Max snapped to attention. Someone was coming through the darkness of the open garage door, someone he knew. All his senses were on alert. Was it Jade? Was it Chase? He wasn't sure at first.

Max realized all the vampires were watching, waiting on edge. When Chase appeared out of the darkness, Max breathed a sign of relief. She was alive. Her clothes were also in burnt in tatters, and she held someone by the waist who was dangling like a rag doll, jerking around as Chase almost literally flew in to the hanger.

Max put down his cup and ran up to the door along with most of the other vampires in the place. She came to a sudden stop. Chase dropped her package, a snarling, hissing vampire Max knew all to well. Max closed his eyes, part of him relieved, part of him horrified.

The vampire hissed at Chase and then saw him.

"Hi, Mr. Maguire. Jade will be so happy to know you're not dead," said Crystal.

"Hi, Crystal," he said. "She already knows."

Crystal tried to jump up but Chase pushed her back to the ground. The tiny girl's once 17-year-old innocent face was twisted it into something crazy, evil. She laughed like a maniac.

Nadine ran up with a robe, which Chase put on.

"I'm glad you're all alive," Chase said.

"Thank God, you're okay," Nadine said. "We've been doing what we can."

Two vampires Max didn't know very well, a man and a woman, grabbed up Crystal and hauled her off.

Tank with his usual non-expression nodded to Chase.

"Thank you everyone. Please get back to work. Every thing you do now is so important."

There were sighs and expressions of relief as they went back to their duties. Everyone except Tank. Max paused.

"Jade was at the high-rise," he said.

"I know. I sensed her."

"Do you know if she's still alive? She was in the escape stairs when the building went up."

Chase nodded sadly. "She's still alive Max." She motioned to Crystal, who was being held off to the side by the two guards. "You know her?"

Max nodded. "She was one of my students, the one I was trying to help."

"The one who got you into this," she said.

"Yes," Max acknowledged. "She's thoroughly drunk the Kool-Aid, in case you haven't guessed."

"I know." Chase regarded Tank for a moment and then looked back at Max. He knew what was coming next. "Can you help us with her?"

"She's not going to tell me anything and I doubt she knows where Jade is," Max said. Chase didn't say anything. He shook his head looking to the ground. After a moment he raised his eyes to meet hers. "I'll do what I can."

"Find a volunteer first," she said.

"I'm really glad you're alive, cause I was not looking forward to a world without you," Max said as he turned and found dinner.

# # #

Max came out of a privacy area that'd been set up, that looked a lot like voting booths. He led his volunteer out, a black young man named Jackson, to waiting chairs and brought him some orange juice and a cookie. Max didn't think Jackson was gay, but he sure didn't seem to mind the experience.

Tank waved Max over and reluctantly he headed in the big guy's direction. Then he caught Jenna looking at him and he stopped and smiled. They shared a lingering stare and then she went back to her work, however not before glancing up at him again. He felt the familiar stir between his legs and then shook it off. As soon as he was staring at Tank any remaining romantic feelings he had were drained out of his body. Max did note that Tank looked pinker, too.

"Max, tell me about the girl," Tank said.

"She's 17. At least she was when this started," Max said. "I don't know how Jade found her, but she's super smart and was my best student. She missed some classes and I went to check on her. She was one of Jade's favorites when I was there. Crystal asked Jade not to kill me, but I didn't get to talk to her much. Jade killed her grandmother, and set it up so it looked like Crystal had moved, so she was never listed as missing. I told most of this to Terry when you guys caught me."

"I know. I wanted to see if anything was missing."

"She's not going to talk to any of us or tell us any good info. She's a true believer, at least she was when I was there, and I really doubt things have changed for her. I got the impression she would die for Jade."

"Chase wants you to talk to her," said Tank.

"Okay," Max said, resigned. Tank started to get up.

"She's not going to respond with you there. You're too big and scary. Send Nadine or Terry in if you need someone else there."

He nodded. "Get Nadine."

Max waved over Nadine and they went toward the office. He really didn't want to replace the memories he had of the office not long before, but it made sense to put her in a room to contain her. Chase was just outside the door staring intently, no doubt studying Crystal with her senses. Chase had changed into the Corps standard uniform, a black t-shirt and pants like Jenna was wearing. Someone must have gotten them in bulk.

"What approach do you want me to take?" asked Max when he came up to Chase.

"Just talk to her." Max nodded and went into the room with Nadine following. The two vampires who'd hauled Crystal off were holding her down even though she was tied down pretty securely. They let go when Max and Nadine entered the room and left.

Crystal struggled against the ropes. "You fucking assholes. Who do you think you are? Jade's going to rip you apart!" She yelled after them. Then just as suddenly, she smiled at Max, her fangs showing.

"Mr. Maguire, how you been?"

"Good, Crystal. What about you?" he asked.

"Oh, you know. Not learning more about the fucking French and Indian War," she laughed.

Max pulled up a chair and sat in it backwards, wrapping his arms around the back of the chair. Nadine stood in the corner and watched.

"I don't imagine so."

"Too many people to kill, lives to destroy. The fun stuff," she said as she struggled against the ropes. Finally she calmed and just looked at him.

"Is Jade alive?" Max asked gently.

She considered him for a moment. "This interrogation thing is not your strong suit, is it Max?"

"Probably not... I'd just really like to give them a reason not to kill you," he said sadly.

"Like that matters. Jade's going to rip Chase's little bitches apart! I'm not important. I'm nothing. And there you are, you traitor. She made you. She turned you into a God and you turned on her!"

"I wasn't anything to her. Just another minion for her to toy with."

"You could have been something," Crystal said.

"No... And I didn't have a choice, any more than I had with Jade. They caught me and it was learn a new way or die. But I'm really, really glad they caught me... You don't have to kill people, Crystal. You can be a vampire and not kill anyone."

"You fool! Where's the fun in that?" She laughed, letting her crazy go. Then she quieted. Like Crystal, Max could hear a conversation in the hanger. It was Savior and Terry. He could sense Chase near them.

"Okay, give me the addresses and I'll look them up on Google Maps. We can take a look at the locations. It might help us find Jade's locations," Terry said.

"The first one is 107 W. Milford Ave.," replied Savior.

"Okay, that looks promising."

"Next, 8520 N. Townsend Street." Crystal's heart rate jumped. Max nodded. So he was just a distraction so they could figure out which locations Crystal was familiar with. He'd play along.

"So Crystal, you might be able to survive this if you talk to me," he said.

Crystal looked away from him as Savior read another address in the other room. Her heart beat was calm.

Nadine touched Max on the shoulder. "Chase will be in soon. We can just wait for her," she said. Max nodded as he fell silent. Another address was read in the hanger with no reaction from Crystal. But the one after she might as well have had cymbals in her chest. Max could see her discomfort as she squirmed against the ropes. A lie detector couldn't have gotten such good results.

They had five good possibilities by the end of their 15 address list. Max didn't have to be silent any longer, but he didn't have anything to say. He really hoped they weren't going to kill her now.

Crystal had started rambling and swearing. "You're all going die. Fucking idiots! Assholes!"

Chase came into the room, ignoring Crystals monologue. "Nadine, please get some chains and bolt her to the floor. Let's not risk her getting loose. Two guards with eyes on her at all times."

"Max," said Chase.

The previous guards returned. Max took one last look at the student he had such high hopes for a long time ago. He left the room and followed Chase. Music began playing which was too loud. He knew it was to cover up any conversations they didn't want Crystal to hear until they could move her. At least they weren't planning on killing her right away.

When there was some distance from the office, Chase stopped. "Thanks, Max."

"I might be able to save her with some time," he said.

"No you won't. I'm sorry. She's not one we can risk it with."

Max felt like his heart was being pulled out of his chest. "What do you need?"

"We're going to hit back," she said quietly. "We're moving at sunrise to another location and then tomorrow night. We're going to hit them all, one after the other."

Max nodded.

"Get some rest. Take care of yourself until go time," said Chase.

Max nodded and went toward the men's room. He saw Jenna glance up, but he just walked away.

He pulled open the door and went in passing a human who was peeing in one of the urinals. Max stalked to the last stall and slammed the door shut. He didn't have to use the toilet, but he needed a moment and there wasn't anywhere else to go. He heard the human leave and Max sunk down onto the toilet, putting his head in his hands.

Too much had happened. Emotions swirled through him and he couldn't stand it. This was what his life came down to? Watching people he cared about being murdered for no goddamn reason? Having to watch one of his kids being put down like a rabid animal because she was too dangerous? Having to snipe a bunch of other Crystals because Jade got to them first? Sobs racked him as he wrapped his arms around his body. None of this was fair.

Anger and grief boiled up in him in a way he hadn't felt for a long time. With Jade he'd hidden in the past using his knowledge of history to protect himself. But now he didn't have anywhere to go.

He just wanted to leave all of this behind. Grab Jenna and escape. Let Chase and Jade have at it and kill each other. Maybe they could hide in Australia or Africa or at the end of the earth somewhere. Of course, Jenna would never leave Chase. Maybe he should just shoot himself in the heart with a bolt and just stop it all, at least for him.

He just couldn't stop crying. What did any of it mean if he couldn't save Crystal when she was right in front of him? None of it was okay. He didn't want to do it anymore.

Then suddenly Jenna was there, wrapping her arms around him and holding him as he let a world of grief flow through him. She began to rock with him slowly, gently, lovingly. He let her calming influence cut through the sadness, slowly easing his emotions into something less dark.

They held each other for a long time. When Max could finally pull away to look at her, he saw she'd been crying too.

"We're a mess," he said without signing. She nodded, smiling.

"I'm sorry about Crystal," she mouthed. Tears threatened to starting raining down again, but he pulled them back, nodding.

"Me too."

## CHAPTER 28

Max and Jenna had managed to sleep together on one of the cots, even though the small beds were definitely made for one person. If they'd tried to have sex, it would not have accommodated that, but sleeping worked.

By morning the hanger was a beehive of activity and trucks and cars headed out, leaving it mostly empty. Max sat with his arm around Jenna as the car sped through the streets. Becca and Savior were facing them on the other seat of the limo, sleeping propped up against each other.

Max closed his eyes and held Jenna's tiny frame. She had fallen asleep with her head on his chest. He could feel her exhaustion which matched his own. She was the only reason he could handle any of this.

Max was not a hero. He wasn't even a good man. Long ago he'd decided he was done being evil, which was how he ended up teaching. He also decided he do whatever he had to to protect his kids, something he'd thought a lot about when school shootings became such a horrible fact of life.

But this was different. Jade would take more kids like Savior and Becca and Crystal and they'd die eventually or they'd become murderers. As long as Jade was alive, she'd do evil deeds. At the beginning Max had decided to kill Jade, no matter what. He wasn't able to do that, but Chase could and he'd have to do what was necessary to help.

Max looked down at the love of his life. Jenna slept peacefully in his arms. She smelled of strawberries, a scent he knew came from her shampoo. He breathed her in. Max knew Jade had to die, and the cost of that just might be Max's life. He was okay with that, though it made him sad to think about leaving Jenna alone. He'd really like to live 800 years with her, but not at the cost of one more kid becoming a monster like Crystal.

# # #

When they arrived at their next location, Max looked around and was surprised. It looked like a summer camp with small cabins surrounding one larger cabin. They were ushered into the larger cabin, which looked like a rustic cabin on the inside, until they went through a door which led to an elevator.

It was a little tight with Max, Jenna, Becca, Savior and Shades in the small elevator. Jenna pushed button number 5, but instead of going up, the elevator went down.

The elevator doors opened up to reveal a hallway that told Max the facility was much larger than he thought it could be. He followed Jenna through a couple more doors and hallways until they reached a large room, a war room with a lot of people zooming about.

"So, this is cool," Max said.

"Very cool," added Savior. Becca smiled and nodded.

Terry, who'd started to heal from his sunburn, approached them, clip board in hand. "Max and Jenna, you're wanted in there," he said, pointing to a door on their right. "Becca and Savior, you follow me. I have volunteers lined up for all of you and then we'll get you started. There are also rooms with cots in case you need a nap at some point."

"Yep! This is so fucking cool!" Savior said.

Max and Jenna headed off to the door and before he got there he knew Chase was on the other side.

He opened the door and saw her behind a large desk, working on a computer. Jenna followed him in the room.

"Sit down," Chase said. They took seats opposite her. "Max thanks for... for what you did."

"She saw me, you know. Jade. If you made it out, I have to think she did too," he said.

"I'm sure she made it out. I didn't see her but I know she's alive."

"Veronica was there too."

"Maybe we got her," Chase said a slight smile creasing her lips.

"We're going to take down the locations your kids have come up with, Max. I want both of you on the raids."

Max felt a pang of worry run through him at the thought of Jenna being at risk. He had very long term plans he hoped to take part in. But he nodded.

"I especially want your rifle covering us," she continued. Max couldn't stop from exhaling a deep breath.

"Okay... Do we have rifles?"

"Yes, we have rifles, and the drones with infrared sensors Savior got for us. It should help separating the humans from the vampires."

"Good... Where's Crystal?"

"Not here. I couldn't take a chance on giving away this location, especially not after losing the high-rise. However, we haven't knocked her out yet either. She may still be useful... Max, you did a great job with the kids. If it wasn't for you and the kids we wouldn't have a strong counter offensive."

Max laughed. "Counter offensive. I'm betting the Civil War generals weren't the only soldiers you've known in your life."

Both the women smiled at him, a knowing look shared between them for a fleeting moment.

"It would be a safe bet."

"Maybe I can get Terry to take odds on it," Max said.

"I want you two to plan the order of targets and how we're going to pull this off. We don't have time to waste, so if you can come up with how to approach this we can nail down that counter offensive... You know what the plan is?" said Chase.

"To kill Jade," Max said casually.

Jenna signed, "To kill Jade."

"To kill Jade," Chase repeated.

# # #

"I think this is the estate Jade will most likely be at," Max said to a large round table of people plotting Jade's demise.

Chase, Terry, Jenna, Shade, Becca and Savior, as well as a few other vampires Max barely knew, listened intently.

"Why this estate over the others?" Terry asked.

"It's her style. It's a lot like the one she lived at when I was with her. It just looks like her... I could be wrong, but I'm feeling like this is the one she'd want, and Jade gets what she wants."

Chase nodded slowly. "I agree. It's a good possibility... That gives us an order for the targets... Rita, Wayne and Paula will be our drone pilots, with Nadine, Savior and Becca watching remotely."

"I could do it. Please, I want to do it," said Savior.

Chase looked at him sternly. "I don't send children into war."

"But..."

"We need you helping remotely, buddy. I need you as my spotters so we can save the humans," Max said gently. "And if it all goes bad we're going to need you as backup too, both you and Becca."

"But who's going to protect you, Max?" Becca asked.

"Are you kidding? Look around you," Max gestured to those around him. "I've got loads of protection."

The kids settled down reluctantly as Chase continued laying out the plans. It was a good plan, but Max couldn't help the uneasy feeling that crept into his stomach.

As they left the table and began to finish preparations for the battle, Savior caught up with Max alone.

"Why can't I be there, Max?" he asked.

"You are going to be there, right in my ear guiding me," he replied.

"But Max..."

"Look, we're an army and when you're a soldier you take orders and do the best you can with those orders. Because the general, who is Chase, knows what's best for the battle ahead. If something does happen to me, or any of us, it will be up to you to continue the fight."

"I don't want you to die." Savior looked like he was about to cry.

"I don't want me to die either," Max said calmly. "I'll try really hard not to, but if I do I'll need you to take care of Becca and Jenna for me. I'll need you to take care of all of them. You're so smart, Savior. You and Becca have made it possible for us to stop Jade and her people. You're like The Next Generation on Star Trek."

"I never saw that one, Max."

"It was a good one. You might want to binge it when you get a chance."

"Promise me you'll try really, really hard not to die."

"I promise I'll try," Max said.

"Okay then. If they need me to I'll be The Next Gen for you."

"It's a deal."

"But if you die..."

"Then I died trying to stop Jade. I'm okay with that."

"I'm not. I'll be really mad if you die... You're the only one who..." Savior's voice cracked.

"I love you too, buddy."

"Yeah... Try not to die. Please." Savior turned wiping tears out of his eyes and headed toward Becca.

# # #

Assignments were given out, the plotting was done, the vampires had gotten a meal, and they had about an hour to rest. Max had other things on his mind besides sleeping though. He saw Jenna from across the war room looking at him and he knew she had a similar idea. If he was going to face death and perhaps the loss of the woman he loved then they were going to fuck like bunnies for as much time as they could.

It wasn't a unique idea. Max saw Terry and Nadine and several of the pairings he knew about vanish for a while. He sprinted across the room and Jenna's smile grew as he snatched her hand and they went off to find a room. They found a few locked doors before they discovered an open room. It was just a couple twin beds with a desk and no personality, but it would do.

No sooner was the door shut and locked than their clothes were off and their tongues were in each other's mouths, along with everywhere else that felt good.

Max was nibbling on one of her nipples and caressing her clit with his fingers when she decided she wanted to be on top. She spun him around until she was straddling him. He'd been amazed the first time she did that, considering how tiny she was, but vampire strength didn't care about size.

Her fingers danced along the shaft of his cock as her tongue caressed his stomach and the pressure built within him. He really wanted to be inside her. He could feel her growing desire as he pulled her hips up to his own and pressed his fingers into her. She began making the wonderful little movements that told him what she wanted.

Max eased his cock into her and they began to move, pleasure filling him up. Their mouths found each other as they fucked, their movements becoming more in sync with each stroke as Max tried to get deeper inside her. He was getting better at holding off his climax while hers built, until they were moving almost as one.

Max knew she could feel his pleasure just as he could feel hers as they rode the wave of his climax and then hers.

Afterward they held each other tightly, not willing to let go. He was breathing hard, something that rarely happened since the whole vampire thing started. He looked at her and realized she was laughing at him. Max started to laugh too. He kissed her gently and with a growing passion.

Considering their time restraints, Max wasn't sure he had it in him, but he managed a second go-around. It was only slightly less exciting than the first round. Then they just held each other, falling asleep connected in every way. He didn't ever want to let her go.

As Max woke with a start he realized Jenna was also

awake.

"Are you okay?" he signed.

"Yes. We'll have to leave soon. Is it wrong I don't want to go fight Jade. I don't even want to think about her."

"No. I wish we could stay like this forever," Max said.

"I've lost more than one love to this war," she said.

"I'm sorry."

"Don't be sorry. If I stop loving then why am I doing this?"

"For what it's worth, I've never loved anyone before you," he said.

She smiled and kissed him. "I thought I couldn't love anyone more than I loved Mason, but Max you're making me wonder about that."

"I did promise Savior I would try not to get killed tonight," he said.

"Good plan," she said.

"Can you try not to get killed tonight too?"

She looked at him lovingly. "I will try."

"Okay. I'd really like to give the 800 year thing a shot."

Jenna nodded and the growing feeling of unease about their coming battle calmed, at least for a little while.

## CHAPTER 29

Whatever calming impact Jenna had on him dissipated by the time the mission was almost ready to go. His gut told him things were going to go badly and he couldn't shake the feeling of dread.

Max caught Chase in her office before they were set to leave.

"So I'm not trying to be negative or anything, but I've got a bad feeling about this. In the Army I learned to trust my gut, and it's telling me all sorts of stuff I don't want to hear," he said.

"Would you have me stop the mission?" Chase asked.

"I don't know. It just feels like something's off, even you catching Crystal," he said.

"Yes, that bothered me too. It seemed almost like Jade wanted me to catch her."

"I'm sorry. My Spidey sense is banging away."

"Well, I've never been one to ignore a Spidey sense," she said with a slight smile. "Let's get the band back together for a chat, the adult band. The kids don't need to be a part of this."

"Agreed," Max said.

# # #

The team stood in a circle and discussed a back-up plan, but with a lot more animation than before, especially from Jenna who furiously disagreed with the direction things were taking.

"No," she signed. "I don't like this. It's a terrible plan, and it's going to get..."

"It's a back-up plan. That's all," Max said.

"I don't like it either," Shades said. "But it could give us a tactical advantage."

"At what cost?" Jenna signed.

"If we're down to Plan B, the cost may well be significant before we even get there," Chase said, her eyes drifting to the floor before looking back up to hold Jenna's glare. As they stared at each other Max felt the history between them weighed heavily. "I'm sorry. We have to be ready."

Jenna slammed her fist into a nearby counter, leaving a dent in it, the sound echoing through the room.

Max took her in his arms. She tried to push away from him at first and then slowly let her body ease into his. He stroked her hair and held her tight. The others left for last minute duties. No more discussion was necessary.

After a few moments Max pulled back so he could look at her. He could feel the anger and worry that welled up inside her. He didn't bother to sign.

"I love you. I don't know what's going to happen, but if Jade wins this one I don't regret one moment of what's happened between us. I don't. Even if we don't have one more minute together. I don't."

Jenna shook her head and then buried her face in his chest. Then suddenly she pushed away from him.

"If one of us dies I'd regret not getting to spend that 800 years with you," she signed. "When I lost Mason I didn't want to live anymore."

"If one of us dies I'd be happy to know that you're fighting on with Chase and the others to turn Jade to dust. I'd be okay with that," Max said.

"I wouldn't," she signed. Jenna shook her head and took a deep breath. Max reached out to stroke her cheek. "But I don't regret our time. I love you too."

They wrapped their arms around each other and held each other for a long time, ignoring the beehive of activity near them. Max had some things to do before they left, especially considering the Plan B of it all, but he just couldn't leave her one moment before he had to.

# # #

As the van pulled out of the compound, Max looked

around at the soldiers sitting in the vehicle around him. Chase's soldiers. He was one of them now. He'd been on enough missions to know that this was different. No joking, no laughing, just the knowledge that this mission was special. Everyone held a grim expression that came with knowing this might be an important battle, maybe even the most important battle.

Jenna was in a different van, set to hit a different target, and Max couldn't bear the thought that he might lose her. He was okay if he died, but he didn't want to live in a world without her in it.

Max watched through the front window of the van as America went by them, all the windows tinted to protect them from the sun. He both loved and hated America, which had failed him and later saved him. Whatever happened with Jade would reverberate through the country one way or another, even if the country didn't know it.

He was very happy though that his kids were safe for now back at the compound, especially since he didn't know what the outcome of the day would be. Savior and Becca hadn't liked one bit seeing him go, but they'd be following the action with the drone cameras. They'd be the spotters using the infrared on the drones, helping him save humans and take out the bad vampires.

He'd had a short talk with them before he left.

"Becca, Savior, I don't know what's going to happen," Max told them. "But it's important if anything happens to me, you two take care of each other."

"Max, we can't..." Becca said.

"That's the most important thing. Okay."

Becca shook her head no and Savior looked away, devastated at the thought. Then he slowly looked back up at Max. "Savior will take care of Becca, and keep fighting."

"If the war is lost, hide. Forget fighting. Run away. Just take care of each other. You both know how to survive now. Run to the ends of the earth if you have to," Max said.

They both looked at him wide-eyed, shocked.

"But Max..." Becca started to say.

"I mean it. If I'm gone, if Jenna's gone, if Chase is gone, don't lose your lives to an impossible fight. Your lives are too important. Got it?" he said.

Savior slowly nodded. And then Becca took his hand and nodded too.

"Just don't let anything happen to you," she said.

# # #

There were three six-man strike teams. Max was part of Strike Team Two, along with Chase, Shades, and some other vampires he didn't know very well, Wayne, Pete, and Rose. Jenna was part of Strike Team One. Chase had purposely separated Jenna and Max, a decision he didn't like but agreed with. It'd be hard for him to focus on his job if he saw her in danger.

After an hour's drive they approached the location of his Strike Team's first target. It was an estate Max felt might be the best location to find Jade, a place that felt too familiar.

The knot in his gut never entirely went away, although it had eased a bit. He prayed Jade would end up on the other side of his sniper's scope, although he doubted God would ever answer a vampire's prayers.

Their first target offered some challenges since there weren't any close buildings or houses. The estate was surrounded by open grassy areas and then by woods. At least that would give them some coverage. A vacant house on the other side of the rear woods outside of the estate provided cover for the strike team. The house had a big garage, which gave them private parking and a place to hide from the sun until sunset.

They set up in the back of the empty house. They didn't waste time waiting for the sun to set. Max and the others hid in the shadows as Chase used binoculars hunting for any kind of surveillance. When she didn't see any, she put a drone out on the patio while Wayne set up the equipment and tied that into a feed that Nadine, Savior, and Becca back at home base could watch. Max knew that the other strike teams were doing the same with their first targets.

Wayne, a short but sturdy fellow who looked only slightly older than Savior, seemed very comfortable with the electronics and he had the drone in the air quickly. Savior had been giving him lessons on drone flying since the idea had popped up. Max and the others watched the laptop monitor as the drone took flight and gave a birds-eye view of the area. At first Wayne flew the drone in a wide pattern not getting to close to the estate. The grounds had a magnificent mansion, a smaller outer house, a pool, a tennis court, gardens and beautiful landscaping. It was perfect for Jade.

While the estate was stunning, there wasn't anyone in sight or any sign that vampires were present. The sun was starting to set so Wayne switched to infrared and got closer to the main house with his drone.

"Chase, I've got to find my perch," Max said. She nodded as he put his ear piece in said "Testing one, two, three," which came through loudly from Wayne's equipment.

Shades helped him with the weapons. He'd have Max's back so Max could focus on shooting the hell out of any vampires at the end of his scope, and not worry about who might be sneaking up on him. As always, Shades wore different sunglasses, and the new ones were an almost subtle shade of purple. Shades didn't often do subtle. Max was glad the big guy had his back. Shades carried a RPG-7 rocket launcher, which they could use to take out any fake windows and otherwise make lots of trouble and noise. They just had to get close enough to use it effectively.

Shades tested his own earpiece and then picked up a duffel bag with his free arm, which was filled with rifles, ammo and grenades for the rocket launcher. The moment the sun was down Max picked up his own duffel and they went out the sliding door and headed toward the woods.

After entering the woods the first sign that they might just be in the right place happened when Max nearly stepped on a trip wire. He stopped suddenly and put his arm up to stop Shades.

"Trip wire," he said quietly. Shades nodded and they both carefully stepped over it. "Chase, either we're in the right place or someone is serious about their security."

"Understood," Chase said over their intercom.

Max and Shades continued more slowly and quickly found more trip wires. "Chase, we've found two more trip wires. I can't disarm them without taking time we don't have," Max said.

"It's okay. Find your perch."

"Will do."

They were half way through the wooded area when Max started looking for the right tree. Trees were his least favorite types of perches. He liked having solid ground or floor under him which was definitely not the branches of a tree.

Max came upon a large tree with lots of branches. He studied it for a moment and then nodded to himself. "This one might work." Max dropped his duffel bag and easily shimmied up the tree, until he was high enough to see the estate. He smiled to himself. In the Army it'd been downright exhausting going through rough terrain, while dragging packs and rifles and ammo. Having the strength of a vampire made it easy.

Max studied his view of the house and examined the trees around him looking for any sign of movement. He was close enough to the big house and had a good view. He could see light coming from the windows of the house, which he knew if this was one of Jade's houses, was actually just a painted board on the inside of the window with a light installed to make it all look real.

This one wasn't going to be as easy as his last target which had actual windows he could shoot out. But Shades' RPG-7 could blow the windows and do some damage.

Max was about a quarter mile from the target, which

would be a snap for the average sniper. But the average sniper had bullets instead of bolts with its mix of steel and wood. Lucky for Chase and her army, Max wasn't average.

"Still no sign of life, Blue," Wayne said through the earpiece.

"None here either," he replied.

Max found the perfect spot in the branches with a clear view of the mansion and went back down to get the duffel bag and filled Shades in. Moments later he was back in the tree and setting up things, while Shades stayed on the ground with the RPG-7, and a bag full of grenades on one shoulder and a rifle on the other.

Max looked down at the big bespectacled man and nodded. He did kind of dig the new purple shades.

Shades nodded back and set off to find his own perch.

Max set up his rifles and bolts so he'd be able to easily grab what he needed to fire.

"Red ready," he said in his microphone.

Moments later he heard Shades say, "Orange Ready."

"We're moving," Chase said through his earpiece.

Max took a deep breath. In moments they'd either rain hell down on the estate or they'd move on to their second target.

Savior's voice came through the earpiece. "Strike Team 1 is a no show for Target A."

"Shit," someone muttered. Max shook his head. He couldn't help but wonder if all the planning was for nothing.

But then Max saw movement at the estate's mansion. "It looks like I've got two guards coming out of the mansion. Can we get the drone in place, Yellow?"

"Just a minute," Wayne said. Seconds seemed to stretch beyond any reasonable point. Max lined up the shot just in case.

"I can see them... Infrared says we've got two vampires," Savior said.

Chase chimed in. "I'm in position. I concur. We've got a vampire house. Fire at will, Red, Orange."

"Red, I'm not sensing any humans on the first floor. And I'm not sensing Jade either. All are targets," Chase said.

"You got it, Blue," he said, lining up a kill shot with one of the guards. He'd already checked the wind and made the calculations he needed for a successful shot. He knew what he had to do.

"Yellow, sweep the exits," she said.

"Roger that," Wayne said.

For a moment it was total silence. Everyone waited for Shades to hit the windows and doors with the RPG. When Max heard swish of the grenade being launched, he nailed the first guard who went up in dust. While the thunder of the grenade sounded off as it went through the air, Max had killed the second guard with another shot through the heart. The explosion hit near a big picture window, just missing it.

In moments Shades had another shot off that took out the window. Chase and the others raced across the grass area vampire-fast to the house.

"That's two down in front of the house," Max said.

"Red, there's five vampires on the first floor, and three vampires on the second floor, two humans. Still checking on the basement. I've also got two in the small house behind. I'm not sensing Jade so far," Chase said.

"Let me know if those humans move," Max said. He had movement on the first floor through the bombed out window, but waited til he had a shot. Suddenly a woman appeared, but Max hesitated for a moment. Was that Maria, from his days with Jade? The one person he thought might be an ally who'd shown him how to use the fancy vampire killing weapon might be in his scope? Max pulled the trigger. Before the bolt could hit its target he realized it wasn't her. He couldn't take a chance, but he was relieved, especially when his bolt hit its target and she vanished into dust.

"Three down," Max said. Shades sent off another grenade which took out another window. Max tossed his rifle onto a branch so it was hanging by a strap and grabbed a fresh rifle.

"We've got two runners from the small house," Savior said.

"Red here, I don't have an angle on them," Max said.

"Purple here, I've got them," Rose said.

Max heard some shots, but he couldn't see what was happening.

"Yellow, get over to backup Rose," Chase said.

"Roger," Wayne replied.

Max found another target in the form of a big man who ran out Shades' new opening. Max fired and hit the vampire in the shoulder. He went down but quickly pulled himself up and tried to run. Chase caught up with him and staked him in the heart with a bolt.

Max saw movement in one of the second floor windows. Someone had broken the window and was trying to get out.

"Blue here, second floor escape," he said to Chase.

"Human," she said. Max eased the tension off his trigger finger. Then he saw another figure behind the escaping woman.

"Vampire, Red." He took the shot and hit the man in the throat. The vampire went down and Max adjusted his weapon to hit the heart as the vamp tried to rise back up. This time Max's bolt hit the mark and the vampire was dust. The woman trying to get out the window screamed and nearly fell. But she caught herself and was able to lower herself toward the ground and dropping the last few steps.

Shades shot off another grenade away from the woman's location, hitting the main door. By that time Chase and the rest of the strike team were in the building and cleaning up the remaining vampires.

Max heard a few shots, but then silence. Max saw Rose pushing one captive back toward the house.

"Red, Orange, hold... Floors one and two are under our control. Heading toward the basement. I felt Jade for a moment, but the feeling's gone. We missed her."

"Fuck!" a man's voice said over the comm. Maybe it was

Shades.

Max realized he'd been holding his breath. He released it, but kept up his surveillance of the area.

"Two more vampires, two humans in the basement. We've got everyone... Red, Orange, come in," Chase said.

Max had no sooner relaxed and was about to stow the weapons than he sensed she was near him. He remembered her, the way she felt, her smell, everything about her. Jade was near. Very near.

Max twisted his head trying to spot her. But she was right there below him, an angry Shades struggled in her grasp. The Vampire Queen Bitch looked as stunning as ever, a slight bemused look on her face.

"Max, Shades, get out of the woods! Jade's there!" Chase yelled.

"I know," Max whispered.

Jade held up Shades' earpiece and said, "Chase is it now? Sorry I missed you. I think I'll take my property back now."

Shades fought to get free. "Jade, he can be useful to you," Max said.

"Oh, Max, really? A sniper? You really are full of surprises," she said as she ripped off Shades' head, his glasses falling to the ground as the big man turned to dust. Before Max could move, Jade was on him and they were gone.

Max fought like his life depended on it, trying to get free of Jade's grasp, but he wasn't any more successful than Shades had been except he wasn't dead yet. He didn't even know how far they'd gone before she dumped him in the backseat of a limo.

He considered trying to run some more, but laughed and sat up in the seat as she slid next to him.

"You're looking lovely," he said as he straightened his disheveled clothing. She took off his earpiece and crushed it.

"Thanks Teacher. I've missed you too... Drive," she said to the driver.

"Sure you have," he said.

"The sniping thing. That's cool. Why didn't I think about that?"

"Because you're living in the past?" he questioned.

"I really thought you were dead until I saw you at the high-rise."

"Some say vampires are dead or undead," he snapped.

She paused for a moment. "Jenna. How interesting. Well, I wouldn't have expected Chase to turn you over to her little pet."

"Well, fuck you. Why don't you just kill me? I'm not worth anything to you," he said angrily.

"Fuck me? What a good idea."

# # #

A couple hours later Max found himself back at another Jade estate, sitting on her bed after having been thrown in a shower and dressed to her liking. It was as though he'd never left.

They were alone and she sat next to him, dressed in one of her dresses that might as well have been her wearing nothing at all.

She touched his leg and he focused on anger making sure she knew how he felt.

"What? No one's been able to give you a good fuck since I've been gone?" he said, letting his anger spill through every word.

"Oh, I've found my amusements. I really thought you and Chase might get it on, but Jenna... So here's what I want. I want to know everything you know. And if you don't give that to me, I'll start killing humans, just one after the other until you spill every secret you have," she said. "Every location, every person, every secret plan, all of it."

"Well, I guess I better start making some stuff up then, because I don't know shit," he said. "You think they trusted me with anything? Seriously? They kept me in a cage until they found out I could shoot. And even in a cage it was better than the cage you kept me in."

"I don't believe you, Teacher. I gave you this amazing gift and you betrayed me."

"They were going to kill me. I told them what they wanted to hear, just like I'll tell you what you want to hear," he said.

Jade pushed Max down on the bed and ran her hands down his body. As before, he couldn't stop his body from responding, especially not since he could feel her desire.

She kissed him, but he didn't kiss back. She stopped suddenly and then pushed herself off him. "Hummm... well, you've got more control than you had before. So how many humans do you think it will take? 10? 20? 30? Maybe I'll just turn a couple of them and set them loose on the others. That'd be fun."

"I don't know anything."

"The problem with you, Teacher, is humans are your kryptonite," she said.

"And the problem with you is you're a fucking bitch." Again he let the anger flow through him as he spat out each word. "Let's not pretend I'm Superman, shall we?"

"Well, you're something. A sniper, in what? The Army?"

"Special Forces. Your people should have done their homework."

"Yes, they should have. But I'm still going to win and you're going to help me do that. You're going to help me kill Chase and her little band of sheep, along with sweet tiny Jenna."

Max flew at her trying to rip her apart, but she pinned him to the carpeted floor. Max spit in her face and when she pulled back in anger, he started laughing.

"You really think you can scare me? You Goddamn evil piece of shit! You're nothing but a fucking bitch and Chase is gonna kill you!"

Jade let Max go and stood. She used a tissue to wipe Max's deposit off her face. "It's only a matter of time, Max. I will break you. I just didn't work hard enough at it the last time."

Jade gave him a long look and then left the room. Max sat up slowly, pain radiating through his side. She'd broken a couple of his ribs, but they started knitting back together almost immediately.

"Well, that was fun," he said to himself.

# # #

Max stewed for what seemed like an eternity before they came to get him. He hadn't had any blood for hours and he was starving.

He was marched down into the basement by three guards and saw Jade's throne and a large cross he had a feeling was set up just for him. The space was set up much like before including human captives held somewhere nearby and an acid vat for disposing of those inconvenient bodies.

Max decided he wasn't going to make it easy on his guards, despite the fact he was feeling weak, so he put on the brakes and starting fighting them. Not successfully, but still he did get some good punches in before they could chain him up to the cross. By the time they were done he wasn't able to move at all.

Some familiar players and some unfamiliar vampires

began to file in, laughing and talking until they saw him. Then there were just hushed whispers. He was kind of glad to see Maria was still in one piece, despite the shocked look on her face. She shook her head and then looked away from him. Her one time fighting partner, Eric, also wandered down, but smiled when he saw Max. They weren't dressed for fighting this time and were wearing street clothes, so Max figured they weren't part of the entertainment tonight.

When Veronica entered the arena she studied Max for a moment with a sour look on her face.

"Hi, Veronica. How you been?" Max asked causally. "Too bad you didn't get burnt up in the high-rise."

She scowled at him and stood next to the throne awaiting the Queen.

Jade floated in in a stunning purple fuck-me dress. Quiet spread through the basement with only a few whimpering humans to distract from the silence.

Jade settled in on her throne studying Max and looking inscrutable as ever, her long blonde hair framing her face beautifully.

"How you doing, Teacher?" she asked.

"Just peachy. You?" he replied. Anger percolated through him.

"I'm doing much better now." Out of the shadows appeared Crystal.

"Hi Mr. Maguire." Max shook his head and sighed.

"Are you surprised we got her back?" Jade asked.

"Everything you do surprises me," he said, his voice low, guttural.

Crystal walked to the throne and stood opposite Veronica as though they were bookends, with Jade in the middle. The vampire queen reached out and stroked Crystal's hair. The young vampire looked at her with such love. His heart broke, knowing she was lost to him.

"We embedded a special tracker in Crystal. It's very hard to trace, and then let Chase catch her," she smiled, beautiful teeth, perfect smile.

Max closed his eyes and let the rage fill him up. As he opened his eyes he asked, "And how did that work out for you?"

"We didn't get as many of Chase's people as we wanted to, but we did get some of our own back. And we learned some things."

"I've always been a fan of education," Max snapped at her. She studied him for a moment and then smiled.

"Was it a useful trip, Crystal?"

"Yes, Jade. I have a full report for you," she said.

"Good. It should be illuminating... Eric."

Without hesitation Eric came out of the shadows and stood before Jade. "Release the Teacher, would you. I need him to have his arms free."

He nodded and then with another vampire set about getting Max out of the chains. Max readied himself. He wasn't surprised he was going to be the main entertainment.

Max fell to the ground when the chains were released. He rubbed his arms and stood. Eric and the other vampire went back to the shadows.

"So what's it going to be?" Max asked.

"Are you ready to die, Max?" Jade replied.

"Sure. Been ready since I was a kid. What about you, Jade?"

"Well, I've got a lot to do yet. A lot of humans to kill. But I'd like to see what you can do with the Saracian Lance."

Max laughed. "Sure. Let's do that." Max spread his arms and bowed. "Why not! Let's get on with the show!"

"I think you need a drink before we get started. Wouldn't want you to get all weak at the knees," Jade said. She lifted her chin slightly and Eric brought in a human man wearing an Army jacket and hat, likely homeless. He was crying and struggling. Eric pushed him into the ring towards Max. The man who had so long ago been a high school history teacher laughed and flew at Eric, grabbing him by the neck and bit down. Eric spun around with Max attached trying to get him off, but Max had a death grip on Eric and drank his blood deeply.

Eric fell to his knees, slamming Max to the ground, which finally released Max's grip. Max rolled and got to his feet.

"That's better," Max said wiping his mouth with the back of this hand. Max laughed as a furious Eric jumped to his feet and rammed him with his head, knocking them both to the ground.

The homeless guy scooted out of the way, while the two vampires fought, spinning, punching, kicking and slamming each other until they flew apart both hitting the ground hard.

"Enough!" yelled Jade. Eric jumped up, snapping to attention looking at Jade, but then glaring at Max, while Max sat up on the ground and smiled. He stood up slowly.

"I'm good now," Max said. "What's next?"

Jade nodded and let a slow smile spread across her face. Max felt stronger with Eric's blood coursing through him. He knew he was probably going to die in Jade's arena, but that was okay. It was all for a good cause, after all.

"Maria, will you die for me?" Maria came out of the shadows and faced her standing next to Max.

"Of course, Jade. I'll die for you."

"I'm not fighting her," Max said.

"Then you'll die," Jade said.

"I guess I will. She's way better than me anyway," he said.

Eric brought out two Saracian Lances and tossed one to Maria and the other to Max. He looked at the weapon and then at Maria.

"Okay, anything for your entertainment, bitch!" Max snapped.

There was a gasp throughout the audience and Maria's mouth dropped open, but she quickly regained her composure.

Jade laughed. "Well Teacher, it looks like the real you isn't hiding from me anymore."

"I'm just a bundle of laughs, aren't I?" he said. "Don't worry, Maria, I can't possibly beat you. It's really not going to be much of a contest."

Max swung the blade a couple times and tried to get the feel of the weapon again. "It's okay," Max said to her. "I'm already dead. Just put me out of my misery."

She nodded, and they waited. The two opponents faced off against each other.

"Begin," Jade commanded.

Max did have a plan, not that he expected it to work, but he didn't have anything to lose by trying.

He'd practiced enough with Maria that he was comfortable with the weapon and after a few swings it started to feel good in his hands again. Max took a swing, Maria responded and swatted him on the butt with the wooden end of the lance. She was toying with him.

Max dove into a roll and came up closer to Jade. Maria swung the sickle end of the lance toward Max's head and he ducked just in time. He spun and swung and dipped and ducked and poked as she gave him a master class in the lance. If she wanted to kill him she could have easily.

Max just kept moving closer to Jade's throne until he took a giant swing that almost took off Veronica's head. She ducked, as the blade end of the lance was embedded in the side of Jade's throne. Veronica rose back up and punched Max square in the nose laying him out flat on his back.

Maria was shocked and just stopped for a moment. Max was bleeding from his nose and mouth as he sat up on his elbows and laughed.

"Well?" Jade asked. Maria responded and brought the blade down to within an inch from his neck. Max was lanceless and just waited. He pushed sad thoughts away. Maybe this was it for him.

Maria held the blade at his neck and then Jade paused long enough that Max thought he might not need another cowboy hat ever again.

"That's enough, Maria." She nodded and pulled the blade away from his neck. "I think I'm not done torturing you yet. It'd be a little too easy for you to just lose your head that quickly."

Max got back up to his feet. "Sorry I missed, Veronica."

The vampire was enraged, but held herself back.

"The show's over. Leave, except for Max and Veronica." Jade never stopped looking at Max as Maria grabbed her lance, while Eric rounded up the human who was supposed to be Max's dinner and secured him. The other vampires in the shadows left. Maria followed the others upstairs and soon the three vampires were alone.

"Let me kill him," Veronica said, venom spilling through each word.

"Not yet. You actually did a pretty good job of acting before, Teacher. I didn't sense this level of defiance in you."

"Yeah, maybe I should get an Oscar," he said.

"I'm not surprised very often, but you... I'm going to have so much fun dissecting you."

In a blur, Jade rose up and came at Max, picking him up by the throat and lifting him off his feet. He struggled, kicking and flailing around, but her grip was too powerful. Finally he calmed his body and relaxed, the only sound was him struggling to breathe.

She cocked her head, studying him, and then brought his face close to hers. "Such a blast," she said, her eyes boring into his as she held him like a rag doll.

Then suddenly an explosion hit the building which shook the ground, and she dropped him. Even Jade stumbled from the force of the blast. She was surprised for a moment, but then she shook her head.

"It's a trap," she said with a laugh. "Of course. You were good, Teacher. A total distraction. Is the tracker in you or Crystal?"

Max tried to scoot away from her. "Guess you'll have to figure it out," he said, his voice rough from her grip.

Dust billowed down the steps toward them and yelling and gunfire ripped through the building.

"I'd guess both, just to make sure in case I killed you. You really don't care if you live or die," Jade said. She quickly turned her attention to Veronica.

"Grab the bug out box and get the fuck out of here... And if you can get Crystal..." she ordered. Veronica nodded curtly and glared at Max, before running up the stairs.

Max scrambled up and tried to make a run for it, but Jade shoved him back on the ground. The force of her hit knocked the wind out of him and he was stunned for a moment.

"I don't think so, Teacher. You're my property and I have plans for you... So many plans," Jade said.

She grabbed him by the hair, pulling him up on his feet. Max tried to spin around to fight her but she pushed him toward the back corner of the basement.

"It'd be easier... if you just killed me, wouldn't it?" Max said, struggling to get the words out.

"Easier, yes," she said, distracted. She threw Max into the wall and he hit hard as she looked back at the stairway. Blood flowed into Max's left eye and down the side of his face as he struggled to move before he regained her full attention. But Jade grabbed him by the back of his shirt and pulled him toward an odd looking area of the wall that looked like it might be an exit, but was walled off.

Jade touched a brick in the wall and an opening in the wall appeared.

"An escape tunnel. How original," Max said. Jade pushed Max through the darkness of the opening but then stopped. She pulled him back and slowly backed them both up. Max could feel tension fill her body and then he knew as he looked into the depths of the dark tunnel... Chase was coming.

## CHAPTER 31

Jade pulled Max back to the far side of the arena and then let go of him. In a blur Chase was standing on the other side of the arena, with only her hair and clothes swinging forward to signify a sudden stop before snapping back in place. Jade and Chase stood facing each other across the arena, their stances wide and ready, their eyes locked together.

Max scrambled up and moved closer to Chase until he was half way between them, but on the outskirts of the arena.

"Max, so glad you're not dead," Chase said, never looking his way. "She's fine."

He released a breath as though he'd been holding it all along waiting to know Jenna was alive.

"Jenna, you mean," Jade said. "Don't know why you kept that one. It's not like she's a brilliant conversationalist."

"You'd be surprised." Chase smiled widely, showing Max dimples he didn't even know she had. "Can you do me a favor, Max? Make sure we aren't interrupted." She reached back and took a gun out of the back of her waistband. She tossed it to Max and he caught it.

"Oh... Okay," he said. Max stepped back away from them. He considered just shooting at Jade. He was a really good shot after all, but he figured Jade would wouldn't be easy to nail.

"Jaad," Chase said with a slight nod. The emphasis was on a hard "a."

"Chaa," Jade responded with her own nod. "It has been such a long time. Missed me?"

"Well, you have kept me busy."

"You're the one who decided to get all concerned about the humans. We could have..." Jade said.

"No, we really couldn't have."

"I'm not the one who changed the rules. Trapped us here."

"You're right. I'm the one who changed," Chase said.

"So don't get all high and mighty about it. And now you want to kill me?" Jade sounded almost hurt.

Max held his gun ready. There was noise on above, but no one was coming down the steps or through the tunnel.

Jade turned and took a few steps along the edge of the arena away from Max. Chase mirrored her, keeping the distance between them.

Max stepped back, farther away from them. Something was about to happen and he didn't want to be in the middle of it.

"Chaa, why waste your time on these insignificant creatures. They're nothing. Nothing but food."

"Not to me. Want to use the lance?" Chase asked noting the Saracian Lance Max had driven into the throne.

"Let's go old school. What do you say. For old times sake... Winner take all?"

Chase nodded slowly. "Agreed."

"Including Max. He's a blast."

"Hopefully he'll figure out a way to kill you if I'm not around. Right Max?"

"I'll give it a shot," he said.

Almost in unison, each slapped her left shoulder with her right hand, and their bodies morphed into ugly, red, devilish-looking creatures with enormous fangs and claws. Max took a step back, shocked. They were the same bulk and height, but completely different. Hideous.

The Chase creature let out a monstrous roar, which the Jade creature replied to. They looked like they were ready to rip each other to shreds and flew at each other, twisting and turning to gain advantage, a ball of two devils trying to kill each other. Blood was spilled as cuts and gouges appeared on the creatures. But then they morphed again and Max had no idea who was who. This time they transformed into green, alien-looking creatures with spikes protruding from their arms and tail. Again they battled, but this time using their tails to do damage. The blood that spilled was yellow and the wounds seemed devastating.

Max felt the wall at his back. He'd backed up as far as he could. As the former vampire queens battled and then transformed yet again into something that looked like it was out of a Godzilla movie, Max saw a blur coming down the stairs. It was Veronica, followed by Maria.

They stopped at the bottom of the stairs and watched the battle and the next transformation. Maria gasped and didn't move. But Veronica found Max in the darkness and flew at him. He knew he couldn't take her in a fight, but he could shoot. Max ignored the show and took aim at the humorless vampire. He shot the gun, hitting her, and she spun out slamming into the wall and landing on top of him.

Max had hit her shoulder and he pushed it in deeper as she screamed. But Veronica was stronger than him and she pinned him to the ground. His gun hand was still loose so he shot her again, this time in the neck. Veronica slammed Max into the wall and ripped the bolt out of her neck. His gun flew out of his hand and Max was defenseless.

Veronica's face was filled with rage, the bolt still in her hand. Maria moved up behind Veronica with a lance and stood there for a moment. Max knew he was dead. Jade might keep him alive, but Veronica would kill him. His life didn't pass before his eyes as he thought it might. Instead he just thought of Jenna.

Veronica raised her hand, bolt pointed at Max's chest, ready to turn him to dust. Max didn't have any moves left. As she started to drive the bolt down Max saw the blade from Maria's lance flash behind Veronica and come down on her neck, cutting off her head. The head bounced off Max's chest and then the body and head turned to dust as the bolt fell on him harmlessly.

Maria stood over Max, the lance having completed it's swing was now down by her side. "Hi, Max."

Max coughed at the Veronica dust he was breathing in. "Hi Maria... Thanks."

"I hated her."

"She was easy to hate," he said. Maria held out her hand and Max took it as she pulled him up on his feet. The battle in the arena between the ever changing creatures was still going on, with terrifying sounds erupting from them. Max had absolutely no idea who was winning or even who was who.

"You better get out of here. I don't know who's going to win this, but..." Max was stopped as one of the creatures stabbed the other in the chest, bringing it to its knees, if those were indeed knees.

Max led her to the escape tunnel opening and she stepped into it. She stopped for a moment looking back and tossed him the lance.

"Thank you. If you run into any of my people just tell them Max sent you," he said as he turned back to the action, and Maria nodded and turned and ran into the depths of the tunnel.

Max stayed in the darkness of the basement and found his gun. It still had some bolts left. Lance in one hand and gun in the other, he waited while the two creatures battled.

Max still had no idea who was who, but one of the creatures was severely injured and losing blood, or whatever fluid they were leaking.

That one had stopped transforming, while the other one kept changing. As the injured creature, a blue and white dragon-looking thing, lay on the ground, the other one stood over it looking like something out of the movie Alien this time. "You lose!" it growled, the words sounding garbled but Max could make them out. It stomped on the dragon, breaking bones, gravely injuring it.

The creature that was winning stopped for a moment, noticing Max. "Kill her, Max. Kill Jade for me," it said.

Without hesitation Max walked into the arena and looked at the injured creature on the ground and the one standing triumphant above it.

"Chase?" he asked.

"Of course. Kill her."

Max nodded and raised his lance's blade above his head. He paused for only a moment as the creature on the ground looked at him, shaking its head and making panting noises, unable to speak. Then he swung and drove the blade of the lance into the stomach of the standing creature. The creature fell to its knees as Max brought the blade down on its stomach again.

The injured creature Max had just saved turned into Chase. She had injuries all over her body.

Max held the lance's blade in the other creature but looked at Chase. "Tell me who was Burnside," Max asked.

Chase smiled weakly. "General Ambrose Burnside... Sideburns," she said, struggling to get the words out.

"I'm so glad I guessed right," he said. Max started to raise the blade, but Chase yelled. "Wait! Get blood on the blade!"

Max nodded and ran the blade through the blood on the ground and then pulled the lance above his head and drove the blade down into the Jade creature's side again nearly cutting her in half.

"I'm glad you guessed right too," Chase said.

Max was about to finish cutting Jade in half when the creature's tail slammed into him sending him crashing to the ground. Max tried to recover, but Jade managed to get up and head to the escape tunnel. Max still had his gun in his hand and he shot her in the head, which stopped her for all of a second before the creature vanished into the tunnel.

Max was about to go after her, but Chase's weak voice stopped him. "Max, you won't be able to stop her. She's already gone."

"What's it fucking take to kill you two... whatever you are?" he asked, frustration filling his voice.

Max returned to the injured Chase. "How did you know?" she asked.

"You never would have asked me to kill her, not like that.

Not if you could do it," he said.

"This is going to take a while to heal. Help me up," she said.

"So you guys are like shape-shifting aliens then, like real aliens, like from another planet aliens," Max said as he took her arm and pulled her up carefully holding her side so she was standing.

Chase looked at him and took a deep breath. "Oh Max, can you manage to not go excited school boy on me and tell everyone what you think you know?"

"It's going to be hard," he said. "How long's it going to take you to heal?"

"Probably a couple days or weeks, or I don't know."

"And Jade?"

"That depends on how much you damaged her. But getting the blood in the wound should help. It could take awhile. Cutting her in half would have ended her, probably," she said.

"Damn it. I wish..." he said.

"You did good," she said.

They heard someone at the top of the stairs coming down. Max was ready to grab the lance again, which would have meant letting go of Chase, but it was Tank.

Max breathed a sigh of relief. He knew they were a sight.

"Did you kill her?" Tank asked Chase.

"No, but she's injured, thanks to Max. It may take her a while to heal."

Tank did his usual guttural growl. "You're injured too," he said.

"Yes, I am," she said. Tank took Chase from Max and he picked her up.

"There are human captives here," Max said.

"Someone will be along to take care of them," Tank said before taking her upstairs.

Max was alone in the arena. He looked back at the escape tunnel and looked deeply into the darkness. He got closer and let his senses flow through the tunnel. He had to make sure she was gone. He hoped Jade wouldn't run into Maria.

There was no one in the tunnel. It was empty. Max looked at the lance in his hand. It would be a nice souvenir. He nodded and then followed Tank and Chase up the stairs.

## CHAPTER 32

When Max got back to Chase's compound, he hit the war room, which was buzzing with activity and had a familiar looking cage with a new vampire inside it.

Savior and Becca ran over to Max. Savior gave him a big bear hug, nearly knocking him off his feet and Becca shyly nodded.

"Max, you're alive! I'm so happy you're alive!" Savior said, releasing him from the hug.

"Hi, Max," Becca said.

"Yep, I'm alive and you guys did a great job. You are both amazing! You found Jade and four of the six locations you discovered were on the money," Max said enthusiastically. He'd already told them this on the phone, but he wanted them to know that what they did was important.

"We did more damage to Jade's organization in one day than... well, I don't know when, but it's all because you two figured out something no one else had been able to figure out. And the drone was amazing. You saved lives."

Becca smiled in her quiet shy way, while Savior was his ever exuberant self.

"Jade took you for like a full day. Are you okay?" Becca asked.

"I'm perfect," Max said.

"There's blood on your shirt," she said.

"Well, luckily I have a hard head and I healed," he gave them a big smile.

Savior suddenly got serious. "Shades... He didn't make it."

"I was with him."

"I'm going to miss him. We also lost Ann with Team One," Becca said.

"I know." The pain of losing a friend like Shades stung, especially someone he wished he'd been able to save.

"There's memorials over there," Savior said nodding

toward a table by the wall. Max saw some of Shades different pairs of sunglasses, and bits of mementos built up, and another memorial next to it for Ann with flowers and pictures and one of her small sculptures. She had been an artist.

"Yeah..." Max knew it was the cost of a war, losing people you didn't want to lose. It didn't make it easy.

"You guys go back to work. I've got to talk to Terry and then find Jenna."

"She was in the kitchen last time I saw her," Becca said.

"Thanks."

Max went to check in with Terry who looked sad and unfocused in a way he never had been. Shades was a good friend of his, maybe his best friend.

"Terry, I'm sorry about Shades. I couldn't do anything to help him."

"I know, Max. At least you made it and Chase called to say you gave Jade something to remember us by," Terry said. "The material we've gotten from the different locations has been invaluable. The kids did great... and you did great."

"How's Chase?"

"More damaged than I've ever seen her, but she'll recover. She said you saved her life," Terry said.

"With help from one of Jade's people, Maria."

"We've been looking for her since you told us about her, but we haven't found her. She must have escaped."

"I hope she didn't run into Jade," Max said.

Father Frank came up to them and slapped Max on the back. "You saved the day, dear boy... We're going to have a memorial tomorrow for Shades and Ann. We're hoping Chase will be able to attend by then."

"I'll be there."

The normally jovial Father Frank looked down and wiped his eyes. "Good," Frank said as he went back to work.

"Hey Max, I've got a present for you," Terry said. He pointed to the new vampire in the cage.

"Isn't that Dodgers guy?" Max asked.

"Yep. He's all yours when you're ready."

"Well, that will be tomorrow's job. I've got to find Jenna and talk to Chase."

"And don't forget I need a full report on everything that happened while you were Jade's guest," Terry said, giving him the deadpan delivery he liked to use. "Everything."

"Believe me, it wasn't..."

"Looks like she dressed you," Terry said, noting the clothing.

"Terry, nothing happened like you're thinking. Nothing."

"Sure, Max. I still need everything in a report."

"Tomorrow... I'm going to find Jenna."

# # #

Max headed toward the kitchen and caught Jenna's scent when he got close. When he saw her, relief, excitement, passion, and desire all flowed through him, and then she saw him. She did not smile. He could feel anger rolling off her. She was mad at him.

Two other vampires were in the room, but when they saw the body language between Max and Jenna, they quickly retreated.

Max went to her, but Jenna stepped away from him.

"What? What happened?" he asked.

"You! You could have died!" she signed, her entire body showing her fury.

"I didn't..."

"You did. You let her capture you! Your fucking Plan B!"

"I did not. I just knew it was a possibility."

"Shades died! You could have died and left me..." Her tears began to flow, but she wiped them away.

"If we'd had more people there to protect me and Shades, more people would have died in the woods. You know that. None of us are powerful enough to take her on. She still would have grabbed me, and no one would have found me without that tracker... You know I would have traded my life for Shades' if I could have," Max said, needing to make her understand.

She turned away from him and he reached out, touching her shoulder. She pulled away from him.

Max felt lost. If she wouldn't look at him, she'd never understand.

He gently reached out again and turned her so she could see him.

"Please... you have to understand. Nothing happened with her."

She signed so quickly and angrily he could barely make out what she was saying. "You think I care about that? If you ever get captured by her again, your only job is to survive. But how dare you put your life at risk!"

Max gently took her hands in his. "I'm sorry," he said.

She pulled her hands away from him. "Your life is worth everything to me."

"And yours is worth everything to me," he signed and said. "A life where Jade no longer exists on this planet is also worth everything to me. You risked your life too. I can't control how this war goes. We risk our lives every time we go out on a mission."

Tears began to flow and he wrapped his arms around her holding her as her sobs rippled through her body. After a few moments, she pulled back, but not away from him.

"You were gone for over a day. I thought you were dead," she signed, the anger beginning to leave her.

"The tracker would have stopped working."

"Not if they found it and dug it out of you. Or she could have kept you until she was able to twist you into..."

"A monster?" he asked.

"Yes."

"I've been a monster in my life. I won't ever be that again, not like her... But I can't promise I won't sacrifice myself if it means saving you or the kids or even the cause. I can't," Max told her.

Jenna looked away from him and slowly nodded. "I know," she signed. She finally looked back into his eyes.

"Maybe we'll just have to accept that like normal humans, maybe we might not have 800 years," he said gently.

"I'd settle for 100."

Max smiled at her. "Let's shoot for 100 then, at least for now. We can always renegotiate later."

A slight smile slowly made its way across her lovely face. "You are not charming, Max Maguire," she signed.

"I've been told I'm a little bit charming," he smiled.

Then she got serious again. "When I lost Mason, I thought I'd never love anyone ever again. It hurt too much."

"So let's promise to live as long as we can manage."

"And never risk our lives without a very good reason," she signed.

Max nodded. "Agreed... Besides we've got our kids to think about now."

She burst out laughing silently. "I guess we do."

Max took her in his arms and kissed her deeply, fully. He knew all he wanted to do was hold her for about a week.

There wasn't much more talking, especially after they made their way to their room. While Max did a lot more than just hold Jenna, there was a fair amount of that too.

It was late afternoon and she was in his arms sleeping, naked. He loved watching her, studying her face, the feel of his hand cupped around her breast, the sensation of the breaths that flowed through her body. She filled him up and made it feel like everything would be okay.

Max's phone buzzed with a text notification. Reluctantly he released her breast and picked up his phone.

"Need to talk to you. Medical One," Chase texted him.

Max really didn't want to move and risk waking her, but the memorial service was coming up and he did need to talk to Chase before he tried to write a report. He carefully untangled himself from Jenna. He couldn't help giving her a kiss on the cheek. Her eyes flickered open.

"I have to go see Chase," Max said. Jenna nodded and he kissed her gently, softly.

Max took a quick shower and dressed in his normal black t-shirt and pants before heading off to find the boss lady.

# # #

Max made his way to Medical. Dr. Foster was studying some x-rays when Max came in. The doctor still had her arm in a sling.

"Max," she replied. "She's in Room 5."

"Thanks, Doc," Max said with a nod.

Max found her room. Chase was in a hospital bed still looking very beat up and weak, but she was awake and smiled when she saw Max.

"How are you, Max?"

"Better than you, I think... Why is it taking you so long to heal?"

"Our blood mixed with a chemical we excrete when we change, keeps our enemies from healing right away," Chase said.

"So she won't be able to heal quickly," Max said.

"And neither will I."

"Wow. So you're an alien," he said.

"Something like that."

"Who else knows?"

"No one, unless Jade has told someone, which I doubt," she said.

"Not Jenna?"

"No. She may have guessed but I've never told her."

"Not even after 800 years?" Max asked.

"If people think we're magic or fantasy, that's easier than knowing the truth."

"And what is the truth?"

"Are you ready to tell me your secret yet?" she asked.

Max shook his head. "It's not something you need to know."

"Well, this isn't something you need to know either."

"Chase..."

"I don't know what your secret is, Max. Some deep, dark thing that you did that scared the shit out of you, I suspect. But it's why you're still here. Why you just saved me when anyone else would have run away with Maria. Why you were able to save two vampire kids and why Maria turned on Jade. It's why we beat her, Max."

He shook his head.

"It's okay," she said.

Max put his head in his hands and rocked. He wasn't ready to spill his guts. He'd never talked to anyone about the horrible things he'd done, not to his father, not on the streets, not in the Army.

"The weight you carry, the battle for your soul, the struggle, I can feel it all," Chase said.

"Jade said you changed the rules. What did she mean?"

"I did. I was worse than Jade. I did change the rules."

"If you're an alien, what does that make me?"

"You know. You're a smart guy," she said.

"What? An alien-human hybrid, maybe?"

"Something like that," she said.

"Something like an alien. Something like an alien-human hybrid... I just want to know," Max said.

"You don't. Believe me, you don't."

"What I do know is that there are more of you somewhere out there and that you changed the rules."

"Like I said, you're a smart guy, Max. But the universe is a big place. All we need to be worried about right now is Jade and taking down her operation before she recovers. You gave us that chance."

Max nodded. "I'll see you at the memorial service," he said. She nodded and he left the room.

As he walked away a chill ran through him. What would it mean if there were dozens or hundreds or thousands of Jades heading for Earth? Chase was right about one thing, he really didn't want to know.

Crystal had been hunting for a couple of nights before she caught the scent. She was lucky Jade hadn't been able to get very far and that the others hadn't found her first.

As she came up to a wooded area a couple of miles from the estate, the smell got stronger and she knew she was close.

Crystal had figured out there was a second tracker in her and she'd dug it out and put it on a truck that was going cross country.

After that she'd been careful, just in case the others were also looking for Jade, but there hadn't been any sign of them since the police left the area.

As Crystal walked through the woods, Jade's scent overwhelmed her. It wasn't until she looked through the brush that she found her, half dead and almost cut in half.

"I've got you now. You're safe," she said.

The young vampire girl picked up Jade as though her weight was nothing and carried her to a car she had taken after draining an unpleasant man who picked her up hitchhiking. His body was in the trunk and she'd deal with that later.

As she put Jade in the backseat, the vampire queen opened her eyes.

"Little one..." she said softly before closing her eyes again.

Crystal smiled. "You're going to be okay, Jade. I'll get you somewhere safe and then get you some humans. I'll take care of you."

Two months had passed since they'd taken down Jade. There was no sign of the Vampire Queen as they dismantled her operation, although people kept disappearing in a way that indicated that Jade's vampires were still causing death and destruction.

Max drove through the familiar Chicago streets, windows open, enjoying the feel of the wind on his face. Chase had agreed to let him have a week off so he could take care of something that still haunted him from his time with Jade.

He looked at his phone and followed the direction of the Maps lady. Terry had finally found the address Max had spent so much time looking for. Max pulled on a face mask, which had been popular since Covid, just in case anyone was watching. He stopped across the street of the Markinson's house. He put on rubber gloves and picked up the manila envelope on the passenger's seat addressed to John and Tilly Markinson.

Max opened up the envelope and pulled out the letter which had Amanda Markinson's driver's license paper-clipped to it. He looked one last time at her smiling, hopeful face and thought of the sad homeless woman he'd chosen to die at Jade's command.

Max had written the letter himself.

Dear Mr. and Mrs. Markinson, I knew your daughter Amanda, although not very well. She was homeless and confused, but I know she loved you. She passed away from an illness and I found her driver's license in her shoe. I don't know where she ended up, but I thought you should know. I'm sorry for your loss. A friend.

He put the license and letter back in the envelope and closed it using the clasp. He suspected it might make her family sadder, but Max thought not knowing would be worse. It had been hard on his mom when he was living on the streets and she didn't know if he was alive or dead, so maybe this would be easier for them somehow.

Max looked around. The street was empty. It was the dead of night so it was unlikely anyone would see him. He got out of the car quickly and put the envelope in the mailbox, then retreated back to the car.

He drove away knowing that no matter what good he did in his life, he'd never make up for what he'd done to Amanda. Or what he'd done to Michelle, his first kill as a vampire. He would have liked to give her family an envelope too, but it was too high-profile a case. There wasn't anything he could do about Michelle, at least not at this point in time.

As Max drove through the streets of Chicago, he felt nostalgic and sad. He missed his old life, but was grateful for his new one with Jenna.

Max looked up into the night's sky. You couldn't really see any stars with the city lights blocking them out. He wondered about Chase's people. If she'd broken the rules, it was certain they'd be more like Jade than Chase. Not a happy thought.

"The universe is a big place," she'd said. He hoped so.

Meanwhile, Chase thought his secret was important somehow. But the secret Max had wasn't just that he'd killed his father. He'd been a destroyer, a villain, an evil that no amount of good could overcome.

Max knew that they thought he was some sort of fucking hero. He was no hero. He knew that. But maybe if he pretended he was a good enough man, then whatever good he managed to do would outweigh the evil. Maybe.

Kat Huddleston is a Chicago-based writer, teacher and artist who loves all things sci-fi. She's was an entertainment journalist for the Syfy Channel's website and for Sci Fi Magazine not all that long ago, and has always had a deep addiction for writing, teaching and creating art. Kat is an award-winning artist who teaches fused glass at The Beverly Art Center in Chicago and her art can be found in several galleries. While she's made a living as a journalist and dabbled in short story and screen play writing, this is Kat's first novel.